❧ SUDDEN TRAGEDY ❧

"What happened here?"

Kori turned quickly. She saw that some of the villagers had gathered up at the top of the sloping beach. They were clustered protectively together, afraid to face this new portent of death and change. But one tall figure separated herself and came walking forward, her moccasins leaving deep footprints in the black sand. Kori looked up and saw her mother staring down at her.

"My wife is dead," said Horeth, sounding lost and confused. "She fell in and drowned." He turned and saw Kori, and his confusion turned to outrage. "It was her fault," he cried, pointing at her. "You killed her!"

by Charlotte Prentiss

Children of the Ice
Children of the Sun
People of the Mesa
The Island Tribe
The Ocean Tribe*

*coming soon

THE ISLAND TRIBE

CHARLOTTE PRENTISS

HarperPrism

An Imprint of HarperPaperbacks

🔥 HarperPaperbacks
A Division of HarperCollins*Publishers*
10 East 53rd Street, New York, N.Y. 10022-5299

This is a work of fiction. The characters, incidents, and
dialogues are products of the author's imagination and are not to
be construed as real. Any resemblance to actual events or
persons, living or dead, is entirely coincidental.

ISBN 0-06-101012-X

HarperCollins®, 🔥®, and HarperPaperbacks™
are trademarks of HarperCollins*Publishers,* Inc.

Cover illustration by Royo

First printing: March 1997

Printed in the United States of America

Visit HarperPaperbacks on the World Wide Web at
http://www.harpercollins.com/paperbacks

❖ 10 9 8 7 6 5 4 3 2 1

To my three cats: Alice, Ben, and Claude

THE ISLAND TRIBE

Part 1:
The Old Ones

1

Lying on her bed of birch boughs, Kori listened to the small sounds of the night. A fire hissed in the corner of her little stone-walled hut. Her brother Oam shifted restlessly on his bed before his breathing quieted and he slipped deeper into sleep. The wind whispered, and Kori heard a scurry of tiny footsteps—a squirrel, or a rat—running across the roof.

Often she would lie awake like this, finding solace in solitude while others slept. She felt warm and safe huddling under the black bearskin that her father had given her when she came of age—and yet, in truth, there was no safety for the people of her tribe.

They had built their homes on a ridge of rock in the center of a wide, slow river. The river protected them from the predators that hunted in forests on either shore, and their location was so remote, no hostile tribes ever came this way to steal or conquer. At the same time, though, there was another danger that could never be erased.

As Kori lay on her simple bed, she felt the ground tremble.

Her eyes flew open. She waited, listening to her pulse tapping inside her ears. For a moment everything was still, and she wondered if the tremor had just been her imagination. Then her bed bucked as if someone had kicked it. She threw the bearskin aside, and rolled onto her hands and knees. Her muscles were warm and sluggish, but fear gave them sudden strength. She sprang up and started across the room.

The floor of polished rock rose under her and hurled her to one side. She threw out her hands to stop herself from hitting the wall, and the rough stones dug into her palms. "Oam!" she shouted, turning toward her brother's bed. "Oam, wake up!"

The embers of the fire in the corner shed so little light, she couldn't see whether he was stirring. Kori was not the type to run or hide; she had more courage than most other women in her tribe. But when the Old Ones shook the ground itself, even brave hunters felt a deep instinctual fear. "Oam!" she screamed. She desperately wanted to flee.

She heard a deep rumbling that seemed to come from everywhere at once, and the floor began dancing. The stone walls made ominous grinding noises, the timber roof creaked, and dirt showered down.

Her brother dragged himself off his bed. He stumbled forward and bumped into her. For a moment they clung to each other, and she glimpsed his startled eyes and felt his breath on her face. Then, without a word, he ran out of the hut. Kori followed him, forcing the flap of goat skin out of her way and ducking through the tiny doorway.

She felt the cold night air on her naked body and heard Torbir, the news crier, blowing his ram's horn once, twice, and a third time. In the light from a yellow moon she saw men emerging from their homes, women clutching babies in their arms, children running, everyone converging on the Meeting Place. Here the villagers threw themselves down and seized big Anchor Stones, ranged in a circle around a fire that cast leaping shadows.

Kori's parents took their places beside the largest stone. Her mother, Immar, kneeled and pressed her forehead against it. Her father, Rohonar, wrapped one arm around it and stood vigilant as the tribe gathered before him. He was their chieftain, so tall and strong he seemed as firmly rooted in the ground as the stone itself.

Kori dropped to her knees behind her family's Anchor Stone and grabbed its rough, pitted surface between her palms. Oam was already kneeling there, and the warmth of him beside her gave her some small feeling of comfort.

Immar lifted her head and threw it back with her eyes closed. Unlike other women of the tribe, she never braided her hair. It blew around her now, in sudden gusts of wind that came from nowhere, as if the Old Ones themselves were breathing upon her. She started chanting, screaming the words into the wind. Kori knew the chant as well as she knew her name; she had heard it from time to time ever since she was born. "Forgive us, Old Ones!" Immar cried. "Have mercy on your people. We honor you. We are your children. Do not punish us!"

Gradually the earthquake subsided, finally ending in a series of short, sharp jolts that made Kori wince as the ground cut into her knees. The rumbling ceased, the ground became steady again, and the gusting wind slowly died away.

For a long moment, no one moved. Kori realized she had been holding her breath; she let it out in a gasp of relief as she slowly rose to her feet. She saw others in the tribe standing, looking at each other, grinning, their faces flushed with the simple pleasure of being alive. Babies were still crying, but mothers could turn to them now and comfort them without fear.

And yet—Kori blinked, wondering why the scene appeared different. Then she realized that the fire at the center of the Meeting Place was no longer the only source of light. An orange glow was emanating from the west, and as she turned toward it, she saw that Mount Tomomor had come to life.

Across the river, far beyond the forest that crowded the Western Shore, the mountain loomed as a low, black, flat-topped triangle against the moonlit sky. A wisp of dazzling fire now burned at its peak, lighting the underside of smoke that was gathering above.

One by one, the villagers saw what Kori had seen. Their smiles faded and they voiced moans of dismay, for everyone knew that Tomomor only woke if the Old Ones were truly angry.

Kori's mother looked toward the distant mountain. She stood and raised her arms. "Tomomor, have mercy!" she called out. "How have we offended you?"

The ground trembled again, but it was just a little spasm, lasting no more than a couple of heartbeats. After that the only sounds were of the night wind ruffling the trees and a faint, distant murmur as Tomomor continued to vent his fury.

Immar called for a chant of respect and regret. Obediently her people seated themselves in a great circle around the fire, old and young side by side, with no concern for status or kinship. As one, they linked hands and began filling the air with song. Kori felt the voices warming her, merging with the sound of her own voice from within, forcing away the fear. It was a good, comforting feeling, but it was short-lived. At the far side of the circle a man named Gloshin slowly stood up, looking embarrassed and apologetic for interrupting the ritual, but still waiting to be recognized.

Rohonar held up his hand and the chanting slowly died. "Yes, Gloshin," he said.

Gloshin was too old to stand straight, and most of his

teeth had gone. He stood with dignity, though, and the tribe looked at him with respect, for he had been a great hunter in his day. Two fingers of his left hand were missing, bitten off by a mountain lion. His sunken chest was emblazoned with scars.

"My brother," he said, peering around the Meeting Place, "Shashin is missing."

There was an apprehensive silence. Shashin lived alone, for his mate had died a dozen years ago, and she had never borne him children. "Shashin!" Rohonar called out in his great voice. He paused, waiting and listening, but there was no answer.

Rohonar's face became lined with concern. He turned to Gloshin's two sons. "Where is your uncle?" he asked them. "Didn't you bring him here?"

The sons glanced uneasily at each other, but they said nothing, and neither of them would return Rohonar's steady stare. The silence deepened and Kori felt cold inside, knowing what must have happened, yet still not wanting to believe that it could be so.

Abruptly, Rohanar turned his back on the circle. He strode swiftly around the Meeting Place and disappeared among the little huts, into the darkness. There was a shocked moment in which no one moved. Then everyone started jumping up, calling to Shashin, hurrying after their chieftain.

Kori felt Oam's hand shaking her shoulder. "Come," he said.

She was four years older than he was, and she resented his habit of telling her what to do. He had always been competitive—determined to prove himself, impatient to share or steal any privilege that she might have. He was no taller than Kori, but much heavier. The plumpness of his face made his eyes seem small, and his mouth was petulant. More and more, she felt estranged from him.

She didn't speak as she got to her feet, and she moved

slowly, not wanting to see what she felt sure was waiting out in the shadows. Oam made a little sound of impatience, then turned away from Kori and hurried after the other villagers, their bare feet scuffing the thin layer of black sand that covered the rocks of the Meeting Place.

For a moment, Kori found herself alone. She stood listening to the distant murmur of Mount Tomomor and the occasional snap of wood in the fire. Then she heard the villagers wailing in distress. She seized a branch from the fire, raised the burning end high, and went in search of the sound.

Three circles of huts were centered around the Meeting Place, their walls made from rocks piled on top of one another, their roofs fashioned from rough-hewn logs covered with baked mud. Kori walked between huts in the first circle, where many of the elders lived. She passed her own home in the second circle and moved on, stepping carefully in the flickering torchlight. She came to the third circle and found all the people there, almost a hundred of them pressed together. Many of them had fallen to their knees, the women sobbing, the men looking grim. Several had brought burning branches like Kori's, and the wavering orange light revealed a great heap of stones—a cairn that had once been Shashin's home.

"People!" Rohonar's voice drowned the wailing of the womenfolk. "Quickly, now." To set an example, he bent and grabbed one of the big stones, hauling it out of the way.

Kori imagined what had happened. Shashin had woken, clumsy with arthritis, weak from old age, and frightened by the earthquake. Before he'd had time to crawl out of bed, the walls had shifted and tumbled, crushing his old body like a seed husk. His blood, even now, must be draining into the fissures in the black rock below, feeding the Old Ones who dwelled there.

Kori feared the Old Ones just as everyone did in her tribe, but when she stared at the ruins before her, she felt something stronger than fear. If this was how the spirits had chosen to punish Shashin, she hated them for it. He had been a kind old man. He had done nothing wrong.

"Kori!" It was her mother's voice. "Help us!"

Kori turned away, feeling sick. She threw aside her burning branch, and as it hit the ground, the flames winked out in a shower of sparks.

"Kori, come *here*!"

There was no affection in the words, and Kori didn't respond. She had reached her twentieth birthday; she was past the age when she should obey orders, even from her mother. She walked away, then broke into a run, hugging her nakedness against the cold air. She ducked beneath scrawny trees that grew in fissures in the black rock of the island, and finally she came to a shallow slope that led to a little bay where the Island Tribe moored their dugout canoes.

Kori ran to the edge of the water and stopped there, squatting down, trying to calm herself as she looked out across the river to the Western Shore. The first gray light of dawn was touching the sky behind her, but the river was still hidden in shadow. Its ripples were limned in orange, though touched by the distant radiance from Mount Tomomor.

Kori stared at the distant silhouette venting streamers of flame. Already she could smell its sulfurous fumes. She thought back to the other times in her life when she had seen Tomomor erupt. Fifteen times? Twenty?

And how many other times had she felt earthquakes shaking her island home, threatening her tribe, sometimes killing people who were too old or young to protect themselves? The number was too large for her to count. Brief little tremors occurred almost daily in this strange, sinister part of the world. Large earthquakes—like the one tonight—struck two or three times each year.

The Old Ones were never satisfied for long. No matter

how many sacrifices Kori's people made, or how often they prayed for forgiveness, they felt constantly threatened.

Kori had never known any other place. Still, she sensed in her soul that somehow this was wrong. Her people were good, generous, decent people; they didn't deserve such abuse.

In a somber mood, she turned away from the mountain. The injustice was so big, she felt impotent in its shadow. One day, somehow, she liked to think that there might be a way to lighten the burden of her tribe, but in the meantime she bowed her head and walked back under the trees to join her kinfolk as they labored over the ruins of Shashin's home.

2

Rohonar was striding around, holding a flaming torch, barking commands to his people while Kori's mother, Immar, stood farther back under the trees, chanting more prayers and words of atonement.

The elders of the tribe had backed away to one side, taking the youngest children and babies with them. Everyone else was hard at work lifting the stones and passing them from one pair of hands to the next. Naked bodies were shiny with sweat in the flicking yellow light. Kori heard the villagers breathing hard as they labored in the cold morning air, and once in a while there was a curse or a muffled cry as the sharp volcanic rock inflicted small cuts on hands and arms.

Kori hesitated, wondering whether to add herself to one of the chains of stone-bearers. She wished, now, she hadn't run away to the river. Her tribe was a tight-knit community; they found it hard to understand or forgive her when she turned her back on them.

So often, she was misunderstood. Even when she tried her best to please her kinfolk, there always seemed to be a gulf—because she found them just as hard to understand as they found her. Even now, as she stood watching everyone laboring so urgently, she felt confused. They seemed so strangely eager to see Shashin's body, even though the sight would cause deeper distress.

Then she realized that they were impatient because they were driven by their grief. Once they uncovered Shashin they could cry out their distress and take him to the Burial Place, where they would chant and pray for him, taking comfort from the rituals and from each other, and then they would feel relief.

For Kori, it was not so easy. Grief was a private thing, and she needed solitude in order to cope with it. Nor could a simple ceremony stop her from remembering Shashin and missing him, feeling outraged that his life had been taken so pointlessly.

Why was she so different from everyone else? Why did they find solace together, while she needed to be alone? These were questions that she had never been able to answer—and this was not the best time to consider them. She realized she should try to atone for turning her back on her people. She stepped forward, squatted down, reached for the largest rock she could find, and took a firm hold on it. With all her strength she was just able to lift it. The pitted, spiky surface was painful against her naked breasts, but she ignored the discomfort. She turned, staggering with the load.

"Kori!" It was her father's voice. "That rock is too heavy. Set it down."

From the corner of her eye she noticed people looking at her. Would they think worse of her now if she gave up and dropped her burden? Would they laugh at her? She always felt so vulnerable to disapproval—so she pretended she hadn't heard Rohonar's command, and she continued carrying the rock away. But after just a few steps a small pebble turned under her foot, and she gave a startled cry as she felt herself losing her balance.

A figure loomed in front of her, heavily muscled, almost as tall as her father. A hand seized her shoulder, steadying her. "Give that to me," said a voice, and the rock was lifted out of her arms.

The man's face was hidden in shadow, but torchlight gleamed on his long braided hair and the edge of his heavy jaw. She recognized him now. His name was Yainar; he led the junior hunters.

Kori watched as he tossed the rock aside. He turned back to her, looked down, and frowned at thin trickles of blood which marked the little cuts on her chest.

In Kori's tribe there was no taboo against nudity. Everyone washed together in the Bathing Place. In the cooler seasons they covered themselves, but during the hottest days of the summer they often spent whole days naked. Tonight, since all the people had run from their homes without pausing to dress, they were all bare-skinned and no one thought anything of it.

Still, Kori felt suddenly embarrassed as Yainar stared at her breasts. He was eighteen, a proud, handsome young man, and not yet paired with a woman. Kori knew she would never be chosen by him; she was two years his senior, and she lacked the kind of shy, delicate beauty that hunters seemed to prefer. She had her father's strong mouth instead of her mother's delicate jaw and gentle eyes—and her fierce spirit seemed to make men feel uneasy.

Six years ago, when she had first come of age, she had approached a man she found attractive—and he had rejected her. A year later she had tried again, with the same result. After that, as the years passed, she had bided her time, hoping and waiting that someone would choose her. A few men had hinted that they wanted her, but they were so unappealing or so in love with their own pride, she couldn't bear to be with them. And so it seemed she was destined to be solitary.

As time passed, she found herself pulling back into her own private world. At the same time, though, no matter how she tried to control her thoughts, she found herself haunted by daydreams, hopelessly unrealistic fantasies in which a man such as Yainar would find himself drawn to her, would bring her gifts, and would treat her with the devotion and respect that she saw her father show to her mother. Sometimes she even found herself imagining a future in which she would somehow inherit her mother's special place in the tribe—although this could never be, since Oam was Rohonar's son, so he would naturally inherit the role of chieftain, and it would be his future wife, not Kori, who would take Immar's role.

Most of all, Kori imagined being held by a man, feeling his hands on her, and feeling herself overwhelmed by the smell of him and the heat of his body. Standing naked in front of Yainar now, she found herself wondering how it would feel if he took a piece of sheepskin and used it to wipe the blood from her cuts. Her face grew hot as she imagined his fingers brushing across her breasts—

She drove the thoughts away for fear that he might sense what she was thinking. She looked up at his face—and found him nodding politely to her. His eyes lingered for just an instant; then he turned and strode back to help the rest of the villagers around the ruins of Shashin's home.

Kori felt foolish and ashamed. "Thank you," she called after him.

He ignored her as he bent down to lift another rock.

At that moment, someone near the center of the ruins cried out. Everyone turned from their tasks and pushed forward, dreading what they would see but feeling a powerful compulsion to look nevertheless. Kori glimpsed the pale color of flesh among the black rocks. An outstretched arm had been revealed, twisted at a terrible angle and mottled with dark blood.

"Shashin," Kori muttered, feeling her fantasies about Yainar displaced by a sudden torrent of memories. She saw Shashin as she had known him all her life, telling stories to the young children, guiding hunters as they fashioned their spears, playing with his grandchildren—Kori felt a physical pain in her stomach. A piece of her world had been stolen from her, crushed out of existence.

"Quickly," Her father's voice was loud and commanding. "Move those last stones."

The villagers crowded one another with renewed urgency. The old man was soon completely exposed, his thin body broken and splashed with red, his eyes staring wide, his mouth open in a silent scream.

Many of the villagers started shouting more prayers to the Old Ones, but Kori saw no sense to that. If the Old Ones cared anything for prayers, why had they allowed this to happen in the first place?

"People!" Rohonar's voice was as loud as the bellow of a bear. He clapped his big hands, once, twice, and a third time.

Gradually the prayers and moans of anguish died away. The villagers turned to Rohonar, and Kori saw hope in their tearful faces. He was so powerful, he seemed to have strength enough for all of them.

"We must not feel anger," Rohonar said more quietly, holding up his hands with the palms facing the tribe. "We live like insects on the body of the land. We are like flies or beetles compared the Old Ones. We have no right to ask why. This is the way it is and the way it must be."

Everyone nodded and sighed, feeling reassured by the familiar words. It was wrong to rebel against the way of the world or search for meaning, because some forces were too great to resist, and some things simply could not be known.

Kori looked at Shashin's relatives. It was always the duty of younger people to rescue elders from their homes in a time of danger, but Shashin's nieces and nephews had failed to do this, and surely they ought to be overwhelmed with guilt. But when Kori found their faces she saw they had been comforted by Rohonar's simple words, and now they seemed resigned to the loss of the old man.

Once again she felt the weight of injustice. It was bad enough to feel powerless against the shaking of the earth and the anger of Mount Tomomor. It was worse to feel that she alone could see a deep and pervasive wrongness that no one else even noticed, as if they were blind.

3

Later, as the sky in the east turned from pink to blue and yellow sunbeams slipped softly through the canopy of leaves, people gathered around Shashin where he had been placed on a bed of branches.

The villagers had dressed themselves in deerskins stained black with fine volcanic sand. Like everyone else, Kori had blackened her hands and feet with charcoal, and her hair was ornamented with raven feathers. It was a symbol of respect for the Old Ones to mark oneself with the color of the land.

Shashin's body was raised up onto the shoulders of his kinfolk, who had hacked off most of their hair with stone axes to signify their grief. The body was carried forward, deeper into the trees, and the villagers formed a slow procession behind it, chanting a death song.

Kori followed along near the end, and she found Oam joining her, falling into step beside her, looking as if he needed her company.

She was reluctant to speak to him. As he grew older he seemed more and more annoyed by her independent spirit and her solitary nature. If she tried to tell him something, he interrupted or contradicted her. If she lapsed into silence, he complained that she was hostile. She didn't know why he was so dissatisfied with her; she only hoped he would change once he was paired.

"Where did you go?" he asked her, murmuring the words so that he wouldn't be heard above the steady cadence of the chanting.

"You mean, when people started clearing the stones of Shashin's home?" she asked him.

He gave a curt nod. "Yes."

"I went to the river. I needed to think."

He grunted. "You showed disrespect for Mother. Surely you heard her calling you?"

She looked at Oam's rounded face, his mouth pursed with disapproval. "I can't always please Immar," Kori said. "Sometimes I must please myself."

Oam grimaced. "You can't *ever* please her."

There was some truth to that, Kori thought to herself, although she had certainly tried over the years to fulfill her mother's expectations. But she resented Oam's tone of voice and his need to scold her.

"When you came back," he went on, "and the rocks were pulled away from Shashin, you just stood there staring at people."

"I was trying to understand how Shashin's nephews could show so little shame," she explained. "It was their fault, after all. They abandoned him in his home."

Oam looked shocked by her words. "But you were the one who didn't seem to care," he said. "Other women showed their grief."

It hurt Kori to feel a gulf of misunderstanding with her own brother. "I loved Shashin," she whispered to him urgently. "Just because I suffer my grief without moaning and wailing, you have no right to doubt it. No right at all."

For a moment they stared at each other. His small eyes seemed to probe her, searching behind her words. "I don't understand you," he said finally.

Kori shrugged. There was nothing she could say.

The chanting died as the procession slowly emerged from under the trees into an open space full of stone houses. For a moment it seemed as if they had somehow circled around and returned to their own homes, yet this village was subtly different. The houses here were built from brown, flat-sided stones instead of rough volcanic rock, and there was no sign of life among them—no children playing, no hunters cleaning and sharpening their spears, no women skinning game, and no babies crying.

In fact, there was no sign that any people had ever lived here. Inside each home the sandy floors were unmarked by footprints, and in the Meeting Place there was no fire burning. Instead, at the center was a wide, circular pit that looked strangely dark and forbidding, as if sunlight could never penetrate it fully. In fact it was a lava tube in the volcanic rock—a vertical hole so deep that no one had ever seen the bottom. Weeds clung to the rim, but nothing grew inside.

Kori shivered. The island was small, and this group of stone buildings was only a short walk from the village where she had spent her entire life. Still, whenever she came here she felt as if she was entering an alien land. The air was always colder here, and it carried a dank smell like old, wet leaves. Often she heard faint whispering and rustling noises that disappeared when she turned her head to listen. The wind blew in gusts that moved first one way, then the other, as if the air itself was tormented by the Old Ones who dwelled in the rock below.

In respectful silence, the villagers gathered around the dark-walled pit. Kori saw the fear on their faces, and this at least was something she shared with them: she hated coming here and feeling the power of the ones who controlled her world.

Rohonar stepped forward toward the Burial Pit, while the rest of the villagers kept their distance. He stood alone for a long moment with his head bowed. Finally he looked up and drew a deep, slow breath. "We have come here," he said, "to surrender one of us, whom we loved."

There was a sad murmur of assent.

"Shashin has been taken from us," Rohonar went on, "but clearly it was the will of the Old Ones. And so we offer him now without anger, without regret."

He signaled to the men bearing the bed on their shoulders, and they moved forward.

"In the beginning," Rohonar intoned, "the Great Spirit created the world. He placed trees upon it, and animals in it. He made the Sun to watch over it and the Moon to renew its life. On this island he placed us: his children."

The villagers chanted their response: "So it was, so it is now, and so it will always be."

"But some of the children were ungrateful. They grew restless and discontent. When the Great Spirit came back to see the world he had made, he found the ungrateful ones fighting among themselves and trying to steal more than their rightful share of the land and the animals on it. This offended him, so he thrust his finger down into the rock to make a deep pit, and he cast the ungrateful ones into it. He told them they would live forever under the ground, where they could no longer defile the world he had made."

Once more, the people chanted: "So it was, so it is now, and so it will always be."

Kori moved restlessly. The air seemed to be dragging at her, stealing the warmth from her body. She felt desperate to get away.

Rohonar turned to the men holding the bed where Shashin lay. He nodded to them, and they lowered one end of it toward the pit. The frail, broken figure of Shashin hesitated for a moment, then started to slide. Suddenly he was gone as if he had never been, and there was just the faintest sound as his body passed through the air, disappearing deep into the rock.

After that, the only noise was of the villagers calling out their ritual farewell:

"Life is given to us. Life is taken from us. We feel no anger. So it was, so it is now, and so it will always be."

The people hurried away. The worst, now, was over. Tonight there would be feasting in the Meeting Place as everyone gathered to speak well of Shashin and praise him for the good and generous things he had done. His spirit was free, sharing the realm beneath the earth with the Old Ones, though he would never share their power. Everyone would want to honor his memory so that his spirit would find peace.

The celebration would be muted, though, by the knowledge that Mount Tomomor was still murmuring his discontent. At some point in the afternoon, if the mountain had not ceased venting fire, Immar might lead people back to the Burial Place and cast a sacrifice into the pit: a goat, perhaps, or a whole deer. No one in the tribe would feel calm until the eruption finally died away.

Kori returned to the village alone, lagging behind the rest of her people. She was still thinking of Shashin, and she was reluctant to begin the work that now lay ahead. In the aftermath of the earthquake there were many practical tasks to be done. The huts had to be inspected for damage. Some of the wooden roofs had fallen and would need to be repaired. Food would need to be prepared for the night's feast. . . .

Kori saw a figure waiting ahead of her, just outside the outermost circle of huts. The figure was a woman, tall but slender, her skin unusually pale, her black hair hanging loose around her shoulders, stirring in the breeze. It was Immar, and clearly, she was waiting for Kori.

Immar stepped forward as Kori approached, and for a moment they faced each other.

"You seem troubled," Immar said softly.

Kori wondered if the words implied concern or criticism. Her mother was a woman of terrible moods. She could show intense affection, clutching Kori and kissing her, holding her so closely Kori felt as if Immar was trying to merge their two selves. But then, unpredictably and instantly, the warmth could be replaced with coldness and cruelty. If Kori seemed forgetful, or if she misunderstood an order or showed a lack of respect, Immar could be merciless. She had beaten Kori often, as a child, and her words could inflict even deeper wounds.

When Kori was six years old, she learned to weave tall reeds from the river. Excited by her new skill, she made a serving basket and gave it to her mother proudly as a birthday present. As Immar received it, though, her smile of pleasure faded and her face showed shock, then dismay, and finally disgust. "I am the wife of the chieftain of this tribe," she told Kori, her voice sounding tense with emotion. "I am a seer and a healer. And now you give me this—do you want me to be a mere serving woman, moving on my knees around the hunters in the Meeting Place?" She glared at Kori, punishing her with her eyes—and then, impulsively, she tossed the basket onto the fire.

Over the years Kori learned there was no way she could ever be sure of pleasing her mother; no way to be certain of avoiding the outbursts of hate. In self-defense she retreated from her—but this created a new round of criticism and anger, and Kori had to live with her own guilt, too, because deep down she still felt a powerful need to win Immar's praise.

Standing under the trees now, in the slanting beams of

morning sun, Kori tried to choose words that would avoid any possible conflict. "It's true," she said carefully, "I do feel troubled—because I miss Shashin."

Immar slid her arm around Kori's shoulders. She started walking, forcing Kori to fall into step. "Grief is painful," she said. "That's why it should always be shared."

With dismay Kori saw the direction that this conversation would take. "I'm sorry I ran off on my own," she said. "I know you don't approve—"

Immar grunted impatiently and gestured with her free hand. "It's not a matter of what I think. It's the way of our tribe. You know people turn to our family for strength and unity in these fearful times."

"This is so," Kori said. She looked ahead to where the houses of her tribe stood just a dozen paces away. People were going about their business, dragging new firewood to the Meeting Place, climbing up and looking for damage on the roofs of their homes, calling out to one another. She envied them the peace of their simple tasks.

"I'm concerned," Immar went on, "that Oam says you spoke against Shashin's nephews."

Kori felt a spasm of anger at her brother, but just as quickly it was followed by resignation. He could never be counted on to respect confidences. "I only said that Shashin might have been saved if his kinfolk had done their duty and carried him out."

Immar stopped. She turned Kori to face her and gripped both of her daughter's shoulders. "Listen to me," she said. She brushed aside a stray strand of her long hair, then lowered her forehead till their faces almost touched. Kori felt the fierceness of the wide, dark eyes, and she saw the tension in Immar's face, pulling the skin tight, making her cheekbones stand out, dragging the corners of her mouth downward. "It is not our way to cast blame," she said. "You know that, Kori. Blame turns people against one another. In this world, we can only survive if we forgive each other. You know that!"

Kori felt trapped. She hated arguing with her mother, yet she refused to yield if it meant betraying her own beliefs. "If no one accepts blame," she said, "then surely—"

Immar's hands clenched tighter and her nostrils flared. She gave Kori a little shake. "Shashin's kinfolk forgot to take him from his home. A moment later, his home was the only one to be demolished by the earthquake. Are you blind, Kori? Do you really think this was just a coincidence?"

Kori hesitated. "What do you mean?"

"Isn't it possible that the Old Ones placed dreams in the minds of Shashin's kin, so that when they woke, they forgot their duties?"

With her mother glaring at her like this, it was almost impossible for Kori to think. "I don't understand," she blurted out. "It makes no sense. Why should the Old Ones do such a thing? And why should we always be punished like this?"

Immar's face acquired a haunted look. "You have *no right* to ask why!" Her arms were so tense, now, they were trembling. Her face was frightening; she seemed possessed. "Do you want to provoke them?" Immar cried. "Do you want them to punish our tribe even more than they have already?"

Immar's lips pulled back from her teeth, and Kori realized that this was not just anger, this was something worse.

Immar's whole body started shaking. Kori turned her head toward the village. "Father!" she shouted. "Oam! Come quickly!"

Immar's legs collapsed under her, and Kori found herself lowering her mother to the ground. Immar's eyes rolled up till only the whites showed. Quickly, Kori seized a piece of wood and thrust it between her mother's teeth, just before the jaw muscles clenched. Then she threw herself onto

Immar, trying to control the wild writhing and jerking of her body.

Kori heard running footsteps and in a moment Rohonar was there, his shadow looming over her. She glanced up at him, feeling ashamed in case her willfulness had somehow provoked this. Would Rohonar be able to see her guilt lurking in her face?

Other people were gathering around. Rohonar gestured at a couple of young hunters. "Lift her shoulders. I'll take her ankles."

Kori saw the young men glance uneasily at each other. Whenever Immar went into this strange state it was always a frightening portent, because only one force had the power to seize her this way.

"To the Speaking Rock!" Rohonar shouted as he and the two hunters carried her away.

The Speaking Rock stood just outside the circle of Anchor Stones in the Meeting Place. It was a huge flat-topped boulder, almost as high as Rohonar himself. He and the hunters lifted his wife up onto it and then stepped back, watching her cautiously as she thrashed and shook under the eye of the sun, gripped by the wrath of the spirits.

All the villagers were gathering, now, and once again their faces showed dread.

Rohonar sensed their anxiety. He turned and raised his arms. He was the tallest in the tribe, and even though he was in his thirty-fifth year, he still appeared to be the strongest. "Be calm, people," he called to them. "This could be fortunate for us. The Old Ones are speaking to her, and soon she will speak to us. We will gain knowledge and understanding. Be calm!"

His wisps of black beard stirred in the morning breeze, and his black-stained mourning robe rippled around him as he turned back to Immar.

Her trembling was diminishing. Gradually, as Rohonar waited by her, it ceased. The terrible tension drained out of her body. Her jaw muscles relaxed, and the piece of wood fell from between her teeth. She lay on the rock for a long moment, panting gently with her eyes closed. Then, slowly, she sat up.

Kori stared at her mother's face. Immar always looked exhausted after one of her fits, but she also looked serene, as if all the malice had drained out of her. This could be deceptive, though, because sometimes Immar would be filled with the anger of the Old Ones and would vent it, in turn, on her people.

Immar breathed deeply. She opened her eyes and looked down at the villagers, squinting in the sunlight and struggling to focus on them. She pressed her fingers to her temples, winced, then threw her hands out from her body as if she were drawing poison from her head. She turned and looked at Mount Tomomor, still venting smoke and ash in the far distance. Then she looked back at the apprehensive faces.

"The houses that we built in the Village of the Old Ones have been damaged by the tremors this morning." Her voice had a strange sing-song sound to it, as if she herself was not forming the words and was merely a mouthpiece. "Stones were broken and must be replaced. This must be done." She took a deep breath and her shoulders slumped. "After that, the Old Ones will be satisfied."

Kori heard a slow sigh of understanding from the people around her. She just stood and stared, feeling confused. She had expected something more, somehow.

Her people had built the empty village around the burial pit as a home for the Old Ones if they should ever be released from their prison underground. The huts were a peace offering, a gesture that had demanded an immense amount of toil and hardship. This, too, of course, had been commanded by Immar, speaking on behalf of the Old Ones.

"We must send a party to gather fresh stones," Immar said.

Summer was already over, and winter was less than two months away. The tribe's store of smoked meat was smaller than it should be at this time of year, and it seemed far more urgent to Kori for young men of the tribe to be out hunting, not gathering rocks and rebuilding homes that would stand forever empty and unused. Still, if this would satisfy the spirits, obviously it should be done. No one questioned that, not even Kori—for she had seen with her own eyes that her mother was possessed.

"Half of the gathering party shall be women, and half shall be men," Immar went on suddenly. "It shall be so." She paused for a moment, looking from one face to the next. "And the gathering party will be led by my daughter, Kori."

For a long heartbeat Kori found herself staring up into her mother's eyes. Immar blinked as if she was surprised by what she had just said. Then, strangely, she smiled.

As Kori watched, Immar slid down from the Speaking Rock into Rohonar's waiting arms. The big man cradled her easily, moving forward while the villagers quickly made way for him and bowed with respect. Always, after one of Immar's fits, Rohonar would take her to their hut, where she would rest for the remainder of the day.

As Rohonar walked away, Kori saw people turning to look at her. A low murmur became an excited babble of words. Kori was only a young woman. Why had the spirits chosen her?

She turned to hide her face, feeling overcome by embarrassment—and by fear of the sudden, strange responsibility that had been placed upon her.

4

Oam stood beside her at the dock where the canoes were moored, while four of them were loaded with supplies. "I suppose it's natural enough," Oam said. "At a time like this—" he nodded toward Mount Tomomor, flaming in the noonday sun "—Mother and Father must stay to watch over the tribe. And I'm needed as a hunter. So, it's sensible for you to be the one to go."

Kori looked at him, wondering if he really believed what he said. He sounded uneasy, unsure of himself. He was jealous, she realized—hurt and angry that Kori had been chosen to lead the gathering party.

When the villagers had first begun to build homes out of sacred stones for the Old Ones around the Burial Pit, Rohonar led the expeditions with Immar at his side. As the years passed, others had sometimes taken his place, but always a man had been in charge. It was almost unthinkable for a woman to take that role.

Of course, in the past the task had been much greater, because many more stones had been needed. It was also the first time that no senior hunters or elders had been asked to participate in the journey; Immar had sent word naming six men and five women to travel with Kori, and all of them were younger then she.

She watched as a group of women carried bundles of smoked meat wrapped in goat skin and placed them in one of the canoes. Yainar was standing close by, taking a special interest because he was one of the young men who would be traveling with Kori. And this worried her most of all.

Yainar was the best hunter of his generation; she couldn't imagine how she would ever give him an instruction or an order. Rightfully he should be in command, and he was obviously aware of this as he marched to and fro, looking irritable as he watched a group of young women making the canoes ready. Food for three days, stone knives and axes, large ox skins for carrying the stones, rope made from braided sinews, poles to be used as sleds—everything had to be carefully stowed.

"The kindling, there," Yainar said, pointing to dried twigs that had been carefully wrapped in cured hide to protect them from water. "It should be at the stern, not at the bow."

Dutifully, the women shifted it, and Kori was torn by indecision. She respected Yainar, but surely it was wrong for him to take the role that had been given to her. Should she challenge him? The idea made her feel deeply apprehensive.

"The fourth canoe," Yainar said, walking across the dock. "It's loaded more heavily than the rest. The burden should be equal."

Kori saw that she would have to act now if she was going to act at all. She summoned her courage and stepped forward. "Yainar," she said quietly, "I must speak with you."

He stopped and turned to her. He stood so proudly, and he was so much taller than she was, it was hard for her not to feel intimidated. It was difficult, also, to cope with the feelings that stirred in her when she faced him.

He was wearing a simple tunic that left his arms bare, and the skin was tightly rounded, glowing brown in the golden sun. Despite herself, she imagined being held by him—

She suppressed the thought. She nodded toward the canoes. "I believe the burdens are equal enough," she said quietly. "Let's leave them as they are."

At first he merely looked surprised. Then, as he realized she was contradicting him, she saw him tensing, looking at her with anger.

Kori stepped closer to him. She forced herself to smile. "I'm sorry," she said softly, "but I have been chosen to lead this party. The Old Ones have willed it, and it must be so."

He paused, and his face became expressionless. It was impossible for her to sense his thoughts. His strength and his hunting prowess seemed to give him such confidence, he seldom showed emotion. He was shrewd and watchful, though, and she had never made the mistake of thinking he was merely a dumb brute. She sensed his intelligence—which made her more interested in him, even as it also made her more nervous about dealing with him.

"What you say is true," he said, speaking carefully, "but how can the leader of the junior hunters take instructions from a young woman?"

She felt her cheeks turning red. "I agree," she said haltingly, "this is a strange situation. So I'll be careful not to speak against you in front of the others."

He gave a curt nod.

"But in return," she said, once again bracing herself to challenge him, "I must ask that you should not speak against me. This way, there will be no strife between us."

His eyes narrowed as he watched her. He hesitated, trying to decide how to respond to her. Then, unexpectedly, he reached out and placed his hand on her shoulder—the same shoulder he had touched when he had steadied her in the darkness the night before. "You have a strong spirit," he said.

"I admire that, Kori." He glanced down, then up at her face. He seemed to be assessing her in the same way that a man might assess a steep slope that he had to climb, or an adversary he was expecting to fight.

Unexpectedly, he looked away. "Do what you want, here," he said. "I must fetch my bedroll and my spear." His hand tightened briefly on her shoulder, and then he turned and strode back toward the village without waiting for her to respond.

Kori watched his strong body as he climbed the slope from the dock, moving with grace despite his size. The women who had been loading the canoes paused in their work, and they too watched him go.

"Kori." It was Oam's voice, coming from behind her. He had observed the whole encounter, and he moved forward now, his plump face creased in a deep frown. "How could you speak to him like that?" He sounded agitated. "He's the leader of the junior hunters. He deserves proper respect."

She turned on him. "I am the daughter of the chieftain's wife," she snapped, "and I was chosen for this task." She watched his face, taking satisfaction from the impact of her words. "I, too, deserve respect," she said. "And now, forgive me, brother, but there is much I have to do."

They set off shortly after noon, four canoes sliding silently through the water.

On both banks tall pines and birches crowded close to the wide, curving river, and thick underbrush made it impossible to see among the trees. Crows and hawks circled overhead, their cries echoing into the stillness. The forest stood motionless, and its dark depths were a forbidding sight.

Kori had placed herself in the first canoe. She wished she could have come last, so that she could watch over the other three, but that would have meant allowing Yainar to take the lead, and if he did, Kori had no doubt he would set a pace that was hard for everyone to follow. She would have to call him back, and he would probably make some disparaging comment implying that she was too weak or wasn't properly able to paddle a canoe.

She still felt intimidated by the role she had been given, but there was some pleasure in the journey itself. She kneeled at the front of her canoe, dipping her wooden paddle. She enjoyed the way it slipped smoothly into the dark river. She liked the feeling as the blade gripped the water like a pair of cupped hands. She also enjoyed being out here away from the tribe, surrounded by the serene mystery of the forest—although Mount Tomomor, still venting fire, was an unpleasant reminder that the spirits she was serving were cruel and unforgiving in their demands. She shivered at the thought of making some error, offending them in a way she couldn't imagine, and suffering their anger.

She remembered the first expedition that her people had ever made to the Gathering Place. She had been only five years old, but still she had noticed the fearfulness of all the people in the party. Her father and mother had both been present, and there were twelve canoes, not four.

In those days the area around the burial pit had been bare and empty, just a table of hard, flat rock where only a few weeds grew. There had been a terrible earthquake. Immar had suffered a seizure that left her slack-faced and exhausted, and the next day she told the people what the spirits had told her: the island would be stricken by fire and thunderbolts unless homes were built for the Old Ones.

Immar said she had been shown a vision of a place upriver where there was an open wound in the land filled with rocks that were specially sacred, since they came from the inner parts of the earth. She demanded an expedition to find this place, gather the stones, and take them back to the island. Her people saw that she was speaking the deeper truth that only came from the Old Ones, so they mounted the expedition that she demanded—even though it terrified them, because the Gathering Place was on the Western Shore, which was taboo.

Many of the elders warned against it. They believed that the Western Shore was a place of strange beasts that possessed great power because they were enchanted by the Old Ones. The Western Shore was also governed by Mount Tomomor, and if people ventured there, he would punish them. Hunters went only to the Eastern Shore; this had been the way of the Island Tribe for as long as anyone could recall.

Still, Immar had been told where the sacred stones lay, and the Old Ones had commanded her to go there—so her people followed.

Even the bravest hunters had been fearful as they ventured onto the forbidden land, but their fears turned out to be groundless. There were no strange beasts—or if there were, the spirits kept them away. The stones were found just as Immar predicted, and the people gathered them and took them back to the island, where they began building houses around the burial pit. There was a great feast and celebration, and in the following years there were many more gathering expeditions. And although the task was long and hard, the people of the tribe began to find pleasure in it. It brought them together and gave them a sense of purpose that transcended the feelings of comradeship they found in everyday chores, because they were joined together in a form of worship.

5

Late in the afternoon they reached a break in the riverbank, an inlet where a stream trickled down, carving its own channel between banks of black sand. Kori took her canoe into this shallow water and jumped out, seizing hold of the canoe and pulling it aground. She paused, then, and looked quickly around while the other three canoes were beached beside hers.

The forest pressed in close to the water, the trees patterned with moss and festooned with ivy. There was a powerful smell of vegetation, and the elusive scent of animals and their droppings. A flock of crows rose suddenly from a pine close by and darkened the sky with their wings. Kori was feeling so preoccupied, she flinched from the sudden sound as they voiced their coarse cries, wheeled away across the river, and were gone.

Kori hoped the birds had been disturbed by her gathering party, not by some fierce predator nearby. She glanced at Yainar, trusting his hunter's instincts more than her own. But he showed no sign of alarm.

She made herself be calm. She went to each canoe in turn, making sure it was dragged firmly up onto the sand, and then she supervised the unloading. Finally she placed a raven's feather in each one to remind the Old Ones that they were on a sacred mission and should not be disturbed.

She turned to the eleven people who had journeyed here with her. She was silent for a moment, trying to judge their mood—and as she did so, she remembered all the times she had seen her father standing in the Meeting Place, pausing and looking down on the villagers. With surprise she realized that he must have been doing what she was doing now, trying to determine what they wanted and what he should say. He had always seemed so powerful, so omniscient, Kori had never imagined that he might need to reassure himself about the tribe before speaking to them.

Facing her now were four young men aged from fourteen to eighteen, with four young wives. The men were standing with their arms folded around their spears, doing their best to look proud and brave. Their wives stood respectfully behind them, glancing uneasily at the forest and at each other. None of them had come here on a gathering journey before.

Standing a little way apart was Yainar, watching Kori calmly, waiting to see what she would say or do. Beyond him stood Derneren, nineteen years old, slow-witted, slow-moving, no taller than Kori, but heavily built and immensely strong. He had lost one eye many years ago when another child struck him accidentally with a spear. His injury made him a poor hunter, but his strength made him useful now, and he had been here before.

Finally there was a woman, Nenara, the same age as Derneren, and almost as strong. She had a shy, gentle nature, but she moved with the mannerisms of a man, and Kori liked her, even though she felt sorry for her. It seemed unlikely that Nenara would ever find a mate in the village.

"It's a short distance to the Gathering Place," Kori said. "There are marks on the trees to guide us. We will camp there, eat, and sleep. At sunrise we'll harvest the stones, and by noon, our canoes will be filled."

She paused, thinking back to other times she had been here. Was there something else she should say? She saw the four young hunters looking restless. "This is a sacred duty," she reminded them. "We stand on the Western Shore only because the Old Ones permit us here. We must respect their power. This is their land. Don't venture off the path even if you see game in the forest."

One of them—a boy named Horeth—was giving her a snide grin. He was a fierce little man with a thin face, sharp features, and small dark eyes. Kori sensed hostility behind his grin, and she knew instinctively that he couldn't be counted on to obey any instruction from her.

She eyed him a moment, then turned to Derneren. "Have you ever ventured off the trail to the Gathering Place?" she asked. She already knew what the answer would be; he was such a straightforward, simple man, he always respected the customs of the tribe.

"Only a fool would leave the trail," he said slowly.

Kori turned back and looked again at Horeth. She watched him steadily and saw his grin fade. Something showed in his eyes: resentment, perhaps, or a new respect—she couldn't tell.

"Yainar," she said, turning to him. "You are the oldest hunter here. You should lead us through the forest."

He seemed faintly surprised. Then he nodded, and she knew she had acted wisely. He would have scorned her if she had tried to claim the skill and experience to guide them.

As they shouldered their packs and moved up the beach, Kori wondered if she should follow Yainar. But then, as she saw him taking powerful strides, she gestured for the others to walk ahead of her. She knew herself too well: if she walked right behind him, she would be far too easily distracted by his body. The knowledge made her annoyed with herself, but she had to admit it was so.

They walked in single file through the trees, stepping carefully on the rocky ground, watching for animal tracks or droppings. Even though she had been here before, Kori felt awed and nervous walking on the sacred ground. Still, there were ax marks on many of the trees along the way, showing the path that had been established by the elders with her father and mother so many years ago.

Abruptly Kori noticed something tugging at her arm. She turned quickly, but it was just a clump of brambles that had snagged her robe. She plucked the brambles off her, then paused, frowning. Some strange white strands were wrapped around the thorns, torn from some creature that had passed this way before her. She peered at them closely. They were the color of sheep wool, but much coarser, like the hair of a bear.

Cautiously, Kori tugged the strands free. She rubbed them between her finger and thumb, then sniffed them. She had never seen animal fur like this before. She felt suddenly cold inside, wondering what beast would have such a white coat.

She looked quickly around. The only sound and movement came from her companions walking ahead of her, disappearing among the trees, unaware that she had dropped back.

Quickly, Kori tucked the white fur inside the pouch where she carried her firesticks and tinder. Was it an accident that she had found this trophy? Her mother, of course, said there were no accidents; everything was the will of the Old Ones.

Kori broke into a run, hurrying to rejoin the rest of her party.

As the sun was setting, they reached the Gathering Place.

The sky above was a thick, rich purple. To the west, streamers of cloud glowed gold, almost looking as if they were reflecting the glow from the summit of Mount Tomomor.

The twelve travelers found themselves in a wide glade where the ground was so stony, only a few weak saplings had been able to take root. The forest formed a dark, living barrier curving around the left side of the clearing, while to the right lay a wall of rock.

Long ago, in some geological catastrophe, a rift had opened here between two sections of the land. One section had risen till it was twice the height of a man, revealing a strip of pale brown rock that had crumbled or shattered into oblong pieces, most of which were still trapped in the wall of the rift. These were the sacred stones.

Kori moved forward through gathering twilight to a circle of ashes and charcoal where countless fires had been built over the years. "Horeth," she called. She turned to the other three young men. "Caruth, Relvan, Leiwan—you should gather dry wood for a new fire before it's too dark to see. Yainar—keep watch, please, while the women unpack our food and bedding."

The people moved to follow her instructions, except for Horeth, who remained where he was. "Gathering wood is not work for a man," he said.

Kori had half expected something like this, and she had already decided what to say. "This is no ordinary place," she told him. "There may be dangers here that we don't understand. You have had practice with a spear. The women have not."

Horeth considered her words. Grudgingly, then, he did as she said.

Kori watched him go, and she smiled to herself with secret satisfaction. In truth she wasn't especially concerned by the dangers of the Western Shore, since the Old Ones themselves had demanded that she and her people should be here. But it gave her secret pleasure to see a man like Horeth doing the work that women were normally forced to do, stooping and rummaging in the underbrush, finding dead-wood and dragging it back.

Meanwhile, Yainar had walked to the wall of rock on the right side of the clearing and was pulling himself up easily from one foothold to the next. Kori watched him as he scaled the rift, reached the top, and stood there looking first to the north, then to the south, silhouetted against the evening sky with his spear in his hand.

She forced herself to turn away. When she'd first come of age, the first man she'd approached had been a young hunter named Ornir. When he rejected her, she felt pain that was so intense, it lived with her still. To be the daughter of the chieftain, and be refused by the men she chose! It was an unbearable humiliation.

A year later, when Kori had chosen another man and he, too, had refused her, she felt forced to admit that her family's special status in the tribe was not enough to compensate for the strangeness, the difference that people sensed in her. She realized, with deep sadness, she might never be accepted by any man.

But now—what should she make of Yainar? She could still feel where he had tightened his grip on her shoulder when she had confronted him while the canoes were being loaded, and she could still see the way he had looked at her with respect. It was hard for her to see his actions clearly through her own haze of desire.

Part of the problem was that he was such a difficult man to assess. There were fewer than a hundred people in the Island Tribe, which meant that to some extent every-one knew each other. But Yainar had always been cautious and reticent, and he spent most of his time with other men. When he spoke he always chose his words carefully, never saying anything that could cause offense. He was polite to the senior hunters and deeply respectful to the elders.

In the four years since he had come of age, he had turned down at least half a dozen women who'd wanted to pair with him. Kori was sure he had no real interest in her. And yet, she still found herself wondering if it was really so.

6

Later, as the stars came out, the gathering party sat around
the fire and warmed the smoked venison and goat meat they
had brought with them. They sang songs of peace, songs to
conquer evil, songs to warn fierce beasts to stay away, and
Kori found pleasure in the simple words. To be isolated like
this, feeling her special status in the group instead of feeling
like an outcast, was new and special.

She was troubled, though, that Yainar had chosen to sit
beside her. Carefully, she avoided looking at him. But that
meant she found herself watching the young couples sitting at
the opposite site of the fire, and she felt envious as the
women moved close to the men and the men casually
accepted the women's presence, knowing they had committed themselves for life. Two of the couples had paired only six
months ago, and Kori saw the men looking at the women's
bodies from time to time with obvious interest. How would it
feel to be desired like that, and to know she could be taken
by a man any night—or every night? The idea was so distant
from her life, she found it impossible to imagine.

As the fire burned low, the singing stopped. Derneren volunteered to stand watch for the first quarter of the night, and Kori agreed. She added more wood to the fire, lay down beside it—and finally dared to look at Yainar where he lay just an arm's length away.

She found him already looking at her. His eyes were somber, half hidden in shadow.

For a long moment, they stared at each other. She waited for him to say something, but he stayed silent. The moment stretched out, and Kori felt tension winding tighter inside her—till she simply had to speak.

"Is there something you want?" she said.

He smiled faintly and shook his head. And then, without a word, he wrapped himself in his blanket of bearskin and turned over with his back to her, so she could no longer see his face.

For a long time Kori lay wrestling with her emotions. She heard the quiet breathing of the people around the fire and the faint murmur of Mount Tomomor, still wreathed in smoke and venting fire, shedding faint yellow radiance from the west. Finally she closed her eyes and managed to drag her thoughts away from the present moment and the enigmatic man lying just an arm's length away from her, but then she heard a new sound that made her suddenly alert.

A faint whispering came from somewhere out in the shadows, away from the fire. She froze, listening. A man was muttering something; then a woman answered.

Kori propped herself on an elbow and looked at the figures in their bedrolls. Everyone seemed to be sleeping peacefully now. But then she realized that two of the bedrolls were empty.

There was a moment of silence, then the whispering again. It was a man's voice, sounding angry. Then a woman, sounding plaintive. And then a scuffling sound, a slap, and a muffled cry.

Kori stood up. She saw Derneren standing atop the ridge where Yainar had stood before, keeping watch. The big man was looking away into the distance as if he had heard nothing out of the ordinary.

Kori wondered if it was her place to interfere. Cautiously she crept through the grass, into the darkness. As the warmth of the fire receded behind her and the night closed around her, she began to feel she was behaving foolishly—but then, without warning, she found two figures in front of her, Horeth and his wife Mima, the woman lying on her back on the ground, the man sitting astride her, holding her down.

Kori stopped and stared. Both of them were oblivious of her. At first she thought they were coupling on the ground, but then she realized Horeth was sitting astride Mima's waist, leading forward, holding her with one hand by her hair while she struggled and whimpered under him. He was whispering something urgently. He shook her, then slapped her face hard. He drew back his hand to slap her again—and Kori acted without thinking. She stepped forward and grabbed his wrist.

He whirled around and stared at her, and for a moment neither of them moved. Horeth looked astonished—and Kori felt equally startled by what she had done.

She found the will to speak. "It's not the way of our people for a man to treat his wife like this," she said.

Horeth wrenched his wrist free from her grip. Cursing under his breath, he released his hold on Mima and got to his feet. Kori found herself staring up into his narrow, bony face, the little dark eyes glittering with malice in the dim light from the fire. "It's not the way of our people," Horeth said, "for a woman to tell a man how to behave." He reached out so quickly, Kori didn't even see his hand till it clutched the neck of her robe, twisting it, pulling her toward him. "You'll say nothing of this," he whispered to her, "because this is not your affair."

The anger in him was frightening—but his behavior outraged her. "Let go of me," she told him, "or I will speak to my father—"

She broke off with a little cry as Horeth made an angry sound at the back of his throat, brought his leg up, hooked his heel behind Kori's knee, and pushed her hard. She found herself falling.

She hit the ground so hard, it knocked her breath out of her. She lay there, clutching her abdomen, unable to breathe. She looked up in shock as Horeth loomed over her.

Then there was the faint sound of a footstep, and a wooden shaft was thrust forward across Horeth's chest, holding him back. Kori turned her head and saw Yainar holding out his spear. "Don't be foolish," Yainar said quietly.

For a moment Horeth looked as if he was ready to fight, but he hesitated when he found himself facing Yainar. For a moment, neither of the men spoke.

Finally, Horeth grunted with disgust. "This is nothing to do with you," he said.

Yainar lifted his spear and rested its end on the ground. "Kori is the daughter of our chieftain," he said. "She was chosen by the spirits themselves to lead this party. Were you threatening her, Horeth?"

Horeth gestured irritably. "We'll say no more of this."

Kori struggled up off the ground. "No," she said. "That is for me to decide."

Horeth turned swiftly. He glared at her, then pointed his finger at her. "My wife was looking at another man. When we were sitting around the fire singing. She was staring at Relvan for half the night. I had reason to punish her."

"But that's not true," said Mima. She got up onto her knees. Her plaintive face turned toward Horeth, then Kori. "I looked at no one."

"Quiet!" Horeth snapped at her, raising his hand warningly.

Many times, Kori had seen Mima sitting and staring off into space while a chore lay half-finished in front of her. The woman was simple-minded; her attention wandered. That was her only crime.

Yainar shrugged. "Why don't you and your wife go back to your places near the fire," he said. "There's heavy work for all of us tomorrow."

Horeth glared at him, then glared at Kori. He grabbed his wife by the back of her robe, hauled her up, and pushed her ahead of him, striding through the grass without looking back.

"He is a small man," Yainar said, half to himself, "who wishes to be bigger." He smiled faintly as if Horeth was a source of idle entertainment. Then he turned quickly and looked to one side, sensing something in the darkness.

Derneren was standing there. "I heard a disturbance," he said.

Yainar relaxed. "It was nothing."

The two men eyed each other for a moment, and even though Derneren was slow-witted, he seemed to understand Yainar's unspoken message. "All right," he said. He turned to go back to his post.

"But I may as well take over the watch now," Yainar went on. "You've done your share."

Derneren stopped. "As you wish," he said. He looked at Yainar, glanced at Kori, then trudged away to join the others by the fire.

Kori paused for a moment, trying to calm herself, trying to decide what she should do.

"What happened?" Yainar asked her, speaking quietly while he watched Horeth, Mima, and Derneren settling themselves back in their bedrolls.

"I saw Horeth hit his wife, and I seized his arm to stop him," said Kori. "He tripped me and threw me down."

Yainar nodded slowly. "You humiliated him."

"Maybe so," she said, "but he had no right to threaten me, and he was wrong to hit his wife."

Over by the camp fire, Derneren tossed some fresh wood onto it and the flames leaped briefly. The light touched the side of Yainar's handsome face: his high forehead, his broad mouth, and his heavy jaw.

He turned away for a moment, looking toward the flickering silhouette of Mount Tomomor. "There is evil in our world," he said, "and it touches all men." He held his spear between his two hands and slid one of them to the serrated flint tip. He rubbed his thumb lightly around the deadly edge. "I believe the evil makes us do things that may be wrong, as you say. Still, you cannot erase it."

"But even if you're right," she objected, "we must still try to control it when we find it in our tribe."

He laughed softly and turned back to face her. Unexpectedly he reached out. His fingers lightly touched her cheek. "You have a strong spirit, Kori. But you are ignorant of the ways of the world."

Kori stepped back, feeling disconcerted by the physical contact and annoyed by his condescending tone. "If you speak of ignorance, remember that I'm two years older than you."

He shook his head. "You know nothing of men. You haven't witnessed the pleasure a hunter takes in killing. You haven't heard men talk about their women and boast about the things they do to them."

"I have woman friends—" Kori began.

"Yes, but they are cautious when they speak to you, because you are the chieftain's daughter. And a woman who is paired will never speak so freely to a woman who is not." Abruptly he turned away from her. "I have to stand watch now. It's my duty." He walked away into the darkness.

She blinked. He had stood with her, looking at her, touching her casually—and now he had turned his back on her. She cursed him silently, then herself for being so easily aroused. Impulsively, she strode after him. "I'll sit with you," she said.

He stopped and looked at her in surprise. "If you wish," he said, "but you'll have to climb the ridge."

"So, I will climb the ridge."

They moved toward it, two shadows in the night. "Here," he said, turning toward her and clasping his hands, cupping them to make a step for her.

She hesitated, then placed her foot on his palms. He hoisted her smoothly, easily, thrusting her up till his arms were stretched above his head. Kori found herself reaching out to the rocks at the top of the ridge, digging her fingers in, pulling herself up in the darkness. And then, a moment later, Yainar was sitting beside her.

"We should sit back to back," he told her. "That way, between the two of us, we can see everything."

"Of course." She squirmed around till her back was touching his. His body was warm. His shoulders were much broader than hers, and she could sense his strength through the contact.

For a while, the only sound was the murmuring of Mount Tomomor.

"I think perhaps there is something you should know," Yainar said at last.

His voice sounded oddly remote. She wished they were looking at each other, so that she could see his face.

"You must know," Yainar went on, "I've bided my time for four years now, waiting before I pair with a woman. But I think I have finally made my choice. I plan to be paired with Tiola."

For a moment the words made no sense. And then, when she understood them, they were impossible to believe. "She's a child!" Kori blurted out.

If Yainar was surprised by her outburst, he showed no

sign of it. "She's young," he agreed, "but she'll come of age before the ceremony. Her thirteenth birthday is at the spring solstice."

He meant it, Kori realized. He had already chosen his mate, even though the girl hadn't yet bled for the first time. "Why are you telling me this?" she said, feeling confused and angry.

He laughed softly. "I thought you might be interested."

Kori hugged herself, trying to understand what was happening and why. She'd told herself not to be foolish, yet she still felt cheated. Why had he looked at her that way and touched her?

"I've talked to other men who are paired with women four or five years younger," Yainar went on. "They say it is good to have a young bride. It makes a pairing more likely to succeed. The man is less tempted by other women, and his wife is more likely to obey him."

"And—this is all that matters to you?" she blurted out, unable to keep the disapproval out of her voice. "You simply want a young woman who will obey?"

"Of course," he said. "If a woman is obedient, there's less reason to punish her."

She pulled away from him, finding the contact suddenly repellent, but then she realized what he was doing. "You're just saying these things to provoke me," she said. "This is just a game to you."

He laughed. "Maybe so." He stretched, flexing his powerful body. "But it's true that I intend to pair with Tiola."

She listened to his voice, and she realized she had to believe this much. "But why have you really chosen her?" she asked him.

He was silent for a moment. When he spoke again, the playfulness was gone from his voice. "I'm an ambitious man, Kori," he said. "I can never lead the tribe, because your brother Oam will inherit that honor. But I hope to be the leader of the senior hunters one day. And Tiola's father currently holds that position."

The truth, she realized, was almost worse than his lie had been. And there was something in the way he was telling her that suggested he was still playing with her, using the words as a weapon, jabbing her with them and waiting to see her flinch.

"Well," she said, trying to remove any trace of emotion from her voice, "you can pair with anyone you wish. It's of no interest to me."

"Oh, Kori." He sighed and shook his head. "You can't pretend, because I've seen the way you look at me. It's true that you really do have a fine spirit. But—you are a strange person, with your wild temper and your ideas about right and wrong. I'm sorry, but I do not desire you."

Despite herself, Kori let out a little cry. "Why are you saying these hurtful things?"

He turned toward her, watching her face in the moonlight. "You asked for the truth. Would you prefer me to lie to you instead?"

Kori thought of all the answers she could give, but none of them would begin to express her real feelings. In anger and frustration she turned around, lay on her stomach, and dropped her legs over the edge of the ridge. Clumsily she lowered herself back down the wall of loose rock. She searched for a foothold, found herself slipping, and fell painfully in the darkness.

She heard Yainar call out, asking if she was hurt. She ignored him as she picked herself up and hurried away through the tall grass, back to the people sleeping beside the fire.

7

The next morning was cold and damp. Heavy gray clouds had settled over the forest during the night, mingling with the smoke that still rose from the peak of Mount Tomomo. The wind was blowing from the west, now, and Kori's throat was sore from the sulfurous fumes. She heard people coughing as they woke in the chill air and roused themselves, stamping their feet and flexing their arms.

Nenara set to work rebuilding the fire. As soon as it was hot enough to warm the leftovers from last night's meal, the people crouched around it, eating greedily.

Hardly anyone spoke. Kori noticed two of the young hunters giving her cautious, curious glances, but as soon as she looked at them, they averted their eyes. Horeth was grimly silent, staring straight ahead at the fire, ignoring Kori completely. Beside him, Mima looked pale and nervous. Her cheek was slightly swollen, and Kori noticed her touch it and frown to herself.

As for Yainar, he was as calm as ever. Kori wondered, in fact, if there was anything that would ever disturb his self-confidence. In a way she envied his detachment, even while she hated him for it.

She finished breakfast as quickly as she could, then scattered the fire and threw dirt over it to discourage people from lingering. "There's work for us to do," she said. "Derneren, you'll pry the stones loose. Nenara and Yainar, you'll help me lower them down and put them on the skins. The rest of you can take the loaded skins to the river." She paused, waiting to see if anyone would object. The young hunters got up and started toward the rift where the rock was exposed, but Derneren held back.

"What is it?" Kori asked. All she wanted now was to finish this task and return to the village as soon as possible, so that she could be alone again.

Derneren cleared his throat. "It's the custom," he said in his deep, halting voice, "to say a prayer."

Kori chided herself. Derneren was right: they couldn't take the rock without the ritual ceremony. But as she stood to recite the words, she found that her mind was blank. She was too preoccupied, too impatient to remember what she should say—and she had never felt deeply about the ritual anyway.

"Shall I speak?" Yainar asked quietly.

Kori gave him an irritable look. "If you wish."

Yainar raised his palms in the ritual sign of humility and surrender. "Old Ones," he said, "we come here to serve you, to obey you, to harvest the sacred stones, not for ourselves, but for your use. If we do not please you, show us a sign so that we may know your discontent. We ask for guidance. We beg for mercy."

"We ask for guidance," the others repeated after him. "We beg for mercy."

There was a long moment of silence. The clouds moved low overhead, driven by a strong wind. The trees bowed and shook their leaves. There was a faint sound as one of the men shifted slightly and his moccasin scuffed the ground. Away by the river, crows barked at each other, their voices almost drowned by the wind.

One by one, then, the people turned away, ready to begin work.

Yainar lagged behind, falling into step beside Kori. "Did I speak the prayer well?" he said.

She refused to look at him. "Well enough."

"And do you think the Old Ones listened? Will they protect us, now, and should we be thankful to them?"

She stopped and stared at him. He was smiling faintly, watching her face to see how she would respond. She sensed that he was mocking her, testing her. But how could he say such things? Had he sensed, somehow, her own confusion about the faith and customs of their tribe? No, he was just toying with her again.

She pushed quickly past him. "I don't want to talk to you," she said.

Derneren went to the rift and started climbing, finding handholds in the raw strata. He reached a place where stones had been taken previously, leaving a deep cavity in the vertical face. He worked his bulk into this cavity, then took from Kori an oak pole with a wedge-shaped tip and forced it into a crevice in the rocks. He leaned on the pole, prying out a perfect chunk of the brown stone.

Nenara and Yainar moved forward. They reached up and took hold of the stone and lowered it down, placing it in a sling made from goat skins stitched together with sheep gut.

Derneren was already levering out another section of stone, grunting with the effort, dislodging a little shower of dirt. And so it went on, till a dozen pieces had been placed in the sling.

Kori turned and found Horeth and Mima waiting close

by. She would have to deal with him sooner or later; it might as well be now. "Carry the first load," she said.

Horeth paused, taking his time to obey. He stepped forward, then, and slid a heavy pole through handles that were stitched to the sling. He beckoned his wife, and the two of them kneeled and raised the pole onto their shoulders. Mima almost lost her balance, and Kori saw that she was barely able to carry the weight because the sling was closer to her than to her husband. Intentionally or by accident, he had given her a heavier share of the load.

Kori felt angry as she saw the two of them moving away, but she was in no mood for another confrontation. She turned for a moment, looking at Mount Tomomor under the lowering clouds. It seemed to her that Yainar was right, and truly there was a force of evil in this world that left no one untouched. The Old Ones punished the men of the Island Tribe, and the men punished others around them. . . .

She drove the thoughts away. More stones were being pried loose. Kori stepped forward and helped to lower them to the ground. Another sling was filled, and then another. The young hunters and their wives shuttled to and fro, taking full slings down to the river and bringing them back empty, and stone by stone, as the morning passed, the task was done.

Eventually Kori went down to the river. Leiwan and his wife were there, loading the canoes. Kori watched them anxiously. Each canoe had been made by hollowing out a massive pine log. They were heavy and strong, but they were not very stable, and if they sat too low in the water there was always the danger of a fierce wind tipping them or flooding them, which would be an unthinkable disaster.

"I think," said Kori, "this will be enough." She turned and started back through the forest.

She was less vigilant now than she had been. This place no longer seemed so strange or threatening. The task was not so challenging, and all she really wanted was to leave.

She stopped. She heard a rustling sound—the sound of a creature moving slowly through underbrush.

Then she heard footsteps coming toward her. She looked and saw Horeth and his wife carrying another load of stones. For a moment she felt confused, thinking that the sounds had come from them.

She stood, turning, trying to see among the trees. The wind blew hard, and the whole forest seemed to shiver. Storm clouds were moving so low, they seemed to brush the upper branches. A pair of thrushes suddenly bolted from a tree close by and raced away with an urgent flurry of wings. The wind blew again, and the trees creaked—and then she heard what she had heard before, away off the trail to her right: the sound of an animal treading warily.

Horeth heard it, too. He dropped the pole he was carrying and crouched, peering into the forest and raising his spear.

Kori looked behind her. The beached canoes were not so far away. She could run to them swiftly enough. She was painfully aware that she had no way to defend herself. Silently she cursed the taboo that restricted women from learning to hunt and defend themselves.

"There!" Horeth said, pointing, staring intently.

Kori looked. She saw a faint movement, a pale blur flitting between the trees.

"Whitebeast!" Horeth cried. He sprang forward, charging into the forest, wading through dead leaves, leaping through the underbrush.

"No!" Kori shouted. She turned and saw Leiwan hurrying toward her from the river. He glanced at her, looked at Horeth—and then he, too, ran into the forest.

"No!" Kori screamed again. "Come back! Do you want to anger the Old Ones? Do you want them to punish us all?" She peered after them and glimpsed them dodging among the trees. In the far distance once again she saw a shape, a creature as big as a bear but far more agile, running wildly, plunging deep into the forest, fleeing from the men—or leading them after it.

Kori heard more footsteps and found Yainar and Derneren running from the Gathering Place. "Horeth and Leiwan!" she shouted to them. "There!" She pointed.

Yainar nodded. He and Derneren both left the trail. Yainar ran lightly, swiftly, soon disappearing among the trees, while Derneren went after him, making a huge amount of noise. Birds scattered, screaming in alarm. Squirrels leaped up into the higher branches, and the wind blew again, moaning through the trees, whipping Kori's hair into her face and thrusting through her robe, making her clutch herself and shiver. She stood alone, waiting helplessly. The sounds of pursuit vanished, and she had the terrible sense that the forest had consumed the men. Then she heard voices. Angry shouts.

She waited, feeling the time drag by. Finally she heard footsteps and saw the figures making their way back toward her, Horeth and Leiwan coming first, Yainar and Derneren coming after them, yelling at them, forcing them back to the trail.

Horeth ran toward her when he saw her. His arms and legs were bleeding from bramble scratches, and his hair was full of twigs and leaves. "You had no right!" he shouted, confronting her.

Yainar strode forward, grabbed Horeth's shoulder, and spun him around. Without pausing, Yainar feinted, then quickly punched the other man's biceps. Horeth's hand opened reflexively and Yainar seized his spear, plucking it away. He took a pace back. "Be calm," he said.

Horeth glowered at him. His face twisted. "It was a whitebeast!" he shouted.

"I understand." Yainar nodded slowly. "But *we* have no right, Horeth. As you well know."

Horeth clenched his fists. Suddenly he reached inside his robe and pulled out his flint knife. He looked at Yainar, then at Derneren, then at Kori. He gave a cry of frustration, then turned to a nearby tree, raised his arm, and stabbed the tree with all his strength. He pulled the knife free, then jammed it into the tree again, and again, till his all strength and his rage were exhausted.

"It would have been a fine kill," said Yainar, moving up behind Horeth and placing his hand on his shoulder. "But the Old Ones allow us here for only one purpose."

Horeth turned, knocking Yainar's hand away. "The Old Ones showed the whitebeast to us!" he cried. "Why would they do that if they wanted me not to hunt it?"

"Perhaps to tempt you," said Kori.

Horeth turned toward her, blinking.

"She speaks truly," said Yainar. "None of us knows the will of the spirits. And we have no right to know."

Horeth grunted in disgust. "I could have killed it," he muttered. He pushed past Yainar and marched away toward the river.

Kori had been frightened by him, but now she realized she pitied him. His anger and his ambitions seemed so small.

She turned and found Yainar watching her. She forced a stiff smile. "Thank you," she said.

He nodded expressionlessly.

"You think it was a whitebeast?" she asked. No one had ever captured the creature. It seemed to live only on the Western Shore, and only a few hunters had ever glimpsed it from their canoes on the river.

"I think it was," said Yainar. He moved quickly past her, following Horeth, taking care not to let his body brush against hers.

Kori reached into her pouch. While Derneren went to pick up the pole that Horeth had been carrying, and Leiwan went back along the trail to summon the rest of the people from the gathering site, Kori stood staring into the depths of the forest, feeling the strange texture of the white fur between her fingers.

8

8

The canoes lay low in the water, barely a hand's breadth above the surface, and they rocked dangerously in the fierce, gusty wind. They were traveling side by side, an arm's length apart, like deer huddling together against the storm. Kori was in the leftmost one, kneeling near the bow with Caruth and his wife ranged behind her. Nenara was in the next canoe to her right, paddling it with Horeth and Mima. Derneren headed the third canoe, and Yainar the fourth.

The river curved briefly to the west, which forced them to face the wind. Kori saw that Mount Tomomor was completely hidden, now, by clouds. Their undersides were black, and where daylight filtered weakly between them it was a sickly yellow, as if the mountain had infected the whole sky with its garish glow and had sent this storm to punish the people who dwelled below.

In the distance Kori saw a gray curtain of rain advancing across the forest. Thunder rumbled, and there was a brief flicker of sheet lighting.

"We won't reach the island ahead of the storm," Nenara said.

"We'll be wise to shelter till it passes," said Yainar.

They were offering her advice, Kori realized. But along this stretch of the river there were sandbars that could easily overturn a canoe. She felt distraught as she looked at the fury of the oncoming storm. Why, she wondered, was she being tested like this?

"I think we can reach the island." That was Horeth speaking. She saw him kneeling behind Nenara, digging his paddle deep, leaning forward, applying all his strength. Gradually his canoe was advancing ahead of the rest.

"I say we find shelter," Kori decided, "on the left bank."

"It may not be safe to turn across the current," Horeth shouted.

Directly ahead, the gray wall of rain had almost reached the river. She could hear it roar as it pounded the trees near the water. Meanwhile, in the forest near Kori, no birds were singing. All the creatures had taken shelter.

The island lay just around the next curve, and the current was urging them on. Still, Kori saw that they could not possibly escape the rain. "To the shore," she shouted again.

"It's not safe!" Horeth shouted.

"The sandbars are behind us," said Yainar.

"Not so!" Horeth yelled at him.

There was a sudden shout of alarm. It was Mima's voice. "Stop!" she screamed.

Kori turned and saw that while Horeth's canoe had moved ahead, Nenara's had started turning. Its prow was closing on the rear of Horeth's canoe, where Mima was kneeling.

"Nenara, turn back!" Kori shouted.

"You said to take shelter," the big woman called. She swore, digging in her paddle, trying to avoid ramming the other canoe.

Mima cried out. She raised her paddle to fend off the canoe that was turning toward her.

"Don't do that!" Kori called out.

The panicky woman didn't listen. She pushed out as hard as she could with her paddle—then screamed in fear as her own canoe rocked backward under her. The left side of it dipped down and water poured in.

"Hold out your paddle!" Nenara shouted. "Hold it out to me!"

Mima turned and threw herself out toward Nenara. The big woman seized Mima's paddle and pulled hard, dragging Mima's canoe upright again, but the younger woman was still so distraught, she kept hauling on her end of the paddle. She cried out again as her canoe listed to the right, now, tipping her forward. She flailed as she lost her balance. A moment later she plunged forward, down into the river.

Her canoe overturned. Its precious cargo of stones rumbled into the river. Derneren, at the prow, and Horeth, at the center, leaped free. Kori saw them hit the water and disappear under the surface for a moment. Then their heads appeared and they started swimming desperately back to the overturned canoe. They seized it and clung to it.

"Mima!" Horeth shouted, looking quickly around. "Mima, where are you?"

"She hit her head as she fell," Nenara called out. "I saw it strike the edge of my canoe."

Kori felt helpless. The storm was almost on them, and Mima, unlike most islanders, was a poor swimmer. As Kori scanned the water for any sign of the woman, the rain engulfed her. It fell like a great waterfall, instantly inundating her clothes, blurring her vision, covering her face. She gasped, barely able to see or breathe. "Mima!" she called out, searching hopelessly through the liquid curtain. Dimly she saw Derneren and Horeth swimming to opposite ends of their overturned canoe. They clawed at it and managed to turn it upright again, and now that it had shed its burden of stones, it sat high in the water. The men clambered into it, but Mima was still nowhere to be seen.

There was a sudden flash, so bright it hurt Kori's eyes. A moment later she flinched and covered her ears as thunder crashed across the sky.

"I'll try to find her," Nenara called.

Kori was still half blinded by the lightning and engulfed by the rain, but she could see the faint gray shape of Nenara standing ready to dive into the river.

"No," Kori called out, "you'll never find her. Stay there!" The storm was so heavy and the light so dim, it would be impossible for Nenara to see anything under the surface of the river.

Meanwhile, the current was carrying them on through the rain, around a curve. Kori couldn't see the island yet, but she knew it was there.

Horeth was still shouting for his wife, leaning over the edge of his canoe, peering hopelessly into the storm.

"Island ahead!" It was Yainar's voice.

Kori saw the rocky, tree-topped silhouette looming through the heavy grayness. This was another source of danger: she knew there were treacherous rocks just beneath the surface at the northern end of the Island Tribe's home.

"To the right!" Kori shouted.

This time, the canoes all turned together.

"Mima!" Horeth shouted, sounding shrill and desperate as he kept trying to see through the downpour. "Mima!"

Strange, Kori thought, that he cared so much for a woman he abused.

"I see her!" he shouted.

The rain was easing off. As the four canoes slowly passed the northern point of the island, Horeth stood up. "There!" he cried.

Kori saw something floating in the water. A pale shape surrounded by something black.

"It's her!" Horeth threw off his coat, kicked off his moccasins, leaped into the river, and started swimming wildly across the current.

Kori saw a beach ahead where the canoes could land safely. She wasn't willing to take them down to the tribe's usual docking place now; that could wait till the weather cleared. She shouted and pointed, and the others followed her. Soon there was a rasping sound as the canoes grounded themselves on a gentle slope of sand.

Quickly she stepped out. She felt the cold river around her knees and rough sand under her feet. She seized the prow of the canoe and heaved it forward.

She turned, then, and looked for Horeth. She saw him swimming back toward the beach, dragging something after him through the rain. He reached the shallow water and stood up, his skin pinched and pale, his eyes showing his shock and dismay. He heaved at the burden beside him and threw it onto the sand. Kori found herself running forward, dropping down onto her knees, reaching out, touching the cold skin of Mima's face where she lay on her back, her long black hair drifting in the shallow water, her lips parted, her eyes closed.

Gradually, the rain stopped. The darkest clouds moved farther on, the thunder sounded away across the Eastern Shore, and for a moment the sky brightened.

The pale light showed a purple swelling on Mima's forehead and water dribbling out of her mouth. Horeth pushed Kori roughly aside, took hold of his wife's shoulders, and dragged her up against him. Her body flopped lifelessly in his hands. "Mima!" he shouted. He shook her again, unable to believe she was dead.

"What happened here?"

Kori turned quickly. She saw that some of the villagers

had gathered up at the top of the sloping beach, attracted by the shouting. They were clustering protectively together, afraid to face this new portent, but one figure separated herself and came walking forward, her moccasins leaving deep footprints in the black sand. Kori looked up and saw her mother staring down at her.

"My wife is dead," said Horeth, sounding lost and confused. "She fell in and drowned." He turned and saw Kori, and his confusion turned to outrage. "It was her fault," he cried, pointing at her. "You killed her!"

9

Kori lay alone on her bed. The clouds had cleared and gentle afternoon sunlight was warming the island. She saw a bright line of light below the door flap and faint radiance filtering down through the smoke hole above the fire in the corner. She wished she could be outside, enjoying the touch of the light, trying to dispel the coldness that gripped her. But she had been banished to her hut, told to wait here alone in the dimness to learn the decision of the tribe.

Kori covered her face with her hands, wanting desperately to understand the world around her and the forces that governed it. She closed her eyes, and inside her mind, she tried to see down inside the heavy black rock beneath her. The Old Ones spoke to Immar; why wouldn't they speak to her? She shared the same blood, and Yainar said she shared the same spirit—

She heard someone talking outside the flap of goat skin covering the doorway. It was her mother's voice. Then the skin was pushed aside, letting in a brief burst of sunlight, and Immar stood with her hands clasped in front of her, gazing at Kori.

Immar had whitened her cheeks with chalk dust, and her eyes and mouth were rimmed with black. She was wearing her finest ceremonial deerskin robe. The lower half was stained deep black, symbolizing the realm of the Old Ones. The upper half was white, decorated with symbols and pictures etched and stained with black berry juices. There were men with spears chasing beasts on the Eastern Shore. The sun was shown as a blazing yellow circle ornamented with gold pyrites. A circle of mother of pearl sewn onto the skin suggested the moon. The front edges of the robe were trimmed with porcupine quills stained in rainbow colors; the neck was bordered with crow feathers, and more crow feathers were woven into Immar's hair.

For a long moment she stood staring at Kori. "All afternoon," she said, "I have asked for guidance." Her voice was a whisper, hoarse from chanting.

Kori stared at her dully for a moment, feeling lost and defeated. "I don't understand," she said, "why you should need guidance." She sat up, trying to find some strength. "Horeth disobeyed me. Mima panicked and tipped the canoe." Her voice rose as she spoke. "I did nothing wrong!"

Immar shook her head. "Horeth says you insulted his pride as a hunter and as a husband. He says you argued against him to prove yourself, even though you knew you were wrong. You wanted to embarrass him, and you deliberately caused his canoe to capsize. And when his wife was drowning, you refused to help."

Kori shook her head violently from side to side. "But none of this is true!" she cried. "Ask Nenara. Ask Yainar. They will tell you who is to blame!"

Immar held up her hand. "Quiet," she said. Her voice was low, but it carried an authority that Kori could never hope to possess. "It is not our way to cast blame."

Kori struggled to understand. "Then if there is no blame—"

"Only the Old Ones can say who shall be judged guilty or punished."

Kori leaned forward anxiously. "And what do they tell you, Mother?"

Immar turned away. "I have heard nothing," she said grimly. "They do not speak."

Kori gave a little cry of anguish. "Then what's going to happen to me?" She felt overwhelmed—by injustice, by loneliness, by sadness for Mima's death. She hated to show weakness, least of all in front of her mother. But she found tears welling up, and she no longer had the strength to hold them back. Great sobs escaped from her as she sat clutching herself on the bed.

Immar walked to her. She reached down, clasped her palms around Kori's head, and pressed it to her belly.

The ceremonial deerskin was heavy and stiff against Kori's cheeks. She smelled the leather and the juices that had stained it, but most of all she smelled the unique scent of her mother, the smell she had known all her life.

"You are my daughter, Kori," Immar said. "This is very hard for me."

Kori twisted her head so she could look up at her mother's face, trying to tell whether Immar was speaking with disapproval or love.

"When I sent you on the journey to gather stones," Immar went on, "I carefully placed no one with you who was older and would defy your authority. I gave you youngsters who would respect your status and obey your commands. And I gave you Yainar, because I'd seen the way you eyed him. He's a fine boy; it would be an honor for him to marry into our family."

Kori felt numb. "You mean you deliberately—"

"I always try my best for you, Kori. You are my daughter!"

Kori's emotions churned inside her. No matter how hard she tried to separate herself, her mother always somehow managed to intervene. She felt violated. "You gave me false hope," she cried out. "Yainar has no interest in joining our family. He rejected me." And she cried again, remembering the pain of the previous night.

"I see," Immar said. She shrugged. "That is unfortunate, but it doesn't concern me. What concerns me is that once again our people have been punished. A storm punished us, sacred stones were lost, a young woman's life was lost, and a young hunter now blames you and hates you." Immar stepped back and raised her arms, spreading her robe like the wings of a great bird. "What am I to make of these terrible things?"

Kori sat wordlessly. She choked back her tears.

"Well, the spirits have not spoken," said Immar. "So we must make our own choices. Come, daughter, before the tribe."

"Before the tribe?" Kori frowned. "Why?"

Immar whirled around. Her eyes flashed in the gloom of the little hut. "A life has been lost. You were responsible. I cannot protect you from the consequences."

"But—" Kori tried helplessly to understand. "When Shashin's life was lost, you didn't force his kin to stand before the tribe."

"This is not the same!" Immar's voice was shrill. "Shashin's kin obeyed the customs of our tribe. They were respectful. They never turned away from their duties. They never behaved willfully and maliciously—" She broke off as if there was a word that was so distasteful, she couldn't bring herself to speak it. She paused a moment, regaining her composure. "You will come," she said again, "before the tribe."

10

Kori followed her mother between the long shadows of the huts in the mellow late afternoon light. She reached the Meeting Place and stopped, staring at the scene before her. All the people of the village had gathered here. All of them were silent, and all of them were looking at her.

Sometimes she had imagined herself at the center of a pairing ceremony, walking forward to meet her future mate while her kinfolk and her friends and the elders showered her with daisies and sunflower petals and other women watched her with envious eyes. Other times she had imagined inheriting her mother's role, so that she could stand before her people as a seer. But she had never imagined standing here like this.

Immar took Kori's arm and together they walked around the edge of the circle while everyone maintained an uneasy silence. Kori heard the fire hissing and crackling, and she heard her own footsteps and her mother's footsteps on the sanded rock. She heard her own breathing, rapid and panicky. There were no other sounds.

Her mother guided her before the Speaking Rock, where Rohonar was already waiting. He was wearing his ceremonial robe of black wolf pelts, the wolf heads snarling silently from his chest and shoulders, with white pebbles where their eyes had been. The robe was trimmed with tassels of black wool, and fragments of volcanic glass were sewn onto it, flashing yellow, reflecting the colors of the evening sky. He wore a headdress of black hawk feathers, and a double necklace of bear teeth. His face was painted black, and he looked a frightening figure—yet as Kori walked toward him, she saw only sadness in his eyes.

"People!" Rohonar held up his hands. "People—" He sounded unsure of himself. His voice was colored with emotion. "There has been so much unhappiness," he said. "Lives lost, terrible portents . . ." His attention strayed to Mount Tomomor, where fire still flickered at the peak. "Something is deeply wrong," he said.

Kori had never heard him sound so confused. She saw no strength in him; no reassurance.

Immar stepped forward. She showed no hint of uncertainty as she stood surveying the crowd. "We must consider," she said, "what must be done." She breathed deeply, drawing herself up with an expression of righteousness. "What matters to us here is that the Old Ones called on my daughter to complete a sacred task. And . . . they were displeased. They brought a fierce storm upon the river. A life was lost. Sacred stones were lost." She turned slowly, eyeing the people gathered around the fire. Her painted face was fierce and grim, her eyes staring wide, her mouth a thin line. "It pains me," she said, "but I sent my nearest kin, and her presence angered them, and we were punished."

The words wrenched at Kori, tearing her inside. Again, she had a sense of awful, unbearable injustice. "Please!" she cried. "I must speak!"

Immar glared at her, but Rohonar stepped between them. "Yes," he said, turning to Kori. "You shall speak."

Kori saw some of the elders nodding their approval. So, she had some small chance to explain herself. But what could she really say? She saw Horeth sitting out among the villagers, watching her with malice in his eyes. She raised her arm and pointed at him. "Horeth, I believe you spoke against me earlier, when I was in my hut and could not answer. But did you tell our people how you violated our taboo when you ran into the forest on the Western Shore? Did you tell them that you insulted the customs of our tribe by beating your wife? Did you explain that you caused the accident on the river by disobeying me twice more?" She paused, feeling herself trembling. "You are the one who has offended the Old Ones," she said. "Not I."

People were turning and staring at Horeth. There was a rising murmur of concern. "You lie!" Horeth shouted, leaping to his feet.

The murmur of concern grew louder. Some people started shouting at Horeth, demanding an explanation.

"Stop." The word was piercing—almost a scream. Kori flinched from the sound. She saw her mother glaring at the villagers. Immar's hands were curled like claws. She was fierce with rage. "This must *stop*," she repeated. "This is not our way. We do not blame. We do not accuse." She turned and eyed Kori. "We do not turn people against each other."

Kori felt beaten by the words. To be rebuked like this, to be treated as if she was her mother's enemy—she looked for any other ally in the crowd. "Yainar," she shouted. "Tell the people that what I said is true. Tell them!"

"This is not our way!" Immar cried again.

"Let him speak," Rohonar said quietly.

Immar turned on him, but he stood firm, although he refused to look her in the eyes. Kori watched in amazement. Never did her parents confront each other publicly.

Immar finally stepped back, drawing her robe around her. "Very well," she said coldly. "He shall speak."

Kori stared at Yainar, willing him to speak. She clenched her fists till her nails bit painfully into her palms.

He took a step forward, and his eyes moved quickly, assessing the people around him. "It's true," he said, "that Horeth ran into the forest near the Gathering Place. But he soon returned. It's true he disobeyed an instruction on the river—although there was some confusion, and no one really understood what we should do. As for him striking his wife—well, she has been taken from us, so we should not speak of this now." He paused, weighing the words he had spoken. "I am not the one," he finished, "to say who might have offended the Old Ones. I am a hunter, nothing more." He turned and went back to his place in the crowd.

Kori felt a renewed sense of betrayal. He could have spoken for her, but how could she have really imagined that he would? He was always diplomatic, careful to offend no one. "Nenara," she called out, looking for the good-natured woman. "Where is she? She, too, saw what happened—"

"Enough!" Immar shouted.

But it was clear, anyway, that Nenara had no desire to speak. Kori saw her standing over to one side, trying to hide behind the man in front of her. Derneren, too, had retreated to the back of the crowd.

"Enough," Immar repeated. "Now," she said, "I am sure that Yainar speaks truly. I am sure, sometimes, Horeth has not been blameless. None of us is perfect. But I am talking about something far more serious: events during the past years, not just the past days."

The crowd was silent again, under the spell of her presence and her voice. They watched her with all their attention.

"For years, now," said Immar, "I have felt—troubled. It's no secret that my daughter and I have had—disagreements." She bowed her head for a moment. "It is a terrible thing," she went on. "But it has to be said. I am troubled in case my own daughter—may be unworthy."

There was a gasp from the crowd. Kori already felt so bruised and betrayed, the accusation hardly touched her until she saw the terrible implications. The Island Tribe had a custom for testing young children. On the child's first birthday, it was left unprotected beside the Burial Pit in the village of the Old Ones. The next day, the parents came back for the infant. If it lived, the Old Ones had judged that it was worthy, and it became a member of the tribe. If its life was claimed, the Old Ones had been offended by it and had taken it because it was unworthy.

Sometimes, though, a child might be so strong, it would live even though it was unworthy. Years might pass before everyone realized the truth: that the child was cursed, it offended the Old Ones and brought punishment and misfortune upon the tribe. When that happened, the cursed one would be cast out—drowned or placed on a raft that was left to float away downstream.

In Kori's lifetime, this had only happened once—to a child of five who had looked whole and healthy, but had never learned to speak. Kori had never heard of an adult being subjected to such treatment. The idea that it should be applied to her was unthinkable.

Kori stared at Immar in horror. "How can you say this terrible thing?" she asked. "How can you?" Then her rage overcame her. She ran forward, seized her mother's robe and tore at it savagely. "You are my *mother*!"

People were getting to their feet. There were cries of disapproval.

"Wait." This time it was Rohonar who spoke. "People, wait!" He moved forward into the crowd, gesturing for them to be calm, demanding that they sit. "Immar did not say she was sure of this," Rohonar said, turning as he spoke. "She said she only *fears* it may be true."

"The spirits have not spoken to me," Immar admitted. "I

prayed for guidance all afternoon. I heard nothing. Therefore—" She drew herself up, looking pained but determined to say what had to be said. "Therefore, we must determine for ourselves where the truth lies. I believe that Kori must be tested. She shall be placed on the Western Shore. If she lives after thirty days, then we will know beyond doubt that she has been found worthy and the Old Ones have protected her. We will welcome her back and beg her to forgive us."

There was a new burst of shouting from the crowd. Kori looked from one face to the next, and she saw some who were outraged and some who seemed concerned, but many more who were silent. They looked uneasy, afraid to speak out against Immar.

Kori turned to her father. She understood, now, why he had seemed distressed when she had come before the tribe. He had known what Immar was going to say.

He saw her looking at him. Awkwardly, he went to her and clasped her shoulder. "This is for the best," he muttered to her, while the noise of the crowd sounded around them. "When you return, there will be no doubt anymore, don't you see? It will heal the rift, Kori. Our people will respect you as they never have before."

She looked up into his face and saw that he was sincere. He really believed that this was a simple answer to a vexing problem. "But how will I care for myself alone out there?" Kori cried. "I am not a hunter."

Rohonar quickly shook his head. "No," he said, holding up his hand. "No, Kori. The Old Ones will not allow you to suffer, because you *are* worthy. This I truly believe. The spirits will protect you."

He had to turn away from her, then, as two villagers strode up to him, both of them complaining that this plan, this punishment, was wrong. He began talking calmly to them, using the same words that he had just used to Kori.

But why did he sound so apologetic? Why did he accept his wife's decree without question? He was the chieftain of the tribe. His people trusted him totally. If he believed Kori was worthy, he could *tell them* she was worthy.

But he hadn't—because he, too, was afraid. The realization overwhelmed her. This powerful man, who had always seemed as tall and strong as an oak, was afraid of the Old Ones, just as his people were. And since his wife spoke on behalf of the spirits, Rohonar must be afraid of her, also. He presented himself as the leader of his people, but he was not.

Kori leaned against the Speaking Rock, feeling weak and dazed as she looked around and saw her world as she had never seen it before, with painful clarity. She looked at the tribe, arguing about what should be done with her. Yes, some were concerned with the harshness of the plan, but sooner or later they would have to do what Immar had suggested. None of them would dare to defy her.

Kori noticed her brother standing to one side. He wasn't talking to anyone; he was looking at the ground, frowning. She watched him steadily, and he glanced up as if he sensed her attention on him. Their eyes met and he flinched as if he was ashamed. Well, he *should* be ashamed. He, too, was a coward, fearful of Immar's power.

But then Kori saw another implication. Her people were worried that if she was unworthy, and if she stayed among them, her presence could cause suffering and catastrophes. Did this mean that her people were afraid of *her*?

She was amazed by this sudden understanding. Always she had thought that because she was different, because they didn't understand her, she was inferior and helpless. To them, though, the opposite was true. She was so strong, she didn't need the comfort of the tribe as they did. She wasn't afraid to be alone. She wasn't afraid to be different.

Kori looked from one person to the next and saw how they avoided her eyes—not just because they were embarrassed, but because she unnerved them. Even now, she wasn't cowering or begging for mercy; she was standing here, confronting them. How many of them would be capable of that, if their positions were reversed?

Finally Kori found herself looking at her mother.

Here was the deepest mystery of all. Immar had admitted that the spirits had been silent. Therefore, she had been free to act in any way she chose. So why had she chosen to cast Kori out, instead of speaking up for her and defending her?

At first there seemed to be no possible answer. Then, just as Oam had sensed her looking at him, Immar turned and glanced in Kori's direction, and in that moment, Immar's expression was unguarded. Kori saw something that she had never recognized before: Immar was wary. She eyed Kori as if Kori might pose a threat to her.

So now the final mystery was solved. Kori had spent so much of her life feeling overwhelmed by her mother's power, but from her mother's viewpoint, Kori grew wilder and more rebellious with each passing year. In fact, Kori was the only person in the tribe who dared to defy Immar, openly and repeatedly. And each time she did, she humiliated Immar publicly. She undermined her power.

Kori saw, now, that she put her mother in an unbearable position. In front of the whole tribe, Kori had spoken out against her. She had challenged Horeth, stirring up anger and dissent and threatening to divide the tribe. The people had started questioning the truth of what they had been told, instead of blindly accepting the truth as Immar presented it to them.

Kori stared at Immar in wonder. *Even my mother is afraid of me,* she thought to herself, *because I am the only one who challenges her strength.*

Then Kori saw the awful consequences. Immar only had two choices. She could ignore Kori, or find a way of forcing her to surrender. It was not in Immar's nature to ignore a challenge; and so, now, she was reaching for any means to regain power over her daughter—even if she had to cast her out alone on the Western Shore.

PART 2:
THE WESTERN SHORE

11

The landscape was serene. The river lay still and bright in the clear morning light, and the sky was a pale, gentle blue. In the far distance, Mount Tomomor had ceased venting its anger and the foul-smelling smoke had vanished on the wind. The world, today, seemed a gentle place.

For Kori, though, the silence and softness of the morning offered no reassurance. Her people would surely take it as a sign that the Old Ones were no longer angry and were satisfied by her punishment. The lesson seemed so clear, even a slow-witted man such as Derneren must understand it.

Kori sat in the bow of her father's canoe while he kneeled at the stern, paddling it across the river with strong, even strokes. A kingfisher swooped down before her, barely brushing the surface of the water with the tips of its wings. Then it soared away, screeching mournfully. The thick forest on the Western Shore loomed ahead, somber and silent, and she eyed it with a feeling of dread.

Behind her, on the island, she knew that all the people of the tribe were standing and watching as she made this grim journey. Some of them, perhaps, had wanted to give her something before she left—a few words of regret, or an expression of hope. She had decided, though, that she had nothing to gain from talking to them. None of them, after all, had had the courage to speak out against this terrible punishment. If they felt guilty now, that was no concern of hers.

She sat in the canoe with her back straight, her head held proudly, refusing to show how scared she felt. In reality she was completely unprepared for the challenge that lay ahead. She had spent the night alone, refusing to talk to anyone. Even when her mother had come for her in the early morning and had escorted her to the canoe, Kori had refused to speak.

Rohonar ceased paddling and the canoe drifted, turning slightly with the current as it approached the shore. The prow gently bumped tumbled rocks that marked the edge of this part of the riverbank. Rohonar turned the canoe with his paddle, then reached out and threw a long thong around one of the boulders.

Kori wondered for a moment what would happen if she refused to get out. Rohonar would try to reason with her, because he was always a reasonable man. But what if she still refused to obey him? Would he actually seize her and lift her onto the land? That would be difficult to do in the unsteady canoe. He might even need to go back and get help from one of the hunters on the island, which would cause embarrassment and make everyone angry.

Still, sooner or later, one way or another, she would be forced to step onto the shore. She had no doubt of that.

Kori sighed and stood up. She turned toward her father and found that he, too, was standing, holding out a spear that he had brought with him. "Kori," he said softly. He frowned, looking deeply unhappy. "This spear belonged to my father and his father before him. It has powerful magic. It will protect you here."

He sounded so troubled, Kori almost felt sorry for him. For most of her life he had been a remote figure, spending far more time with the elders and the hunters than with his family. Sometimes he brought her little gifts: shells that he found when he went hunting on the Eastern Shore, pieces of glittering colored volcanic glass, animal claws and teeth, or fine trophies, such as the bearskin that she slept under each night. But he always seemed to avoid being with her at home.

Kori understood why, now. It was Immar who ruled the home, deciding which chores needed to be done and who should do them. Immar dressed Kori when she was little, bathed her, fed her, and told her the legends of the tribe. Immar taught her how to skin deer, string beads, stitch moccasins, and cook fish. She filled Kori's days so completely, there was no room left for Rohonar. And perhaps he was glad of that, because he felt uneasy being so close to the center of Immar's power. He preferred the company of men, who respected him as a bold hunter and never guessed that beneath his bravery in the wilderness, he was secretly afraid—of his wife.

Kori accepted the spear from him. She weighed it in her hand, trying to sense the magic that he mentioned. The shaft was perfectly straight and beautifully finished, burnished with musk oil, engraved with fine spiral lines filled with white guano, and ornamented with tassels and feathers. It was an excellent spear—but to Kori, it was nothing more than that. She couldn't sense its magic any more that she could hear the voices of the Old Ones.

"Thank you," she said, looking up at his face. She wanted to say something more, to tell him that she understood him now, but something stopped her from speaking the words. Understanding, she realized, was not the same as forgiveness. She still couldn't forgive him for being weak and not defending her.

He stepped closer to her, making the canoe pitch under

them. She was startled by the idea that he might try to embrace her—but no, he stood alongside her with his back turned to the island and his shoulder touching hers, and then he reached inside his robe and pulled out a bundle wrapped in plantain leaves and tied with a thong. "This is for you, Kori," he said in a low voice. "Smoked fish and venison. Enough for three days."

She blinked. This was unexpected, and it was kind of him—but no, it wasn't enough! If he wanted to help her, why hadn't he *really* helped her? She took the bundle from him, but the inadequacy of it just made her angrier, till she couldn't contain her emotions anymore.

"You're the chieftain of our tribe, Father," she blurted out. "Why do you have to behave like this, hiding your actions from the people on the island? Why can't you command them, instead of being ruled by them?"

He shifted uncomfortably and looked away. "It's true I am the chieftain, Kori, but my power is nothing compared with the power of—of the spirits." He touched her arm, urging her to hide the package inside her own tunic. "Quickly now," he said. "You must go. The Old Ones will protect you, I have no doubt of that. Thirty days from now, I'll return to find you here. Then we will be able to put all this behind us and begin anew." He nodded, reassuring himself that what he said was true.

She stared at him, looking for any sign of uncertainty. No, he had made his decision. He was not going to go back on it.

Grimly, Kori picked up her bearskin bedroll, which she had been allowed to bring with her. It was neatly rolled and tied. She slung it over her shoulder, then climbed up the sharp rocks, steadying herself with one hand and holding her spear in the other.

She reached the top and hesitated. She knew she should turn and say good-bye to her father, but if she did that, she would weaken. She might even cry.

"Good-bye, Kori!" he called after her.

Faintly, from the island in the center of the broad river, Kori heard the villagers shouting their own farewells. It was a mournful sound and it filled her with fury. If they were so sad to see her go, they should never have allowed this to happen.

She stood up, still with her back turned to them, and she stepped from the rocks onto the land. As she did so, her anger compelled her to make a vow. She would return, and when she did, she would be older and wiser and stronger—so strong, no one in the tribe would ever dare to mistreat her again. Even her mother would be forced to yield to her.

At first she felt proud as she walked through the forest. She hadn't cried or begged for mercy. She had been defiant to the end. Who else in her tribe would have had so much courage?

But soon she found her spirit weakening. The land here was subtly different from the Gathering Place upstream and totally different from the Eastern Shore. The trees were thinner, like animals that had been starved and were barely clinging to life. The bushes and weeds were pale, as if the rays of the sun never reached this dim, sinister place. The earth was gritty underfoot, and when she kneeled and touched it, she found it wasn't normal soil at all. It was like gravel or powdered rock.

Kori paused and glanced around. All her life she had heard stories of strange creatures that dwelled here—from whitebeasts to snakes that were so large that they could swallow a man whole. Her people believed that sometimes the Great Spirit would take pity on one of the Old Ones and allow his spirit to roam the Western Shore in the body of a lizard. Even on the island, lizards were never killed. They were sacred creatures.

Kori had never known what to believe. Maybe this truly was a place where the Old Ones had so much power, only a fool would trespass. Or maybe something bad had happened long ago, and the real truth had been lost from one generation to the next.

Kori stood for a long moment, listening. Birds were calling to each other in the treetops. Insects hummed in the shafts of sunlight. High up, a black squirrel leaped from branch to branch, then paused and eyed her, twitching his tail.

These creatures seemed normal enough, yet still her skin prickled and she felt insecure. She repositioned the bearskin on her shoulder and shifted her grip on her spear. Could she really live here alone for thirty days? After she ate the food that her father had given her—what then? She had no skill as a hunter, since women were forbidden to hunt in her tribe.

Suddenly the time ahead of her seemed like a black void that was going to suck the life from her body. She felt herself trembling. She feared the Old Ones; she didn't trust them to protect her. So far as she could tell, they had never protected anyone from anything. There was far more cruelty than mercy in the way they treated her tribe.

Maybe she should turn around. She could camp right on the shore of the river, where her people could see her from the island. If they watched her lying there, slowly starving, day after day, surely they'd help her. Surely her mother—

No! Kori angrily shook her head. She would never humiliate herself that way. If she gave in and begged for mercy, she would be a slave to her mother forever.

Kori searched for a way to evade the situation she'd been put in. Maybe she could swim back to the island under cover of darkness and steal food from her tribe's caches. That pleased her, stealing from the people who had betrayed her. Yet the idea hurt her pride. If she was going to prove to her people that she was braver and stronger than they had ever imagined, she had to *be* brave and strong.

She felt her mood of defiance returning more powerfully

than before. She realized she would rather risk dying in the forest than humiliate herself by begging for help or stealing.

She turned and strode forward. Many times, in the past few years, she had tried to sense the spirits and hear them speak. It maddened her that only Immar had this special gift. Well, Kori was standing on their land now. Here was her chance to confront them. She vowed to walk deep into the forest—all the way to Mount Tomomor, if necessary. If they chose to punish her or kill her as they had killed Shashin, so be it. At least she might learn their true nature before she died.

12

Around noon, Kori stumbled on a dense thicket of blackberries. A flock of crows had been pecking at them; she beat the bushes with her spear, forcing the big birds to rise up in a flurry of wings. Some of them circled around her, screaming and diving close, threatening to rake her arms or her face with their claws. She grabbed stones and gravel and bombarded the birds till they finally retreated to high tree branches, still complaining angrily.

The crows had eaten most of the berries that were easiest to get, but Kori found she could still harvest a rich crop by reaching deeper into the brambles. She ate one handful after another till her fingers were stained dark purple from the juices and her stomach began to cramp. Finally she turned away, realizing that she was thirsty.

She felt suddenly ashamed of her own foolishness. She'd been so concerned with pride and defiance, she'd ignored her most basic needs. Water was so plentiful for the Island Tribe, they took it for granted. Even on the Eastern Shore there were so many small streams, hunters never had to go far to quench their thirst. But here Kori had no idea which way to turn.

Of course, she could always return to the river. But her vow of defiance refused to allow that option, and the vow was the source of her strength.

She thought of the birds and the squirrels she'd seen. They needed water. She'd seen deer tracks, too, and footprints from larger game. There must be water!

She stood and listened, but there was no sound of a nearby stream. She looked around, then made an arbitrary decision. She started walking quickly to the south.

The sun flashed through gaps in the canopy of leaves. It led her onward. And as she walked she found the land sloping down. Soon she heard faint sounds of water, and she saw that as the slope steepened, the trees ended. She ran forward—then gave a little cry of fear as she glimpsed what lay ahead.

Kori found herself stumbling clumsily down a steep slope with gravelly soil sliding under her moccasins. She cursed herself for letting her thirst sway her judgment and make her behave as stupidly as a young child. She threw out her arm and hooked it around the last sapling before the land dropped almost vertically to a narrow, winding ravine, a miniature canyon clogged with jagged black rocks. Water was tumbling over them, gleaming in the sun. And just a short way upstream were three beasts standing in the water, bending their heads and drinking. They were creatures so strange, she felt fascinated by them even as they filled her with fear.

She clung to the tree, trying to breathe silently through her open mouth and trying not to move for fear of scuffing the ground and releasing a shower of small stones. Surely, she thought, the beasts must have heard her. She glanced up, wondering if she could climb the tree if she had to. The trunk was so slender, she could close her hands completely around it. She didn't think it would take her weight.

She turned back to the beasts in the stream. They were shaped like wolves, but each of them was the size of a bear, twice as big as any wolf she had ever seen. Their coats were striped black and brown as if their skin had stolen the pattern of sunlight striking through the trees. Their snouts were long and tapering, pink at the end, and their teeth were curved—not as fearsome as the tusks of a boar, but she guessed they could rip out her stomach if they chose.

One of them paused in its drinking and looked up. Kori saw beads of water clinging to the coarse hairs around the animal's black lips. It swallowed noisily and turned from side to side, sniffing the air.

There was no wind, but the motion of the stream created a faint current of air. Kori prayed it would be enough to carry her scent away. Perhaps the noise of the water splashing over the rocks had been loud enough to conceal the sounds she'd made.

Her arm was beginning to ache, but she ignored it. She clung motionless to the sapling, waiting. Finally the giant wolf lowered its head and continued drinking.

Kori glanced over her shoulder. There was another tree a little way up the slope, just out of reach. She desperately wanted to retreat to the relative safety of the forest. She clasped her spear, turned it, and pressed its stone tip against the trunk of the tree that she was clinging to. Cautiously, then, she pushed herself up the slope, moving hand over hand up the shaft of the spear till she reached the next tree and could throw her arm around it.

Bit by bit she retreated until she could hunker down behind some bushes. She paused there, breathing heavily, peering at the animals down by the water. They drank some more—and then, without warning, they all turned and started leaping through the stream till they reached the opposite bank. They scrambled up it, and she saw they had feet like a cat's, each armed with four long, black, curving claws. Finally the animals disappeared into the forest.

Kori slowly stood up, trying to calm herself. Perhaps the stories about the Western Shore were true after all. Half a dozen skilled hunters might hope to kill one of those giant wolves, surrounding it and weakening it the same way they would gradually sap the strength of a cornered mountain lion. But mountain lions were usually found alone. If the giant wolves roamed in packs, Kori saw no way that men could ever kill them.

She looked down at the stream tumbling around the rocks. She desperately wanted to go down there, catch the water in her cupped hands, feel it against her face, and relish the coolness of it in her throat. But she didn't dare to show herself now, and if she waited till after dark, it might be even more dangerous. Many carnivores preferred to hunt at night. Their vision might be better than hers, and this would be an obvious place for them to come in search of prey.

Kori wondered if the Old Ones were tormenting her. They had led her to the water so quickly—and now she was too fearful to drink.

Cautiously, she started walking parallel with the stream, moving uphill and staying just inside the edge of the forest. She was much more alert now and paused often to listen and sniff the air. The sixth time she did so she heard a distant braying sound, like the bellow of a mammoth but higher pitched.

Kori clutched herself and shivered. Why did these creatures lurk here in this wild country? Why had no one ever seen them down at the edge of the river? Perhaps, she thought, the rocks at the river's edge were so high and steep, the animals couldn't reach that broad stretch of water, so they had no use for it. Or perhaps the power of the Old Ones was as great as people claimed, and the animals were only allowed to roam inland from the Western Shore.

Kori moved on, walking as silently as she could and constantly glancing around. She trekked steadily west, following the line of the stream, but still she found no place where she would feel safe to expose herself.

Eventually the afternoon sun began sinking ahead of her, and through small gaps in the trees she saw that it would soon slip behind Mount Tomomor. The forest would be plunged into darkness then, and moonlight would barely penetrate the leafy canopy.

She had to find a place to spend the night. Could she sleep in the high branches of a tree? And even if she found a place that was comfortable and safe enough, would her thirst allow her to sleep? She let out a cry of frustration. Her people knew how ill-equipped she was, as a woman, to fend for herself, and her mother knew that too.

Kori's thoughts were interrupted as her foot slipped and her ankle twisted under her. She grabbed a tree to stop herself from falling and felt a stab of panic; a sprained ankle could be a fatal injury here, rendering her helpless in the face of any predator.

Then she looked down and saw why she had lost her footing. There was a tiny channel in the land, barely wider than her foot, hidden under ferns and bracken. Kori bent down and tore the foliage aside. Beneath it she found a bare trickle of water seeping through the grainy soil toward the stream in the ravine.

Kori eyed the water. Even if she pressed her face into the crack she didn't think she could manage to drink from it. And there wasn't enough for her to cup the water with her hands.

Then she saw the answer to her dilemma. Quickly, she started digging with her fingers. The black soil was so loose and gravely, she had no trouble scooping out a hollow.

She made a basin in the ground. Then she waited.

It took longer than she had hoped, but after a while the hollow she'd scooped out was half full of water. She cupped her hands in it, raised them, and drank, still alert for any signs of life around her. The water had a bitter, mineral taste, but she ignored that. She drank again, then waited for the basin to refill, and drank still more. Finally she unpacked the food her father had given her and greedily ate some of the venison.

She felt a little more confident now. The food warmed her and made her feel stronger, but she still needed to find somewhere to spend the night.

She moved on, pausing often to look to either side, behind her, and above. She saw a pine tree that was much fatter than the others around it, embraced by a thick growth of ivy. In a year or two the pine would die as the ivy engulfed it completely, but now it was still alive and strong. Kori thrust her spear through the center of her bedroll, then slung it onto her back and adjusted its thongs so that it hung between her shoulders. She seized the main stalk of the vine, which was so large she could barely close her fingers around it. Hand over hand, finding footholds in the web of ivy, she started hauling herself up.

She reached a point where two heavy branches protruded close together. Here, she thought, she might be safe. She sat on one of them for a moment, quieting her breathing as well as she could and listening to see if any creature had been attracted by the commotion.

The forest was still reassuringly silent. The sun was almost setting, and most of the birds had stopped singing. Soon the nocturnal animals would be prowling—but not yet.

Kori brushed pine needles from her robe. Sitting up here in the tree she was overwhelmed by its rich fragrance. The pine cones were heavy and swollen at this time of year, so she seized one and cracked it open, hoping to find pine nuts.

Sure enough there was a cluster of the pale, soft, fingernail-sized delicacy. She ate them greedily—then realized she had no time to harvest more. She had to make herself secure before darkness fell.

She placed her bedroll in the notch between two branches, then took her flint knife from the little pouch that she always carried, which also contained firesticks and tinder. She chopped off some tough pieces of ivy and used them to tie her spear securely to the main trunk of the tree. Then she unrolled the bearskin, sat on the two branches, and wrapped it around her. She leaned back against the tree trunk. It wasn't comfortable, but she thought it would be bearable.

Carefully she started cutting thick pieces of vine, using them to tie herself to the tree. The light was growing so dim, she could barely see what she was doing. Still, she forced herself to work slowly and methodically. If she dropped the knife, she might lose it forever in the darkness.

She wrapped half a dozen lengths of vine around herself and the tree, then used another few pieces to lash her legs to the branches under her. Finally, she was satisfied. She stowed her knife back in her pouch.

A breath of wind passed through the forest, and the pine shifted slightly. Kori hugged herself inside her bearskin. She prayed that it wouldn't rain. The sky had been clear all day, and the weather seemed dry—but it surely wouldn't stay dry for all the thirty days of her exile in this wilderness. How would she cope if a thunderstorm struck? Would she have the courage to build a fire to dry and warm herself down on the forest floor? What would she do if it attracted some hideous creature?

Kori told herself not to think about all the things that could go wrong. She had survived her first day of solitude; surely that was enough.

She tried to sleep, but each time the wind blew, the tree

shifted and creaked under her. Ants and spiders started exploring her neck and ankles, and she couldn't get rid of them without unwrapping herself and exposing herself to the cold night air. Her skin itched, and the rough, lumpy bark of the branch under her was digging into her thighs.

Meanwhile, down in the forest she heard small animals rustling through the undergrowth, and in the distance she heard the same eerie braying sound that had startled her before. A while later she thought she smelled the musky odor of a lion, and there were splashing noises from the stream.

For a while it seemed she would never manage to sleep. Finally, though, she was so exhausted, her eyes fell shut.

She woke with a start. The moon was high in the sky, barely visible through the forest canopy. Kori found herself breathing quickly, her pulse racing. What had woken her so suddenly? There had been a sound like someone shouting.

Then she heard it again: a howling noise, so loud it made her flinch. It was one of the giant wolves, she realized. She heard the animal crashing through the forest. It howled one more time—and others joined it.

The crashing noises came nearer. Kori strained her eyes and saw a bulky shadow moving below her—then another, and another. There were ten of the creatures moving in a pack, scouring the land for prey.

One of them paused at the foot of her tree. She heard it sniffing the air. It raised its head as if it could see her, and it howled.

Kori felt an overwhelming, irrational need to climb higher. She found herself fumbling instinctively at the vines. She had to close her eyes and clasp her two hands together, clenching them tightly, forbidding herself to do anything that would make a sound. She told herself that the giant wolf hadn't seen her. Even if it had, there was no way it could climb. Its claws were for seizing and holding prey, not for climbing trees.

The dark shadow of the giant wolf circled the tree, still making sniffing sounds. The rest of the pack moved on, but this one animal lingered behind. It reared up on its hind legs and Kori heard it pawing at the trunk, its claws rustling through the ivy and scouring the bark.

Kori wondered if she might be able to kill it. The branch where she sat was only about three man-lengths above the ground. Even with her lack of skill, surely would be able to strike such a large target with her spear.

But could she kill it with a single throw? She imagined the spear embedding itself in the wolf's body, and the wolf whirling around, snapping at the spear with its powerful jaws and breaking it in two. Or the wolf could simply turn and run through the forest, taking the spear away with it.

Kori shuddered at the thought of losing her only weapon. She couldn't afford to take even the smallest risk of that happening. To sit here and do nothing was excruciating; yet there was no alternative.

The wolf circled the tree one more time, then rubbed the side of its massive head against the trunk, marking it with its scent. Then it snorted and loped away, its huge paws thudding on the soft ground as it went to rejoin its pack.

Kori found herself trembling. She felt terribly alone, and she couldn't hold back a sudden resurgence of bitterness and resentment toward her mother and the rest of the tribe. They had placed her here to test the will of the Old Ones, but as far as Kori could see, she was the only one being tested. She didn't believe the Old Ones cared any more about her life than they'd cared about Shashin's.

Surely, she had been sent here as a punishment, nothing else. First Immar had sent Kori to lead the stone-gathering journey, which she must have known would be arduous for a young woman. And now she had found an even greater challenge to break Kori's will.

Well, Kori thought to herself, it wouldn't work. The challenge would make her stronger, not weaker.

Once again her bitterness renewed her courage. She settled herself on the tree branches and willed herself to fall back into sleep. The forest was even noisier now than it had been at sunset: she heard owls screeching, the tiny voices of voles, the rasping squeals of bats, and dozens of rodents rooting through dead leaves and pine needles on the forest floor. Then she heard a distant roar that she was sure came from a mountain lion. That worried her, because a lion could easily climb the tree where she sat. Still, she had her spear. She told herself she could stab the face of any big cat that tried to reach her. And if she kept a firm grip on her spear and didn't throw it, there'd be no risk of losing it. In fact, she told herself, it would be good fortune if a mountain lion tried to climb up to her.

Was that really true? She didn't know. She was like a man chanting songs about his great strength before he went to hunt. The more she told herself that she was strong, the more she found herself believing it—until, finally, she was calm enough to fall back asleep.

13

She woke at dawn, chilled and aching but proud to be alive. She stretched and shook herself, slapping her arms and thighs as hard as she could to warm them.

Then she froze. Another animal was sniffing at the foot of her tree.

Cautiously, Kori peered down. At first she couldn't understand what she saw. The creature was four-legged, with a long tail and a long snout, but it was nothing like the giant wolves. It was a huge lizard with scaly skin, almost the size of a man.

Kori stared at it in awe. Surely, this great creature must be the source of the legends she had heard about Old Ones being allowed to roam the land in lizard form on the Western Shore. Had it been sent here to test her?

Kori felt fiercely hungry after her meager meals the previous day. She couldn't help looking at the lizard as a source of food. To kill it would mean violating a taboo—yet she no longer felt scared of that. In fact, she took it as a challenge. She had no respect for the Old Ones now; she despised them for their random cruelties. Even if they chose to punish her, she didn't see how they could hurt her any more than her own people had already.

She loosened the vines binding her to the tree and flexed her limbs impatiently, trying to work the stiffness out of them. Meanwhile, the big reptile seemed to be losing interest. It turned away from the tree and paused, moving its head slowly from side to side.

Kori made a hissing sound.

The lizard ignored her. It took a slow step in the direction of the stream in the ravine.

Kori seized a pine cone and threw it, striking the lizard on the head.

The creature was stupid—so stupid, Kori didn't see how it could possibly contain the spirit of an Old One. It whirled around, blinking its yellow eyes. Its long tongue flicked out, tasting the world around it, trying to understand what had just happened.

Even if it was just a lizard, not possessed with any spiritual power, it could still be dangerous. Was it carnivorous? Its jaws looked fearsome, though not as frightening as the giant wolves. From the way it moved, she didn't think it could run very fast. If she threw her spear and merely wounded it, she thought she would have a good chance of chasing it, seizing the spear, dragging it out of the beast and striking it again—unless, of course, its scaly hide was too tough for the spear to penetrate.

Kori slid her spear free from its resting place. She raised it and took a slow, deep breath, trying to steady her trembling hand. Could she really do this? Maybe she was being foolish, but sooner or later she would have to kill to eat, and this dumb creature would feed her far more thoroughly than rabbits or squirrels.

She directed all her attention to the lizard, till she was aware of nothing else. She took careful aim. She focused all her willpower, all her strength on the muscles of her arm. She drew in her breath and held it—and then she cast the spear.

She didn't wait to see if it struck its target. She swung down from her branch, seized some dangling vines, and let herself drop. The vines ripped free in a shower of bark fragments, but they helped to break her fall. She crashed into some bushes, rolled over, and jumped up, taking quick, urgent breaths, full of fear but determined to kill her prey.

The lizard was making a terrible hissing, gasping sound. The spear had struck it in the back, just behind its left shoulder. The shaft was buried deep and blood was pooling around it. The lizard turned and snapped angrily, but couldn't reach the spear.

Kori told herself she had no choice. She had to retrieve her weapon. She seized her knife and ran forward, screaming wildly.

The lizard turned toward her. Its jaws opened wide and its tongue flashed out.

Could its tongue be poisonous, like a snake's? Kori didn't dare find out. She danced to one side. The lizard was slow, as she'd hoped, and it was distracted by the pain of the spear. She ran around it and then, in desperation, she threw herself on its back.

The skin was tough, rough, and cold. There was no way for her to hold on. She felt herself sliding as the beast reared under her. Instinctively, she hooked her arm around its neck. Her knife was still in her hand. She jerked her fist upward, stabbing the knife into the lizard's throat and slicing farther up till blood suddenly started flowing.

Kori found herself being thrown free. She thudded down onto the ground, still clutching her knife, her arm now slick with blood. For a moment she stared up in terror as the lizard seemed to see her and came toward her, its jaws gaping, showing dozens of cone-shaped yellow teeth.

But the creature was more concerned with its wounds than with her. It made a whining, screaming sound and pawed futilely at the gash in its neck.

Kori jumped up again, ran forward, danced around the side of the lizard, and grabbed her spear. She pulled it free, trying not to turn it or wrench it for fear of ripping away the flint head. She jumped back, hesitated, then flung the spear again, this time aiming for the lizard's mouth.

The shaft flew between the great jaws. The serrated stone tip of the spear penetrated the roof of its mouth and sank into the lizard's brain. The beast reared up, then fell over on its side. Its legs twitched helplessly. It writhed and shook, hissing and gagging. It pawed futilely while she watched with a mixture of horror and excitement. And then, finally, the creature shuddered and lay still.

Kori crouched down, gasping, staring at the lizard, waiting to see if it was really dead. She found herself laughing suddenly, for no reason. She clutched herself, feeling her fear turn to exultation. She stood up, threw her head back, and let out a shout.

Her limbs felt weak and rubbery. She was dizzy. She leaned against the pine tree, breathing hard, while the beast lay dead in front of her. She forced herself to take hold of her emotions. She had to think carefully. Too often she'd heard stories of young hunters who were so excited by their first kill, they acted recklessly.

She stood for a moment, calming herself. Would she be punished now? She imagined how horrified her people would be if they could see what she had done. They would pray for forgiveness; they would chant together, late into the night.

Kori glanced around. The forest was no different from before. The earth did not suddenly open under her feet. Mount Tomomor did not erupt in fury. Either the Old Ones hadn't noticed what she'd done—or they simply didn't care.

But she realized she had to think of practical things. Clearly she had to skin the lizard and cook as much of it as she could. The smell of roasting meat would attract other creatures, which would be dangerous for her—but if she didn't cook the meat, it would last only a day or two before it spoiled.

Kori reached for her firesticks, then realized there was a higher priority. If she was chased by some predator, she didn't want to leave without her bearskin. She turned to the pine tree, seized the vine, and forced her shaky arms and legs to obey her. Somehow she managed to climb back to her perch, where she grabbed the bearskin, rolled it, and flung it down to the ground.

Clumsily, she followed it. She paused, listening. The forest was still quiet. She pulled her spear out of the lizard's fearsome mouth and placed it with her bearskin, where she could grab them instantly if she needed to. Then she took her flint knife and started work, cutting parallel strips of flesh from the lizard's soft underbelly.

Even its stomach-skin was so tough, the knife was soon dull.

Kori paused for a moment, thinking of the times she had seen men sharpening their weapons. They behaved as if it was a sacred ritual, yet it had always seemed relatively simple.

She searched around on the ground until she found a large shard of sharp volcanic rock. She placed the flint knife on a smooth, hard stone, then carefully tapped it with the sharp rock, knocking away tiny flakes and exposing a fresh edge. Then she set to work again, sawing with the knife till her muscles were so weary, she had to stop.

By this time her arms and chest were covered in blood, but she didn't dare venture down to the stream to wash herself. She went back to the tiny pool she'd dug yesterday and drank from it, then used the remainder of the water to rinse her hands.

Now it was time to build a fire. She gathered dry wood

and leaves, took out her fire sticks, and placed the one with the socket on a firm, level stone. She sprinkled the driest tinder around it, kneeled down, and took the drill stick between her palms. Her people normally said a prayer to the spirits before making fire, but since Kori had just committed one of the most terrible crimes that her people could imagine, she was no longer interested in mouthing prayers. She was gripped by a new mood of defiance.

She started spinning the drill stick, pausing to sprinkle more tinder around the point of it, then spinning it again, till the first tiny embers glowed. She blew on them, added tiny amounts of powdered leaves, blew on the embers some more—and the first flicker of flame came to life.

Bit by bit, she added to the flame till she had a good hot blaze. She waited till the fire consisted of hot embers, then skewered the chunks of lizard meat on strong twigs and rested them on forked sticks that she jammed into the ground. The meat started hissing and spitting, giving off the most unbearably delicious smell. Kori realized she couldn't wait till all the meat was cooked. She grabbed the nearest chunk and started gorging herself on it raw. The flesh was very tough and it had a strange taste, more like a bird than a beast. But it quickly satisfied her craving.

She stopped eating and sat for a while, turning the cooking meat from time to time. Flies and ants had already converged on the lizard's bloody carcass. A couple of large hawks were lurking in the trees above, and finally one of them mustered enough courage to come swooping down and rip off a piece of flesh with its beak. Kori stood up and screamed at it, but it escaped with its bloody prize and retreated from her.

So far, no other scavengers had come to eat their share, but surely that was just a matter of time.

She was taking one wooden skewer of cooked meat off the fire and getting ready to cook the next when she heard stealthy footsteps approaching. Without hesitation she threw the hot cooked meat into her bearskin, folded it into quarters, seized it by its corners, and stood up, throwing it over her shoulder. She grabbed her spear and stepped close to the pine tree.

For a long moment, nothing happened. The animal in the bushes must have heard her movements, and now it was pausing, displaying caution equal to hers. She felt glad of that. It meant that the creature wasn't starved and crazy with hunger. Maybe it was just a bobcat, in which case she could throw it some scraps and it would leave her alone.

Then the sound of stealthy footsteps resumed. Kori slipped behind the tree and tensed, ready to climb or run. She saw tall flowering weeds nodding and swaying as the animal pushed forward. There was a soft crunch of dry leaves, and then, with a jolt of fear, Kori saw two large, golden eyes peering out from the bushes just beyond the lizard's carcass.

She had seen mountain lions carried home dead by proud hunters, but she had never seen one alive. The beast crept forward, its black nose flexing as it tested the air, its white whiskers pulled back flush with its plump, furry cheeks. Its ears were flattened, its eyes were half closed. For a moment Kori was transfixed by its power, its grace, and its beauty.

Then it saw her peeking out from behind the tree and it stopped, staring.

The lion was no more than a dozen paces away. She knew how fast it could cover that distance if it chose to leap at her. She told herself that it had no reason to attack her. There was a bloody, fresh-killed feast right in front of it. Still, Kori felt a pure, overwhelming fear as she looked at the lion.

She was tempted to run, but any sudden movement might panic the animal, which would make it far more dangerous. She also felt an instinctive urge to climb back up the pine tree, but the lion could climb it as easily as she could.

In an agony of suspense, she waited.

The big cat sniffed tentatively. It eyed Kori again, then resumed creeping forward. It nudged the lizard's carcass with its snout, licked it, and she heard the cat's fat pink tongue rasping over the lizard's scaly body. Once again, the cat paused. Then it closed its fearsome jaws around the lizard's nearest leg and started backing away, dragging the carcass with it.

Kori watched with horrified fascination as the big brown cat hauled the carcass all the way out of sight, into the nearest bushes. There was a long pause. Then Kori heard the mountain lion growling softly, and there was a cracking, crunching noise as it bit into the lizard's rib cage. Finally she heard the beast purring as it devoured the meat.

Kori let out her pent-up breath. Once again she felt weak and shaky. The cat had acted just as she had hoped—just as hunters had described in their stories around the campfire. A mountain lion would never fight unless it needed to. Almost always, it could be bribed with food.

For a moment Kori imagined somehow befriending the beautiful creature. That, she knew, was a hopeless dream. She had seen the primitive look in the lion's eyes. It prowled alone, and it killed alone. This forest was its home, and it lived well without any need for her companionship.

Kori hesitated. She thought of the meat bundled in the bearskin and the uncooked skewer waiting beside the campfire. That meat belonged to her and she resented having to leave without it.

She shook her head. It was far wiser to leave with one skewer of meat than risk losing her life for the chance of leaving with two. She started moving slowly backward, stepping as silently as she could. Finally, when she was a score of paces from the tree where she had spent the night, she turned and ran.

14

For the rest of that day she followed the edge of the ravine where the stream flowed, moving continually farther west toward Mount Tomomor. Late in the afternoon she found that the slope became steeper and the trees were thinner. The soil was more gravelly here, littered with large chunks of sharp-edged rock that forced her to move slowly, watching where she placed her feet. A breeze was blowing toward her, and the air seemed colder than before.

Finally she emerged from the forest onto a wide expanse of furrowed stone that stretched ahead of her as far as she could see, barren and forbidding, gradually curving upward until it become Mount Tomomor itself.

Kori had lived on a small island all her life, sometimes making brief journeys along the river and into the forest on the Eastern Shore. She had never seen so much clear, empty space, and she had never dreamed that she would dare to tread on the actual slope of the mountain. Staring at it, she found herself growing dizzy. Instinctively she took a step backward and reached out to touch the bark of a nearby tree.

The bare vista and the empty bowl of the sky made her feel as if she were falling.

The sun was directly ahead, not far from the mountain's flat peak. The curving rock gleamed in the oblique light, making it look like a vast river that was stuck in time but could resume flowing at any instant. She half expected it to come roaring down upon her and sweep her away.

She closed her eyes and leaned against the tree. She reminded herself that she had faced a mountain lion; surely, she could face a mountain.

Once again she looked at the dizzying vista of rock. This time she forced herself to study every detail. There were big misshapen boulders with ragged, spiky edges. There were rifts and chasms, patches of gravel, and furrows that looked as if they had been made by giant claws. If any land belonged to the Old Ones, surely this was it.

At the same time, though, Kori saw that she might benefit from venturing onto it. There would be no animals for her to hunt; the only life she saw consisted of pale yellow grass growing in small clumps in fissures in the rock. The forest called to her, because it was familiar—but she knew from the previous night that it offered no real security. In truth it was a brutal place where the strong hunted the weak, and no refuge was entirely safe.

She now had enough food for at least the next three days. And if there was no game out here in the wasteland—well, that meant she should be safer here, because the land would attract no predators.

She looked to her left, at the ravine where the stream flowed. It snaked farther up the mountainside, and this was all she needed to make up her mind. She was going to need water as much as food, and she would be far safer drinking from the stream out here where she could easily see if animals were nearby.

Tentatively, she moved forward. The rock underfoot was

so spiky and sharp, it almost pierced her moccasins. But this, too, gave her confidence: the rock would be painful for any predator's paws.

She started following the edge of the ravine as it wound up the slope. She had the sense of walking where no human being should be, invading a land that was so cruelly barren, it reminded her of the Burial Pit back on her island. But she forced herself on, and she found that if she angled her eyes down and avoided staring at the empty sky, the open space didn't disturb her so much.

Maybe, she thought, all the land had looked like this when the Great Spirit made it, before he created trees and bushes and animals and people. Was this, in fact, a place where the Great Spirit himself still dwelled? The thought gave her a cold, tingling sensation that radiated across her shoulders and down her back. She turned suddenly, half expecting to find something—spirit or beast—pursuing her. But the vista of rock was empty all the way back to the forest, which stood like a wall of green at the bottom of the slope.

Kori turned slowly, looking carefully in every direction. The space was as empty as before. Nothing stirred. Surely it would be safe now to satisfy her thirst.

She ventured down into the ravine and drank, pausing often to look and listen. There were some distant bird calls, and she heard the murmur of the wind across the tumbled vista, but there were no other sounds.

She climbed back out of the ravine just in time to see the disk of the sun slipping out of sight behind Mount Tomomor. The sky was now a dazzling blend of yellow and green around the mountain, but the land was plunged into shadow. She blinked in the sudden dimness and frowned. About a hundred paces away, almost directly ahead of her, she saw a wavering yellow point of light.

Kori stood and stared at it for a long time, trying to

understand. The yellow spot looked like a campfire; there was no denying that. But how was this possible? So far as she knew, no one in her tribe had ever ventured into the forest on the Western Shore. Certainly no one had ever trespassed into this wasteland. Could the flickering yellow point be a small piece of the fire from the top of Mount Tomomor that had somehow taken root with a life of its own?

Once again she felt frightened. At the same time, fear was beginning to seem like a friend to her. She had been terrified of the lion—yet she had survived. She had been frightened of killing the lizard—yet nothing bad had happened to her. In fact, she was beginning to believe that every time she was bold, she reaped a reward.

She moved forward cautiously, clambering around great boulders and across swatches of black rubble like charcoal embers where a vast fire had burned. As the landscape grew darker around her, the flickering yellow point of light grew brighter.

Surely, it *had* to be a campfire. It was burning like a little beacon on top of a big slab of rock that reminded her of the Speaking Rock where her mother lay and listened to the spirits. And now, as Kori paused and peered into the darkness, she saw a silhouette up on top of the rock beside the fire. It was a person; she was sure of it. She saw an arm move, throwing more wood onto the fire, and sparks danced up into the air.

Could he be a spirit taking mortal form? Her people believed that when they died, their spirits went into the earth forever, to share the realm of the Old Ones. But perhaps her people were wrong, or maybe there were things they had never learned.

Kori crept closer, trying not to make a sound. She stared so intently at the mystery in front of her, she placed her feet carelessly. A little outcropping of rock broke under her weight, loosing a sudden cascade of stones that rattled away, down into the ravine beside her.

The figure near the fire jumped up. Kori froze, cursing her carelessness. She was only a dozen paces from him now. She hoped she was hidden, standing among the rocks in the gathering darkness. He, though, was clearly outlined against the sky. He was dressed in white, but it wasn't a deerskin robe or a sheepskin, it was . . . different.

"Whitebeast," she whispered to herself, feeling awe.

Suddenly he was gone. She blinked, and for a moment she really did believe he was a spirit who had vanished back into the rock where his real home lay. But then she heard his feet scrabbling over boulders, and she glimpsed him leaping up the steep slope. She realized, with amazement, that he was running away from her.

Kori was overwhelmed with a sudden, desperate need to explain this mystery. If she ran from him as he was running from her, she would never know who he was or how he came to be here. She forced herself forward in the semidarkness. She could hear him breathing hard as he clambered over the rough stones. Then she heard a shout of surprise and a cry of pain.

Kori stopped. Was he really hurt, or was this some kind of trap? She stood for a moment, trying to decide what to do.

She couldn't bear to turn around and forget what she'd seen. She imagined herself returning to her tribe one day, standing in the Meeting Place, describing everything she had done and seen on the Western Shore. She imagined the faces of the hunters, resentful yet forced to admit her courage.

But none of this could ever be if she failed to pursue this mystery. Her fear still told her to run back to the forest, but she forced herself to move forward step by step, struggling over the rough terrain.

She reached the edge of a gully—and there he was, squatting at the bottom, clutching his ankle, groaning softly.

Kori paused for a long moment, staring down at him with wide eyes. Even in the faint light she could see that he was of normal flesh and blood. He was not a beast; he was a man wearing a strange white fur. He had fallen and hurt his ankle. He was in pain.

But if he wasn't from her tribe—who could he be? She had never considered that other tribes might exist. No one in the Island Tribe had even suggested such a thing. The Island Tribe believed that they alone had been created by the Great Spirit as his only children.

Once more she summoned her courage. "Who are you?" she shouted at him.

He stared at her. Quickly he reached for his spear, which had fallen beside him. His fingers closed around its shaft, but there was no way he could throw it, squatting at the bottom of the narrow gully, with his shoulders against the wall of rock.

"Who *are* you?" Kori called again.

His face was a vague pale shape in the dimness, staring up at her. Haltingly, he spoke—but the words were a string of strange sounds, as meaningless as the cries of a baby.

And yet, some of them seemed almost familiar. Kori realized that they were like her own language echoing back from a distant mountain.

"My name is Kori," she called down to him.

"Uroh," he called back to her. He said something more that she didn't understand, although there was a word that sounded like "name" in her language. Then he repeated the sound he had made before: "Uroh."

His voice calmed her. Even though the words were foreign, the voice was human and it was gentle. He wasn't shouting a challenge or a cry of warning. He wasn't speaking like a hunter facing his prey.

She had risked so much already; did she dare to risk any more? Once again she considered turning away and retreating. But that was even less tolerable than before. She had to stay here. She had to understand where he came from. "Do you need help?" she called to him.

There was a silence. She realized that he was trying to understand her, just as she had tried to understand him.

"Help?" she repeated.

He shifted a little, and she heard him gasp with pain. "Help," he said—although the word sounded strange in his mouth. "Yes, help."

Moving with great caution, Kori started lowering herself down the side of the gully. He couldn't use his spear against her, but he might have a knife. Still, if she kept her distance, she'd be safe. He was injured, after all.

She kept pausing and checking on him as she made her way down, but he didn't move. He seemed genuinely unable to put weight on his ankle. He watched her as she came closer.

The sky was almost totally black now, but the moon was already up, and it lit his face. He looked young, perhaps seventeen, and his hair was cut in a style she had never seen before. In her tribe, the hair of men and women was always braided. It was only cropped if someone was grieving, and then it was hacked till it was no longer than a thumb-knuckle. This man's hair had been cut evenly so that it hung around the level of his jaw.

His mouth was firm, but his eyes were full of wonder as Kori reached the bottom of the ravine and turned to face him. He hesitated, then opened his hand, releasing his grip on his spear. It fell, clattering against the rock.

She stood, wondering if she could trust him. She kept a firm grip on her own spear as she edged closer to him.

"Friend," he said. At least, that was how the word sounded. He nodded to her and held out both his hands, palms toward the sky. "Friend!"

She paused. His white coat seemed to glow in the moonlight. "Whitebeast," she said, smiling to herself. She reached inside her pouch. The fragment of white fur was still there. She stepped forward boldly and reached out, comparing the wisp of fur with the robe that he wore. Suddenly, she laughed.

He frowned at her, not understanding. Well, why should he?

Kori almost tossed away the shred of fur, then thought better of it. She tucked it back in her pouch.

She glanced down at his ankle. He was keeping his weight off it, but it didn't look as if it was broken. Quickly, she squatted down. She placed her spear on the ground in front of her, where she could grab it quickly if she needed to. Tentatively, she reached out to him.

He flinched instinctively as her fingers touched the bare skin of his leg. Kori, too, found herself pulling back from the shock of physical contact. His skin was warm, no different from any man's in her tribe. But he was not from her tribe. He was from somewhere else, somewhere unimaginable. He was alien.

She touched him again, more boldly this time, feeling the bones as her mother had once taught her. The flesh was swollen around the joint, but it was just a sprain, nothing more.

Kori thought for a moment. She didn't know how to explain herself to him. Well, he would just have to trust her. She picked up her spear, holding the shaft just below the flint head, then took hold of the hem of his robe with her other hand. Before he could stop her, she began sawing the spear through the white hide, cutting a strip that was as wide as her hand.

He made a startled protest, then lapsed into silence as she took the strip that she'd cut and wrapped it tightly around his injured ankle. Finally she took two thongs from her pouch and tied them tightly around the hide.

She straightened up and dusted her hands. She nodded to him, and slowly, he smiled. He bowed his head and said something that she couldn't understand. Its meaning was clear enough, though. He was thanking her.

Kori glanced around. He wouldn't be able to climb the steep sides of the gully, but if she helped him along it a little way there was an easier place where they could both get out. She bent, picked up his spear, and held it with hers. "Lean on my shoulder," she told him.

He frowned at her.

She took his arm and drew it across her shoulders. The closeness of him made her nervous, but she told herself not to think about his strangeness. She started helping him along the narrow, rock-strewn channel toward the place where they could climb back up to the rough, bare, rocky slope.

15

A little later, when the moon was so bright it dazzled her to look at it and the stars burned fiercely in the clear, dark night, Kori sat with Uroh on top of the flat rock where she had first seen him.

It hadn't been too difficult to help him out of the gully. Steadying him as they walked across the furrowed ground had been harder, especially since she had trouble keeping her own footing in the darkness. Getting him back up onto the flat rock had been almost impossible, but it made sense for them to retreat there, because its steep sides made it safe from any predator she knew.

He lay with his leg stretched out, watching Kori as she added wood to his campfire. She saw that he had a good supply of kindling from the forest, and another white skin like his robe had been laid out as a bed to sleep on. He possessed a finely made backpack of a design she had never seen before. There were two flint knives, firesticks, a pouch containing thongs and bone needles, even a spare pair of moccasins. He was far better equipped to travel than she was.

As the flames leaped up, she turned and peered at him more closely than before. His short hair still looked strange to her, but his smile was reassuring. He had a wide, friendly face.

"You," he said. "Island Tribe."

She drew in her breath. The words were unmistakable. How did he know about her people?

Then she remembered all the times when hunters had come back to the island in their canoes, claiming they'd seen whitebeasts running through the forest on the Western Shore. Of course this man knew about her tribe. He and his friends had looked across the river at her island. He might have spent days watching her people.

But what was he here for? What did he want? Could she make him understand her questions? "You." She pointed at him. "Uroh. Where?" She pointed south, then north. She spread her hands and stared at him questioningly.

He hesitated, but only for an instant. He turned and pointed farther west, up the slope that led to the summit of Mount Tomomor.

Kori felt a moment of panic. Had she made a terrible error? Was he a spirit taking human form, after all? Surely no tribe could live in that arid wilderness, up near the mouth of the mountain where fire burst out and suffocating smoke engulfed the land.

"Far," he said. He made a motion with his hand indicating the slope of the mountain and beyond it. "Many days. Far!"

Kori blinked at him. This made even less sense. "There's no land there," she said. Mount Tomomor marked the edge of the world. The idea of something beyond it was absurd.

He didn't understand. She tried to explain herself three times. Finally, in desperation, she drew a picture in the fine black dust on the flat rock where they sat. She showed the river, which sprang from a mountain to the north, marking the northern edge of the world. She showed Moun

Tomomor at the western edge. Another range of impassable mountains bounded the eastern edge. And to the south—she hesitated. No one had ever ventured more than four days to the south. The forest was so thick, men had to cut their way through it. The river became narrow and flowed so fast over treacherous boulders, no one had ever tried to navigate through it. Her people believed that the river flowed off the edge of the world, and only a madman would be stupid enough to follow it.

Uroh slowly shook his head. He pointed to her drawing of Mount Tomomor, then moved his finger farther west and drew another mountain, and another beyond that. He pointed to himself, then to the third mountain.

Kori felt dizzy. Everything he told her about himself was impossible. And yet—he existed. And to her knowledge, no one in her tribe had actually tried to venture beyond the limits of their world. So how could the elders be certain when they told young children what was true?

Kori felt doubt gnawing at her, and it made her nervous. If she rejected one thing that the elders said, why should she believe the other things? How could she trust them at all?

Kori looked into Uroh's face. Was he lying to her? No; he was looking puzzled, as if he couldn't understand why she should doubt him. He was telling her something that was obvious to him.

She turned away from him. She saw a bucket of deerskin sitting close by her on the rock, containing a small puddle of water. She grabbed the bucket, turned, and took it with her as she lowered herself from the flat boulder.

Uroh shouted a question to her, but she didn't even try to understand the words as she strode away. She felt confused and angry—with Uroh for making her feel so ignorant, but most of all with her people. They were so frightened of the land, they didn't dare explore it, but they still pretended to know everything.

She realized she was angry at herself as well, because she had been foolish enough to believe everything her tribe had told her.

Kori found her way down to the fast-flowing stream in the ravine. She filled the bucket, wondering how many other things she believed might not be true. Those sacred rocks that her people had brought back to the island with so much effort—were they really sacred? Was anything about the Old Ones true? Did the Great Spirit himself even exist?

She balked at that, because if there was no Great Spirit, the world couldn't exist. It must have come from somewhere. And yet no one had ever seen the Great Spirit, or touched him, or heard him speak.

But that wasn't quite true. Her own mother heard the spirits speak. And when the earth shook or Mount Tomomor spouted fire, how could these things be explained if there were no spirits under the earth to make it happen?

It was all too difficult, too big for her to cope with. First she needed to know simple, everyday things about this strange young man she had found: what he wanted, how his people lived, and why he was here alone.

Kori made her way back to the flat rock by the light of the moon and climbed up onto it, spilling some of the water on her leggings but not really caring. She saw Uroh sitting close by the fire, and she felt embarrassed by the way she had run from him. "Here," she said, holding out the bucket. "Water. Drink."

"Water," he said, smiling. It was still the same word, though his mouth stretched it strangely. "Thank you," he said as he took it from her.

Kori sat cross-legged on the rock. She felt convinced now that he was no danger to her. "Are you hungry?" she asked as she opened her bearskin, revealing the cooked meat.

"Hungry." He nodded. He didn't reach for the food, though. Maybe he didn't think that was polite. Or maybe he was afraid that the food might be poisoned. Kori picked up two chunks of the lizard meat and held them out to him. He hesitated, then chose one. She nodded and started eating the other. He grinned happily and followed her example.

"Good," he said, and smacked his lips. Then he paused. "You hunt?"

"Yes," said Kori, feeling a moment of great pride.

He frowned. "My tribe—no women hunt."

"They don't hunt in my tribe, either," Kori said. Quickly, before she could stop herself, she started telling him what had happened to her. It was difficult, because she had to keep repeating words that he didn't understand. Bit by bit, though, she was learning his different pronunciation. She told him everything: about her mother, and the trip to gather sacred stones, and the death of Mima, and the decision of the tribe to place her here, to be tested.

At the end of her story Uroh was silent for a long time. He sat and stared at her with wide eyes. His black hair lay half across his forehead; he brushed it aside. "You are very brave," he said finally.

Kori had been feeling apprehensive. She had listened to herself telling him everything, and it made her sound like such a misfit. But now, with surprise, she realized the look in his eyes wasn't doubt, it was admiration.

"And your people sound cruel," he went on.

Kori thought of her tribe: her brother, her parents, her other kin. Suddenly she wanted to cry. His kindness undermined her courage. It made her want to borrow some of his strength.

But he was injured, she reminded herself. And even though he seemed decent, he was still a stranger. She must be cautious—at least for a while.

"Perhaps my people seem cruel," she said carefully, "but they live in a cruel world. They have been punished so many times by the Old Ones—" She broke off.

He was frowning again. He didn't understand.

Suddenly Kori knew that he didn't believe in the Old Ones. He was too carefree. He didn't fear his world.

"I'll explain some other time," she said quickly. "Tell me, why did you run when you first saw me coming toward you?"

He laughed. "It was hard to see you in the twilight. You were walking so boldly, holding your spear, and your face and arms were bloody—"

Kori glanced down at herself. She was still marked with the lizard's blood.

"I thought you might be a man who had come here with other hunters who were hiding back in the forest," Uroh went on. "Up on this rock, I'm safe from animals but easy for a hunter to kill with his spear. And I only have one spear of my own. Farther up the mountain," he jerked his head toward Mount Tomomor, "there's a place where I can hide from an enemy's spears and throw rocks down on him. That's where I was running to."

Kori wondered why he made his explanation in such detail, with such a serious expression. Then she realized he was defending his pride. He had fled from a young woman. Worse still, he had slipped and hurt his ankle, and she had helped him.

"But why are you here alone," she asked him, "with only one spear?" A sudden thought came to her. "Did your people cast you out, like me?"

He shook his head. "My people have a custom. Every young hunter must go out alone to prove himself."

Kori thought about that. "My people have seen your young hunters in the forest." She reached out and touched the white fur of his robe. "They think you're animals. They call you whitebeast."

Uroh laughed. He threw his head back and showed his strong white teeth. His laughter was full and uninhibited.

Kori thought she had never heard anyone sound so untroubled by the world.

"Why do your hunters come down to the river?" she persisted. "And why do they always run and hide?"

Uroh's smile faded. He looked at her seriously. "My people watch your tribe sometimes because we are afraid of you."

Kori blinked. "You are afraid of us?" It was another idea that was almost impossible to believe.

Uroh spread his arms. "Your hunters throw spears at us! They try to kill us!"

Kori slowly rubbed her face with her hands. Her head was aching. "This is all so strange," she murmured. "Everything here is strange. This open land where nothing grows—"

"The lava?" he asked.

She gave him a questioning look. "Lava?"

He nodded. "When the mountain spits fire, the lava runs down the slope like blood. But then it cools and turns to rock."

"I understand," said Kori. The idea seemed bizarre, but she was tired of seeming ignorant. And she was exhausted, she realized—mentally and physically. Her fear had subsided, leaving her empty. "May I stay here by your fire?" she asked.

"Of course." He made it sound as if it should have been obvious. "It may not be an accident that we have met. There's such a thing as fate, or at least, my people think so. If you and I are chosen by fate, we'd be foolish to defy it. We must find out why we have been chosen, and what we can gain from it."

"I don't understand this word 'fate,'" said Kori. "But I like the sound of what you say." She got up off her bearskin and shifted it a little, placing it on the exact opposite side of the fire from the white fur where he would be lying. "I hope I can trust you, Uroh," she said, feeling a twinge of apprehension at the idea of closing her eyes in his company.

He gave her his wide, carefree grin. "Here," he said. He picked up his spear and held out the end of the wooden shaft. "You can sleep with both the spears. And my knives, too." He tossed them to her. "I know that you won't hurt me. You could have killed me when you found me in the ravine, but you brought me back here. Now you have my weapons; you can trust me in return."

Kori stared at him in wonder. She had never known a man who was so relaxed, so friendly, so willing to give her his time, his words, and even his weapons.

She placed the two spears and the flint knives carefully on her bearskin, then lay down beside them. "Thank you, Uroh," she said. She tried to return his carefree smile, but her face felt suddenly wooden with tiredness. As she turned on her side and rested her head on her arm, she felt her awareness slipping away. Within moments, she was asleep.

16

She woke with the sun in her eyes. She lay for a minute, squinting into the glare, enjoying the warmth on her body . . . and gradually she remembered where she was.

She thought of everything that had happened the previous day, and she felt overwhelmed. But it was a good feeling: a feeling of power and freedom that she'd never imagined she could have.

At the same time, of course, she was homeless now. She looked down the hillside, past the forest that stretched into the distance. Somewhere down there was the island where her people lived. What were they doing now? Were they thinking of her? Had they forgotten her? She felt a sudden pang. There had been a sense of security, a feeling of belonging—but that wasn't true. She had never been safe, and she had never been truly happy. It was painful to admit, but it was undeniable.

She rolled over, deliberately turning her back on the forest and the island that lay beyond. She found herself looking at Uroh. He was lying on his side in his strange white furs, still sleeping despite the bright morning sun. His black eye-lashes gleamed in the oblique light, and his broad face seemed just as relaxed and friendly now as when he had been talking to her in the firelight. His full mouth curved up slightly at the corners, so he seemed to be smiling even while he slept. Kori marveled at his serenity.

His robe had fallen open, revealing the smooth, tanned skin of his chest. Kori pushed herself up on one elbow and peered at his body. He was slim and lean, not a heavily mus-cled giant like Yainar. Still, his muscles looked strong. She studied the hard, flat shape of his stomach, then found her-self peeking lower, down to the shadowy triangle below his abdomen—

He made a little sleepy sound and moved slowly, stretch-ing. Kori pulled back, shocked by her own boldness. She found that his brown eyes were already open, watching her. His smile deepened. She glimpsed his even white teeth. "Kori," he said softly.

She gave an awkward laugh. "I was just looking at your furs. I've never seen furs like that. I was wondering, what beast—"

He sat up and pulled the furs around him. "They come from the great white bear," he said. "It lives in the cold lands far to the north."

"A white bear?" She tried to imagine such a thing.

"They're strong and hard to kill. But their furs are the warmest of all." His eyes narrowed as he watched her face. "Do you want to touch it?" He held out his arm, reaching across the ashes of the campfire, which had burned out dur-ing the night. Shyly, Kori leaned forward and combed her fingers through the dense fur. It was even thicker than her black bearskin. She dragged her fingers down his forearm, then stopped abruptly as she found herself touching the skin of his wrist.

She pulled back. "I wonder why it's so white."

"Because the mountains where the white bear lives are covered in snow for the whole year. The bear is cunning: he wears white to hide himself from our spears."

Kori gave him a sharp look. "But you said your people live farther to the west, not the north."

Uroh hesitated. "That's true." He looked embarrassed. "Yes, our tribe doesn't live in the north. We trade with other tribes who live there, and that's how we get the white furs."

Once again Kori felt her mind becoming overloaded with impossible ideas. "*Another* tribe? You mean, there are more than just my people and yours?"

He grinned. "Many more. Many tribes. Perhaps hundreds. Who knows? Perhaps they were all one tribe long ago. Some people set out in one direction, some people set out in another. They made their homes in different places. And each tribe learned to speak a little differently."

Kori pulled up her knees and wrapped her arms around them. She sat like that for a long moment with her eyes closed, hugging herself, trying to imagine the world being ten times as big as she'd always been taught—no, a hundred times. And whole tribes journeying to new homes instead of always living in the same place. Then they would meet each other and trade with each other. The concept was frightening. It made her feel so insignificant.

She looked back at Uroh. "My people have always lived on the island," she said, "since the beginning of time. So these other tribes—they must be descended from ours. Maybe—maybe their first people were exiled, like me!" She felt a rush of pleasure at making this deduction. But the pleasure faded as she saw his amused expression.

"Every tribe says it gave birth to the other tribes," he told her. "No tribe wants to believe that it is just one of many. But memories are short. How do you know where your people really came from?"

His calm, logical tone suddenly irritated her. "You think

you know everything," she snapped at him. She stood up quickly and pulled her robe around her with sharp, angry movements. "You just sit there and laugh at me for being so ignorant."

"No." His smile vanished. He bent his good leg and managed to struggle up onto his feet. "No, I would never laugh at you, Kori." He broke off, grimacing with pain as he put too much weight on his sprained ankle. He stared at her helplessly.

She grunted in annoyance and stepped quickly to him. "Don't stand on it," she told him. She took his arm, hooked it around her neck, and tucked her shoulder under his armpit. "Sit," she told him. "Lean on me. Slowly, now."

Bit by bit, she lowered him till they were sitting side by side. She was so close to him, she felt the warmth of his body. His musky smell seemed to close around her. She glanced at his face and found it almost touching hers. Quickly, she pulled away.

"I never meant to make fun of you," he told her, looking deeply serious. "I know more about the world just because I've seen more of it. I admire you, Kori. You're strong and brave—as brave as any hunter."

Never in her life had a man said such a thing to her. Kori felt even more confused than before. Her stomach felt queasy. It was hard for her to swallow. She turned away, biting her lip, trying to calm herself. Absent-mindedly she noticed that when he had struggled to his feet, he had kicked over the little leather bucket.

Quickly she picked it up. "I should get more water," she said. She managed not to look at him again as she scrambled down the back side of the rock and hurried to the stream.

A little later they rebuilt the fire and ate more of her store of lizard meat. Once again she placed herself carefully opposite him, keeping the fire between them. Her emotions were still churning inside her, and she knew that if she let herself, she could think about Uroh in the same way she had thought about Yainar. He wasn't as handsome as Yainar, or as strong, and she wished he hadn't cropped his hair in such a strange way. His eyes, though, were magical; they lingered on her as if he gained actual pleasure from staring at her. And they had such a dreamy, distant look, they never made her feel uneasy the way she did when Yainar stared at her.

Uroh's face was pleasant, too, with his friendly mouth, so often smiling, and his well-spaced features. More than anything, though, she found herself responding to him because he seemed so interested in her. He hadn't tried to touch her, and he had been respectful and polite, but the way he talked to her and the way he looked at her made her feel as if he had more than just a friendly interest, and if she let herself she could easily imagine him shedding his strange white furs, revealing his slim, strong body, touching her, holding her—

She shook her head quickly. What was wrong with her, thinking like this? Uroh was a stranger, a man from an unimaginable place, and she knew nothing about him. He had a charming smile, but that meant nothing. He had flattered her, praising her strength, but strength was the last thing a man looked for in a woman. His compliment was probably his way of telling her that they were equals, like brother and sister. She found it easier to talk to him than anyone in her own tribe—but this, too, could be her imagination. And even if it was true, it certainly didn't mean he desired her. She was determined not to make a fool of herself with him as she had with Yainar.

"We'll need more meat soon," she said, keeping her voice calm and matter-of-fact as she licked her fingers clean and then drank from the bucket. "And you won't be able to put weight on your ankle for another two days."

He frowned. "I think perhaps tomorrow—"

"No. Two days." It pleased her that she could feel certain of one fact in the world, at least. "My mother is a healer. She taught me these things. So, I will have to hunt for the two of us."

Privately, she lacked the courage that she put into her voice. The idea of picking up her spear and returning to the forest made her feel dismayed.

"There is an alternative," said Uroh. "May I tell you?"

She hesitated. His voice was gentle. There was no hint of mockery, and it would be foolish of her to refuse advice on this subject. Obviously he knew more about hunting than she did.

"Please do tell me," she said. "I confess—I've had very little practice with a spear."

"Well, a spear is a fine tool, but only if you need a deer to feed a whole tribe, or a bearskin to serve as a blanket, or some fine antlers or teeth to show as a trophy. For just the two of us, a snare is the best method." He paused, looking at her cautiously. "Do you know how to set snares?"

Kori looked down. She said nothing.

"Don't feel embarrassed," he said, "just because I have knowledge that you lack. It may not be a custom in your tribe for people to trap game."

"For men, perhaps," Kori said. "But not for women."

He shrugged. "Well, then, your people have kept this knowledge from you. You have no reason to feel ignorant."

He told her, then, all the different ways that thongs, vines, sticks, and rocks could be used to trap small creatures. He explained how to find a path in the forest where foxes or opossum or rabbits often pass by. He showed her how to make a noose, and then he spread out some ashes from the fire and drew pictures in them with a pointed stick, showing Kori how to tie the noose to a sapling, bend the sapling, and hold it with just a tiny twig. Any animal that touched the noose or the sapling would release the twig, and the noose would seize the animal by its leg or by its neck and jerk it high into the air where it would be helpless—and also out of reach of other predators that might want to claim it.

Uroh drew a picture of a deadfall, and of a pit with sharpened stakes in it, and he explained the best way to place bait and the caution she should use approaching any animal that was trapped and fighting for its life. She marveled at the way he described these things. His explanations were so clear, so methodical, she hardly had to ask any questions.

There was a strange, special pleasure sitting here with him in the bright sun, learning from him. She had no fears or anxieties even though she was supposedly in a land ruled cruelly by the Old Ones. He was so cheerful, so relaxed, he made her feel secure.

Finally, when the sun was near its noontime place in the sky, Uroh told her that he had nothing more to say. She smiled at him shyly and thanked him. "I don't mind learning from you," she said, "because you treat me as an equal."

He looked surprised. "Well—I think of you as an equal."

"Even though I am a woman?"

He shouted out his cheerful laughter. "You are no ordinary woman."

A feeling of warmth had been growing inside Kori, but now it suddenly disappeared. She looked away, feeling as if he had slapped her. It was like a curse, this strong spirit of hers, which was so obvious that even a man from another tribe could tell that there was something strange about her.

"Yesterday I set snares all along the edge of the forest," Uroh was saying, unaware of her thoughts. "I'll tell you where they are. After you harvest the game, you'll set the snares again. It should be simple."

Kori forced her thoughts back to the present. There was a task that needed to be done, and if they wanted to eat, she would have to do it.

*   *   *

A little later she was picking her way over the rills and fissures in the rocky slope, heading back toward the forest with an empty sack slung over her shoulder and her spear in her hand, just in case.

If Uroh was really right, this slope had been a mass of viscous liquid long ago. She tried to imagine how it must have looked.

But it was more important to eat than think. She strode on down the hillside, eager to reach the forest before the light started to dim and predators emerged from their lairs looking for creatures to kill and eat.

17

Kori marveled at how simple it was to harvest the snared game. Following Uroh's instructions she seized each animal by its back legs, loosened the snare with her free hand, then quickly whirled the prey and dashed its head against the nearest tree. Resetting the snares was trickier, and she felt nervous and vulnerable crouching in the forest, waving flies away from her face while she tried to balance the force of a sapling with the tiny scrap of wood that kept it in check. Still, she fixed the last of the snares well before sunset and felt proud of herself as she made her way back to the high, flat rock where Uroh was waiting.

Then she thought of something that took away her feelings of pride and replaced them with anger. If it was so simple to set a snare and feed herself from the land, why hadn't any of her people told her how to do it? Why had her father given her just a few scraps of meat instead of knowledge and tools that she could have used to keep herself alive?

Perhaps the idea had never occurred to him. She was a woman, and everyone knew that women couldn't hunt. That was why Rohonar had given her a spear that was full of powerful magic. He'd assumed that without the magic she would be lost.

Kori grimaced and kicked a loose piece of stone, sending it flying away and out of sight, down into the ravine where the stream flowed. There was a faint, distant splash.

As she climbed back up to the high rock she felt even more grateful to Uroh. By teaching her how to trap game, he had given her much more than the skill to feed herself. He had helped her to see her life differently, as something that she could control.

He greeted her with a broad grin and a shout of welcome as she climbed up to join him, and he cried out with pleasure when he saw the game that she was carrying. "Good, Kori!" he said, clapping his hands.

"It was simple," she said, feeling embarrassed by his praise, but enjoying it all the same.

He waved his hand. "Simple or not, it would have been hard for me to do it with my ankle. And were you able to set the snares?"

"Yes."

He grinned. "And was that simple, too?"

"No, it was much more difficult. But I managed it," she added quickly.

He winked at her. "If women ever found out how simple it is to trap game, they'd lose all respect for men, wouldn't they?"

Kori stopped and thought for a moment. "But you are a man, Uroh. Does that mean I should lose respect for you, because you have told me these things?"

He fell silent, and she couldn't read his face. Finally he gave her a shy, cautious look. "Is that how it is, Kori? Have you lost respect for me?"

She now saw something in him that she hadn't seen before. In some ways he was less sure of himself than he seemed. "I respect you all the more," she said, "for having the courage to treat me as your equal."

He looked at her doubtfully. Then he shrugged. "Well, I am the way I am," he said. "But instead of talking like this, we should skin the game before it gets dark." He frowned. "I talk too much. I'm a dreamer, Kori. I lose track of the practical things."

Kori reached for the flint knives and handed one to him. He took one of the rabbits, she took the other, and they worked together in silence for a moment, cutting through the belly fur and peeling the skin back. "Are all the men in your tribe like you?" she asked him.

He took the rabbit's head in his left fist and dragged its skin back with his right hand. "No one is like me," he said. His voice was neutral, but Kori saw a hardness in his face. "As I told you, I'm a dreamer. And although you say you respect my courage, other people don't feel the same way. They don't respect me, because I'm not a fighter."

Kori paused and gave him a look of concern. "The men in your tribe fight each other?"

He shrugged. "Of course. It's the nature of men to fight. How else can they learn who's strongest and should serve as their chieftain?" He gave her a curious look. "And how can a tribe learn to defend itself against other tribes if the men don't practice fighting among themselves?"

Kori realized she had stumbled on yet another strange concept. She paused for a moment, trying to imagine men hunting each other as if they were hunting game. It was a deeply disturbing idea. It sickened her.

She looked down, found herself holding the entrails from her rabbit, and set them aside. She washed her fingers absent-mindedly in the little water bucket. "So, tribes fight each other."

Uroh gestured with his flint knife. "They fight for land, or for women, or for honor. It seems your people have been fortunate living here, cut off from other tribes. Even so, surely your menfolk fight among themselves sometimes."

Kori quickly shook her head. "In my tribe everyone stands together. They put aside their differences. They have to, to be strong enough to face the Old Ones."

Uroh took his rabbit skin and stretched it out carefully on the rock. He picked up the body of the animal and skewered it on a straight, pointed piece of hardwood. "This is very interesting," he said. "Your people turn their anger toward these spirits you talk about, instead of each other. Is that how it is?"

"Perhaps. But what about you, Uroh? You say you don't fight like other men."

He gave a strange, distant smile. "When men in my tribe want to fight me, I tell them to hurt me as much as they want. Hurt me more! Hurt me more! I won't fight back."

She looked at him in concern. "And what happens?"

"Oh, they get angry with me, and they insult me, and they lose interest. Or sometimes they do try to hurt me—but their anger makes them stupid, so I turn it against them somehow." He grimaced, taking no pleasure in the conversation. "Fighting wastes the strength of a man. It wastes the strength of a tribe. If your tribe has found a way to live without fighting, they're very fortunate."

For the first time, Kori saw some value in the code her people lived by. Finally she felt ready to ask the question that had made her too uneasy before. She leaned forward, looking at him intently. "Tell me, Uroh," she said. "Do you believe there are spirits?"

Uroh skewered Kori's rabbit on the same spit as his own, then set them over the flames. Carefully, he added more fuel to the fire. "I don't know what I believe," he said. "I watch the world, and I see many mysteries." He spread his hands. "If there's no rain and the streams dry up and the animals die of thirst—is that because the spirits are angry, or because the Sun God is angry, or for some other reason?"

"So . . . you don't know the answer?"

"How can anyone know the answer?"

Kori looked into his tanned face, so amiable and open, with a hint of a smile always lurking at the corners of his mouth. She had the sudden strange impulse to take his hands in hers and hold them, just for the pleasure of feeling the warmth of his skin, feeling joined with him physically—because, she realized, she was feeling joined with him mentally in a way that she had never known before.

The thought frightened her, because she didn't trust her emotions. She looked quickly away, saw the leather bucket, and grabbed it. "I must get fresh water," she said, hurrying to the rear of the rock.

Later, as the sun set, they ate their fill of the meat. Kori lay down on her back on the bearskin and looked up at the stars. She couldn't see Uroh, because he was on the other side of the fire. Still, she sensed his presence.

"Tell me more about these Old Ones," he said after a long silence.

Kori started explaining the faith of her tribe. She repeated the phrases she had heard so often from her mother and father, but tonight the words tasted strange in her mouth. They came from a different place, a different world, where people were fearful and she had never found the peace of mind that she felt at this moment.

Uroh was silent for a while when she finished speaking. He took a piece of wood and tossed it on the fire, sending yellow sparks whirling up to join the brilliant silver dust strewn across the sky. "My people," he said, "believe that the Sun God created the land, the forests, the animals, and the tribes. Then the Moon God gave each animal and each person a soul—a spirit—so that it could create children. And

just in case there might be a time when there were more animals, or more people, Moon God created extra spirits, which
she placed in the sky. And those are the stars. And when
someone dies, his spirit goes up to become another star."

Kori waited. She finally realized that he wasn't going to
say anything more. "That's all?" she asked, feeling disappointed.

He chuckled. "That's all."

Kori pushed herself up on one elbow and looked across at
him. "But when Mount Tomomor shoots fire into the sky,
how do your people explain that?"

Uroh reached lazily inside his robe and scratched his
chest. "They say that Mother Earth has stolen some fire from
the Sun God, because she's jealous of his power."

"And this doesn't scare them?"

"No, because they aren't close enough for the fire to burn
them, and it cools soon enough."

Kori found herself feeling amazed by the simplicity of his
view of the world. "What about earthquakes?" she asked.

Uroh shrugged. "Sometimes Mother Earth has a fever and
she shivers. After a while, the fever passes."

"But aren't your people frightened?" She thought of poor
old Shashin. "Isn't anyone killed when earthquakes destroy
your houses?"

"We don't have houses. We live in tents. If a tent falls
down, it doesn't hurt anyone." He gave her a quizzical look.
"If I lived in a house made from stones, maybe then I'd be
frightened."

Kori felt momentarily confused. It was such an obvious
thing to say, yet it had never been obvious to her before.
"The rocks are part of the earth," she said, remembering
things she'd been taught when she was just five years old.
"The Old Ones are always angry at their fate, and sometimes they punish us, but if we respect them, and worship
them, and give them sacrifices, they will protect us. The

spirits are in every rock, so if we build our homes from rock, the Old Ones will be pleased, and they will be with us always." She shook her head helplessly. "These words sound foolish to me now, yet all my life I've believed that they are true."

"And they may be true," said Uroh, grinning. "Who's to say? Who can ever tell?" He tilted his head curiously as he looked at her. "Is that why your people take their canoes upriver and gather rocks from the Western Shore? To build more houses?"

"Yes." Kori leaned forward, feeling a little leap of excitement. "Uroh—was that you, a few days ago, running through the trees?"

He drew back. He looked at her in sudden suspicion. "Was that you who tried to kill me?"

"No!" She flinched from the thought. "No, no, I tried to stop them!"

He eyed her for a moment longer, then slowly relaxed. "I'm glad of that," he said.

She reached inside her pouch and fondled the little scrap of white fur. "I may have saved your life," she said. "Horeth was so excited to see a whitebeast—" She paused. "So it was you in the woods. Does that mean you're the only one from your tribe roaming the land here?"

He shrugged. "There were some others here in the spring, but not now."

"Why were you watching us when we were stone gathering?"

He laughed. "Mount Tomomor was spitting fire, so I went into the forest to be away from him." He watched her for a moment longer, and his face shimmered in the heat above the fire. "Kori?" he asked.

There was a new note in his voice that made her feel instinctively cautious, though she couldn't say why. "Yes?" she said.

"I must ask a favor. Could you look at the hide that you bound around my ankle? It feels very tight."

So that was all he wanted. Well, if the dressing was tight, she should loosen it immediately. She scrambled up, moved around the fire, and squatted beside him in the darkness. Gently, she touched his skin. The swelling had diminished. In fact, the thongs were actually a little looser than before. She gave him a puzzled look. "It doesn't seem too tight to me."

He sat up so that he could look directly into her face. For a long moment he studied her, saying nothing.

Kori shifted self-consciously. "What is it?"

"Nothing."

"So why are you staring at me like this?"

"Because—well, I think you are beautiful."

She felt as she had been riding in a canoe—and suddenly the canoe was gone, and she was floundering in the river. She reached out to steady herself where she sat. She felt like laughing, but she couldn't laugh.

"What's the matter?" he asked. "Did I say something wrong?"

Nameless feelings were flowering inside her, and she felt horribly confused. "You said something that isn't true," she said. Her voice sounded abrupt. The words were too loud. She wished he would stop looking at her.

He didn't look away. His soft, dreamy brown eyes were still watching her. "I know what I think," he said, "and I think it is true. You are beautiful to me."

She wondered if he was mocking her. She looked quickly down at her hands. She had tried to conceal her thoughts and feelings from him, but maybe he had sensed them, just as Yainar had sensed that she desired him. And now Uroh was going to tease her and play games with her—just like Yainar. She looked away and noticed the water bucket with only a puddle left in the bottom of it. With a shaky hand, she reached out to grab it.

His hand moved faster than hers. He seized her wrist and held it. "Not this time," he said.

"Stop!" she protested. "Let go of me!"

Quickly he released her. "What's wrong?"

"You're being cruel to me." She felt like crying.

He shook his head, looking amazed. "No, Kori. No, I'm only saying what I believe. What's cruel in that?"

She hesitated, then gave him a quick, doubting look.

"Look," he said, "I want you, Kori. There, I've said the words." He blinked. "Are you already paired with someone?" His expression changed to match his plaintive tone of voice, and she realized with surprise that he was unsure of himself.

"I'm not paired," she said. It was hard to speak.

He moved closer, slid his hands under her arms, and pulled her against him. She shook from the shock of contact as she felt the strength in his lean body. She tried hard not to respond, but still she felt herself growing excited. Wasn't this what she had wanted with a man for so long? So why did she feel such an overwhelming impulse to push him away now? Why did she want to turn and run? "This is wrong," she muttered.

"For us, it's not wrong," he said. He smiled at her. "Are you frightened, Kori? You're such a brave hunter. How can you be scared of me?"

"Because—because I don't know if you speak truly. I know I'm not beautiful. The men in my tribe shun me."

He made a little noise of disapproval. "The men in your tribe must be fools. I do speak truly. I desire you, Kori."

Suppose—suppose she yielded to him. The thought terrified her, but suppose she did. "We aren't paired," she whispered.

Quickly, confidently, he shook his head. "We make our own customs here. We're not in your tribe, or mine. We are our own tribe."

His words stirred something inside her. "Do you really believe that?" she asked, trying to see his face in the darkness.

"Your people rejected you. Why shouldn't you reject their customs?"

It was true, Kori realized. She owed no debt of obedience. It was an incredible thought. She was truly in charge of her own self. The people who had cast her out meant nothing to her now. Her spirit soared as her inhibitions fell away. "And you really want me?" she asked.

He nodded. "Yesterday," he said, "when you first came running after me—I glimpsed your face, just before I fell. In fact, that's why I fell. I saw you were a woman. I was so surprised, and—there was something about your confidence, the way you stared at me—I felt this great need to know you. Even after I hurt my ankle in the ravine, I could have dragged myself out somehow. But I didn't. I just lay there waiting for you." He laughed and shook his head ruefully. "I was risking my life, but I stayed there."

Kori felt her own desire surging up so strongly, she felt as if she was drowning. She turned to face him—and impulsively, he took her cheeks between his hands and pressed his mouth against hers.

Was this the way it was supposed to feel, to kiss someone? She didn't know. She felt shy because her mouth was clumsy against his. She pulled quickly away from him. "I'm sorry," she said. "I don't really know—"

"Shhh." He took her shoulders firmly but gently and pressed her down onto his blanket of white fur. "We must teach each other."

Her pulse was still running fast—just as fast as when she'd found herself face to face with the mountain lion in the forest. But she trusted him now, or at least she thought she did, as long as he would stay here with her.

"Sooner or later you'll go back to your tribe," she blurted out, feeling a new wave of uncertainty and distress.

"Maybe I should bring you with me." He looked into her eyes.

"You mean it?" The idea was inconceivable.

"I just know I want to be with you." Tentatively, he slid his hand inside her furs and brushed his fingers across her breasts, exploring the shape of her body.

Kori shook and cried out. She'd imagined this so many times, but now that it was happening, it was nothing like her fantasies at all. She felt the weight of his body as he leaned against her, and she felt her own physical weight against the blanket on the hard, cold rock. She smelled him and tasted him as he kissed her. The feelings were powerfully physical, shockingly real. But when his fingers moved lower across her abdomen and touched her thighs—now she felt the kind of desire she'd imagined so often. Her skin felt hot, and she was wet inside, and she wanted him with an intensity that scared her.

"Wait," she said. She grabbed his arm. "Wait. I can't—we don't know what may happen to us. You talk about taking me to your tribe, but it's too much for me to think about now. If I should get pregnant with you, what will happen to me?"

"A child only grows when a man plants his seed in a woman." His brown eyes looked directly into hers. "Surely your people know that this is true?"

Kori tried to remember things her mother had said. Yes, Immar had told her this, but what did it really mean? "What must I do?" she whispered.

"Just trust me, Kori. I won't give you my seed. Not unless you ask me for it." He slid his hand lower, between her legs.

She gasped. Could she trust him? She felt as if she didn't have a choice anymore. The need for this had been trapped inside her for so many years, it seized her like a wild animal and shook her till her thoughts were in fragments, leaving nothing but a longing that was so strong, she couldn't reason with it. Instinctively she reached for him—then checked herself in embarrassment.

He took her wrist and guided her fingers to him. She drew in her breath in surprise. He was so big; how could he ever fit inside her? She remembered some of the stories she'd heard from women warning her that there would be no pleasure in the first time, and maybe not the second time or the third time, or ever.

"Be gentle," she told Uroh as she felt his naked body pinning her to the rock.

She couldn't tell if he heard her. He was staring at her with wide eyes, as if he was just as amazed as she was to find himself coupling with her in this arid wilderness. He ran his fingertips over her forehead, her cheeks, her lips, proving to himself that she was real. With his other hand, he pushed himself inside her.

It did hurt, just as she'd been warned, and she gave a little scream. But he paused for a moment, looking at her with concern. Kori shifted under him, pulling her knees up, and now when he moved into her she felt pleasure competing with the pain. And then he pressed harder against her and she no longer noticed whether it hurt or not, because she felt as if she had captured him. Instinctively she clenched her muscles to hold him inside. She never wanted to release him. She wanted to be coupled like this forever.

He groaned, and she saw in his face that it excited him when she clenched on him. She wrapped her arms around him, wrapped her legs around him as well. She clung to him, kissed him, and he stiffened in her arms. He jerked his hips quickly, then pulled out of her with a startled cry. His body shook and he slumped down on her, panting.

She stared at him in confusion. Then she felt wetness on her thighs, and she realized he had climaxed outside her.

For a moment she felt empty and cheated. But she realized it was just as well he had pulled out of her when he did.

And then, as her mind cleared a little, she realized there was no hurry. Uroh looked dazed and he was panting as if he had just dragged a deer back from a hunt. She snuggled against him, waiting till he caught his breath. Surely, he would want her again before the night was over.

18

When she woke the next morning she felt as if she was reborn. It amazed her that so much could change in a single night. She had been self-conscious and ashamed of her desires. She had been awkward and insecure, convinced that she was unattractive to any man. But now—now, she felt renewed and complete. She felt like a bud that had been tightly clenched in on itself and had suddenly opened.

She lay with her eyes closed for a moment, enjoying the strange little aches in some of her muscles. She was sore inside, but she enjoyed the feeling. She was proud of it, like a hunter showing off scratches from a fierce beast that he had killed.

Kori yawned and stretched and then sat up. She looked down and saw smears of blood on the insides of her thighs. So the stories that women told were true: a man really could make a woman bleed.

For just a moment, Kori felt terribly guilty. She had violated one of the strictest taboos of her tribe. Her mother would be horrified. This should have been a most special night, preceded with days of chanting and feasting and prayer to the spirits. The pairing of a chieftain's daughter was a momentous event for the tribe. And now—now, it could never happen! She had been defiled by a stranger whom she barely knew.

She shook her head angrily. Her tribe had cast her out. She owed them nothing. In fact, she found herself taking savage pleasure imagining how horrified they would be if they could see her now, lying naked with Uroh on the sacred ground of Mount Tomomor itself. This, surely, was a greater act of defiance than all her other petty rebellions put together.

Kori turned and looked at Uroh beside her, sleeping peacefully. His robe was open, revealing his genitals. Kori edged closer, remembering how she had wanted to look at him on the first morning she had woken with him. She had been too ashamed, then—but not now.

She stared in wonder. The thing that had been so frightening last night was no different now from a boy-child's.

Did she dare to touch it? Well, Uroh had wanted her to touch it last night. He had placed her hand on it, and it had given him pleasure.

Gently she closed her fingers around the flesh. She held it—then gave a cry of surprise and pulled her hand back as it stirred under her palm.

She looked up at him and found him craning his neck, peering down at her, his eyes still half-closed with sleep. Slowly, he grinned. "Last night you were timid," he said. "And now you're bold."

Her first impulse was to hide her face in shame. But no; that was another habit from her childhood. Uroh had taught her to question the customs of her tribe, and she had left that part of herself behind, hadn't she? Bravely, with an effort of will, she managed to look him in the eye. "You told me to be bold," she said.

He nodded slowly. "I like your courage. It excites me."

"Really?" This was something that she still found hard to believe. She thought of Yainar and his desire for an obedient woman. "Most men prefer a woman who obeys them. Someone who knows her place."

He shrugged one shoulder. "I already told you, I'm unlike most men. Obedient women are boring. If I can win a bold woman like you—that makes me feel as if I must be a very powerful man."

He seemed sincere. But then, he always seemed sincere. She only hoped it was really so.

She allowed her hand to stray back to his groin. "You don't mind if I do this?"

"It feels nice, Kori. But if you rouse me again, I shall want to have you again."

"And is that such a bad thing?"

He smiled faintly. "The hunters of my tribe have a saying. A man should only couple with a woman once in a night. If he couples twice, he'll sleep so soundly afterward that he'll never hear his enemies. Three times, and he'll be so weakened that he won't be able to fight them. Well, Kori, you already had me twice last night. And you see how I slept through the dawn. So perhaps the rest of the saying is also true."

Kori looked around at the open expanse of rock. "You have no enemies here," she said. She looked at his ankle. "And so long as you're injured, you won't be able to fight anyone anyway. It seems to me there is nothing for you to worry about."

He threw his head back and laughed.

She moved up and lay upon him, shamelessly pressing her breasts against his chest out here in the bright morning sun, alone in the wilderness.

Later they ate cold rabbit and the last scraps of lizard meat

Uroh ate as if he was starving, and Kori smiled to herself, proud that she'd been able to rouse him again. He was still glancing at her body now, even though she had covered herself with her robe.

"You really do think I'm desirable," she said.

He gave a short laugh. "That's clear enough."

She thought again of Yainar, who was obsessed with his ambitions, and Oam, always worrying about his status in the tribe, and all the young hunters trying to prove their strength and skill. It felt so good, now, to be able to laugh at them instead of feeling crushed by their indifference.

She turned back to him. "But what about the women in your tribe, Uroh? Did they desire you?"

"Some of them." He finished the last scraps of meat and wiped the grease from his fingers.

Kori felt a little stab of concern. "You don't mean—you are paired?" She realized with dismay that she hadn't even asked him this the previous night.

He grunted, looking uncomfortable. "No, I'm not paired."

Well, that was a relief—assuming he was telling the truth. She sensed he was still hiding something, though. "So how do you know the girls desired you?" she persisted. "What happened, Uroh? Am I not—" She couldn't finish the question.

He shot her a quick look and she saw she had hurt his feelings. "Kori, I have my pride," he said. "Surely you understand?" He paused, staring at her, and he saw that she didn't know what he meant. He sighed. "There have been no others but you," he said gruffly.

And now, suddenly, she did understand. His people looked down on him because he was too quick to dream, too slow to fight. He had been rejected not just by the other hunters, but by the women of his tribe.

She moved close and kissed him gently on the cheek. "I'm sorry, Uroh," she said.

"Don't pity me!" His voice was unexpectedly loud.

"Of course not!" She shook her head. "I admire you, Uroh. I desire you. I—I adore you."

The words came out before she could hold them back. She was amazed by her ability to say them.

He lowered his head and gave her a brooding look. "If we were from the same tribe," he said, "would you pair with me?"

She blinked. "Well—of course," she said. "Otherwise, why would I have given myself to you?"

Slowly, he relaxed. She realized his shoulders had been tense and his fists had been clenched tight. She watched as the muscles lost their tension on by one. And then, finally, he grinned. All the worry was erased from his face. Once again he looked carefree. "Good, Kori," he said. "I'm glad. We should invent a ceremony for ourselves. What do you think of that?"

The idea delighted and frightened her, both at once. She wasn't ready, yet, to imagine such a thing.

She looked down, and she saw the bucket sitting on the rock close by. "Is it all right now," she said with a shy smile, "if I fetch us some water?"

Later, after she washed herself in the cold stream, she took water back and washed Uroh. Then they lay together till noon, enjoying the autumn sun, and Kori found herself talking to him about the kinds of things she always used to think about, lying awake at night while Oam slumbered nearby. These were questions that she had long since learned not to mention to other people, who became irritated or impatient with her. Questions such as why do some trees shed their leaves in the winter, while others don't? Why do birds choose to sing? Why should the sky be blue in the daytime but black at night?

Amazingly, she found that Uroh had asked himself some

of these same questions—and many more. It was magical to spend time with him like this, just thinking and talking about the world.

In the afternoon Kori went to gather more game from the traps. She came back with two more rabbits and a woodchuck, and she also brought more wood for the fire. He greeted her just as happily as he had the previous day, and this time he had a gift for her. Shyly, he showed her a white shell that he had carved painstakingly with his flint knife, fashioning it in the shape of a bear. He had drilled a hole in it and strung it on a leather string.

"A white bear," Kori said, turning the object over in her hands. In her tribe people decorated their clothes, but she had never known anyone with the skill to make an object that was a model of something. She didn't even have words to describe the idea.

"I made it just for you, Kori." He looped the thong around her neck so that the bear hung between her breasts. "This way, a piece of me will always be with you."

She felt deeply moved. Then she looked up sharply. "Are you thinking of going away from me?"

He looked shocked, then embarrassed. "I am happier with you than I have ever been," he said.

She felt somewhat reassured. Still, when she let herself think about it, their days here were like stolen time. Sooner or later the seasons alone would force them to make choices that she was frightened to think about.

Not yet, she told herself. She needed one more night. Tomorrow she would ask the difficult questions.

When the next morning dawned, the weather was cooler with high, thin clouds creeping across the sky behind Mount Tomomor. It had been a cold night, and for the first time Kori felt the bite of autumn in the air. Time had seemed to cease while she was with Uroh, yet that was a dangerous illusion. In a few more months winter would claim the land. Many animals would disappear underground, hiding till spring. The land would be thick with snow. Normally, in her tribe, she would be working busily, laying in stores of smoked meat, firewood, and dried berries.

"Uroh," she said, as she wiped the remains of their breakfast from the rock beside the campfire and tossed the animal bones onto the rocks below. "Uroh—when do you have to return to your tribe?"

He was sharpening his spear, nibbling flakes of flint with his fine, even teeth. He turned to look at Kori and slowly rested the shaft across his knees. For a long moment, he said nothing. His face became blank.

Kori shifted uneasily. She didn't like it when his happiness disappeared like this. "I don't have to go back to my people—ever," she went on, forcing herself to say the words, although the idea still frightened her. When she thought of her mother, her father, or her brother, she missed them despite herself. They were her kin; how could she just abandon them?

Because they had abandoned her, she reminded herself. She tried to harden her feelings, remembering the cruelty of her tribe. Why would she ever want to be with them, if she could be with Uroh?

He turned and looked away over the rocky mountainside. "I've been wondering," he said slowly, "if it's foolish to think we could have a tribe of our own, Kori."

At first the idea amazed her, but then, as she thought about it, it seemed childlike. She found herself smiling. "So you would be the chieftain, and I would be your mate, and our children would be the people of the tribe?"

He laughed. "Maybe *you* would be the chieftain."

She smiled—but her smile quickly faded, for this was no time to sit and dream. "The winter is hard, Uroh. It's too hard for us to survive in the wilderness alone, with no stores and only two spears."

He looked crushed by her words. He said nothing.

"You really are a dreamer," she said. "And I'm glad of that, because your dreams make me think of things I've never thought of before. But we must be practical. Sometime before the first snow, we will need to be part of a tribe."

"I suppose this is true," he said very quietly.

Kori waited, but he didn't go on. "Maybe," she said, "my own people—"

"No!" He glared at her and made a slashing movement with his hand. It was the first time she'd heard him speak so sharply, and it startled her. "I couldn't pledge myself to people who treated you so cruelly." He shook his head. "No," he said again.

In a way, Kori felt relieved. She couldn't imagine how her people would ever accept a man whom they thought of as a whitebeast from the Western Shore. She waited for him to go on, but he lapsed into silence. The wind blew and she shivered, pulling her robe around herself. There was something inside him, an indecisiveness, a conflict that she didn't understand.

"Well," she said finally, when it seemed as if he would never speak, "you did say, on our first night—"

"I said I would take you to my tribe." Still, he wouldn't look her in the eye. "I would like that, perhaps. For the winter, at least."

Kori felt a new uncertainty growing inside her, eating away at the trust she had begun to feel for Uroh. "Perhaps?" she said. She moved over to him and placed her hands on his shoulders. She gave him a little shake. "Uroh, look at me!"

Reluctantly, he obeyed.

"Do you remember what you said?" she asked him. "About being paired with me?"

He blinked. She felt him stiffen. "Of course I remember!" he sounded offended. "Kori, I want to be with you. There's no question of that." He shifted uncomfortably. "I'm just not sure how my people—" He hesitated. "Perhaps I should go to them a few days from now and explain what's happened between us."

She frowned at him. "You really do care for me," she said.

"Of course!" Once again he was offended that she should doubt him.

"But didn't you look ahead, Uroh, when you spoke about taking me to your tribe? Didn't you try to imagine if there would be any problems?"

He looked down. He moved his shoulders uncomfortably. "Sometimes I don't think as carefully as I should."

She felt a spasm of anger, but then, just as quickly, she forgave him. If he was more practical and less of a dreamer, she wouldn't feel so comfortable with him, so happy with him, and so interested in him. She had to accept him as he was and make allowances for it. If this meant that she had to be the one to make plans and think ahead, she was willing to shoulder that burden.

"So tell me," she said, "what we can do."

He eyed her for a moment, and from the look on his face, she saw he was thinking about coupling with her again.

"Uroh, this is serious," she told him, hardening her voice. She tucked her robe around her body, concealing her nakedness from him.

He sighed, looking defeated. "When my ankle is healed," he said, "I should go to my people. Then, after that, I can come back for you."

"You mean you want me to wait here alone?" She was shocked to discover how much the idea scared her.

"Maybe not." She saw him struggling to make a decision. "Perhaps you should come with me."

"But why is it 'perhaps' again? Your people have watched

my people on the island, so it won't shock them to meet me. And since you say there are so many tribes, surely there must have been other times when a woman and a man from two different tribes have mated together."

He nodded quickly. "That happens often. In the spring—"

"Perhaps we could pretend we've never coupled together," Kori went on. "We could have a formal pairing ceremony—if your tribe has ceremonies like that."

"That's a fine idea." He forced a smile. "You're right, Kori. But can we talk about this a little later? First I must find out if my ankle is strong."

She wanted to object. She wanted to tell him she had a right to know what he was thinking, and she needed to know why he was so nervous about taking her to his people. But she sensed that if she tried to force him to speak, he would become more and more evasive, and he would retreat from her.

Perhaps that was how he had become such a dreamer in the first place, because his kinfolk and the other boy-children had tried to force him to do things or become something that was impossible for him. He had hidden from them inside his mind, just to hold on to his sense of self. Kori could understand that well enough, because she had done the same thing.

She decided she was willing to let the subject drop—for a while. But she looked at Uroh with a new feeling of caution. He was warm and gentle and a fine companion. He had skills that he could teach her, and she liked to imagine mothering children by him. She thought she could trust his sincerity when he made a promise. But he might make the promise so blindly, he couldn't be trusted to look ahead into the future.

He turned away from her and started unwrapping the strip of hide around his ankle. He cupped his hands around his leg and slid them slowly down, testing gently. "It's much better," he said. He flexed his ankle. "I think it's strong enough for me to walk a little, Kori."

"Be careful," she warned him as he rose to his feet. "It's only been three days."

"No, it's much better." He put his weight on it, then turned to her and grinned. "It's been hard for my pride, lying around here while a woman brings back food. Let's walk together, Kori." All his pensiveness had disappeared as quickly as it had come. He seemed carefree again.

19

Now that she was with Uroh, she saw the land as she had never seen it before. He pointed out that the hillside was made from separate layers of lava, from the many different eruptions. Each new flow had erased all life—but within a year, life returned. He showed her where grasses had taken root in little cracks and crevices in the rock. The roots of plants seemed soft and pliant, but they could split the rock, given time. Small trees would split the rock again, and eventually it would turn to gravel, then sand. The land where the forest grew had been lava-rock, long ago.

"And so a soft, living plant is more powerful than the hardest stone," he told her. "Something that bends and yields may be stronger than something that cannot change its form."

She thought about what he had said. Did that mean she might be stronger than the people of her tribe, with their strict faith and their unchanging rituals? She didn't *feel* stronger. Yet here she was now, surviving in this wilderness because she had been able to change herself.

"How do you know all these things about the land?" she asked Uroh as they moved farther down the slope and approached the edge of the forest.

"My people watch and learn," he said. "And see, here." He pointed to a ridge just before the edge of the forest. "Those fingers of rock, there, are like the dribbles you see where water spills down. That was as far as the lava flowed in the last great eruption, ten years ago." He walked ahead and stepped down carefully from the rock to the forest floor. "Feel," he said, digging his fingers into the loose soil. "It's still the same rock, broken into pieces."

Kori saw that he was right. "Then we're not safe here," she said, glancing back at the ominous bulk of the mountain. "If lava flowed this far before, it could flow again."

"That's so," said Uroh. "But the mountain gives us warning, and the lava flows slowly. We'll always have time to move farther down the slope and be safe."

He led her a little deeper into the forest. He pointed to plants whose roots were good to eat and other plants that were poisonous. He showed her where woodpeckers had drilled holes in trees and had hidden hazelnuts in them, which a hungry person could dig out if there was nothing better to eat.

But the most important thing Uroh had to teach her wasn't a list of rules telling her what to do and what not to do. More than anything he showed her how the forest could be her friend, rather than her enemy. A thorny thicket might conceal a predator—but it could conceal her, too. The fear she had felt when she was here before gradually yielded to a new feeling of harmony and understanding, although at the same time she saw that it would take her months or years to acquire a hunter's true, deep instincts for survival.

At noon Uroh found a place where a narrow trail snaked through the woods. He got down on his hands and knees and sniffed the earth. "Deer," he said, pointing to some droppings close by. "And wolves." He moved a little farther along and kicked a much larger dropping that crumbled into dust. "A black bear was here, but many weeks ago." He went farther along the trail, bent down, took a long thong from the pack he carried, and strung it loosely between two trees so that it crossed the trail close to the ground. He found a length of dry wood, leaned it against the thong, then balanced a rock on it. Finally he threw some dry leaves across the thong to conceal it.

"I don't see how that's going to trap anything," said Kori.

"It's not meant to. Come, this way." He moved back along the trail for fifty paces and tied a similar thong there. "If any large creatures come here," he told her, "a stone will fall, and we'll be warned." He nodded to the brambles. "Even a bear prefers not to force his way through thorns when there's a path he can follow. So, we can eat without fear now."

They spent a while gathering berries from the brambles, then sat together on a rock beside the trail. They ate some rabbit meat that they'd brought with them, together with the fruit that they'd just gathered. As they sat quietly, the forest gradually came to life around them. Birds and squirrels that had hidden themselves before now moved through the branches high above. The squirrels chattered; the birds sang. Kori heard finches and doves, rooks and sparrows. She watched a flock of swallows suddenly take flight, wheeling through the trees, bursting out briefly through the forest canopy, then coming back to rest on high branches as if they were practicing for the journey they would soon make to the south.

In the brambles opposite her, down near the ground where there was a tiny space below the thorns, she heard a scuffling noise and saw a small, dark eye. It was a muskrat, she realized, sniffing the air, trying to decide if it was safe to forage. All the animals were bolder at this time of year, knowing there was only a short time left to fatten themselves before the onset of winter. The thought made Kori pause, and it dampened some of her pleasure at being with Uroh. She couldn't stop herself from wondering what was going to happen to her.

Uroh reached out and touched her arm. She turned and opened her mouth to speak. He touched his finger to his lips, then bent his head slightly and pointed to his ear. He sat there in silence, listening.

What had he heard? Kori forgot about her concerns. She strained her ears, but she heard nothing, just the same bird songs as before.

Uroh grabbed his spear. He nodded along the trail, then pointed toward the high branches in that direction. Kori looked and saw nothing, then realized that the birds up there were scattering, flitting from tree to tree. Finally, she heard what Uroh had heard: the faint sound of a large animal moving cautiously toward them.

"Should we go?" she asked him, whispering softly, directly into his ear.

He shook his head. Perhaps, Kori thought, he wanted to impress her with his hunting skills. That made her nervous, because she had heard too many stories of men who were injured or killed while trying to prove their bravery. Then another, even more disturbing thought came to her. He might want to spear a large animal so that if he didn't take her with him back to his tribe, she would have enough to eat while he was gone.

Uroh slid off the rock where he'd been sitting and placed his feet carefully, silently on the ground. He bent his knees slightly and raised his spear till it was just higher than his shoulder. He moved his other shoulder forward, then stood motionless, staring wide-eyed along the trail.

Even though she felt apprehensive, Kori couldn't help noticing the power in his slim body, the way his shoulder muscles and biceps were bunched, and the way his back was curved, poised to put every shred of his strength into the throw. His face was calm, but she saw him straining his senses, alert for the smallest sound or movement. Really, she thought, he was beautiful. And despite all her anxieties, so far as she could tell, he was hers.

Something heavy fell. The noise wasn't loud, but to Kori it sounded like a crash of thunder.

She jumped, then realized it was the trap that Uroh had placed. At the same instant she saw him casting his spear, throwing himself forward with it. The shaft flew through the forest, straight and true. It disappeared among the trees— and there was a cry of pain.

Uroh froze. His face changed. He turned and stared at Kori in horror. The cry sounded like no beast she had ever heard. It sounded human.

Uroh turned and seized Kori's spear, which she'd been holding across her knees. He ran forward.

Kori hesitated, then went after him. Sunlight and shadow patterned his white bearskin as he raced through the forest. *Whitebeast*, she thought. He really did look like a frightening animal leaping among the trees.

He stopped so suddenly she almost collided with him. She seized hold of his shoulders from behind and pressed close to him, peering around him, afraid of what she might see.

She heard Uroh draw in his breath, and she felt him stiffen. At first she saw nothing; then she made out the figure of a man lying on his back among the dead leaves on the ground, futilely grappling with the spear that was embedded in his chest. He raised his head, saw Uroh staring at him, and let out a shout of fear.

Cautiously, Uroh moved forward. The man on the ground instinctively tried to wriggle away, but blood was flowing freely around the spear and he was in too much pain to move far. He reached clumsily for his own spear, lying close by.

Uroh took three quick strides and stamped on the spear, holding it down. He turned to Kori. His face was anguished. "Who is he?" Uroh cried. "What's he doing here?"

Kori moved forward. The face of the wounded man was briefly lit by a patch of sun—and she saw who he was.

For a moment she thought she would faint. The world seemed to tilt, and she reached out to Uroh to steady herself. Then she stumbled forward and fell down on her knees. She placed her hands on the wounded man, to prove to herself that he was real. She felt his chest heave as he stared up at her, groaning with pain. She felt the warmth of his blood.

"Oam!" she cried. She reached out and touched his forehead, his cheek.

"You know him," Uroh said.

She turned and stared at him. "He's my brother!"

There was a long, frozen moment. Uroh took a step back. He rubbed his arm quickly across his forehead. "I thought he was a wild beast. You know I did! It was an accident!"

"I know. I know." She was staring back at Oam. Uroh's spear had flown so fast, it had passed between Oam's ribs and all the way through his chest. There was so much blood, she couldn't imagine how to stop it. Oam was panting, making throttling sounds, and his lips were already rimmed with red foam. If she pulled the spear free, it would only get worse.

She felt herself crying. She reached out with a shaking hand and stroked Oam's hair. She knew with absolute certainty that he was going to die.

"What's he doing here!" Uroh shouted. "Your people never come to the Western Shore. They never come into the forest. Never!"

"Hush," Kori said to him. "It's not your fault, Uroh. I'm not blaming you." She turned back to Oam and stared into his eyes. "Were you looking for me? Is that why you're here?"

He nodded weakly.

Kori was overwhelmed with anguish. Why did this terrible thing have to happen? Was this how the Old Ones were choosing to punish her?

"People—people protested," Oam said, choking out the words. "Said it was wrong, you were cast out."

"They did?" She felt dizzy. It was hard for her to believe. And yet, Oam was here. He could only have come here if the tribe approved it.

"Father—wanted you back. Mother refused. There was a meeting. Many people said, punishment was too severe." He gasped, turned his head, and vomited up blood.

"Oam!" Kori cried. "Oam, I'm sorry!" She fell down on him and clung to him. "I didn't know—" She broke off, crying helplessly.

He reached up and she felt his hand on her shoulder. "Mother spoke to the spirits. Told me to come for you, it would be safe. Been here two days. Looking."

Kori imagined her mother lying on the high rock listening to the voices—or pretending to listen. What difference did it make? It had been another lie. Oam had not been safe. He had not been protected. He had come here to his death.

"Thought you'd stay by the river," Oam gasped.

Yes, of course he would have thought that. No one in the tribe would have expected Kori to go boldly into the forest.

Oam was squinting past her, up at Uroh. "Who is he?"

"It doesn't matter." She pressed her cheek against his. "Thank you, Oam. Thank you for coming for me."

"Help me, Kori."

She pulled back and looked into his eyes. She saw the fear. Then she looked again at his terrible wound. There was a huge circle of thick, rich blood on the ground around him. "I can't help you, Oam," she said, barely managing to speak the words. She felt her chin quivering, her stomach churning. It was terrible to know that she could do nothing.

"Then take me back," Oam gasped. "Don't leave me here."

He looked terrified now—not just of dying, but of being left here on this sacred ground.

"Promise me!" He stared up at her with wide eyes.

She nodded. "I'll take you back to the island." That was the least she could do for him. "Of course I promise, Oam."

He looked relieved. Then he grimaced with pain. He gripped her hand eagerly, clumsily. "Thank you, Kori. I'm sorry. Sorry for all—"

He closed his eyes. His face was white. His forehead was covered in sweat. He was trembling. His teeth chattered. His head tilted back and his face contorted. His grip on her hand tightened till it was painful and then it relaxed.

She stared at him as he slumped on the ground, limp. All the life had left his body.

20

For a long while Kori squatted with her eyes tightly closed, hugging her arms around her knees and trying not to think or feel. She couldn't cope with the emotions that roared inside her: the confusion, the grief, and the anger at what had happened.

She felt as if she had been cruelly tricked. For a few short days she seemed to have found peace of mind; but of course it had been just an illusion. She felt as if she had been running through a meadow, relishing the sun on her body and the earth under her feet—and now suddenly the meadow was gone, the sunlight was gone, and she was falling into a deep, dark pit that had always been there, if only she had been sensible enough to notice it.

"Kori."

She heard Uroh's voice and felt him touch her shoulder, but his voice seemed far away and the pressure of his hand was barely perceptible in the storm of her grief.

"Kori!" He shook her, gently at first, then harder.

She resisted for as long as she could, but finally she

opened her eyes. The world was blurred. She wiped tears from her eyes and found him squatting in front of her, staring at her anxiously.

"We can't stay here," he said. "It's not safe here." He gave her another little shake. "Do you understand? Animals will smell the blood." He nodded to Oam's body.

It took her a moment to understand what he was saying. At first she felt annoyed with him for showing so little sympathy or remorse, but then she realized he was right. If Oam was left lying here, he would be devoured by predators.

"We have to take him to the river," she said. She forced herself to stand up. Her limbs were stiff and aching. She was cold. She shivered and clutched herself.

"The river?" Uroh stared at her uncomprehendingly.

"Yes!" She glared at him. "Weren't you listening? Didn't you hear what he said?"

He stepped back, wounded by her tone of voice. "He spoke with the accent of your tribe. I couldn't understand him."

She paused for a moment, trying to get her emotions under control. "I'm sorry," she said. She took a slow breath. "Oam—my brother—is terrified of this place. He was very brave to look for me in the forest. He thinks the slope of the mountain is possessed by the Old Ones. He begged me not to leave him here."

"But the river is at least a day's walk away," said Uroh. "And it's well past noon. And there are only two of us, Kori. How can we possibly carry him there?"

"I made a promise!" she cried. "He came for me, don't you understand? He risked his life for me." She started crying again. She had never imagined that Oam would do such a thing. Of course, his mother had told him to do it and had promised him that the spirits would protect him. Even so, she felt overwhelmed by his act.

Uroh stared at her helplessly. "You made a promise," he

said, "which cannot be kept. What you want to do cannot be done."

"It can be done!" She glared at him. "We'll tie him to a pole and carry him on our shoulders. We can do it!"

Uroh sighed and shook his head. "Kori, Kori—my ankle has not yet fully healed, and he weighs more than either of us. We'll have to rest often, so it will take at least four days to make the journey. And where will we spend the nights? How will we protect ourselves? How will we protect him?"

She sniffed back her tears. "We can find a way. I promised to take him back."

"After four days, his flesh will be decaying."

She turned and glared at Uroh, then felt her spirit draining away. He was right, she realized. She had promised the impossible.

"We can place him up on the rocky slope," Uroh said gently. "We can cover him with stones to stop the birds from feasting on him. If the people of your tribe want to come for him and take him back to the island, his bones will still be there."

Kori laughed sourly. "Most people in my tribe would be too scared to come here."

Uroh spread his arms. "Well, this is the best we can do."

She cursed herself for the words she had said to Oam. Still, there was no point in agonizing over it now. The sun had long since passed the zenith. If they were going to do anything at all, there was no time to waste.

"I'm sorry," said Uroh, "that this terrible thing happened." He moved closer to Kori and put his arm around her shoulders. "You know it was an accident."

"Of course it was an accident." She managed a weak smile for him. "I don't blame you, Uroh. I blame my people—my foolish, superstitious people. They were the ones who cast me out. And they were the ones who sent him to look for me and cost him his life."

*   *   *

Uroh pulled his spear from Oam's chest. He cleaned it, then added Kori's spear to it and slung them both between his shoulder blades, under his backpack. He stooped and lifted Oam under his arms, and Kori lifted him under his knees. Together, then, they carried his body out of the forest.

Kori quickly realized that Uroh had been right: taking her brother all the way back to the river would have been an enormous task entailing terrible risks. Just moving him up onto the rocky slope took most of her strength, and she saw Uroh limping, wincing whenever he put too much weight on his wounded ankle.

They placed Oam between two large boulders. Kori stood and looked at him for a long moment, knowing that this would be the last time she would ever see his face. Despite the terrible wound in his chest and the blood on his shoulders and around his mouth, she had the eerie sense that he was still really alive. It seemed as if she shouted loudly enough, or shook him by the shoulder, he would open his eyes. Why was the life force so fragile, and where did it go? There *must* be some human spirit that left the body at the moment of death. Had it already slipped down into the earth, as her people believed?

Kori realized she had never felt so confused and lost. All her old beliefs had been shaken, and no new ones had taken their place.

"We should cover him," Uroh said quietly, "before the sun sets."

Kori nodded. She squatted down, placed her brother's spear beside his body, then started resting large stones around him. A shadow passed across her and she looked up quickly, feeling suddenly fearful, but it was only a buzzard passing across the face of the sun. She squinted at the wheeling black shape and took satisfaction in knowing that she was preventing the bird from feasting on her brother's flesh.

Building a cairn took longer than she expected. The sun had almost slipped behind Mount Tomomor when Kori was finally satisfied with her work. She stood for a moment beside Uroh, staring at the heap of stones.

"My people would tell us that his spirit is another star in the sky, now," Uroh said.

"And my people would say that he has joined the Old Ones in the rock beneath our feet." She looked at Uroh, and he looked back at her.

He spread his hands. "Neither of us knows what is true."

She looked at him in irritation. "Doesn't it bother you to feel that way?" she asked him. She understood a little better why her people maintained such a rigid faith. Any belief was better than none at all.

"It troubles me," Uroh agreed. "But it's better to be unsure than to believe a lie. And I think if I spend enough of my life looking at the world and learning things, perhaps I really will find out what's true." He shouldered his spear. "We should make ourselves safe for the night."

Kori followed him across the rills and furrows of sharp, dark rock. "So you think you can learn truths that even the wisest elders of your village have never known," she said. His arrogance amazed her.

Uroh turned and smiled sadly. "Perhaps I can't," he said. "But I have to try."

There was no food for them that night. They had eaten all their stock of game, and there had been no time to go back to the forest and empty the snares. Still, Kori didn't feel like eating anyway. She didn't feel like talking, either, and Uroh seemed to understand that. She lay close beside him, enjoying the warmth of the fire on her back and the warmth of his body against hers. She closed her eyes and let her mind wander back through her past, through all her memories—all the times when she had been with her brother, watching him grow up, talking to him, arguing with him, trying to cope with his temper tantrums and his need to prove that he was stronger and smarter than she was.

She realized, now, that in his own strange way, he had cared about her. But he had been too insecure, too intimidated by her to show his real feelings. What a waste that was! She blamed herself for not having seen what lay inside him. How many others of her kinfolk would have shown her more warmth if only she had let them?

Gradually she felt herself drifting, watching scenes from her childhood inside her head. Then she saw Oam all grown up, just the way she had seen him a little earlier when she had placed him out on the rocks and started covering him with stones. His wounds had gone, though. He was whole and strong and healthy again, wearing nothing but a loincloth, so she could see his plump, rounded body. He was grinning happily at her, like a baby.

She felt sudden joy. How seldom she had seen him smile, over the years! But then, just as quickly, she felt melancholy regret. "I'm sorry, Oam," she said. "I'm so sorry for everything."

He was still smiling. Her words didn't affect him. "My death was not for nothing," he told her. "Look what I've found. Let me show you."

He reached up with both arms as if he was about to dive off a high rock into a river. But he was nowhere near the river. He was standing out on the rocky slope, near the cairn where they had placed his body. Kori stared in confusion.

"Watch." He started sinking into the rock in front of her eyes. "Come with me, Kori!"

"No!" she cried.

"Trust me. It's safe. Come!" He had sunk to his waist.

She took a step closer. "Oam, I can't follow you." It hurt her to say the words, but he was asking too much of her. She would do many things for him, but she couldn't die for him.

"You'll be safe!" he called to her again. The rock was up around his shoulders. In a moment he would disappear.

"Don't go!" she cried. She took another step forward— and the rock turned to vapor under her feet. It absorbed her as easily as if she had stepped off a cliff. She cried out in dismay. But there was nothing she could do to stop herself. She sank down—and the bright sunlit world disappeared. She was immersed in darkness. She flailed in panic. Her hand touched something. Oam's hand! She gripped it fearfully. "I can't see you," she called to him.

But then they emerged somewhere, a vast underground cavern. There was still no light, but somehow she could see him anyway. "Look!" he called to her. He turned and swung his arm around at the great empty space.

Kori turned quickly. "But there's nothing here," she said.

"Yes." He let go of her hand and started moving away from her. "You must share this knowledge, Kori. Tell our parents. Tell our people. There is nothing to fear."

She stared at him in confusion. "Come back, Oam."

He wasn't listening to her anymore. His figure was receding. "There is so much to explore, Kori. And I have no fear, here. I can be free."

"Oam, come back!"

He didn't answer. He was a tiny, distant shape, then he was gone.

She felt herself being shaken. Someone's hands were on her shoulders. Cool air touched her cheeks. Her bearskin lay beneath her.

She opened her eyes and found Uroh's face close to hers. "Wake up, Kori," he was saying. "Kori!"

"Yes." She nodded quickly. "Yes. I'm awake." She blinked, focusing on the hard, bright world around her. She drank in the colors, desperately wanting them to drive away the dark residue of the dream.

"Were you calling to your brother?" Uroh asked her. "Were you dreaming of him?"

"Yes." She rubbed her face with her hands. She sat up and seized Uroh's arm, gripping it tightly, reassuring herself with its warmth and strength. "It was a frightening dream, Uroh. Where do dreams come from? Do your people know?"

He laughed softly. "From the spirits—so people say."

Kori nodded. "Yes. From the spirits." She took a deep, slow breath. "I believe there are spirits. I believe Oam's spirit spoke to me, in my dream." She looked around and found herself facing the bulk of Mount Tomomor. "But there are no Old Ones." She spoke clearly, loudly, bravely.

Despite herself, she felt frightened. It was the first time she had dared to speak the words. Even now, she feared retribution. But no: Oam had shown her. The earth below was empty.

Uroh laughed softly. "If dreams are put into our minds by spirits, maybe the Old Ones were deceiving you, Kori, showing you something that is false."

She shook her head, feeling impatient. "This isn't a game, Uroh." The last of her indecision and confusion were gone, now. She saw the world with a clarity that amazed her. "I have to go back," she said.

"You have to go where?" He was watching her curiously. "Back to your brother's cairn?"

"No." Her impatience intensified. Why couldn't he understand? "No, Uroh, to my people. Otherwise, Oam will have died for nothing."

Slowly he understood what she was saying. His expression changed; he looked shocked. "You mean you will leave me here? You don't want to be with me?"

She paused and eyed him carefully. He had seemed quite willing to think about leaving *her* here, while he went to talk to his tribe, for reasons he had still not explained. But she didn't want to think about that now. There was a new burning purpose inside her. "I have to tell my people," she said, "that Oam has died. This they must know. But more than that, I have to tell them what I've learned from his spirit. I couldn't honor my promise to take him back to the island—but I can still take the message he has given me. If I don't do that, he will have died for nothing, and I will feel the burden of guilt upon me for the rest of my life."

Uroh was staring at her, looking deeply shocked. "But what message is it, Kori? What could be so important?"

She shrugged. "I have broken every taboo. I have defied the spirits in every way. And I am unharmed. And my brother, who was told that he would be safe here, protected by the Old Ones—he is now dead. So there are no Old Ones." She said the words even louder than before. "Oam showed me this. He placed on me the obligation to show it to my people."

He pulled his arm away from her. He gathered his robe around him. "I don't understand," he said. "You owe your people nothing."

"No, Uroh! My debt is to my brother! He lost his life for me here, surely you can see this. And I promised to take him back, and I failed." She felt tears stinging her eyes. She clutched at her robe, fretting at it with her fingers. "So I must take his message. I must. My people live in fear, Uroh. They are constantly afraid, and for no reason. This is wrong. You must see it's wrong."

Uroh looked thoughtful. "But they may not want to hear this from you," he told her, speaking softly. "They may feel even more afraid if you try to take their beliefs away."

She could tell his words were well intentioned, but they maddened her. "People have died because of their superstitions. A man named Shashin died, because his house was made of stone, and it fell down upon him. A woman named

Mima died, because we made a foolish journey. My own brother died. I was cast out, and I could have died. This is wrong!"

He was silent for a long moment. The wind whispered around them. The only other sound was the gentle rushing of the stream in the ravine a dozen paces away. It was another cool morning out here on the rocky slope, and the sky was filled with high, pale clouds. Kori shivered.

"And what will you do," Uroh asked, "after you give your people your message?" He was no longer arguing with her intentions. He could see the force of her will, and there was a new look of caution in his eyes. She realized he must feel threatened by her; he was no longer the center of her attention, the center of her life.

Well, of course, she did still need him, and he should realize that. "After I tell them what I have learned," she said, "then I will be free."

He looked at her skeptically. "Won't you want to stay with your people?"

She thought for a moment, but a moment was all it took. "No," she said. "I see now that they cared for me, more than I ever realized. But I don't think I will ever feel truly a part of their world and their lives. I just have to do my duty for Oam, that's all."

"All right," he said. He stood up and tucked his robe tighter around himself against the wind. He looked away from her, scanning the landscape to the east. "You should have company through the forest. I'll come with you."

"To my people?" The idea filled her with apprehension.

He shook his head. "Not to your people."

"Then what will you do?" She squinted up at his face and shaded her eyes against the bright sky.

"I'll go with you as far as the river," he said, looking down at her. "And I'll wait in the forest—to see if you return."

He didn't trust her, she realized. She quickly scrambled

up and hugged him, pressing her body close to his. "Of course I'll return!" she said, clinging to him.

"I believe you intend to," he said. "But as I told you, Kori, I believe there is such a thing as fate. At first I thought, when I found you, we were fated to be together. But now—now I am not so sure if fate will allow it. And this is something neither of us can know."

PART 3:
REVELATIONS

PART 3
REVELATIONS

21

Together they crouched among tall reeds that grew between the forest and the river. The sun was almost setting behind them, and the sky above was a rich, dark blue. The river lay in shadow, stretching away from them to the distant Eastern Shore. The water was so flat and still, Kori could barely see the current.

"Are you still sure you want to do this?" Uroh asked softly.

The island lay directly opposite. As always, a fire was burning in the Meeting Place; she could see the distant point of light flickering. Faintly she smelled the rich human odors of her tribe and the aroma of cooking meat. Soon, she knew, people would be gathering for the evening meal. Mothers would feed their children. There would be storytelling.

"Yes, I want to go there," Kori said. Her feeling of obligation was as strong as ever. There was truth that must be told.

"How will you get to the island?" Uroh asked.

"There are men upstream, fishing from canoes. The fish grow bolder when the light gets dim. Fishing is always best in the evening. But soon, they'll return to the island, and I'll call to them."

"I see no one," said Uroh, scanning the river.

"They're around the next bend, but they'll be back soon enough."

He nodded. His face was solemn. He had been in a somber mood all day, while they made their way down the slope and through the forest.

"You know I'll only stay on the island for one day, two days at most," she told him. "I'll tell them about Oam's death, and there'll be a ceremony for him, and then I will tell my people what I learned from him, from his spirit. And then I'll say my final farewells, and I'll be back here with you again."

He looked away. "So you say."

She frowned at him. She knew he felt uneasy about her plan, but she wished he would show a little more trust in her.

"I'll show you where I'll be waiting for you," he said, moving back under the trees.

"I would like to see that." She edged back from the river, then stood up and brushed black sand and fragments of dried reeds from her leggings.

He started walking downstream, moving through the forest with swift confidence, as if he'd often been this way before. She followed him, finding it difficult to keep up.

After a while he stopped and glanced around. "You see that big rock on the riverbank?" He pointed. "And the mossy tree with the twisted trunk? We turn inland here."

Kori tried to memorize the landmarks before she followed him deeper into the gloom of the forest.

He walked just far enough for the trees to close in around them so that they were completely hidden from the river. Then he stopped again. "See the thicket, there?"

Kori peered into the semidarkness. She saw a dense mass

directly ahead: bushes and brambles laced with vines, nettles, and poison oak. It looked ugly and impenetrable.

"Come," said Uroh. He led her a little way to the right, then paused where a blackened tree had been felled by lightning. It rested at an angle. "Can you climb?"

"That?" She gestured to the tree. "Of course."

He tucked his spear under his pack, then stepped up onto the slanting trunk. Leaning forward, grasping it with both hands, he made his way up it.

She followed him and saw that it took her above the thicket. She looked down and saw a tiny clearing, a little circle completely enclosed by the tangled underbrush. A massive pine tree stood there, festooned with ivy.

Uroh swung across to the pine and lowered himself down it to the ground. Kori followed, and she found herself surrounded and protected by the surrounding mass of vegetation. It was a perfect refuge, hidden and protected from humans and animals alike.

She looked down and found herself standing on a soft carpet of ashes. "How did you ever find this place?" she said.

He shrugged. "By chance." He shed his pack, kneeled down in the dim light, and groped under a heap of leaves. "I think I left wood here. Yes."

She watched while he started a fire. It was a relief when the flames came to life, driving away the oppressive darkness. She saw him smile with satisfaction, and she realized it was the first time he had smiled all day.

"You'll wait for me here?" she asked him.

He nodded. "Yes."

Now it was her turn to feel insecure. "I'll come to you tomorrow or the next day," she said, "and you'll be here? And then we'll go together to your people?"

"Yes," he said again, less emphatically than before.

Kori sighed. "Uroh, be truthful with me." She squatted down opposite him with the flames between them, so they could see each other's faces in the yellow light. "Are you afraid that your people won't accept me?"

"No." He shook his head decisively. "No, they have to accept you."

"Then what's the matter?"

"This has been a special time," he said. "Alone together, with no one interfering in our lives. It won't always be so easy, Kori." He pulled his spear out from under his pack and ran his hand along the shaft. Then he turned it and thrust its point into the forest floor. "You know, I wish your brother had never found us."

Kori grunted with irritation. "Yes, if he had never found us, he would still be alive today. But your wishes will gain you nothing. Nor will your fears. We will face the world together, Uroh. And I don't believe it can be any more difficult than when I was first cast into this forest on my own."

He looked at her wearily. "You have a lot of courage."

"Yes, I have. Don't you?"

For a moment she saw his spirit return. "Of course I have courage!" He frowned. But then, slowly, the fierceness faded and his somber mood returned. He looked away, retreating back into his own thoughts.

Kori sighed. "I must go. I need to find the people in their fishing canoes before they return to the island."

"All right." He stood up.

She stood and hugged him. He pressed his mouth hard against hers—so hard, it almost hurt her. Yet again, she wondered what was wrong with him. He reminded her of the way some children behaved when they were learning to swim, thrashing around and fighting with the water instead of relaxing and letting it hold them. Yesterday he had been calm, moving easily through the world. Today, he acted as if the world was his adversary.

Well, she had tried to get him to share his feelings with her. There was nothing more she could do now.

He released her abruptly. "Don't mention me to your people," he said.

"Don't mention you?" The words caught her by surprise. "But why not? None of our hunters will come to this shore, Uroh. They're afraid."

He grunted. "Maybe you'll make them less afraid if you take away their superstitions. I don't want them to know about my people, Kori. It's safer that way. Promise me you'll say nothing."

Why hadn't he mentioned this before? She felt angry with him. There was no time to talk about this now. "But what about Oam?" she protested. "How can I explain his death?"

Uroh frowned. He gestured impatiently. "Tell them—tell them he was stalked by a mountain lion. He killed it, but it wounded him, and the wounds were so serious, he died. Tell them anything, Kori. But let your people go on thinking that my people are whitebeasts."

She thought about it. "All right," she said reluctantly.

"Good." He squatted down beside the fire again. Its flickering light showed his face, still grim and brooding.

"Good-bye," said Kori.

He threw wood into the flames. "Good-bye, Kori. I'll be here when you return."

A little later she was back by the river. She felt nervous now. Uroh had made her feel secure during the past few days, and he had erased her sense of isolation. But just as quickly, she felt he had taken away what he had given her. Now that she was alone again, some of her old fears returned. Could she really confront her people with what she had learned? What if they questioned her vision of Oam's spirit? What if they refused to listen?

For a moment her determination wavered. Maybe it would be better just to tell them that Oam had died and say nothing more. She could stay just long enough for the mourning ceremony, and then she could slip away, back to Uroh. . . .

No. If she did that, she would betray Oam, who had died in an effort to protect her.

The sky was dim purple now, almost black. She peered into the darkness and listened. At first she heard nothing, and she feared she was too late. Then, faintly, she heard the splash of a canoe paddle.

She felt thankful that it was a still, quiet night, allowing sounds to travel across the water. "Hello!" she shouted. She cupped her hands around her mouth. "Over here! It's Kori! Here on the Western Shore!"

She held her breath and listened. At first she heard nothing, then a distant, puzzled shout.

"Here!" She screamed the word so loudly, it hurt her throat. But loudness alone might not be sufficient. Sound echoed strangely along the riverbank. People in fishing canoes might never be able to locate her just by listening.

Kori felt annoyed with herself. She should have thought of this. In fact, if she hadn't been so worried about Uroh, she *would* have thought of it. Quickly she kneeled down. There were some dead, dry reeds among the rocks on the shore and some dry grass. She fumbled in her pouch, pulled out her firesticks, and put them together, working by touch alone in the darkness. Swiftly she started twirling the drill-stick between her palms. She paused and felt for its hot tip. She sprinkled tinder on it, then twirled it some more.

Another curious shout sounded from across the water. She ignored it. There was a faint red glow from the sticks in front of her, then a tiny flame.

She fed it swiftly. There had been no rain in several days—not since the storm that had assaulted her stone gathering party. The reeds were very dry and caught fire easily. Moments later, she had a fire burning. She stood behind it, catching its light, and now she shouted again.

She heard a paddle dipping, and gradually the sound came closer. She threw more fuel on the fire.

A voice called again, and this time she heard her name. Then, finally, she saw the canoe. She guessed it was the last of the fishing canoes returning to the island.

"Kori, is that you?"

She recognized the voice. It was Pistu, a kind old man who had broken his foot as a child and was never able to hunt with the other men. He spent half his life out on the river, casting nets. Almost always, he worked alone.

The canoe bumped up against the rocks on the riverbank. Kori saw his wrinkled face in the light from her fire. He was peering at her fearfully, as though she was an apparition.

"Pistu, it is truly me," she called to him. "There's nothing to fear."

He stood in the canoe for a long moment. Nets of knotted thongs were piled at his feet. Kori saw the firelight gleaming on fish scales, and she smelled the fresh catch.

"Oam was sent to find you," Pistu said finally.

"I know." She picked her way over the rocks, moving cautiously, afraid of stumbling in the faint light. She lowered herself slowly into the canoe and dumped her black bearskin beside the fish nets.

"Where is he?" Pistu's face was still lined with doubt and fear. This had been a courageous act for him, allowing his canoe so close to the land of the Old Ones.

"Oam—has died," Kori said. She was suddenly sickened by the idea of having to lie about her brother's death. Yet she had given her word to Uroh. She felt trapped, and it made her angry. She could see that Uroh would feel cautious because her people had hunted his people as if they were beasts. But that was because they hadn't known the truth. They'd thought Uroh's people *were* beasts.

Kori grabbed a spare paddle that she found in the bottom of the canoe. She pushed out from the shore.

"Oam is dead?" Pistu was staring at her in shock.

Grimly, Kori started paddling the canoe. "A lion killed him, Pistu." There; she had told the lie. Silently, she begged Oam's spirit to forgive her.

"So you saw him, then."

Pistu was old, but he wasn't stupid. Kori realized she would have to be careful in what she said. "I saw him," she agreed, "but I was too late to help him." She remembered suddenly how Oam had looked as his life left him. She could still feel his hand on her wrist, gripping tightly.

She suddenly wanted very much to be back on the island, in the warmth and light of the fire in the Meeting Place. "Let's go across the river as quickly as we can, Pistu," she said. "It's best if I tell my story to the whole village, because it is not a story I want to tell more than once."

22

As the canoe finally reached the island, Kori saw many people holding flaming torches and peering into the night. They had heard her shouts and seen the fire she'd started on the Western Shore. Like Pistu, they stared at her fearfully, not quite ready to believe she was of human flesh and blood.

Kori climbed up onto the stones around the dock where the canoes were moored. She found her father striding toward her from among the crowd with his arms outstretched. A moment later he was hugging her.

A tormented mixture of emotions overwhelmed her as she was engulfed in her father's embrace. He was happy to see her, he was welcoming her, and now other people were clustering around, shouting greetings. The smell of her father and his clothes was like the smell of home, and the faces of the people were faces she had known all her life—yet everything seemed wrong and strange, because the smell wasn't Uroh's smell, and the meaning of home, for her, had changed.

As her father released her she turned and smiled shyly at her friends and kinfolk. Then she saw her mother.

Immar's eyes were gleaming in the torchlight, and they were watching Kori intently. As always, Kori had the strange sensation that those eyes could look behind her face, into her spirit and her mind.

Immar slowly frowned. She glanced from Kori to Pistu. "Where is Oam?" she called out in a clear voice that cut through all the shouts of welcome.

The noise of the crowd slowly died down. Kori stood, wondering how she could possibly say what needed to be said. She had fought and killed a great lizard. She had been face to face with a giant cat—yet still she felt nervous of her mother.

Still, she remembered the vow she had made when she first found herself alone on the Western Shore. She would not allow Immar to intimidate her. "You sent Oam to look for me," Kori said, "and I believe you told him he would be safe." She took a deep breath of the cold night air. "But you were wrong."

The silence, now, was absolute. The faces that had been smiling in welcome now looked distraught. From the corner of her eye Kori saw her father take a step backward.

Immar looked at Kori in confusion. "Where is my son?" she said.

"He was badly wounded." Kori felt herself weaken as she remembered, again, the sight of Oam dying. "I couldn't save him. There was nothing I could do."

For a moment Immar closed her eyes. Her nostrils flared as she breathed deeply. She was trembling with emotion, but even so, she maintained her self-control. She turned suddenly to the people around her. "Go to the Meeting Place," she told them. "Go there!"

The people stirred uneasily.

"Please go!" Immar repeated. She turned to Rohonar. "You should wait there with them."

Rohonar looked confused. He was still looking at Kori, shaking his head in disbelief. "Oam is dead?" he whispered.

Immar strode across, pushing through the crowd. She took Rohonar's arm. "Go with our people," she said more gently but just as insistently. "They need you. Take them to the Meeting Place. I will join you soon enough."

Rohonar nodded slowly. He turned away, so shocked he couldn't speak. He started walking toward the Meeting Place, and the crowd followed him.

"Kori, come with me," said Immar, grabbing her arm. "You're filthy. You must be cleaned. You'll tell me what happened. Then we will tell the tribe."

Kori found herself being marched toward the Bathing Place, a shelf of broken rocks that allowed easy access to the river. Abruptly she wrenched her arm free. "You have no right," she said, "to treat me like a child."

Immar's face was barely visible in distant firelight from the Meeting Place. She moved closer to Kori—so close that Kori could feel her breath.

"You will do as I tell you," Immar hissed at her. She seized Kori and shook her, then stepped back, staring at her with an anguished expression. "How is it possible," she said, "that you are alive and he is dead?"

Kori stared at her mother. "It was an accident!" she cried out.

Immar made a sound of disgust. "I should have known better. Your father roused them all—I had no choice. I had to send Oam." She suddenly seized Kori by both shoulders and shook her violently. "Why do you live? Why did he die?"

Kori found herself crying. This was all so wrong, so different from what she had hoped for. "Mother," she said, "why do you treat me this way? Why do you hate me so much?"

Immar took a slow breath. She paused for a moment, and suddenly her rage was gone. "I don't hate you, Kori," she said tonelessly. "But if one of you had to die, I regret that it was Oam." She gestured to the Bathing Place. "If you don't want me to wash you, wash yourself. Then come to the Meeting Place and we'll decide what to do with you."

Before Kori could answer, Immar walked quickly away.

When Kori ventured back to the circles of huts she heard her people chanting. It was another song of mourning and regret, another song of humility, begging the Old Ones for mercy and forgiveness. At first the sound filled Kori with sadness, for yet another person from her tribe had lost his life. Then she found her sadness yielding to impatience, because there was no point in all this chanting and prayer.

She ventured into the Meeting Place and saw that her mother had quickly donned her ceremonial robe and was leading the chant, while Rohonar stood close by, looking pale and lost, and the villagers sat cross-legged on the ground. Men were comforting their wives, women were holding their babies, and all the young hunters and elders and children were singing the familiar words.

"One of us has been taken," the people sang. "One of us has gone. If we angered you, O spirits, forgive us. Please forgive us. Be gentle with our people. Be kind to us in our homes. We praise you for your wisdom. We beg you for your mercy. Forgive us, please forgive us."

Kori stood in the shadows, waiting. She saw old Torbir, the news crier; Horeth, whose wife had drowned; Derneren and Nenara; and so many others she had known all her life. She knew their faces better than she knew her own, and yet as she watched them sing, they were like strangers to her.

She noticed Yainar sitting just a dozen paces away, with Tiola, his future bride. He was just as handsome as she remembered, singing with his head thrown back, his face so proud, his chest so broad, the skin gleaming in the firelight where it showed between the inside edges of his robe. She remembered vividly how she had desired him and how she had felt when he rejected her. But none of this mattered now.

Finally, after a long time, Immar held up her arms and the chanting stopped. An old woman named Seri started walking among the people carrying a heavy leather bucket of broth, quietly offering it to the elders of the tribe to soothe their dry throats and warm them against the chill air. Many people were weeping quietly, overwhelmed by the sadness of losing the chieftain's heir. Others merely looked dazed, exhausted by all the upheavals of the past weeks.

"I have lost my son," Immar called out to the silent crowd. Her voice was unsteady, colored with emotion. "This, I think, is the greatest grief a woman can know."

There was a murmur of agreement from the villagers gathered around.

Immar drew herself up. "Still, it is the will of the Old Ones. Therefore I accept it as our fate. We have no right to ask why."

There was another murmur, louder than before.

"Kori." Immar turned and looked squarely at her. "Come before us and tell us what happened to Oam."

Reluctantly, Kori walked forward. Now that she saw her people again she doubted her power to say anything that would sway them. Still, she remembered what Oam's spirit had shown her, and what he had asked, and what she had promised him. She couldn't leave his message unspoken.

Kori glanced uneasily at Immar as she joined her in front of the Speaking Stone, but Immar showed no sign of anger now. Her face was grimly composed.

"When did Oam find you?" Immar asked.

"Yesterday." Once again Kori wished she hadn't promised to lie about his death. After all, her whole purpose here was to tell the truth. "I found Oam wounded, in the forest, a day's journey from the Western Shore," Kori said. "He was bleeding so fast, there was nothing I could do."

There was a murmur of dismay from the people facing her.

"How was he wounded?" Immar asked. Her voice was gentle, almost sympathetic, but Kori still sensed her mother's quick intelligence, and she was wary of it.

"I'm not sure what inflicted his wounds," Kori said, avoiding her mother's eyes, knowing their ability to sense the smallest lie.

"But this is not so." It was an old man's voice, from the back of the crowd. It was Pistu, Kori realized. "You told me the wounds were from a mountain lion."

Kori felt her face redden. "Well, I saw lion tracks, and there was blood on Oam's spear," she said. "And the wound in his chest looked like—"

"Oam was a good young hunter." A man named Hurinara rose slowly to his feet. He was the most respected of all the elders. "He would never be so foolish as to anger a lion."

Kori felt trapped by the questions. "Perhaps the beast was hungry," she said, "and Oam might have been careless. He must have felt nervous being on his own, on the Western Shore."

"Well," said Hurinara, "did he *tell* you a lion had attacked him?"

Kori clenched her fists, feeling frustrated. This was not what she'd come here to talk about. "He had so little strength," she said, "there was hardly any time for us to speak before he died."

Hurinara shook his head. His long white hair hung almost to his waist. His face was scarred and mottled with age. His teeth were all gone, yet he stood with pride, and there was no hint of doubt when he spoke. "The big cats aren't hungry at this time of year," he said. "They have all the prey they can eat."

"Then maybe I'm mistaken!" Kori cried. "I found him dying. That is all I know."

Hurinara still didn't seem satisfied. He stayed on his feet, confronting Kori. "How did you live in the forest?" he asked her. "You were gone many days."

Kori felt disconcerted by the new question. "I ate small game. And berries," she said. She felt suddenly annoyed with this old man and his suspicions. If he insisted on doubting her—well, she could certainly tell him the truth on this subject. "Also," she said, choosing her words deliberately, "I speared a lizard. It was a huge beast. Almost as big as a man."

There was a cry of horror from the crowd. Hurinara stared at her in shock.

Immar glared at her. "You killed a creature that could have been possessed by an Old One?"

"I had to eat, Mother," Kori said, turning to face her. "It was you who placed me there. Did you want me to die? Should I have starved to death for fear of offending the Old Ones?"

"This is not the point," Hurinara protested. "You stand here now and *boast* of this—"

She turned back to him. "I am not boasting. I am saying what happened. And look: I still stand before you now. I was not punished."

"*Oam's death* may have been your punishment," Immar told her.

Kori found herself getting angry. Why did they have to be so hostile to her, even now? Why were they so critical, instead of praising her courage? And how could her mother dare to blame her this way?

"That cannot be so," Kori said. She stared at Immar, trying to understand the mind that lay behind the mask of cold disapproval. "You sent Oam to the Western Shore because the Old Ones spoke to you and told you he would be safe. Isn't that true?"

Immar's mouth became a thin, angry line.

"Did the Old Ones lie to you, Mother?" Kori persisted. "If

that's so, why do we ever bother to listen to them? And if they took the life of a good, dutiful person like Oam, who never offended them, and they spared my life even though I insulted them and defied them on their own sacred ground—well, then, what does it matter what we do?"

There was a murmur of discontent, rising as she spoke. She saw the faces of the people around her, and she realized with frustration that many of them would never listen to reason, because reason could never speak louder than their fears. They wanted her to share their faith—or be silent. And that was *all* they wanted.

"I have heard enough," said Immar.

"But there's more I must say," Kori protested. Even though her task now seemed hopeless, she still had to honor her obligation. And if just one or two people listened to her—well, perhaps that was sufficient. "Listen to me," she went on. "After Oam died—his spirit came to me. He spoke to me. He showed me—he showed me the realm of the spirits underground." She took a breath, knowing what she had to say, but not knowing how to say it in a way that the people would tolerate. "He told me—there are no Old Ones."

Now there was a roar of disapproval. Hurinara was still standing in front of her. He raised a shaking hand and pointed at her face. "Quiet!" he shouted at her. "We sent Oam to bring you back to us because your punishment seemed too severe. But if this is how you speak to us, there's no place for you in this tribe!"

There were shouts of agreement.

Kori stared at the crowd in despair. What would it take, she wondered, to prove what she had learned? She spread her arms. "If there are Old Ones," she cried, "let them strike me down and end my life where I stand before you all!" She paused, waiting. The clamor died as people watched her fearfully.

"You see?" Kori yelled at them. "You see? I live! I say to you what Oam said to me: there are no Old Ones." She looked at the faces in front of her. The villagers were yelling at her again, telling her to be silent and show respect.

"Stop her!" someone cried.

"She's a danger to us all," someone else shouted.

"I hope you are satisfied, Kori," said Immar, glaring at her. "No matter what we do for you, you defy us, you insult us, you bring shame and danger upon us—"

"You did *nothing* for me!" Kori screamed, shaking with a wave of anger that was so powerful, she could barely stand. "You cast me out! You wanted me to *die!*"

"She is unworthy." It was Gloshin, Shashin's brother, shouting at her now. "Shashin died because of her."

"Shashin died because your sons forgot to rescue him!" Kori shouted back. "And if I am unworthy, why have the Old Ones allowed me to live?"

"You killed my wife!" Horeth cried, stepping forward with hate in his eyes.

"No, you killed her!" Kori yelled at him.

All the villagers started moving toward her. She had never seen them like this, with such malice in their eyes. She felt her rebellion weaken in the storm of their anger. They had turned from an audience into a mob. She looked at them and felt afraid.

Her father strode forward. "People!" he shouted. "People!" He stood in front of her, holding up his hands. "People, this is not our way!"

The villagers hesitated. They still trusted Rohonar; they were not ready to defy him.

"Kori was alone on the Western Shore," Rohonar called out. "She saw her brother die. Her faith was tested cruelly. It would have broken a weaker person."

"It makes no difference," old Hurinara cried. "She must not be allowed to speak this way."

"I'll deal with this," said Immar. She seized Kori's arm. "Derneren!" she called.

The big, one-eyed man came striding forward, looking reluctant but, as always, obedient. "Take her to her old hut," Immar said. "And keep her there. Then we can decide what to do."

23

"Thank you," Kori said to her father as he walked her to the hut, with Derneren following behind. "Thank you for standing up and speaking for me."

Rohonar grunted. He said nothing. His face was hidden in shadow; she couldn't imagine what he was thinking.

"It was brave of you to stand between me and the rest of the tribe," Kori went on. "I didn't expect it."

Still he said nothing.

They reached her hut, but Kori hesitated outside it. "Father, there is no need for this now. It's foolish to keep me here. I am willing to leave the tribe again. You can let me go—"

"*Quiet*, Kori." He sounded exasperated. She had never heard him speak to sharply to her. "You will do as your mother says. I want no more rebellion, no more strife."

"There doesn't need to be strife," she said. "Just let me leave. Wouldn't that be the simplest way?" She thought suddenly of Uroh, waiting for her in the forest. She saw his face in her imagination and felt a deep, desperate yearning. She had been so foolish to imagine that her tribe would listen to what she had to say, just because they felt guilty for casting her out and had sent Oam to find her.

There was no point in staying here any longer. She had fulfilled her obligation to Oam; she had stated the truth. She tugged at her father's robe. "Let me go back to the Western Shore," she said.

"Go back?" He looked at her as if she was crazy.

"I only cause trouble here. Your life will be simpler without me—"

"No." He pressed his hand to his forehead and stood for a moment, gathering his patience. "No more of this foolishness, Kori. Go into your hut. Do as Immar says." He turned and strode away.

Kori watched him, feeling another wave of frustration. When she had been afraid to leave the island he had abandoned her on the Western Shore. Now that she wanted to leave, he was keeping her here. It made no sense.

"Go inside," said Derneren. He grabbed her arm.

"Let go!" she protested, trying to pull free. Could she run from him? He was slow-moving and stupid. If she could get to the dock and seize a canoe, none of the villagers would dare follow her across the river.

"Go inside!" he shouted at her.

· His grip was painful. She couldn't free herself. He hustled her forward, grabbed the back of her neck with his other hand, and bore down with all his strength, forcing her to stoop. She cried out in outrage as he pushed her into the hut through the low doorway.

She stood for a moment in the dimness, breathing hard, imagining all the ways in which she might hurt Derneren, or distract him long enough for her to escape. But she could tell that none of them would work. She saw his feet directly outside the door. He was guarding her conscientiously, doing his duty.

She groaned with frustration and slumped down on her bed. She looked across the little hut and saw Oam's bed, where he had slept beside her for so many nights. So often, he had been maddened by him, but now the hut seemed terribly empty, and she was haunted by her memory of him lying in the forest with his face full of fear and his chest gushing blood.

Without warning, the door flap was pushed aside and Rohonar came into the hut. Kori turned and looked at him in surprise. He was carrying some kindling, some coiled thongs, a piece of elderwood resin, and a small stone dish. In his other hand he carried a sputtering torch.

Without speaking, he kneeled in the corner and quickly started a fire. He placed the resin in the stone dish where it would catch the heat from the flames, then turned to Kori.

He brushed dirt from his hands. His eyes were brooding. His mouth was tense, turned down at the corners, drawing lines in his face that normally were barely visible. He looked older than when she had last seen him. "You thanked me for protecting you in the Meeting Place," he said. "I have come to explain to you, Kori, why I chose to do so."

Kori waited. She saw there was no point in arguing with him—at least, for the time being. He had come here with something to say, and he would not be happy if she interrupted him.

Rohonar moved across and sat on Oam's bed. He looked down at it and a shadow of grief crossed his face, but it only lasted for a moment.

He looked up at Kori. "When I took you to the Western Shore," he said, "I felt unhappy. The decision to place you here for a month . . . was not a good decision." He shifted uneasily. "It's hard for me to speak this way," he said. He fell silent, clasping his hands and staring down at them. The fire hissed in the corner, lacing the air with its smoke. Outside

the hut, Kori heard footsteps of villagers on the sandy, rock
ground and people talking, arguing with each other.

"It was wrong to cast you out," he said finally.

She had never heard him speak so frankly this way
against her mother. She was moved by it. And yet—
surely, any father should have known it was wrong t
abandon his daughter where her life would be in danger
Now that she saw him wrestling with his feelings, she sa
behind the proud, stern mask that he had worn for s
many years. She saw that on the inside, he was a simpl
man—simpler than she had ever realized.

Kori thought back over the years. Every time he had mad
a decision, Rohonar always asked for advice from the elder
and his wife. She'd imagined that he was a shrewd leade
who knew it was better to reach a consensus than impose hi
will, but now she knew better: he asked for help in makin
decisions because he wasn't able to do so on his own.

Of course, he was unaware of her thoughts. He was sti
wrestling with the challenge of speaking frankly to her abou
himself. "After I left you on the Western Shore," he went on
"I talked to the elders. Many of them—most of them—
thought your punishment was too severe. But they had sai
nothing, because I had said nothing, and I was your father
So it was my responsibility, Kori. That's why I sent Oam t
find you and bring you back." He nodded to himself, satis
fied with the way he had explained it. "And that is why
spoke out tonight in the Meeting Place. I was trying to mak
up for what happened."

His concern was good to hear, and she was gladdened b
it, but she also felt disillusioned. She had always admire
him. Now she saw she had admired what he seemed to be
not what he really was.

"But listen, now," he went on. "If you want my support
Kori, you must help me in return. I cannot defend you if yo
make everyone your enemy." He leaned forward, lookin

deeply serious. "A river doesn't try to pass through a mountain," he said, speaking the words slowly and distinctly, watching her to make sure she was paying attention. "And a tree doesn't try to stand straight in a storm. The river takes an easier path. The tree bends its head."

"You mean I should yield to other people," Kori said. Again she felt disappointed. Was this all he had to say?

He nodded vigorously. "Our people are your people. When you see the caribou migrate in the spring, do you see one of them turn and run against the herd? Can you imagine what the consequences would be?"

Kori sighed. So many times, she had been told to bow and bend. "What if the herd is running the wrong way, Father? What if there is one caribou who stands a little to one side and sees better than the rest? What if she sees the herd is running toward the edge of a cliff? Should she blind herself and run with the herd, even though they will all die?"

He scowled at her, and she saw she had stepped beyond the limits of his tolerance. "You are a young woman, Kori. You are not a seer. You are not the chieftain. You have too much pride. You should know your place."

She turned her face aside, forcing herself to swallow the words she wanted to shout in reply.

"Listen," he went on. "When you returned to our island tonight, people were amazed. They expected you to be hungry, weak, and begging for forgiveness. Instead, you were more wild and defiant than you have ever been before. You even defied the Old Ones themselves." He spread his arms. "You frightened everyone, can't you see? And now, because they fear you, they hate you. They think you must have made some terrible pact with the Old Ones against our tribe. How else could you say such terrible things and not be punished?"

There was a short silence. Rohonar was breathing heavily. He was flexing his hands as if he wanted to seize something—anything to end this whole vexing, troublesome business. Abruptly he stood and went to the fire. He came back carrying the little stone dish and placed it on the floor beside her bed. Then he picked up the leather thongs.

"No!" Kori cried. "You cannot tie me!"

"It must be done." He seized her left ankle. "If you struggle, Kori, I will fetch people to hold you." He wrapped the thongs around her ankle and knotted them tightly.

"But why!" she cried out.

"Because people fear you." He glared at her, then seized her right ankle and started tying the other ends of the thongs around it, leaving a small amount of slack between her legs—no more than the length of her forearm.

"Just let me return to the Western Shore!" she cried.

"It is too late for that." He took out his flint knife and trimmed the knots. "Hold still." He picked up the dish of resin, poured a little onto each knot, and blew on it till it cooled. There would be no way, now, she could untie them with her bare hands.

"Now listen," he said, standing up. He pointed his finger at her. "If people are frightened enough, Kori, they try to destroy the thing that frightens them. Do you understand?"

She stared up at him in confusion. "What do you mean?"

He grunted in disgust. "It will not be exile next time, it will be worse than that—unless you repent and apologize and beg their forgiveness. Then, perhaps, I can speak for you again, and protect you again. But not until then."

He didn't wait for her to reply. He gathered his robes around him with a proud sweep of his arm and turned his face away. He ducked through the doorway and was gone.

For a long time, Kori lay looking at the fire, wondering how much truth was in his words. Was he just trying to scare her? She liked to think so—yet he was such an honest man, she was sure he would never say something that wasn't true.

Should she really humiliate herself? Should she lie and grovel to people who had always resented and shunned her, just to protect herself from their anger and gain her freedom? She wasn't sure if she could do that. Her father was right: she had too much pride.

Outside the hut she heard more people walking past. She strained her ears and caught some of the words they were speaking. "Danger to us all," a man was saying. "If she wasn't Rohonar's daughter—"

"She has an evil tongue." This was a woman talking. "An evil tongue and an evil mind."

Kori groaned. She seized her bedroll, spread the bearskin on her bed, and threw herself down on it. She pulled her legs up; the heavy thongs snapped tight between her ankles, reminding her of her new status as a prisoner.

She cushioned her head on her arm and raised her other arm so that it covered her ear, muffling the sounds. *Uroh,* she thought, wishing she could somehow send the words to him where he was probably sleeping in the clearing in the forest. *I miss you, Uroh. I'm sorry. I should never have come back here. I will return to you as soon as I can.*

Finally, in a state of exhaustion and despair, she fell asleep.

24

Light flashed across her eyes, waking her. She sat up blinking and saw that someone had drawn the door flap aside, letting in a brief glimpse of the bright morning sky.

For a moment Kori was filled with hope. Were they releasing her? Then she saw that someone was coming in. The door flap fell shut behind him, plunging the hut back into semidarkness, with just a dim, diffuse glow filtering through the smoke hole above the fireplace. The fire itself had long since burned out.

"Who's there?" she asked, peering into the gloom. The shadowy figure was tall and broad-shouldered, but he wasn't her father.

"Yainar." He moved forward, bent down, and placed something on the end of her bed. "I brought you breakfast."

"Oh." She leaned forward and found a shallow basket containing some scraps of meat, some dried fish, and some berries. At first she felt nauseated by the thought of eating, but then she realized she should conserve her strength. If she allowed herself to grow physically weak, her spirit would be weaker, too.

She picked up the basket and held it in her lap. Quickly, mechanically, she started eating.

Yainar squatted down near the door and placed his spear across his knees. "Derneren is no longer guarding you," he said. "He's at the ceremony for Oam, by the burial place."

Kori paused, absorbing this news. "But I'm still a prisoner?"

"Yes. Immar told me to make sure you don't leave the hut."

She resented his tone of voice, so confident of his authority over her. She still remembered the awful, hurtful way he had rejected her, and the way he had refused to speak for her before she was cast out, when she was desperate for someone to take her side against Horeth.

"I don't understand why I am being kept here," Kori said, in a low, sullen voice. "It makes no sense."

Yainar grunted. "That may be so."

She peered at him, feeling surprised—then suspicious.

He turned his spear idly, caressing its smooth shaft. "No one knows what to do with you, Kori. They're scared and confused. Naturally their actions make no sense."

She could see him more clearly now that her eyes had recovered from the brief flash of bright light. He was watching her idly, as if none of this was important.

Kori finished the food and pushed the basket aside. "So I frighten them," she said. "But clearly, I don't frighten you."

He laughed softly. "I don't think the spirits listen when you speak. I don't think they care what you say. Otherwise, they would have struck you down long ago."

He sounded so calm and sure of himself, just the way she remembered him. But perhaps she should be grateful that one person, at least, wasn't looking at her as if she were a threat to the tribe.

"Perhaps the spirits don't care what *anyone* says," she told him. "Perhaps they just don't care about our tribe at all."

There was a short, cautious silence. "I have wondered about these things," he said.

She felt even more surprised—and then, more suspicious. He had toyed with her before. She had learned not to trust him. "Why are you speaking this way?" she asked. "Aren't you afraid what people would think, if they heard you?"

"No one will hear me." He turned the spear again and ran his thumb over the edge of its flint point. "They are all at the ceremony. And even if you told them, Kori, that I had questioned the faith of our people—who would believe you?" He laid the spear across his knees again and folded his arms.

She was stung by what he said, all the more because it was cruelly true. "So speak to me frankly, then," she told him. "Tell me what you really believe. Do you share our people's faith?"

He laughed. "I don't think about it, Kori. I say what I need to say, and I do what I need to do. I am a practical man."

She tried to see behind his words. "You mean you just tell people what they want to hear, so you can get what you want?"

His laughed died. He looked at her soberly. "Yes," he said. "That's what I do."

She felt disgusted. "If a person doesn't speak the truth, surely his words are worthless."

This time he was silent for many heartbeats. She began to wonder if she had offended him, and he had decided not to talk to her anymore.

Eventually he stood up and moved to Oam's bed. His face caught a little more of the light, and despite herself, she was reminded how handsome he was. In the past, she'd been overwhelmed by his presence; and then, when he rejected her, she'd been equally overwhelmed by her feelings of hurt. Now, though, it was different. She felt clear-headed, because she wasn't obsessed anymore with the need to find a mate.

could look at Yainar and feel interested in his sharp, cal-
ating mind. And even though he had been hurtful to her,
could appreciate the strong, straight line of his nose, his
ady eyes, his heavy jaw and his massive, rounded shoul-
s. Her emotions no longer ruled her; she ruled them.

He studied her just as she was studying him. "You are dif-
ent," he said. He wasn't speaking in his usual offhand
le. He sounded curious. "You're more sure of yourself
n you used to be. I see it in the way you look at me."

"Perhaps," she said. She felt annoyed that he had judged
so accurately.

He grunted. "You are a strong woman, Kori. Perhaps too
ong—and too caught up in this need of yours to speak the
th. Perhaps if you learned to speak more cautiously, as I
, you could make friends instead of enemies. And then
u might get more of what you want."

"You mean yield to the tribe?" She grimaced. "I already
ard my father tell me that."

Yainar gestured disparagingly. "Your father yields to the
nd," he said, not bothering to hide his contempt. "This is
t what I mean. I mean you should only *seem* to bend, and
cunning to achieve your goal."

She was shocked by the way he spoke. She had never
ard anyone in the tribe speak so coldly, so cynically. "You
n't respect my father?"

He shrugged. "That doesn't concern us here."

She shifted on her bed, drawing her knees up and draping
bearskin around herself so it shielded her from him. "So
at do you want from me?"

His face became intensely serious. "I have a need for
owledge. I want to know about the Western Shore."

"The Western Shore?" His curiosity surprised her.

He shrugged as if it should have been obvious. "I'm an
bitious man, Kori, and a bold hunter. If you can venture
to the Western Shore, why shouldn't I?" He settled himself

on the bed, still holding his spear between his hands. "Is it strange and frightening place? Did you see spirits walkin the land in the moonlight?"

She wondered how much she should tell him. One part her still resented him and wanted to give him nothin because she was sure she would get nothing back from hi On the other hand, if she kept talking to him, perhaps s could distract him from his task of guarding her. And in fa she yearned to tell someone what she had done, simp because she was proud of it.

So she started telling him her story, from the mome when her father had abandoned her. She described ever thing except Uroh, and of course she repeated her lie abo the way in which she found Oam.

Yainar was a good listener. In fact, Kori couldn't remer ber any time in her life when a man had paid such clo attention to what she said—except for Uroh, of course. On in a while Yainar would interrupt and ask her to clari something or add more detail, but mostly he sat in silenc He even showed respect.

"The lion that you saw," he said when she had finally fi ished. "The one that stole the body of the great lizard fro you. Do you think it could have been the same one wh killed Oam?"

Kori hesitated. He asked the question casually, but sl had learned by now that there was nothing casual about hi "Perhaps not," she said cautiously.

He gave a curt nod. "I agree. The lion you saw was we fed, and it didn't attack you, so why should it attack him He pondered for a moment. "But lions don't share their terr tory. Where one roams, you seldom find another. So, Kori don't believe a lion killed Oam."

She felt disconcerted by the way his mind worked, draw ing such quick conclusions. It had been bad enough facin Hurinara last night in the Meeting Place. It would have bee

r worse dealing with Yainar, and she was glad he hadn't
uestioned her then. "So perhaps a bear killed my brother,"
he said, trying to make herself sound uninterested.

"Or perhaps a wolf," he said, still watching her. "Or per-
aps a whitebeast."

She flinched. She felt herself go cold inside as he spoke.

"Strange," he went on, "you haven't mentioned the white-
easts. We know they are there. Did you see none of them
n your journey?"

Her face reddened with embarrassment and anger, and
he hoped he couldn't see it in the dim light. "I know noth-
ng about the whitebeasts," she said in a low, tight voice.

He grunted. "You are lying to me, Kori. I see it in you,
nd I saw it when you spoke in the Meeting Place." He
miled faintly. "What did you say to me? If a person doesn't
peak the truth, her words are worthless."

She wrestled with her emotions. "Tell me why I should
peak truly to you," she suddenly blurted out. "You can take
nything I say, and use it to suit your own purposes. And I'll
eceive nothing from you in return. And I'm powerless. You
re my guard. I'm your prisoner."

He inclined his head. "This is true," he said softly. "But it
oesn't have to be so."

She glowered at him. "What do you mean?"

"Think, Kori. Our world is different now that Oam is
one. Your father has no heir. So any man who pairs with
ou will be the future chieftain."

She stared at him, feeling stunned. He was so cold-
looded in his ambition, and yet there was something
mpressive about that. He had an aura of power that swayed
er even though it disturbed her. "What are you saying?" she
hispered. "You would pair with me just to gain the power
ou want?"

He waited, saying nothing, watching her steadily.

She felt shaken and, in a way, amused by the irony. Here

he was now, almost offering something she had wanted badly. And now, it meant nothing to her. "I could never pair with you," she said.

He raised his eyebrows. "Because I rejected you before? Put aside your pride, Kori. Listen. I can show you how to make people serve you instead of hate you. Don't you understand? You are strong—perhaps stronger than anyone in this tribe. You have your mother's power, if you choose to use it."

The statement was so unexpected, so bizarre, she didn't know how to react. She let out a short, derisive laugh. "You think I listen to the Old Ones?"

"No, no." He sounded impatient. "I don't even know that she does hear voices. Maybe she does, or maybe her sickness feeds her imagination, or maybe she puts the voices in her own head, like—like the way you can make yourself see patterns when you rub your eyes."

Once again his tone was so dismissive, she felt stunned by it. She had never dreamed he had so little respect. "Have you—ever spoken of this to others?" she asked.

He laughed. "Of course not."

She stared at him, feeling amazed that she had never known, never guessed his real feelings. "Do you think," she said, "that any other people in the tribe share your outlook. Are some of them secretly—"

He waved his hand dismissively. "You saw them in the Meeting Place. They believe what your mother says, and they fear it. Oh, there may be some hunters who feel as I do, that the Old Ones show less interest in us than Immar would have us think. Still, they believe the Old Ones exist."

Kori nodded slowly. "I see. So what did you mean when you say I have my mother's power?"

"I mean you are a strong person, as she is. I thought she couldn't fail to break your spirit or destroy you. But now I see I was wrong. Your exile just made you stronger. You may be even stronger than she is." He scowled at her. "But only if you learn to use your strength properly! It's crazy, the way you're acting now. Your strength is destroying *you*. Don't you see?"

She just sat and stared at him, trying to assimilate everything he said. "I don't think you understand," she said. "I'm not interested in these plans of yours. All I want is for my people to let me leave and return to the Western Shore."

"Leave?" Now it was his turn to sound astonished. His eyes narrowed. She could almost hear his thoughts humming like a swarm of bees as he searched for a reason behind her desire. Suddenly he seized his spear and thumped the end of it on the floor. "Oam is still alive! He's waiting for you there!"

"No. No." She held her head in her hands, once more feeling scared by the way he leaped to a conclusion. "I just want to go back," she said, not knowing what else to say. "No one likes me, here. It was good to be on my own."

He made a derisive sound. "You can't survive the winter on your own." He pushed himself up and stood before her. "Look inside yourself, Kori. Forget this foolishness about leaving the island. If you really want to leave, why did you come back here? If you really care nothing about our people, who do you try to persuade them to think as you do? The truth is, you yearn for power over them." He turned and started toward the doorway. "I can help you, Kori. I can teach you how to be powerful instead of being powerless." He nodded slowly. "Think about that."

25

For a long time she lay on her bed, just as she used to when Oam was alive. Faintly she heard the wind blowing, the leaves rustling, birds calling—thrushes and finches, and sometimes a kingfisher down by the river. And then, rising and falling on the wind, she heard her people chanting where they were gathered at the Burial Place.

It lasted a long time, as she had known it would. The death of the chieftain's son was a cause of overwhelming grief at any time, and today there was an even greater need to reaffirm the tribe's customs and beliefs.

The chanting lasted all through the afternoon. It made Kori feel impatient. Her people could be fishing, gathering berries, building winter stores that would increase their chances of survival, instead of praying for help from Old Ones who didn't exist or didn't care.

She tried to shut the chanting out of her mind. She looked at the door flap. There was a small gap beneath it—a slice of light that showed her just a glimpse of Yainar sitting outside, guarding the hut, his shadow slowly lengthening on the black sand.

Her loyalty was to Uroh, there was no doubt about that. Yet as she lay alone on her bed she remembered Yainar's proud, dangerously handsome face. The idea of pairing with him was impossible, yet as the day wore on she couldn't resist building a fantasy about it. How would the tribe react—her mother, especially? And if she were Yainar's mate, how would it feel to couple with him? Did different men make love in different ways, just as they held a spear differently and paddled a canoe differently? Maybe she would never know the answer to that question, but it amused her to think about it.

And how would it feel to inherit her mother's position one day and have real influence over the tribe? Yainar had told her that this was what she really craved, and he'd sounded so sure of himself. But, she decided, he was wrong. She didn't want to control other people; she just wanted to find a place where other people didn't control *her*.

Her thoughts were suddenly interrupted. The door flap rustled and once again Yainar stood in front of her. "They're coming back," he said.

Kori looked at him, feeling startled. Then she realized the distant sound of chanting had stopped.

"Your mother will want to see you," Yainar went on in a low, urgent voice. "Don't defy her. For your own good, Kori. Do you understand? Remember, there's a difference between bending and seeming to bend. Remember!" Quickly, then, he ducked back out of the hut.

Kori felt instinctively angry at him for telling her what to do. But there was no time to think deeply about it because already there were voices outside and footsteps. People were walking back to their homes, and she caught snatches of their conversations. They sounded unworried, now, and satisfied. The order of their lives had been restored.

Everything was the way it had always been, the way it always would be.

The door flap opened, and this time it was Immar who appeared in front of Kori. Her face was daubed with ash and black mud to signify her mourning. Her hair had been hacked so ferociously with an ax that only some short, ugly tufts were left. She was wearing her ceremonial robe, but it, too, had been defaced. It was hanging in ragged strips, with all the ornamental feathers and quills shredded and the precious stones gone.

Kori stared at her mother in dismay. The self-mutilation was so extreme, for a moment Kori found it impossible to think. Then one clear, bitter thought came to her: if Kori had died on the Western Shore instead of Oam, would her mother have mourned this way for her?

Immar stood with her arms hanging by her sides. She stared down at Kori with her shoulders slumped, looking infinitely weary. "I hope you have had time to think about the trouble you caused us last night," she said.

Kori wondered what she could possibly say. She had only spoken the truth. If the truth caused damage, should people be protected from it?"

"Our people's faith has been restored," Immar went on. A muscle tugged at the side of her face. Contrary emotions seemed to be surging inside her. She looked away from Kori's eyes. "Still," she said, "people fear you. They fear you will say more terrible things that could cause us all to be punished." Immar breathed deeply. "They fear you may even destroy our tribe."

"Then it would be best if I am exiled again," Kori said.

Immar stiffened. "It pleases me," she said, stammering over the words, "that you are willing to punish yourself for the good of us all." She hesitated. "But you were exiled before, and you returned to cause more anguish and fear than ever." Immar took another slow, deep breath. "No, you must stand before the tribe, you must confess your sins, you must beg for forgiveness, and you must surrender to the will of our people. After that you will be given chores and kept under guard. You will be treated as a child until you show us that you deserve to be treated as an adult."

The words came out so swiftly, Kori realized they had been carefully rehearsed—probably approved by Rohonar and the elders.

"And if you cannot submit," Immar finished, "then—" She paused. For a moment she closed her eyes, and she swayed slightly as she stood before Kori. "Then, your body will be given over to the Old Ones. You will be cast into the pit."

Kori gasped. "But I am your daughter!" she cried.

Immar looked at her face, but she avoided Kori's eyes. "You are my daughter, but you threaten my tribe. If I must choose between the life of my tribe and the life of my daughter, I must choose the life of my tribe, no matter how terrible that may seem, because I cannot betray my people."

Kori scrambled up, feeling her emotions gathering like a storm. "And what does my father say of this?"

Immar gestured casually, as if the question was irrelevant. "He hopes you will surrender yourself so that he can be the first to forgive you."

Kori tried to imagine it. Even if she could really stand before the tribe and apologize and renounce her beliefs, it sounded as if she would have no freedom for weeks or months. She would not be allowed to return to the Western Shore. She would lose Uroh. The thought was unbearable.

She clasped her hands. "Please," she said, "just let me go. I promise I will never return."

Immar quickly shook her head. "If you leave now, my people will forever live in fear."

Kori felt tears of frustration and anguish welling up. "They only live in fear because you choose to frighten them! *You* are the one they fear, with all your stories of evil spirits and terrible punishments!"

Immar raised her hands. "Enough," she said. Her voice was unsteady. "I can't listen to you, Kori. You have until sunrise tomorrow to make your decision. Be humble, repent, and you can still be welcomed back among us."

Immar turned away quickly, before Kori could speak. She ducked through the doorway and was gone.

As the light slowly dimmed outside, Kori felt overwhelmed with despair. The choice she faced was no choice at all: between death and a life that would be barely worth living. She almost felt tempted to choose death, for this way at least she could stand by her beliefs and defy her people to the very end.

But would they really carry out their threat? Kori remembered the look in the eyes of the villagers surging toward her in the Meeting Place, and she thought that many of them would be willing to—to dispose of her. And Immar had been distraught, delivering her awful message. She was clearly facing the prospect of not only losing Oam, but losing Kori, too.

Kori slid off her bed and managed to walk to the door, taking tiny steps with the thongs stretched tight between her ankles. She crouched down. "Yainar," she called in a voice that was barely more than a whisper.

There was no reply.

"I want to talk to you," she said, louder.

"Kori, I can't speak to you." He said the words calmly and clearly, with no attempt to hide them. There were people out there, Kori realized, who would notice if he went into the hut. He must have been commanded to stay outside.

She gave a little groan of frustration. Surely, there had to be something she could do. She imagined Uroh waiting patiently for her. If only she could reach out with her mind and tell him what had happened. Even then, though, how could he help her?

She looked around the little hut. Two beds, an empty food basket, some ashes where the fire had been—that was all she saw. Could she cut the thongs by rubbing them against the stone walls of the hut? Probably not. All the jagged edges on the inside walls had been chipped off when the hut was built, so that no one could be hurt accidentally. And even if she freed her ankles, she didn't think she could outrun Yainar.

Could she escape unnoticed, somehow, during the night? She didn't see how. The walls were of solid stone, with no window. The roof was built from many layers of wood and hard-baked mud.

Kori threw herself back on her bed. She couldn't imagine what to do.

Later, Derneren came in and gave her some dinner. He put it on her bed without a word, then crouched down and started a fire.

She watched him as he moved slowly, methodically, ignoring her completely. How comforting it must be, she thought, to be so unworried by the world.

"What should I do, Derneren?" she blurted out suddenly. Her solitude was distressing her so much, she was willing to talk to anyone— even him.

Derneren glanced at her in surprise. He paused for a long moment, staring at her with his one good eye.

"I want to leave my people," Kori said. "I want to go and never return. But they won't let me leave. What should I do?"

"Pray to the Old Ones," Derneren said, turning away. "The wisdom of the spirits is greater than ours."

She laughed bitterly as he left the hut. "Thank you, Derneren!" she called after him. "Didn't you listen to what I said last night in the meeting place? Don't you understand *anything*?"

She fell back on the bed, her cheeks wet with tears.

She lay sleepless for a long time, listening to her heartbeat and her breathing and wondering how it would feel to die. Would her spirit be liberated, as Oam's had seemed to be? Would she roam the inside of the earth, or would she drift up to the stars, as Uroh's people believed?

She found no comfort in any of those ideas. She wanted to live, she realized; she wanted it with a deep, overwhelming intensity.

When she finally managed to sleep, she dreamed again of Oam. She was lying at the edge of the river while he swam to and fro in front of her. He was grinning, frolicking in the water. He kicked up fountains of spray that gleamed in the sunlight. "You can be free, Kori!" he called to her. "You can!"

She wondered what he meant. Was he urging her to end her life? "I don't want to die," she called out to him.

"You don't have to," he shouted back. "You're a woman, Kori. A desirable woman. Look at yourself."

She looked down—and saw that she was naked. Her body glowed gold under the sun. She wondered if she should cover herself, but when she tried to sit up, she found that she couldn't move. Her limbs refused to obey her. "Help me, Oam!" she called out.

But he had vanished. The river was calm and still, as if he had never been there. Then she saw someone walking toward her along the shore: a slim, boyish figure in white furs, carrying a spear. "Uroh," she called, feeling a wave of excitement.

He had already seen her. He strode toward her, shedding his furs. He stopped in front of her, his cropped black hair shining, his naked chest gleaming with perspiration. He stood looking down at her body, and she saw his chest heave as he drew a deep breath. Then he kicked off his leggings and she found herself staring at his genitals. She blushed at the sight of them.

"You see how I want you, Kori?" he said. "I'd do anything to have you now."

"Then set me free!" she called to him.

He kneeled before her, then lowered himself upon her. She felt his hot flesh against hers—and suddenly she was free. She spread her arms and wrapped them around him. She opened her thighs, and he entered her.

She cried out—and woke with her pulse racing, her body tingling, her skin feeling hot. Someone was entering the hut, she realized. She heard him moving, and she knew instinctively that it was Yainar.

She almost laughed, thinking suddenly of Derneren. In his simple way, he had been right. She had not gained wisdom from the Old Ones, for she knew they had never existed. But the wisdom of the spirits had guided her. Oam had shown her precisely what she must do.

26

"I heard you cry out," Yainar whispered to her.

"Yes," she whispered back. "But it was just a dream. What are you doing here? Isn't Derneren supposed to be guarding me?"

Yainar moved to the foot of her bed. She saw his profile outlined in faint red from the last embers of the fire in the corner. The light gleamed briefly on the polished flint tip of his spear. "Derneren has gone," Yainar said. "I told him I couldn't sleep, so I'd guard you for the rest of his watch."

Well, Kori thought, that was fortunate. Her plan was clear now, but as sleep fell away from her mind, she found herself feeling fearful. Could she really do what had to be done?

"Listen," Yainar said. His voice sounded more urgent than when he had spoken to her the previous day. "I'll tell you what you must say, and how you must say it. People are calmer now, Kori. I believe you can manage this."

"What?" she asked.

"When you stand before the tribe, you can pretend you were driven half mad by being cast out onto the Western

Shore. You can say that you lost your faith when you saw your brother die. Admit that you resented your mother—everyone knows that you do, so there's no point in denying it. Tell them you wanted to hurt your mother after she exiled you. The truth of this will make people more willing to believe you when you say you realize, now, you were wrong. You are ashamed. You see it was your own fault that you were cast out. You're grateful to your mother for giving you one last chance. You love her, you love your people—"

Kori couldn't bear to listen to any more. The idea of saying such things was so abhorrent, it made her feel sick. "All right," she said. "You're very clever, Yainar, and I believe it could work."

"I'm sure it can," he said, sounding quietly confident.

"But what happens afterward?" she said.

"Well—" In the darkness, she heard him shifting slightly. "They'll scold you and they'll want people to watch over you. I will arrange to guard you some of the time. After a while I'll tell them you've truly changed. And then—in the spring, perhaps we may take the next step."

She smiled to herself. "You mean you would really pair with me, just to inherit my father's place?"

"That depends," he said cautiously. "First I have to be sure of you, Kori. You will have to learn not to speak out. Perhaps you're right that our people shouldn't live in fear. Perhaps we should be free to explore the Western Shore. But these things can only be done if we work toward them slowly and carefully."

Kori could see, in his own way, he was right. But she could also see that she would never have the discipline to do what he wanted. "I respect your wisdom," she told him. "What worries me, though, is whether I can really trust *you*."

He looked at her in surprise. "But I've confided in you," he said, sounding offended. "I've spoken frankly."

"But you weren't honest with me in the past, were you?"

He grunted. "Things were different then."

"You rejected me. You were hurtful to me, Yainar. You told me you weren't attracted to me. So how can I even imagine pairing with you?"

He was silent for a long moment. "I do find you desirable," he said.

"You do?" She loosened her robe. "Feed the fire, add some kindling to the embers."

He hesitated. She guessed he didn't like being ordered around by a woman. But then his curiosity got the better of him. She saw his silhouette move as he went to the corner and did as she said.

Meanwhile, Kori opened her robe and unlaced the waist of her leggings. She waited impatiently, feeling anxious and unsure of herself. If it weren't for her days with Uroh, she would never have been bold enough to behave like this.

Finally a yellow flame flickered into life, driving away the darkness. Yainar stood up. He turned toward Kori—and stopped.

She was lying on her back, naked, with her arms resting by her sides. She stared back at him shamelessly. "If I pair with any man, Yainar, he must want me as a woman, not just as a way to seek power for himself."

He was silent for a long time. She saw a mixture of emotions in his face: caution, interest, reluctance. She still couldn't tell, though, if he desired her—and she felt a pang of doubt.

"I apologize if I offended you when we were at the Gathering Place," Yainar said slowly. "At that time I had to stop your fantasies about me, for both our sakes."

She shrugged. "Maybe so. But I still need proof that you are interested in me now."

He laughed uncertainly. "You mean I should couple with you? Here in this hut?"

"Why not?" she said, though the words made her so nervous, she found it hard to speak.

"But—we are not paired."

"No, we're not," she agreed. "Does that bother you so much? It seems to me, you have no great respect for our tribe's customs. The only customs you respect are your own."

He stared at her body, then looked away, then looked back again. Kori felt some hope. He did seem to want her, but he was nervous.

"If someone finds us—" he began.

"How can anyone find us?" She made an impatient sound. "This is the only way, Yainar. If you want me to take you seriously, you must prove yourself to me."

He gave her a sharp look. "And if I don't? You'll sacrifice your life?"

"Of course not. No, I will take your advice, either way. I will make peace with my tribe. But after that, if you expect to take advantage of the status my family has given me—" She shrugged.

Inside herself, she was beginning to feel desperate. He was so cautious, she was beginning to think that she couldn't tempt him after all.

Slowly, Yainar's hand strayed to the belt that held his own robe closed. "I've always admired your spirit, Kori," he said softly. "I've always wondered, though, if a woman with so much spirit can ever really give herself to a man."

Kori thought of Uroh. She smiled. "If I am with a man I respect, who respects me in return, I will gladly give myself—as long as he truly desires me."

He watched her face, searching for any sign that she was deceiving him. Finally he seemed satisfied. "All right, then," he said. He opened his robe and let it fall to the floor, exposing his chest.

He looked so powerful, Kori felt a new wave of cold

doubt. She was a mere woman; how could she do what she had planned? But she thought again of her dream. She was sure that the dream had spoken truly.

Yainar leaned his spear against the wall while he took off his leggings. Kori couldn't restrain her curiosity; she eyed his crotch. She felt guilty, betraying Uroh this way. And she was so anxious, it was hard for her to think. Still, she was relieved to see that Yainar's genitals were swollen with lust.

He moved toward her, then remembered his spear. He turned and picked it up, stepped around the bed, and laid it beside the bed on the floor. Cautiously, he kneeled beside her. "I don't know if this can be done," he said, "with your ankles tied."

"Perhaps you should cut the thong," she said.

"Is what you want?" His voice was sharp. He jerked back, his eyes full of suspicion.

"Of course not!" she snapped at him. "You wouldn't be able to repair it, and we'd both be in disgrace. How would I make a confession before the tribe if it looked as if you tried to help me to escape?" She paused. "I was just joking," she said more softly.

She saw him slowly relax. *Good,* she thought. *He trusts me more now.*

"Perhaps I should turn on my side," she said. "I've been told it can be done that way."

"All right."

She rolled onto her left side and pulled up her knees. She was facing away from him, now, but she could sense him watching her, looking down at her buttocks. The birch boughs creaked under her as he shifted his weight. She felt the heat of his body, and then his hand touched her flank. Her emotions were in such turmoil, she couldn't tell what she was really feeling. Perhaps a part of her really did want to be taken by him, just to satisfy all those bygone yearnings and prove to herself that she had some power over him.

More than anything, though, she felt afraid.

His hand touched her shoulder, then ran around and cupped her breast. She heard him draw in his breath sharply, and she closed her eyes for a moment. *Forgive me, Uroh,* she said inside her mind.

Yainar spread his knees wider apart. His genitals nudged Kori's thighs. He was breathing heavily, bracing himself with one hand and reaching down with the other.

Kori raised her head and looked back at him. All his attention was on coupling with her. He was just on the point of pushing himself inside her.

She drew a slow, deep breath. She rolled suddenly onto her back, pushing him away from her. She saw him giving her a startled look as she pulled her knees up till they were almost touching her chin. Then she kicked out with all her strength.

Her heels smacked into the side of his face. The blow sent a blunt pulse of pain through her, but she hardly noticed. She glimpsed him rolling away, crying out in surprise. Instantly she reached down, seized his spear, and hurled herself after him. She was clumsy with the thong binding her ankles, but she didn't dare to stop and cut it. He had the reflexes of a fine hunter. She would only have a brief moment in which to grab the advantage.

She found him lying on the floor, starting to get up, looking furious.

"Stop!" she hissed at him. She raised the spear, aiming squarely between his eyes.

He hesitated. He glanced quickly from the spear to her, judging his chances of grabbing it away from her.

She edged back a little, leaving a safer space between them. "I'll do it," she warned him. Her voice was shrill, even though she tried to quiet it. "I'm defending my own life. I'll take yours if I have to. I will!" She glared at him, baring her teeth and tensing her arm, ready to hurl the spear.

He flinched from her. "Kori—"

"Lie on your stomach on the floor," she snapped at him. "And don't make noise. If you make noise, I will truly kill you."

"On my stomach?"

She realized he was trying to delay her, to give himself more time to think of a way to overcome her. She made a quick, wild stabbing motion, almost touching his face with the point of her spear. Despite himself, he flinched.

"Quickly!" she hissed at him. "I'm desperate. I'll do anything. I don't care. Anything to get out of here."

"All right!" He held up his hands, and with excitement, Kori realized he believed she was speaking the truth.

Slowly, Yainar lay facedown on the floor.

Kori stared at him. An overwhelming feeling of power swept through her, so intense that it made her feel weak and shaky. She really could kill him, she realized—not that she had ever intended to. Quickly she used the spear to cut her own bonds close to one ankle. Then she cut the other end of the thongs, near the other ankle. That left her with two lengths, each as long as her forearm.

"I'm going to tie you," she said. "I won't hurt you if you don't resist. But the spear is here beside me. I will use it if I have to. I swear I will."

Cautiously, she squatted down. She lowered her hips till she was sitting on his head, pressing his face into the rough floor. He could wriggle and writhe, but he couldn't touch her.

"Put your wrists together behind your back," she said.

He didn't move. "What do you think you're going to do?" he asked her. His voice was tight and trembling—not with fear, but with rage. She was humiliating him as no woman had ever humiliated a man in her tribe before.

"I'm going to go back to the Western Shore. Now do as I say!"

He made a sound of disgust. "You're crazy."

"Maybe so, but I'm not like you. I can't stay here and lie about what I believe." She seized one wrist and dragged it to the center of his back. She seized the other and crossed it over the first. To her relief, he didn't struggle. Maybe he really was afraid she would kill him.

"You will die in the snow," he said. Then she felt him stiffen under her. "Unless—" He paused. "There must be other people out there!"

Even now, his mind was too sharp for her liking. Her hands shook as she tried to tie his wrists. She said nothing.

"You're a fighter," he said. "That's obvious. You'd never sacrifice your life. So there must be people who you think will help you."

"Hush!" she told him, wrapping the thong and knotting it.

He swore softly. "I see it now. Those whitebeasts are not beasts at all. When we were at the Gathering Place, when I chased Horeth into the forest, I glimpsed the whitebeast there. It walked on two legs. How stupid I've been. He was a man!"

Kori paused, trying to steady herself. It didn't matter, she thought, that Yainar had guessed the truth. He still wouldn't be able to convince other people. "Perhaps you're right," she said. "But even if you are, it's of no concern to you now. Bend your knees. Lift up your heels."

He was grimly silent for a long moment, and he didn't move. "You will regret this," he said finally. "I will cross the river myself, one day, and I will find you and punish you for what you're doing now."

That chilled her. He sounded as if he was making a solemn vow. She was terrified to think what he would do if he ever did find her.

But she had no choice. "You can threaten me all you want," she said. "I have to do this, because I won't stay in this tribe."

He didn't answer. He still didn't move.

She leaned forward, seized one of his ankles, and dragged it up. She tied the second thong around it, then looped the thong around the other one binding his wrists. She hauled on it, forcing him to bend his leg till his heel touched his hands. She hesitated. She'd planned to tie both his ankles, but the second one didn't matter. He'd be sufficiently disabled with one leg tied.

She knotted the second thong, checked one last time to make sure that the knots wouldn't slip, and got up off him.

"Kori."

"What is it?" she asked as she grabbed her leggings and robe and quickly dressed.

"I give you one last chance not to make an enemy out of me."

"Does it hurt your pride so much to be defeated by a woman?" She slipped her feet into her moccasins.

He made any angry sound. "I was sent to guard you. When people find that a woman overcame me and escaped—just think what this will mean."

She hesitated. She saw, suddenly, that people would mock him and laugh at him. His status would be gone. All his ambitions would be ruined.

She had been fearful of his strength, but now she saw his weakness. He was terrified of losing respect. And wasn't that why he wanted to be chieftain, so that every single person would respect him?

Perhaps it was wrong of her to sacrifice him like this, just to get what she wanted. He had wanted to use her to get what he wanted, in his own way, but he had seemed willing to help her in return.

She squatted down beside him. "I regret this," she said, "but I don't know what else to do. My own life is at stake, remember that. What other choice do I have?"

He squirmed on the floor and managed to turn his face

toward her. "Make it seem that you escaped while Derneren was on guard. Pull stones out of the wall, or cut a hole in the roof—"

She shook her head. "I've already thought of these things. It's not possible, and there's no time. It will soon be light." She sighed. "I'm sorry if this seems unjust, Yainar. You know, even though you were hurtful to me, you are the only person on the island who has ever taken me seriously and shared some of my feelings." She smiled to herself. "And I know now, you really did desire me."

"Kori—"

She stood up quickly. "I have to do this. There's no other way." She seized his spear. "I wish you well."

She ducked out of the hut and was free.

27

She ran lightly among the huts. Dawn was not as close as she'd feared; the night was still completely dark. The moon was low in the sky, smeared by cloud. Its light was dim, but she knew her way well. She was sure-footed and silent as she ran out of the village and down toward the dock where the canoes were moored.

She paused on the rocks for a moment and listened apprehensively. Maybe she should have forced something into Yainar's mouth to stop him from shouting. She cursed herself for being too impatient to think of that. Still, no sounds were coming from her hut, and she realized he wouldn't want to attract attention. He would probably try to free himself before dawn so that no one would find him tied naked on the floor. Maybe he would even find a way to save his pride by inventing a story about how she had managed to escape.

Well, that wasn't her concern now. She turned to the canoes. Should she take one and release the rest, so that no one could follow her? That might be the most sensible thing to do, but the thought distressed her. Her people had labored so long and hard to create those canoes, hollowing out pine trees with stone tools. Kori herself had helped with the work. It seemed deeply wrong to destroy it.

Well, she told herself, it didn't matter if she left the canoes moored where they were, because no one would risk pursuing her onto the Western Shore. Yainar had vowed to follow her, but surely that wouldn't be permitted—certainly not now, when the tribe was still so fearful over Oam's death and everything that Kori had said.

She jumped into the smallest canoe, untied it, and pushed it out into the river. She kneeled in the stern and started paddling swiftly, turning into the current so that it wouldn't carry her downstream. Several times she glanced behind her, half expecting to see torches being lit and people gathering on the shore, shouting threats at her. But the island lay in darkness except for the dim glow of the fire in the Meeting Place, and there was no sound.

Kori realized, suddenly, she had achieved something that none of her people would have thought possible. She had overwhelmed one of the strongest men in her tribe. She had freed herself. She felt a sudden urge to stand in the canoe and yell out her pride.

With difficulty, she calmed herself. She still had to find Uroh, and she had to face all the uncertainties about him and his people. Well, she felt equal to that challenge now.

She saw the Western Shore looming in front of her, and she stood up, leaning forward, reaching out for the rocks at the river's edge. She steadied the canoe, then jumped out of it.

She hesitated. Should she let it go? She certainly had no intention of returning to the island. Still, it felt wrong to throw away something that was so valuable. She took the heavy thong attached to the prow of the canoe and wedged it between two rocks. Then she grabbed Yainar's spear and clambered over the rocks, into the forest.

The moon was a little higher now and had risen above the band of clouds. It was shining from the east, across the river, in among the trees. She decided she wouldn't need to start a fire and light a torch. There was just enough light to see by.

She started moving parallel with the river, tracing the same path that she had followed with Uroh. She didn't share his easy confidence in the forest, though, and she paused often, listening. Two owls were screeching to one another somewhere, and their harsh voices made Kori shiver. There were rustlings and scuttlings near her feet—then she stepped on a dry twig and a flurry of black shapes appeared from nowhere, swarming madly into the air above her. She heard wings beating and saw pointed black silhouettes wheeling chaotically across the river. Bats, she realized. She felt a moment of fear. Her people regarded bats as a bad omen.

Well, she didn't care what her people thought anymore. She moved on, pacing through the trees, and finally she saw the first landmark that Uroh had pointed out to her: the tree with the twisted trunk. And there was the other landmark, the large rock on the riverbank silhouetted against the water glittering in the moonlight. She smiled with relief. She was close now.

She turned and moved into the forest. It was denser and darker than she remembered it, but the moon was just visible through the trees, and she kept it directly behind her.

Suddenly she bumped into a tree trunk and recoiled, cursing herself for being too impatient. She sidestepped it and found herself walking through the fine, clinging strands of a spiderweb. She rubbed her face angrily with her sleeve. The big thicket had to be close by. She drew in her breath to shout to Uroh—then stopped.

She heard men's voices.

She stood transfixed, feeling a cold wave of apprehension spreading through her belly. How could there be men here? An awful suspicion formed in her mind. Had Yainar escaped

omehow and made his way ahead of her, bringing others
with him? But no, that was inconceivable.

She crept forward, listening intently. There were two
men talking, and one of them sounded like Uroh. Both of
them were speaking his people's tongue. At first she had
trouble understanding them, because her ears had adapted
back to her own tribe's speech. Then she caught a few
words: ". . . the Island Tribe."

Again Kori crept forward. The forest was almost totally
dark here, and she walked with both her hands outstretched.
Her palms suddenly encountered brambles, and a nettle
stung her ankle. Surely, this must be the thicket. She pulled
back, ignoring the pain, and turned, straining her eyes in the
darkness. Yes, now she saw the slanting tree, only a few
paces away.

". . . not safe," she heard one of the men say. She was sure
it was Uroh.

"Well, they'll be there before dawn."

"But I say—"

"Say what you want, Uroh. It's too late."

There were footsteps, then a rustling sound. Kori realized
one of the men was climbing the ivy that sheathed the trunk
of the big pine tree in the clearing. She quickly crouched
down as she heard a gentle creaking noise, then the sound of
feet scuffing the dead, fallen tree as the man shinned his way
down it. He grunted as he lowered himself to the ground,
and then he came stepping through the forest. For a moment
she panicked as she saw him looming up and thought he was
going to walk right into her. She flinched and crossed her
arms over her head—but he missed her, passing so close she
felt his legging brush against her knee.

He moved on past her, toward the river. She wondered
for a moment if he could have been Uroh—but no, his scent
was different. So, Uroh was still in the clearing.

Kori remained crouching, forced herself not to move. It

tormented her to have to hide like this, doing nothing while valuable time passed. Finally, after the forest had been silent for many heartbeats, she decided it was safe. She hurried to the slanting tree and scrambled up it.

A moment later she was able to look down into the clearing. She saw a small fire burning and a figure squatting beside it, staring into the flames.

"Uroh," she whispered.

He jumped to his feet and looked up, peering nervously into the branches above him.

Kori swung across to the ivy-covered pine and started down it. "Uroh, it's me, Kori."

"Kori!" He sounded excited, but he looked shocked. "Why are you here at night like this? Are you all right?"

She dropped down to the ground. She misjudged the height and landed hard on her heels—the same heels that had already been bruised when she kicked out at Yainar. But she didn't even notice the pain. She peered at Uroh's face with a terrible mixture of feelings: love, suspicion, and fear. She wanted to hug him, to hold him—but she couldn't. "Who was that man?" she demanded.

Uroh stared at her. He didn't answer.

Kori felt a wave of anger. Without thinking, she swung her arm and hit the side of his shoulder with her first. "Tell me!" she cried. "I risked my life to be here tonight. To escape my tribe. To return to you. Don't you understand that?" Suddenly she realized she was crying, and that made her angrier still, to feel her emotions writhing out of her control and to realize how much she cared for Uroh.

"Kori!" He reached for her.

She flailed her arms. "No!"

He seized her wrists and held them. "Kori, be calm. Hush!"

She struggled for a moment, then realized it was pointless. She couldn't deny her need for him. "Just tell me who he was and what's happening," she said, turning her face away from the firelight so he wouldn't be able to see the tears on her cheeks.

"His name is Onnoru, and he's from my tribe—"

"I know that! I heard that! What did he want? How did he find you here?" She looked down and realized what should have been obvious before: the carpet of ashes in the clearing was so thick, it must have been created by many fires—more fires than Uroh could have lit in the month of his solitary wandering on the slopes of Mount Tomomor.

Kori wrenched her wrists free and stepped back. "This place is known to your people."

"Well—yes, it is. I told you my people have watched your island. Scouts often camp here."

"Scouts? What does that mean? Is Onnoru a scout?"

"Yes, he is."

"And you, are you a scout, too?" She glared at him, watching his face with close attention, just as Yainar had watched hers, looking for the slightest sign of deception.

Uroh shrugged uneasily. "I suppose—"

"You lied!" It was almost too much for her to bear. She had trusted him so much. She had given herself to him and sacrificed her bond with her tribe for him, and he had deceived her.

He held his head between his hands. "Please don't be angry with me, Kori. Please."

She looked at his startled face and realized she wouldn't get anywhere by raising her voice. He hated confrontations. He would retreat from her, just as he had retreated from his own tribe. "All right," she said, trying to speak more quietly, "just tell me why you lied."

"I thought—you would be afraid of me, if you knew my people had sent me to keep watch on your people. I wanted you, Kori. I still want you. More than anything."

Well, he seemed to be telling the truth about that, at

least—although she was no longer sure how much to trust her own judgment about Uroh. But there was so much she didn't understand. "Why do your people watch the island? And what were you saying to Onnoru about it being unsafe? You must tell me everything, Uroh. I can't stand it if you hide things from me."

He squatted down by the fire. "Sit with me, Kori," he said.

"No." She folded her arms and stood staring down at him.

He looked up at her face, then shook his head despairingly. "All right, I'll tell you everything," he said. "My people used to live far to the north."

"That's not what you told me," she interrupted him. "You said you live to the west, and you trade for your white bearskins with a tribe to the north."

He nodded helplessly. "I know. I know. I didn't want to admit to you—we were forced from our land by another tribe. We have been searching for a new place to make our home. I'm not a fighter, like most of our menfolk, so they sent me forward as a scout with three others. We found your island, and our chieftain decided—he decided we should take it as our own. The location is so secure, we would never again have to fear being driven from our homes."

Kori looked at him in horror. "You mean—your people plan to *steal* it from mine?"

Uroh held his head between his hands. "They will attack your people and drive them off, or force them to surrender and serve my tribe."

Kori tried to imagine it. Her people were so timid, so fearful; if a hostile tribe attacked them, they would panic like startled deer. Some would fight back, but most would flee or be killed. Or, worse, they would slump to their knees and pray to the Old Ones to save them.

She shuddered. She had no love for her tribe anymore, but she had no desire to see them slaughtered. "Tell me now," she said grimly purposeful. "When did you find out about this plan? Did you know about it when you first met me?"

He turned his face away. "Yes," he said in a sad, low voice. Then he tried to gather his strength. "You have to understand, Kori, how much I risked for you. If they had found me with you up there on the rocky slopes—I would have lost everything. They would have cast me out or killed me. I took that risk just for you."

"But they would have killed me, too!" she cried. "You risked *my* life, not just your own. And you didn't even tell me!"

"I'm sorry." He put his hands over his face. "I was afraid you'd leave. I just wanted you. I told you, I felt we were fated to have each other. I felt it in my soul. I still do. Somehow, I knew we would manage to be together."

Finally she understood. He was such a dreamer, so hopelessly estranged from hard realities, he preferred to put his trust in his strange ideas about fate. He had just hoped for the best.

She felt a wave of despair. All the anger drained out of her; there was no point in being angry with him now. "All right," she said. "You had no malice in your heart. But when you lie, Uroh, it destroys trust. Never lie to me! The truth is all I care for. Never lie!"

He took his hands away from his face and looked up with a mournful, lost expression. "Please forgive me, Kori. I didn't mean any harm by it. I never wanted to hurt you. I just thought it was for the best."

She shook her head. "Maybe I can forgive you in the future, Uroh, but now, there are still things I need to know. What did Onnoru mean when he said, 'they'll be there before dawn'?"

Uroh looked back at the campfire. His sighed. "He was telling me our warriors will attack tonight."

"The island? *Tonight?*"

He nodded hopelessly. "I argued against it. I knew you

were there, so I was terrified that you'd be killed. But my people don't respect me. My words are worthless."

Kori stepped backward. In a sense, none of this was her fault or her responsibility, and since her people had been willing to sacrifice her life, it made no sense for her to be concerned about theirs.

And yet—that wasn't quite true. Most of the people on the island were decent enough at heart. They had only treated her badly because Immar had made them so fearful. They had acted in self-defense.

Kori grimaced with the effort of trying to weigh such a huge, terrible problem. Suppose she hardened her heart toward her people and turned her back on them. Then what? She suddenly saw why Uroh had been so reluctant to take her to his tribe. She felt paralyzed, trapped between two awful alternatives. Her tribe was so afraid of her, they were ready to kill her. His tribe was so ruthless, they would kill her, too.

She looked at him, wondering if he understood all of this. She guessed that he did, for he'd had a long time to think about it. And she saw that there was no point in asking him what to do, because he didn't know. That was why he'd done nothing all along. He was helpless.

"Is there any hope," she said quietly, "of peace between your tribe and mine?"

He shook his head. "I've argued for it. But no one takes me seriously. They see that your people are weak because they've lived in isolation so long. You have hunters, but you don't have warriors. It should be an easy battle. So why should my people bother to make peace?"

"Because it is wrong to kill and steal!" she cried, feeling outraged by his words.

"Yes, Kori. I know that. But the leaders of my people see the world differently. They steal from the weak with no regret, because they have no respect for them."

Kori groaned and turned away. "Well, one thing I've learned is that I am strong." She took a deep breath, wishing fate could have allowed her to hold on to her feeling of freedom and excitement for just a little longer. But there was no point in self-pity. "I suppose," she said, "it is up to me, now."

He gave her a confused look. "What do you mean?"

"I have to do something. I can't sit and do nothing. This is a terrible thing that your people plan to do."

"You think you can stop it somehow?" Clumsily, he scrambled up. "Kori, you're crazy."

She shrugged. "Perhaps. But look, Uroh. If I stay here alone with you in the forest, we won't survive the winter. If I go to your people with you and ask them to accept us, they will kill me and punish you for hiding your attachment to me. Isn't that so?"

He looked away. His face was sad. "I think we should just wait," he said. "The battle will pass. And perhaps things will work out differently from the way we expect." He turned to her again, seizing hold of her hands and staring into her eyes. "I truly believe we are fated to be together. I know that it's so."

She loved him for his gentleness, his accepting nature, and his agile mind. But at this moment, she hated his lack of spirit. There was a gulf between them that she had never seen before. "The world won't take care of us, Uroh," she said. "If we want something, we will have to fight for it."

He shook his head, looking pained. "Fighting wastes the strength of a man. It is not my way, Kori. And I don't believe you can change fate."

"I'm sorry, Uroh." She felt herself starting to cry. She hated to abandon him like this, while they were so estranged from each other. But her conscience gave her no choice. "I don't feel the way you do," she said. "Stay here if you must and wait for me. I hope you'll do so. I will try to come back to you. But I must go now."

28

She hurried back toward the river, feeling her way between the trees, pursuing elusive glimpses of the moon. At this moment she felt hurt by Uroh, disappointed in him, even betrayed by him. But suppose she could rediscover her feelings for him. Was there really no way to save herself, save him, and recapture the contentment that she had known so briefly?

Clearly, they couldn't survive the winter without stores of food and a secure shelter. Could they *steal* the food they needed? She hated the idea. And even if they succeeded, how would they find a safe place to live? Uroh's people roamed the Western Shore. The two of them would be in constant danger.

Would it be possible to strike out in a new direction and find a completely different tribe that was less warlike than Uroh's, less superstitious than Kori's, and willing to take them in? She had no idea whether such a thing was possible. It sounded like one of Uroh's fantasies, and she wasn't willing to gamble her survival on it.

So—could she persuade his tribe, somehow, to adopt her, perhaps if she pretended to be his prisoner? No, they wouldn't trust her, especially if they'd just fought and killed her people. They'd be afraid she would try to take revenge on them. And they might be right.

She was left with only one option, which sickened her and made her feel weak with despair: she could only survive if she rejoined her own tribe. And now, her situation would be even worse than before—because by knocking Yainar down and leaving him tied naked, she had made an enemy of the one person who had offered to help her.

She finally emerged from the forest and stood for a moment, breathing hard, staring blankly across the river, wrestling with her awful predicament. Really, she decided painfully, Yainar had been right. She had been far too reckless, far too headstrong, making enemies instead of friends. She had used her strength against herself. She had never stopped to think how much she depended on the goodwill of her people and the security they offered.

She wondered if she could get back to the island in time to free Yainar, before anyone else found him. Would he forgive her? And if they could then warn everyone and *defeat* the warriors from Uroh's tribe, would that change everything? It still wouldn't solve her predicament with Uroh, but maybe if her people forgave her and freed her, she could bring food to Uroh in some hiding place in the forest throughout the winter.

The task sounded so impossible, the idea of it made her feel weak inside. But her other choices seemed worse, and Uroh just wanted to sit and do nothing. Well, maybe he was right—maybe the two tribes would annihilate each other, and then she and Uroh could take over the island and live there alone together, gorging themselves on stores of food that had been intended to feed more than a hundred people through the winter.

Kori grunted in disgust. She wouldn't waste any more time imagining such foolishness.

She ran quickly along the edge of the forest till she found her canoe, still tethered where she'd left it. How glad she was, now, that she hadn't cast it adrift. She stepped in, pushed it away from the shore, and started paddling quickly toward the island. The eastern horizon was still untouched by any hint of dawn, and the darkness closed around her. Her muscles were weary from lack of sleep, and she shivered in her robe. Still, she forced herself on.

She looked carefully to either side while she paddled, searching for any sign of movement and wondering how the warriors from Uroh's tribe would make the journey across the river. They were mountain people. Could they build their own canoes? Would they know how? She wished she had questioned Uroh more closely, but it was too late to go back.

The night was still and the river was calm. Surely, if there were men out on the water, she would see them easily in the moonlight. But no matter how she strained her senses, she saw nothing. The only sound was of her paddle dipping into the river, and the water making faint chuckling noises as it flowed around her canoe.

Kori reached the island and tied her canoe with the others. As she stepped out of it, she felt a sudden wave of anguish. It was so humiliating to be back here again, so awful to return to the place from which she had freed herself.

But this was a matter of survival, she reminded herself. Her pride had to take second place. She climbed up from the dock and hurried toward the village. Once more she ran lightly among the huts of her tribe, glancing quickly around, alert for any sound, but everything was silent; no one stirred.

She reached her own hut and stopped outside, trying to quiet her urgent breathing. She trembled at the thought of facing Yainar, and she wished she could go to her father instead, or an elder such as Hurinara, or even old Torbir, the news crier, and give them her warning about the attack from Uroh's people. But they believed their tribe was the only one in the world. They would never accept what she said. Also, the only way she could hope to have Yainar as an ally was if she set him free.

She turned and pushed her way through the door flap, and she almost tripped over him where he lay on the floor. "Hush!" she told him urgently, as he made a startled sound. She saw he had turned around so that he was lying on his side with his bonds near the embers of the fire in the corner, and she realized he had tried to burn the thongs binding him. That must have taken a lot of courage; the thongs were so tight against his skin, there was no way to burn them without burning himself as well.

"Kori?" His voice was full of disbelief.

"Yes." She kneeled quickly beside him.

"Why are you here?"

She wondered how to explain in such a way that he'd believe her. "You were right," she said, "about the white-beasts. They are men. And one of them became my friend. But—I have just learned—he lied to me." It hurt her to admit it, but she couldn't escape the fact. "His people—the whitebeasts—they are a homeless tribe. Other people stole their land and forced them to leave their land. Do you understand?"

There was a long silence. "They are a tribe, a separate tribe like our own?"

"Yes. The world is larger than we ever imagined. There are *many* tribes. And sometimes, they fight one another."

Yainar groaned. "Why do you come back here to tell me these things? What do you want? Perhaps everyone was right after all, and you are truly crazy."

She couldn't stand it. She seized him by the shoulders and

shook him violently, banging his head against the stone wall. "Listen to me, you have to listen!"

He made an angry sound at the back of his throat. "Show some respect."

She tried to calm herself. She released her hold on him. "I'm sorry. I'm truly sorry. Please listen. I heard my—my friend, talking to another man from his tribe. They want to steal our island from us. They will kill us and take what they want."

Once again he was silent for a long moment. "How can such a thing be done?" he said.

Well, at least he was considering what she had to say. He wasn't just dismissing it. "They would hunt us like animals," she said, "and chase us away or slaughter us."

He grunted. "How can you be sure of this?"

"I am certain," she said, trying to make herself sound confident, knowing that he would never trust her if she sounded like a hysterical woman. "They will be here tonight, do you understand? I heard them say so."

"Tonight? You say these men are going to come to our island and try to kill us *tonight*?"

"Yes! Why else do you think I would come back here to you, Yainar? I know you hate me now, after what I've done. Do you think I'd return if I had any choice? You told me that I've made you my enemy, but you are the only one I can talk to about these things, the only one who may believe me."

"I see." He grunted with discomfort. "Well, if you want me to help you, you'll have to cut the thongs."

She hesitated, feeling apprehensive. "What will you do? Will you warn everyone?"

"I'll go out and look for these warriors you talk about."

She thought about that. Perhaps it was the best she could hope for. "Will you hurt me?" she said. "Are you angry because of what I did? You know I was just trying to save myself."

"Perhaps I would have done the same thing in your place," he said. "Now cut these bonds, Kori, if you're serious about what you say."

She really had no other choice. She took her spear—his spear—and felt for his wrists. He jerked and grunted with pain, and she realized his skin was raw where he had tried to burn the thongs, which were stiff and charred. He might have succeeded in freeing himself, she realized, if the fire had lasted longer.

She sawed the thongs with her spear, first freeing his ankle, then his wrists. He rolled over, straightened his leg, and groaned. He wriggled his shoulders and flexed his wrists. "You tied me tightly," he muttered.

"I was afraid of you," she said.

He laughed without humor. "You should be." He turned toward her. "Now give me the spear."

She hesitated. There was a new, commanding tone to his voice. And then she heard something else—something that made her freeze motionless, with the breath cramping her lungs.

"Kori," he called to her. "Give me the spear!"

She reached out, fumbled in the darkness, found his face, and pressed her hand across his mouth. He made a muffled noise of surprise; she pressed her palm harder, silencing him.

Kori squirmed closer to him where he sat on the stone floor of the hut. She touched her lips to his ear. "Outside," she whispered. "Listen!"

For a long moment there was no sound. Then, faintly, there was a footstep.

Kori felt a prickling sensation across her scalp. Sometimes a villager might have trouble sleeping and would step out for a walk under the moon, but this was not the sound of someone taking a casual stroll. This was the sound of a hunter stepping stealthily, stalking his prey.

Now she heard something more: a smothered sound, so faint it was barely audible. And then a breath of wind blew in under the door flap, and she smelled something on the night air. For a moment she found it hard to recognize; and then she shuddered as she realized what it was. It was the smell of blood.

She felt Yainar stiffen beside her, and she heard him draw in his breath. He groped urgently for the spear, trying to seize it out of her hand, but he failed to find it in the darkness. At the same moment Kori heard another footstep, this time directly outside her hut.

She felt horror sucking at her stomach. Without knowing what she was doing, she leaped up and blundered backward till her shoulders slammed against the rear wall of the hut. At the same moment, the door flap slowly opened and the figure of a man pushed inside, moving with extreme caution. He paused, turned—and saw Yainar squatting on the stone floor.

"Kori!" Yainar shouted, throwing himself to one side. At the same instant, the intruder raised his arm to cast his spear.

The door flap had lodged opened a little way, allowing faint moonlight to penetrate the hut. Kori glimpsed Yainar holding up his hands as if he could somehow deflect the spear. She levered herself away from the wall, pushing against it with all her strength. She drew in her breath and screamed, an inarticulate cry of rage and fear. She saw the figure whirling to face her. She brought up her spear and stabbed it like a long dagger directly into the stranger's face.

He made a terrible sound, a gargling cry, as he toppled to the floor. She fell down on top of him, banging her knees and elbows. She jerked the spear free then stabbed him again, this time in his chest. Once more she pulled the spear up, then plunged it down.

"Kori!" The voice was in her ear, painfully loud. "Outside,

get outside!" Yainar dragged her off her victim. He wrenched the spear out of her hands and threw himself ahead of her, out through the doorway.

Kori stopped for a moment. She was shaking uncontrollably, still gripped by terror.

She turned toward the doorway, then turned back, kneeled beside the man she had attacked, and groped in the darkness. He was still making awful coughing, gasping noises. She tried not to hear them as she found his spear, took it from him, then followed Yainar out of the hut.

A slim streamer of faint gray light was touching the eastern sky. Kori peered into the gloom and saw Yainar standing three paces away, looking startled and fearful, his eyes wide, his body in a defensive crouch. She looked in the opposite direction and saw two strangers running among the huts, their furs ghostly white in the dimness. One of them saw her, and he threw his head back and screeched like an owl.

It served as a signal. More warriors suddenly started emerging from other huts nearby. With a deepening feeling of dread she realized they had been killing her people in their sleep.

"Wake!" Kori screamed. "My people, wake!"

The warrior who had seen her took two paces toward her. She glimpsed his face daubed with black mud and his hair cropped shoulder length like Uroh's. He whirled his arm and cast his spear.

Kori found herself falling. Dimly she realized that Yainar had thrown her down. The whitebeast warrior's spear grazed her shoulder and hit the outside of her hut with the sharp sound of flint against stone.

Kori saw Yainar crouching beside her, trying to scramble back into the hut. "No!" she shouted at him. "They're retreating, don't you see?" It was true: the warriors were leaving the village. Kori realized there were relatively few of them—perhaps no more than twenty. They had crept onto the island under cover of darkness, knowing that they were hopelessly outnumbered. Now that she had sounded an alarm they were escaping while they still had a chance to do so. Kori suddenly remembered the thought that had passed through her mind earlier in the night. "The dock!" she cried. "We must get to the dock! They'll untie all the canoes and leave us stranded!"

Yainar hesitated, then nodded. He jumped up with Kori beside him and together they chased after the last of the running men.

To either side of her, in the huts that Kori passed, she heard sleepy voices calling puzzled questions. She saw one of the villagers poking his head out from his dwelling, staring at her in shock. But how could she possibly explain what was happening? There was no time. She ran as fast as she could, with Yainar just a couple of paces ahead of her. Together they emerged from the last circle of huts and looked ahead down the slope to the river. At least a dozen hunters in white furs were already leaping into the Island Tribe's canoes. A dozen more were still converging on the dock.

Kori wondered how they had crossed the river originally. But there was no time to consider that. She saw the warriors crowding together, filling four of the canoes and cutting them free from their moorings. Then she saw what she had dreaded all along: one of the men turned and raised his spear, ready to slash the thongs that moored the rest of the canoes.

"No!" she shouted. She stopped, pulled back her arm, and cast the spear that she had taken from the man she'd slaughtered in her room.

She threw herself to the ground as the shaft flew away from her. She saw her quarry hesitate, startled by the sound of her voice. The light was still so dim, though, he didn't see the spear as it arced toward him. He fell silently with an expression of disbelief as the head of the spear dug deep into his chest.

Three canoes full of the warriors now cast off and were paddling away across the water. Only four men remained in a fourth canoe by the dock. One of them moved to do what his companion had tried to do and cut the remaining canoes loose. Kori heard a footstep close beside her where she lay on the ground, then she saw Yainar running ahead, casting his own spear.

His adversary was more alert than Kori's had been. He saw what was happening and ducked down—but still the spear hit him in the shoulder, and he yelled with pain.

Another man, right beside him, stood and hurled his spear. Yainar fell into a crouch and the shaft flew harmlessly above him.

Now there were more cries from the village—cries of shock and fear as people emerged from their homes. The last warriors at the dock looked at the gathering crowd of villagers and abandoned their plan. They pushed their canoe out into the river.

"Quickly!" Kori said, scrambling up onto her hands and knees. "We must go after them!"

Yainar grabbed her shoulder. "No," he said.

She looked at him in confusion. "But we can pursue them!"

"Kori." His grip tightened. "Kori, there are only two of us. And we have no spears now."

She looked around, feeling disoriented. "But—others will help us."

Yainar shook his head. "You know full well, Kori, none of our people will dare to follow those men to the Western Shore." He stood up and grimly brushed dirt from his clothes. He watched the warriors as they disappeared across the water, till they were lost in the semidarkness. He turned, then. "We should go back to the village. We must consult our elders about this. And we must find out how many of our people have been killed."

29

People were running from one hut to another, shouting and moaning in distress. Kori saw a woman dragging her child from her home, his small, lifeless body wet with blood. She saw a hunter standing motionless, holding his dead wife in his arms, staring at her in disbelief. Babies were screaming. Children were crying. Everywhere people were shouting for help, but there was no help.

"Your whitebeast friend," said Yainar, seizing her arm. "Did he know the warriors would come here and kill people in their sleep?"

"No!" Kori cried out.

Yainar seemed unconvinced. "But he did know his people planned to kill us one day. And he deceived you."

Kori dragged herself free. The idea that Uroh had known, and hadn't warned her, was suddenly unbearable. She turned and ran, trying not to look at the dead and wounded all around her, trying not to hear the cries of pain and grief, till she reached her own hut.

She ducked inside—but here was another terrible sight.

The man she'd speared was lying on the floor, his head thrown back, his eyes wide, his mouth gaping. His face was covered in blood from the wound where her spear had plunged into his cheek. There were two more deep wounds in his chest, and his furs were saturated. Kori's moccasins made sticky noises as she moved, and she realized that the warrior's blood had flowed so freely, it covered almost the whole floor.

She stood clenching her fists, staring at the man's face. He looked to be no more than twenty years old, a hunter like the young men in her own tribe. Yet he had come here to do this terrible thing, killing people in the most cowardly way she could imagine.

This, she thought, was what Uroh had rebelled against when he refused to fight. She understood him better, now—far better than before. Still, she was tormented by the fact that he had lied to her.

Kori fingered the little shell-replica of a bear that still hung on the thong around her neck. Feeling weak, overwhelmed by grief and confusion, she turned and blundered out of her hut—and found herself suddenly face to face with Torbir. She stopped, staring at him. She had known him all her life; he was as familiar to her as the shape of Mount Tomomor. Seeing him now, surrounded by this bloodshed, made her feel as if she was being torn in two.

"Your mother," Torbir blurted out, staring at Kori strangely. His gnarled hands reached clumsily for Kori. "Mother is calling for you."

It took Kori a moment to understand what he was saying. "Is she hurt?"

Torbir tried to speak—and failed. He nodded helplessly.

Kori paused for a moment. She tried to imagine how she would feel if her mother died. Immar was so strong, so fierce, the idea was inconceivable.

Torbir tugged at her robe. "Hurry," he told her.

"Yes." Kori nodded, turning away. She started walking, then broke into a run, trying not to see the carnage around her.

Moments later she reached her parents' home and found Derneren standing outside, looking dazed, with blood all over his hands, arms, and chest. "Are you all right?" Kori stammered.

He looked down at himself, then up at her. "Not my blood," he said. He gestured with an awkward jerk of his arm. "Mother wants you."

"And my father?"

Derneren shook his head. His simple face creased into an expression of misery. "Dead," he said.

Kori blinked. She touched her hands to her cheeks, reassuring herself that she, at least, was alive. "They killed him," she whispered. She wondered if she had really heard what Derneren had said.

"Go inside!" he shouted at her.

Kori pushed aside the door flap. This was where she had spent the first fourteen years of her life, sleeping on a small bed in one corner, till she came of age. In this room she had seen her brother born. Here was where she had tried so hard, so often, to win her mother's approval—and here was where she'd learned to fear her mother's rage.

The smells were overwhelmingly familiar: wood smoke, deerskin, musk oil, herbs, and bundles of reeds that had been laid out to dry across the rafters. She saw her father's spears standing in one corner, a fishing net neatly rolled and resting against them. His fine furs and her mother's robes were hanging against one wall. Three pairs of moccasins were lined up inside the doorway.

Kori stepped forward. As her eyes adjusted to the dim light, she saw her mother and father lying together on their simple bed at one end of the hut. Kori hesitated, afraid of moving closer, but Immar heard her and was already looking at her. "Here," she said, gesturing weakly to the side of the bed.

With a deep sense of dread, Kori crept forward. She saw her father lying beside her mother with his eyes closed, and she remembered many times when she had seen him resting here after hunting on the Eastern Shore. He looked so peaceful now, she half expected him to sit up and welcome her, but there was a huge dark stain on his chest, and as she ventured closer she saw more blood that had trickled from his mouth.

"They killed him," Immar whispered, seeing Kori staring. "I woke, and a man was in here. I was confused. I thought, for a moment, he was Oam, back from the Western Shore." She closed her eyes for a moment. "But then he killed my husband, and he speared me also, and he left me for dead." Her voice sounded full of wonder, as if these things were too strange for her to believe.

Kori fell to her knees. "Why didn't you cry out?"

Immar shook her head. "I was afraid they'd hear me and come back." She winced as she struggled to breathe. The air made a rasping noise in her throat and lungs. She coughed and cried out in pain. "Is there water?"

Kori looked around, finding it hard to focus on anything. Finally she saw a water bucket in one corner. She went to it, filled a leather cup, took it back to Immar, then hesitated, half expecting her to reach out and take it. But Immar lay motionless.

Kori was seized by conflicting feelings as she raised the cup to her mother's lips. Never had Immar asked or allowed Kori to aid her like this. Always, Immar had been too proud, too fierce, too strong to accept anyone's help—and Kori found herself suddenly wondering why. What was so terrible about being helped?

"Thank you," Immar whispered, after she had drunk half of the water. "That's enough."

Kori set it down on the floor. "Are you badly hurt?"

Immar ignored the question. "I need to know if other people in our tribe were killed."

"Yes," said Kori. "Many." She hesitated. "Mother, if you're badly hurt, let me see the wound. If you're bleeding, we must stop the flow."

"No." Her tone was cold. It allowed no room for discussion. "Now tell me. These men, these killers—they were from the Western Shore?"

Kori sighed. As always, she was not going to be allowed to say what she wanted to say. "Yes, Mother," she said.

Immar forced a stiff, sour smile. "So there are other tribes. Ours is not the only one. I always wondered."

Kori looked at her sharply. "You always—"

"Take my hand."

It took her a moment to make sense of what her mother said. The request was so unusual, so unexpected. She groped under the fine bearskin that covered Immar where she lay on the bed, touched her mother's arm, and flinched, finding it coated in congealing blood. Clumsily, Kori moved her fingers down till she found her mother's fingers.

Immar gripped Kori's hand with fierce strength. "Now listen," she said. "This is important. Are you listening?"

"Yes." Kori watched her mother's face, not knowing what to think or expect anymore.

"You know, when I was a child, Rohonar's father was chieftain."

Kori nodded. Of course she knew this.

"He was a fierce man," Immar went on. "He pitted other men against each other." Her mouth twisted with distaste. "Because of him, the hunters took many risks. They fought each other. Some were injured. Some even died. This island was a violent place. Women suffered."

Could that be so? Kori had never heard it said before. But there were a lot of things that people avoided saying.

"Your grandfather died when he tried to kill a mother bear defending her cubs," Immar continued. "I had already paired with Rohonar. I vowed then that the violence would end. I'd noticed men put aside their rivalries in times of crisis, so I found a way to scare them." She gave Kori a strange, twisted smile. "You said I frightened my people. Well, you were right. I did. For their own good."

Kori felt dizzy as she heard the words. They were spoken so callously, with such righteousness. How could her mother take pride in deceiving her own kinfolk? What had given her the right to do such a thing? And then, as Kori realized the implications, she felt outraged. "But you didn't tell me!" she cried. "You deceived me, too! You made my life—" She broke off, unable to speak, feeling tears running freely from her eyes. "Why?" she cried. "Why did you hurt me so?"

Immar gave her a look of disdain. "You always defied me. Always rebellious. I couldn't trust you. Not till you learned to obey."

Kori tried to drag her hand free, but Immar held it tightly. Her eyes lost focus, as if she were looking through Kori to another place far away in history. "Ever since I was a child, I had my—my fits. I heard voices. Sometimes they told me if an earthquake was near. Sometimes they said things that I couldn't understand. But I learned to—to interpret them. To warn my people."

"Even when you heard nothing?" Kori cried out.

Immar shrugged. "Sometimes."

Kori struggled with her emotions. "It is *wrong* to deceive our people," she blurted out.

Immar squinted, focusing on her with difficulty. She scowled. "Don't lecture me with your right and wrong!" She breathed deeply. "It was for their own good. You didn't see how it was before. All your life, you've benefited from what I chose to do. People are generous now. They forgive each other. They love each other, because they turn their hate against the Old Ones. And I gave them things to work for. The sacred stones." Her mouth twisted in an awful smile. "It was I who found the Gathering Place on the Western Shore."

Kori shook her head, unable to cope with the wrongness of it all. "And when I wouldn't obey you, you wanted to—to get rid of me."

Immar gave her a scornful look. "I wanted to teach you a lesson, nothing more. I sent you to the Western Shore—I thought you'd huddle by the river, and people would see you, and they'd take pity on you, and bring you back, and you'd be grateful." She grunted with disgust.

Kori stared at her mother. "You thought I'd just . . . do whatever you wanted?" She gave a short, sharp laugh. "And when you said I'd be *killed* if I didn't obey you—was that a bluff, too?"

"Of course." She coughed and groaned. "Kori. Listen to me. I want you to pair with Yainar. Do you understand?" She gripped Kori's hand harder, till it was painful. "He's a good, obedient man, like your father. Promise me!"

Obedient? Kori thought of what she had learned about Yainar, and she almost laughed at the way Immar had deceived her people, while being deceived herself. "I can't promise to pair with Yainar," she said, keeping her voice low and calm.

Immar's jaw clenched and the muscles tightened in her neck as she struggled to sit up. But she gasped with pain and slumped back on the bed, struggling to breathe. She coughed again, and her mouth was suddenly rimmed with red. "It is my dying wish!" she cried.

Kori stared at her mother and once again she felt her emotions tearing her inside. "Let me get help," she said.

"Stay!" Immar tugged at Kori's hand. "You mustn't destroy what I've built, Kori. Listen! This is what you must tell our people. They are being tested. Do you understand? The Old

Ones sent these whitebeasts. To test our faith. The spirits tested *your* faith. You were deceived by them. You know better, now. Our people must defend their island. The whitebeasts will attack again. This will be the ultimate test." Immar's face suddenly lost its strength, and her jaw quivered. "Please, Kori, say this to our people!"

With amazement, Kori realized that her mother was crying. "Mother—"

"Tell them!"

Kori wrenched her hand free. "You tell them!" she cried. She backed away. "I'll bring some elders. You tell them! They'll believe *you*!"

Without waiting for her mother to respond, she turned and ran outside.

The sun had risen. The daylight dazzled her. She slumped against the wall of the hut and stood for a moment with her eyes closed, taking deep breaths, trying to stop herself from shaking.

"Kori?"

The voice was familiar. She opened her eyes and saw Yainar standing in front of her, flanked by Hurinara and three other elders. Derneren was with them, and several junior hunters.

"What happened in there?" Yainar said, reaching out and grabbing Kori's shoulder. "Derneren wouldn't let us go inside—"

"Go in!" Kori gasped. "She needs to talk to you. Quickly, go in!"

Hurinara moved closer to Kori, eyed her doubtfully for a moment, then ducked into the hut. One by one the other elders followed him, and then Yainar went in after them.

Kori closed her eyes again. Maybe, she thought, her mother would live. Immar had such willpower, surely it was possible. Kori found herself hoping desperately that it would be so. The last thing she wanted was the burden of Immar's legacy, because there was no way she could be true to it. She could never deceive her people and claim it was for their own good.

The door flap rustled beside her, and she saw Yainar emerging. She wondered why he was coming out so soon. "What is it?" she asked. Then she saw his expression, and she realized she knew the answer.

Yainar nodded slowly. "Your mother has died."

PART 4:
RETRIBUTION

30

One hut in the tribe was larger than all the others—large enough for a score of men to sit together in a circle. Here, the chieftain and the elders could gather to talk and argue and reach an agreement on what was best for the tribe. Here, also, they could decide when to hunt, on what day to celebrate the end of winter, and when pairings would take place.

No woman had ever entered this hut. The Island Tribe clung to the tradition of a man leading them. They knew that Immar had a different kind of power, bestowed by the spirits. Still, even she had always been excluded from the Elders' House.

Today was different. Today, Kori entered the house.

Yainar led her in, and she saw a small fire surrounded by twenty mats woven from reeds, placed in a circle. Eight of the mats were empty; on the remaining twelve, elders sat.

Hurinara was in the place of honor, on the far side of the fire, facing the door. His back was rigid, his eyes impassive, his mouth a thin line. He was wearing his ceremonial clothes: a headdress of eagle, hawk, crow, and owl feathers;

leggings stitched from scores of fine soft moleskins; and a robe of elk skin. He wore a necklace of bear teeth, and he held a spear ornamented with feathers from blue jays and redwings.

Kori thought she saw his wrinkled face tighten with disapproval as she stepped across the threshold. Finally, though, he inclined his head, allowing her and Yainar to kneel.

For a long while there was silence, and Kori felt it pressing in on her, maddening her, because surely there was no time to waste. She knew better, though, than to speak before she was spoken to. She sat without moving, trying to be patient as well as she could.

Finally Hurinara spoke. "You are here," he said, "to answer our questions. We must act, but before we can act, we must understand. This is a very grave matter, because our tribe has never been in such a state of danger."

He spoke slowly, formally, and she found it difficult to remain silent. If it was so important to act, why did he waste time talking about it? At the same time her own survival was now linked inextricably with the survival of her people. She could no longer afford to make enemies.

Hurinara turned to Yainar. "Do you know, yet, how many were killed?"

"Twenty-two," he said. "And several more wounded. I think the whitebeasts would have killed us all if they had had the chance."

"So," said Hurinara. "Are we certain these men are truly men, as we are? Are we sure they are not Old Ones?"

"One of them is lying dead in my hut," Kori said. "He seems a mortal man. I speared and killed another who was trying to cast all our canoes adrift."

An elder named Jojokin leaned forward. "You cast a spear?" he stared at her with a mixture of disapproval and disbelief.

Kori nodded. "I took it from the warrior who came into my hut."

"I cut the bonds tying Kori's ankles," Yainar interrupted quickly, "so she could defend herself."

"Wait," said Jojokin. He had a reputation for quibbling over details. "Who killed the warrior in your hut?"

Kori hesitated.

"I did," Yainar said.

Jojokin shook his head. "But what were you doing in her hut, Yainar? You were supposed to be guarding it outside."

"I went into the hut," Yainar said calmly, "because she called to me. She was thirsty and needed water."

Hurinara gave him a stern look. "If you had stayed outside, you would have seen the invaders. You could have shouted an alarm."

Kori couldn't stand it any longer. She held up her hand. "May I speak?"

Hurinara glared at her. "What do you have to say?"

Kori saw that this might be her only chance to exert any influence here. "The whitebeasts are searching for a safe haven where they can spend the winter," she said. "They were forced from their land in the north by another tribe—"

"*Another* tribe?" It was Gloshin speaking this time. He glanced at the others in the circle, then stared at Kori with undisguised animosity. "First you ask us to believe that we share the world with a second tribe. And now there is a third?"

"I believe there are many," Kori said.

There was a murmur of disbelief.

"The world is far larger than we ever knew," Kori insisted.

"But these whitebeasts," said Hurinara. "How can you be sure that the Old Ones did not create them—to test us, perhaps?"

Kori sighed. "I have told you what I was told, and what I believe. The whitebeasts were forced to give up their land, so they feel they have a right to steal our land in turn. But they are men and women and children, they are human beings, not beasts." She hesitated. She knew what she wanted to say—what she *had* to say, if she was ever going to see Uroh again.

"Perhaps," she said tentatively, "if we show them that we will fight back fiercely if they attack, but we are willing to share our land with them if they come in peace, there will be no need for any more bloodshed. Our island is large enough for many people."

The elders stared at her in disbelief. They started voicing their shock, their outrage. The murmur grew to a cacophony. Some of them got up onto their feet to denounce her.

"Enough," said Hurinara. He pounded the floor with the end of his spear. "Quiet!"

The outburst slowly subsided. Kori looked down at her hands in her lap. Once again, she had merely succeeded in outraging people instead of persuading them to listen to her.

"These beasts killed more than a score of our people," Hurinara said. "We can never live in peace with them."

"My own mother and father have died," Kori countered. "What does it benefit me to kill the whitebeasts in revenge? How can it help any of us?"

"Quiet!" Hurinara's jaw jutted out. He pointed at her and his finger trembled with anger. "You are a woman. You must be silent, now."

Kori saw that if she tried to speak more, she would be sent out of the house. She sat mute, staring at the floor in front of her.

"I don't think you can be trusted," Hurinara went on. "I don't understand your dealings with these whitebeasts. I think you may have collaborated in some way with them."

Another of the elders coughed politely to show that he wished to speak. "She did take the life of a whitebeast who was trying to cut loose our canoes," he said.

Hurinara gestured dismissively. "She has no skill with a spear. She may have been trying *not* to hit him. We cannot be sure of anything, except she has threatened us all, and these whitebeasts came here after she spoke against—against the Old Ones." His voice dropped with respect as he said the words. He turned to Yainar. "What are your thoughts on all this?"

Yainar inclined his head respectfully. "I sent a dozen youngsters out around the island. One of them found three rafts made of logs lashed together with vines on the beach at the northern end of the island. This is how the warriors came here from the Western Shore."

"Ah." Hurinara nodded. "And your young men are still watching the river in case of another attack?"

"Of course."

"Very good, Yainar. We must see that our island is well defended. Now, what else?"

Yainar didn't hesitate. "I would like to take six hunters to the Western Shore, to track the whitebeasts. We know now that the Western Shore is safe for people, because Kori went there and returned. If we track the whitebeasts, we may find where they are hiding and how many of them there are. Then, perhaps, we may attack and kill them all." He spoke quietly, confidently, looking from one elder to the next. "I believe we must kill them," he said, "to be safe."

There was a murmur of concern. An elder named Grebir leaned forward. "You want us to hunt them like animals?" he said. He was a cautious man, always warning people about dangers. "We will be massacred," he complained. "Even if the Old Ones allow us to set foot on their land—"

"But we may all be killed," said Yainar, "if we don't hunt them."

"The risk is still too great," Grebir said.

"The Western Shore is no place for us to venture," another elder said.

"I'm not so sure," said Hurinara. "I like this young man's spirit. You know, I remember when Rohonar's father was still alive. There was more fighting spirit in those days."

So it was true, Kori thought.

"We must discuss this plan," Hurinara went on.

Kori could see how much influence the old man wielded among the elders. They would complain and express their doubts, but in the end, what was Yainar asking? Only for a small number of men. He had carefully suggested a plan that would create the least amount of risk for the tribe and would also allow him, a junior hunter, to take a commanding role.

She tried to imagine what would have happened if Immar hadn't died. She would have gone into one of her fits, she would have been lifted up onto the Speaking Rock, and then she would have opened her eyes and told the tribe that the Old Ones were testing them, and her people must defend their territory. There would have been no rash talk about chasing the whitebeasts onto the Western Shore. Everyone would have rallied together, and they would have waited patiently knowing that sooner or later the whitebeasts would attack again. And probably, if the tribe stayed on the island, they would be able to defend themselves, because their island was such a secure refuge. Only a foolish man, eager to prove his courage, would venture away from it.

Perhaps, Kori thought, this wild male spirit could never be controlled. Perhaps the only safe solution was to turn it against an imaginary enemy. In that case, although it sickened her to have to admit it, Immar might have been right.

The elders were arguing among themselves now. Kori watched them with fatalistic detachment, knowing she would not be allowed to speak and knowing that they wouldn't listen to her anyway. She saw Hurinara rising to his feet, while the other old men fell silent. With surprise she realized that the meeting was over.

"It is decided," Hurinara said, standing proudly in his fine clothes. "Four men will go with Yainar, not six, and they shall be junior hunters. They will explore the Western Shore and search for the whitebeast warriors." He nodded to himself, then turned to Kori. "And you will accompany them, in case—" He looked at her doubtfully. "In case your knowledge of the land may be useful." He raised his spear and smote the shaft's end on the ground.

"It is decided," the elders echoed.

31

Yainar's hut was filled with trophies testifying to his prowess as a hunter. The pelts of lions and pumas covered the walls. He owned more than a score of spears. Elk and deer antlers and necklaces of lion teeth hung from the ceiling. A huge section of mammoth hide covered most of the floor, bequeathed to him by his father, who had died from injuries he sustained on that hunt.

There was no bed of birch boughs, just a big brown bearskin doubled over at one end of the hut. At the other end his tools were meticulously laid out on a square of bleached deerskin: flint knives, axes, shapers, and bone drills. Lengths of hardwood stood around the fireplace, drying slowly. Other lengths had been stripped and planed; still others had been soaked in musk oil and were waiting to be burnished.

"You should sit there," said Yainar, pointing to the bed of bearskins.

Kori did as he said. "Why do you keep this?" she asked, pointing to a tiny squirrel pelt that had been carefully mounted on a rectangle of birch bark above the bed.

"My first trophy. When I was five." He went to a corner where fish nets were piled with discarded scraps of leather, and he started rummaging through his supplies. "You understand, Kori, I spoke for you. I have taken responsibility for you, because I still believe you can help us if you choose."

"You speak as though I'm a child," she said angrily.

"Not a child, a rebel. Can you deny that you've rebelled against everything our tribe believes in?"

She looked at him defiantly. "You don't believe in most of it, either."

"I'm sensible enough, though, to keep my beliefs to myself." He turned, holding some thongs. "Now, since I cannot trust you, I will have to restrain you again."

She stared at him in disbelief. "Why?"

His face tightened. "Because I can't trust you. Remember, you are my responsibility now."

She looked at the thongs with a feeling of dread. "How will I walk with your men on the Western Shore if my ankles are tied?"

He shook his head. "Not your ankles, this time. You must be free to walk or run. But the elders were shocked that you had thrown a spear." He moved closer to her. "There'll be no further danger of that if your wrists are bound. It will also be a reminder to everyone that you are under my control."

She folded her arms and lowered her head. "And if I refuse?"

He shrugged. "Then I cannot take you with our party. You'll be a prisoner in your hut again. Which do you prefer?"

She thought of being confined to her hut. That would be intolerable. On the other hand, if she went to the Western Shore, she might have some faint chance of seeing Uroh—or protecting him, if the hunters found him.

"I will go with you," she said reluctantly.

"Hold out your left wrist," he told her.

"You forget," she said, "I saved your life. When the

warrior came into my hut and was about to kill you, if it
hadn't been for me, you'd be dead by now. And I was the
one who shouted the alarm. Isn't this so?"

Yainar sighed. "Yes, and you are the one who struck me a
savage blow." He touched the side of his face where her heels
had hit him, and Kori saw that the skin was swollen and a
bruise was forming. "You abandoned me naked on the floor,"
Yainar went on. "You came back and freed me, but only
because it served your purposes. So, Kori, obviously I cannot
trust you."

Reluctantly, she gave him her wrist. He carefully wound
one of the heavy thongs around it and knotted it, tightening
it with his teeth. With a flint knife he trimmed the thong as
close to the knot as possible. "Now the other wrist," he said.

It was terrible to be treated like this, but what other
choice did she have?

She gave Yainar her right wrist and watched as he
wrapped the second thong around it, threading it through
the first, so they were linked. Once again he tightened the
knot and trimmed it. Then he went to the fire in the corner
and fetched some elderwood resin, just as her father had
done when he hobbled her ankles. Carefully Yainar poured it
over one knot, then the other. He blew on it till it cooled,
then moved back, satisfied.

"You understand, Kori," he said, "I still have my ambitions. Hurinara will act as our chieftain, but only for a short
while. Sooner or later, if you learn to control your tongue
and reassure people instead of turning them against you, the
tribe will want to see you carry on the line of your family.
This is a natural desire, and it will be natural for your mate
to be the chieftain, especially if he is a strong, brave hunter
who has proved his courage and his judgment."

Once again she tried to imagine what he had in mind, and
helplessly, with a feeling of utter dismay, she realized that
now, it might be the best prospect she could hope for if there

was no way she could be with Uroh. At least with Yainar she would have some status in the tribe.

He was watching her carefully. "I think you are beginning to see sense at last," he said. "And now that your mother is gone, perhaps you will be less rebellious, too." He nodded to himself. "But you still have a lot to learn. Lie down on your stomach." He pointed to the bed of bearskins.

She hesitated. "Why?"

He leaned closer to her, till his handsome face filled her view. He was looking at her in a different way from before, and she felt a strange premonition. His eyes were brighter, and his teeth were showing between his parted lips. He almost looked as if he wanted to devour her.

He reached out and gently stroked her cheek. "You know," he said, "when we were out at the Gathering Place and I said you were not attractive to me, I lied. You are a good-looking woman, Kori."

With no warning, he slapped her with his open palm. It was a powerful blow, and she found herself falling, crying out, landing painfully on her shoulder on the furs.

"But when I tell you to do something," he snapped at her, "you will obey me."

Kori looked up at him in shock. He still seemed as calm as before, still measuring his words, but she saw a hunger in him now—the hunger of a hunter.

"You have no right!" she cried.

"No," he said. "*You* have no right. You are in my custody, Kori."

"Even if I were paired with you, you would have no right to treat me this way." She started to scramble up.

He reached out so quickly, she barely saw his hand. She yelped with pain as he grabbed her by the neck, swung her around, and threw her facedown on the furs. He stepped over her, then sat down on the small of her back, pinning her. "I see I have to teach you to obey me," he said. He seized her by the hair and jerked her head back. She opened her mouth to scream—and found something being thrust between her teeth. It was a piece of rolled goatskin, she realized. A thong was strung through it. Swiftly, Yainar knotted it behind her head, and she realized with fury that all of this had been planned.

She made helpless, desperate noises as he seized her leggings, dragged them off, and threw them aside. He stood up, then, and placed one foot upon her neck, holding her firmly while she writhed and kicked her feet. He grabbed a bundle of thongs and swung them, lashing them across her naked buttocks.

Never had she imagined being treated like this by a man. It filled her with rage—all the more because he was doing it so casually, with such idle contempt. He whipped her again with the thongs, and she flinched from the pain. He lashed her again, and again, till her buttocks felt as if someone had sprinkled glowing embers across them. She tried with all her strength to twist away from him, but it was hard for her to move with her hands tied together, pressed between her stomach and the bearskin under her. She screamed, but the goatskin filled her mouth, muffling the sound.

Finally Yainar stepped back and tossed the thongs aside. He stood for a moment, looking down at her, and she heard him breathing heavily. "You will learn," he said, "that it's painful to defy me. What you did to me in your hut—you will learn *never* do that again."

She turned her face toward the wall, refusing to look at him.

"Now," he went on, "there is another thing we have to settle."

She heard the rustle of skins as he shed his robe. He kicked off his leggings and she felt the heat of his body as he kneeled behind her.

Kori wriggled onto her side. She raised her hands and pushed herself up. If she could get up onto her feet—

He seized her ankles and jerked them hard, straightening her legs and throwing her flat again. Then he fell down on her, pinning her with his weight. His breath was hot on her neck. She felt his chest against her back, rising and falling rapidly.

"You offered yourself to me in your hut," he said with his lips almost touching her ear. "I have not forgotten that, Kori." He seized her by the hair and gave her a little shake. "If a woman offers herself, she should expect to be taken." He turned her head to one side so that he could see her face. Her cheek was red where he had slapped her, and he trailed his fingers across the inflamed skin, watching her flinch from him.

Then he reached down to his crotch, and she felt him guiding himself between her thighs. He moved with such assurance, she was sure this couldn't be the first time he had forced himself on a woman. She wondered how many girls in the tribe had been assaulted by him and had been too afraid to tell anyone afterward. The thought enraged her. Then she remembered how she had wanted him once, and she was filled with fury. He was charming, handsome, and utterly confident. He had even revealed himself as a rebel not so different from her. But underneath—underneath, he cared only for power. That was why he was doing this to her now.

He forced his knees between hers, then reached down and raised her hips. Kori wasn't bothering to struggle any-more; she could see he was going to take her, and if she kept trying to defy him, it would only anger him again. She tried to pretend she was not here in his hut. She thought of the forest, and the rocky slope of Mount Tomomor, and Uroh—

She cried out behind her gag as Yainar forced himself into her, and she realized it was wrong to think of Uroh now, while she was being defiled like this. It was an insult to her sweet memories.

Yainar seized her by her shoulders and jerked his hips once, twice, and a third time—then his hands clenched and Kori felt his muscles stiffen.

She suddenly realized he was not going to pull out of her. She felt panic. The idea of bearing his child was so awful, it filled her with fear. She squirmed with wild desperation and managed to pull her hips away from him just as he reached his climax.

He slumped down, gasping, then made a tormented sound. He seized her again by the hair and shook her. "Why did you do that?" He twisted his fingers in her hair till she shrieked with pain. "Why?"

She turned her head and saw him glaring at her. His cheeks were flushed and his forehead was damp. The hunger that she saw before had disappeared. It was replaced now with simple anger.

He fumbled with the thong tying her gag, managed to loosen it, and jerked the goatskin from her mouth. "Why?" he demanded again.

Kori swallowed. She licked her bruised lips. "You think I want to bear your child?"

He dropped her down onto the bearskins and kneeled over her for a moment, panting. "You're right," he said. His voice had changed. His anger had gone and he had regained his normal control. He was calm again. "We are not paired." He laughed as he turned away and pulled on his leggings. "In my mind—in my mind, I was already the chieftain of this tribe, and you were my mate."

Kori saw that something about her had blurred his thoughts and weakened his grasp on reality. Could it merely be her family status?

He put on his robe, then untied his braids and shook them out. Calmly he started to rebraid them. "So," he said, "now you know how it feels to be taken by a man." He kicked her leggings to her. "Did it hurt?"

"Yes," she said. With her hands tied together, it was hard for her to dress herself, but not impossible. "What I don't understand," she said as she struggled into her leggings, "is that not so long ago, you told me you admire my spirit."

"That is true." He seated himself cross-legged on the floor and watched as she covered her nakedness. "But I also admire the spirit of a mountain lion. It is the way of a man to conquer that spirit."

Suddenly she understood. "And that is all you want," she said. "To conquer me as if I were an animal."

He shook his head, frowning. "It's not the same." He rubbed his jaw thoughtfully. "All I require is that a woman defers to a man. She can still be helpful, she can give useful advice—as you will, Kori, when you're with us on the Western Shore. You alone have been there. You may be able to guide us. Even so, I will be the one who makes the decisions and gives commands. You cannot do that."

She thought of him leading his small group of young warriors through the forest, and she knew instinctively that he would be so determined to prove himself and win acclaim from his people, he would expose everyone to unnecessary hardship and danger. And what if he found poor Uroh? How could she stop them from killing him—or torturing him?

"You seem worried," Yainar said, studying her features with shrewd eyes. "You're thinking about the journey we'll be taking, yes? What is it—you think we'll find that white-beast who deceived you?" He leaned forward intently. "And maybe old Hurinara was right, just for once. Maybe you do have some loyalty there."

She laughed sourly. "The whitebeasts killed my parents. They would have killed all of us. How could I have any loyalty to them?"

He was still studying her. "There was no blood when I

took you just now," he said slowly. His jaw clenched and his face changed as his anger returned. "You coupled with one of them! Yes, when I was with you in your hut, you were so bold with me—you showed off your body as a virgin never would."

"But none of this is true!" Kori protested.

He sprang up suddenly and paced across the floor of his hut. He seized a spear and whirled around. He glared at Kori. "Your whitebeast lover is still there on the Western Shore. That's why you wanted us to make peace with them, so you could have him. Isn't that so?"

"No!" Kori cried again.

He shook his head. "You don't deceive me, Kori." He turned his spear between his hands. He ran his thumb slowly over the sharp edge of the flint and once again she saw the hunting hunger in his face. "We will kill all of those whitebeasts," he said, caressing the weapon. "And when we find the one that defiled you—I promise you, he will die an especially slow and painful death."

32

He left her alone for most of the afternoon. She heard him briefly outside the hut talking to Hurinara, arranging for more hunters to be posted along the shore of the island; and then he was gone.

She lay for a long time on the bearskins in his hut. She knew she could get up and leave if she chose, and perhaps she should help her people cope with the chaos that had been inflicted by the warriors. Somehow, though, she lacked the strength. She had hardly slept, she had lost all her closest kinfolk, she felt exhausted and abused, and she hated the idea of appearing in public with her wrists tied.

So she lay on the skins, facing the wall, trying to forget all the terrible things that had happened. And after a while, she slept.

When she woke she saw men entering the hut. There was Yainar, Derneren, and three others, all aged eighteen or nine-teen. One she recognized as Nikoro: a thin, intelligent, wild-eyed youngster, prone to sudden moods but fiercely loyal to Yainar. Then there was Siew, good-natured, amiable, and strong, although he walked with a limp and was known to be inaccurate with a spear. Finally there was Euri, shy and quiet, a man who always tried to do what others wanted because he hated any form of disagreement.

So, Kori thought, these were the young men who would be journeying with Yainar to the Western Shore. Looking at them, she realized that Hurinara must have little confidence in this expedition. All the strongest, experienced hunters would remain on the island, protecting it; the ones who would follow Yainar were expendable.

Undoubtedly Yainar was shrewd enough to realize this, but he gave no sign of it. He was smiling and slapping the men's shoulders as they entered the hut, and they were grinning, looking proud that they had been chosen.

"Kori," Yainar called to her, "there's food in the Meeting Place. Bring some for my men."

They fell silent, turning and looking at her where she lay on the bed of furs. She felt her cheeks redden as she wondered whether they could guess that Yainar had forced himself on her. She wanted to tell him to get his own food, but once again she knew that if she defied him, she would pay for it later. Was this how it would always be, obeying Yainar's whims for fear of him punishing her?

No, she told herself. Sooner or later there would have to be an opportunity to free herself from her bonds and her servitude. She didn't yet see how it could happen, but it *had* to happen.

She stood and walked among the men to the door. She felt their stares as she brushed between them.

"Kori will be coming with us," Yainar said. "She will be useful, I think. I realize she has caused unrest here, but all that is under control, now."

A couple of the men saw the thongs joining Kori's wrists and grinned self-consciously. Kori bit back the words she longed to say and ducked out of the hut, tense with anger.

She found mostly women and children at the Meeting Place, chanting and praying for their dead kinfolk. Kori tried to avoid being seen as much as she could; she moved around the edge of the circle, keeping in the shadows, hiding her wrists in the folds of her robe. Still, many people turned and looked at her. Some seemed cautious or hostile, but others looked at her with regret, and she realized they were wishing she were better suited to inherit her parents' roles. Without Immar, there was no one to speak for the Old Ones. Without Rohonar, there was no one standing strong, making people feel secure. Hurinara was here in the Meeting Place, moving from one family to the next, trying to reassure his people, but he was a frail old man. The villagers looked scared and lost.

Could Kori ever guide them? She shied away from the idea. People should guide themselves, not hope that someone else would do it for them.

She went to the fire, where the carcass of a boar was roasting. Awkwardly, with her wrists tied, she cut sections from it, nodding and acknowledging the embarrassed greetings from people close by. She piled the meat on a piece of bark, then quickly ran back to Yainar's hut.

She found the men sitting in a circle, listening earnestly while Yainar discussed his strategy. All of them were holding weapons—knives, spears, and wooden clubs—which they toyed with and gestured with while they spoke. Kori looked at their weapons, then at their faces, and she saw boys wanting to be men, and men wanting to hunt other men. So, this was the spirit her mother had spoken of.

Kori set the food down in the center of the circle. She suddenly missed Uroh more than she could bear, regardless of the lies he had told her. Her days with him on the rocky slope of Mount Tomomor seemed so distant and unreachable, she was filled with despair.

The men hardly noticed her as she left the food and

moved back to her place on Yainar's bed, and as she sat there silently watching them, she saw that they only picked absent-mindedly at their meal. There was something on their minds that was far more important than women or food: the prospect of revenge.

Later, after the men returned to their own homes, Yainar came and sat beside her. He looked pleased with himself, and she saw that this was what satisfied him most: to lead a party of men and be warmed by their respect.

"We'll set out before dawn," he told her, stretching out his legs and leaning against the stone wall. "I took a canoe and traveled up and down the river today, close to the Western Shore. I saw a place where it looked as if trees had been felled."

She watched him warily, wondering why he was telling her this.

"That's where they built their rafts," he explained. "The riverbank is not so steep there. It slopes down."

"But why should they return to the same place?" she asked.

"Because they stole some of our canoes, and the canoes are too valuable to be discarded. They must have wanted to pull the canoes out of the river to hide them from us."

She saw that he was probably right.

"So perhaps you have some confidence in our journey now," he went on.

Was he looking for approval from her? The idea revolted her. "I believe we'll probably be killed," she said calmly, "because the whitebeast warriors have had more practice than you at hunting men and murdering them."

His smile faded, and his eyes were cold. "Do you want me to punish you again?" he said softly.

"You asked my opinion," she said, refusing to be intimidated by him. "You wouldn't want me to lie to you."

He thought about that for a moment. She saw him glance toward the bundle of thongs that he had lashed her with before, and she tensed herself for the possibility that he would use them. But then he seemed to change his mind. "Take off your leggings," he told her.

Kori thought of disobeying him, but there was no point. She bared herself, silently vowing that one day, she would not only escape from him, she would destroy him. He knew nothing of that, of course. He sat watching her through half-closed eyes, moving his hand to touch himself under his own clothes. Then, when she was naked from the waist down, he gestured for her to turn over.

"Must it always be like this?" she asked. "On my elbows and knees, like an animal?"

"It's a woman's duty to serve her man in any way he chooses," he said as he moved behind her.

Maybe, she thought, he didn't know there were other ways in which to couple together. It would be dangerous, though, to try to tell him. He might take it as an insult to his manhood, or he might assume she had acquired her experience from Uroh.

She winced with pain as he took her as roughly and quickly as he had before. She hated him for his arrogance and his callousness. Her only consolation was that this time he remembered to pull himself out of her before he climaxed.

"We will sleep, now," he said after he finished. He stretched out on the furs, reached for one of the thongs that he had used to lash her, and knotted it around the other thongs binding her wrists. She saw he took care to tie it tight and close between her wrists, so that she wouldn't be able to reach the knots even with her teeth.

He took the other end of the thong and tied it around his own wrist, so she was tethered to him. "There are many spears and knives in my hut," he explained. "I'll sleep more soundly, Kori, knowing that you cannot reach them."

The thought of killing him hadn't occurred to her. She wondered for a moment if she could do it, but the idea turned her stomach. There had been too much bloodshed already. She wanted less, not more. And if the villagers ever found that she had killed a man like Yainar, she was sure they would show her no mercy.

"You will sleep there," he said, pointing beside his bed.

"On the floor?" She stared at him.

He shrugged. "This is my bed, not yours." He picked up a sheepskin and dumped it beside her. "Pull that over you if you're cold."

She watched him with disdain as he lay down and turned his back to her. Soon, she told herself, she would find a way to move against him—provided she survived the journey that he had planned.

33

She woke suddenly, with her pulse racing. The floor was trembling. Instinctively she peered around in the darkness, looking for Oam. So many times he slept through earthquakes. So often, she had to waken him and warn him—

But of course Oam was gone, and her parents were gone, and she was in Yainar's hut, lying on the hard floor. He was already sitting up, jumping to his feet, dragging her with the thong that linked the two of them. "Come on!" he shouted at her.

She struggled after him, out of the hut. She saw a light that she thought, at first, came from the rising sun. But it came from the west, and she realized that Mount Tomomor was erupting again. The yellow fire at its summit cast a sickly glow over the forest and the river.

The earth tremor died away, but Mount Tomomor continued venting fire. Kori felt shocked. Usually there was a lull of several months, at least, between one eruption and the next. "The people will be fearful," she said, "especially since they don't have Immar to guide them anymore. You may find it hard to persuade your men to set foot on the Western Shore. They'll believe—"

"They'll believe whatever I tell them." He cut her off coldly. He glanced quickly around. "In fact, we should set out now. Dawn can't be far away." He glanced at the thong attaching her to him, and he untied his end of it. "You should go to the dock," he said. "Pick out the best canoe for the six of us. We'll be there soon enough."

He turned and ducked back into his hut.

Kori walked slowly among the huts. People were emerging, looking exhausted but fearful, and hurrying to the Meeting Place. Soon, she thought, there would be more chanting, more begging for mercy from the wrathful spirits.

She walked out of the village, down to the dock, and stood there in the darkness, looking out over the water. She remembered coming here alone after Shashin died, and she marveled that her world could have changed so much in such a short time. That made her think of Uroh, and she wondered if he could see her standing here from the Western Shore. Where was he now? What was he thinking? Was he thinking of her, waiting for her?

"Kori!" the voice came from behind her, and she heard footsteps. She turned and saw Yainar leading the four other men. Their faces looked sallow in the dim, flickering light.

Yainar stopped beside her. "Did you pick a canoe?"

"That one," she said, choosing one at random.

"Seat yourself in it." He turned to his men. "Siew, stow these spears. Derneren, take these food bags."

The men glanced at each other uneasily. "Perhaps we should wait," said Siew, "till the Old Ones are less angry."

Yainar grunted with annoyance. "We are their children, their chosen ones. Remember that! We have been dutiful. We have served them loyally. Why should they feel any anger toward us? No, they are angry that the beasts in their white furs have taken so many of our loved ones. They are angry with the men we seek to kill."

"But we can't be sure," said Nikoro. His thin face turned to each person in turn. His large eyes looked nervous. "Now that Immar is gone, we can no longer know what the Old Ones say."

Yainar gestured at Kori where she was seating herself in the canoe. "See, Immar's daughter. Does she seem afraid? She knows there's nothing to fear on the Western Shore. She's been there and returned. A mere woman!" He turned back to his men. "And *you* are still scared?" He paused, eyeing them. "Well, are you? If you are, speak now. I won't have any cowards on this journey."

He waited. No one met his eyes. No one answered.

Still, he wasn't content to leave it there. "Derneren," he said, "are you afraid?"

"No." The word was clear and plain.

"Euri? Siew? Nikoro?"

"No," they answered—and Kori saw their courage returning. Somehow it had helped them to be challenged. Yainar had scoffed at their fears, and now they were agreeing with him, sharing his disdain and his casual confidence.

"Finish loading the canoe," Yainar said. "We must hurry. I want to be upstream before dawn."

They showed no further hesitation as they obeyed him.

The paddles dipped silently, and the canoes moved slowly upstream. The black water was touched with yellow as Mount Tomomor continued to cast its flickering light, and Yainar guided the canoe closer to the Western Shore, where the forest cast a long shadow.

Kori felt nervous to be traveling so close to the land, and she found herself crouching low, half expecting a hail of spears to come flying out from among the trees. But she could see that Yainar was right; so long as they stayed in the shadow, they were virtually invisible in the night.

As they followed the curve of the river around the northern end of the island, Yainar murmured a command and the men ceased paddling. The canoe drifted on, gradually slowing against the current. Yainar turned it slightly, and the bow edged close to the shore. There was a faint rasping sound from below as the canoe grounded itself less than an arm's length from the tumbled rocks on the riverbank.

Kori threw out a thong to tether the canoe, then climbed out and onto the rocks, moving awkwardly with her wrists tied. She waited, feeling exposed and frightened, while the men quietly unloaded their spears, bedrolls, and packs of provisions and joined her, one by one. Without a word, the burdens were divided and shared.

Everyone paused, then, looking toward Yainar. Kori saw tension in the men's faces and fear in their eyes. Yainar turned from one to the next, clasping each man's arm, patting each man's shoulder, nodding to them reassuringly. He turned, finally, to Kori, and gestured for her to follow directly behind him. Then he started creeping through the night, stooping down, placing his feet with exaggerated caution on the ground, which was littered with stones and gravel. The forest was almost totally dark; the only light came faintly from the river, where ripples reflected the distant glow from Mount Tomomor.

Kori kept as close as she could to Yainar's back. He was taller than she, and his body shielded her, giving her some slight feeling of security. She heard Derneren plodding along behind her, the gravel crunching softly under his moccasins and the leather straps of his pack creaking gently as he moved. The sounds were almost drowned, though, by the constant, distant murmur of the erupting volcano, and Kori found herself feeling grateful for that.

Yainar paused without warning and she almost bumped into

him in the darkness. He reached behind him, steadying her with his hand on her arm. Slowly, then, he crouched down.

She followed his example and peered ahead—and she saw what he had seen. The trees at the edge of the forest, by the water, stood in an unbroken line. A little farther in, though, there was a clearing, and when Kori breathed slowly, smelling and tasting the air, she caught the scent of men.

Yainar turned and pointed. There was a gap in the shoreline where rocks had been heaved aside, leaving a narrow, sloping path down to the water. Clearly, this was where the warriors had built their rafts and launched them.

Yainar took his spear and slid it into the bundle of other spears strapped to his back. He started crawling ahead on hands and knees, moving with extreme caution. Kori copied him as well as she could, though it made her anxious to edge forward, moving slowly, pausing and listening, searching for the slightest sound.

They reached a point where bushes and tall grass at the edge of the forest had been flattened. Yainar turned inland here, crawling close to the edge of the path that the warriors had made. Kori felt her pulse quickening and she silently questioned his decision to take such an obvious way into the forest. Surely, she thought, it would be better to crawl through the protective underbrush. But no; that would create far too much noise. There was no choice: this was the only safe way to proceed.

The trees closed in around them, cutting off the faint radiance reflecting from the river. Then a new source of light came into view. Up ahead, in the clearing where a score of trees had been felled, a fire was burning.

Yainar crawled right to the edge of the clearing and stopped, hunkering down behind some bushes. He tugged at Kori's arm, gesturing to her to move beside him. He beckoned to the four men, also. Soon they were all crouching shoulder to shoulder, peering through the web of vegetation at the camp site that lay just a dozen paces away.

Kori saw two men in white furs sitting astride a fallen log, facing away from each other, back to back, each holding a spear. More spears were standing close by, planted in the ground. Beside the fire, two other men were sleeping. Kori shuddered at the knowledge that these men had slaughtered so many of her people and would slaughter her, too, if they could. At the same time she found herself urgently peering at their faces, feeling a wave of relief as she saw that none of them was Uroh.

Yainar shifted his position slightly and pointed. In the shadows behind the fire were some long, dark shapes. They were the canoes that had been stolen from her tribe.

Yainar turned to Derneren. He edged close to the big man, whispered something in his ear, and gestured quickly. Derneren nodded and started crawling to the left, around the edge of the clearing, staying out of sight behind the natural wall of foliage that grew to knee height.

Yainar went to Siew, next, and gave him instructions. Siew nodded and started crawling away to the right, circling the clearing in the opposite direction.

Finally Yainar beckoned Kori and the other two men. They edged close and bent their heads to his. "Wait," he whispered.

Waiting was an awful torment. Kori felt the hard ground under her, stealing heat from her body. The pack that she wore was heavy on her back, and its straps were tight around her shoulders, making her arms feel numb. She glanced at Yainar and saw him squatting patiently, as if he had no need ever to move from the position he was in. In the faint firelight his face was serene, though his eyes were wide and alert.

Kori wished more than anything that she could leave this place. Perhaps this was the hardest part for her, feeling powerless, forced to accept Yainar's judgment, all the while knowing that she might lose her life if he erred.

And still Yainar waited. Kori tensed as she saw a flicker of movement, and she drew in a breath, feeling a renewed wave of fear—but it was only one of the guards, who had been sitting on the log, standing up and tossing another piece of wood on the fire. He sat back down, and once again Kori found herself trying to calm her fluttering pulse.

When the moment came, it came so quickly that she hardly saw what was happening. There was a faint sound from the opposite side of the clearing—a rustle of foliage that she would have thought was the wind if the night hadn't been so still. One of the guards turned his head, and at the same moment, he made a startled noise, a grunt of surprise that turned into a cry of horror. A spear was embedded in his chest. He lurched to his feet, grabbing at the shaft, his mouth falling open in shock. Suddenly his white fur was splashed with red, and he toppled to the ground, shrieking.

His companion jumped to his feet and Kori glimpsed his startled face as he looked around. At that moment another spear came from nowhere, thudding into his right shoulder.

Kori sensed Nikoro tensing beside her, eager to leap to his feet, but Yainar reached out quickly and grabbed his arm, restraining him. Meanwhile, the figures who had been sleeping by the fire were standing up, looking around in confusion. The wounded man yelled to them. He pointed to the far side of the clearing. The men by the fire seized several spears. They crouched down, peering into the underbrush with their backs turned to Yainar, Kori, Nikoro, and Euri.

Yainar leaped to his feet, seized a spear from the bundle on his back, and cast it in one smooth movement. It struck one of the warriors between the shoulder blades and he fell on his face. Euri and Nikoro were leaping up, now, casting their spears, and suddenly the warriors in their white furs were both lying on the ground, twisting and struggling to escape from Yainar and his men, who came leaping into the clearing, their faces full of killing lust, more spears in their hands.

34

Kori stared at the fallen men. Her pulse was still running fast and her face felt flushed. She felt dizzy; it was hard to swallow. More than anything, she was glad to be alive, but at the same time she was horrified by the carnage. The men were not dying quietly. They were screaming, vomiting, and thrashing on the ground. She could hear their blood hissing as it gushed from their wounds.

Yainar and his men gathered around their prey, watching them with wide-eyed fascination. Then Yainar bent and slit the throats of the three who were most seriously wounded, and their screaming ceased. For a while there was a ghastly bubbling sound, but then even that faded into silence.

Only one of the warriors was now left alive. He was the one who had been wounded in his right shoulder. The spear was still embedded there, and he was lying on his back, propped against the log, staring at Yainar and his companions with an expression of terror.

Yainar moved toward the wounded warrior. He squatted

down in front of the man, took hold of the spear and turned it slightly, screwing it deeper into the wound.

The warrior's jaw clenched tight. Sweat broke out on his forehead. His legs kicked out and he gasped, arching his back.

"Where are the rest of your people?" Yainar said. His voice was quiet, but he wore the same intent, hungry expression that Kori had seen when he assaulted her. He was savoring this, she realized with revulsion. She couldn't stand it; she had to do something.

She ran across the clearing and seized his arm. "Stop!" she shouted at him.

He swung his arm and flung her aside. She found herself falling, landing hard on the ground. She stared at him in surprise—and when he looked at her, he, too, seemed surprised.

"The whitebeast doesn't understand what you're saying!" Kori cried out to him. Cautiously, she got up onto her feet. "Your words are strange to him. Can't you see that?"

Yainar frowned at the wounded man, then at Kori. "His language is different from ours?"

"Yes." It tormented her to have to look at the warrior, but she forced herself to do so. She squatted down beside him. "You understand me?" she asked, trying to speak with the accent she had learned from Uroh.

He nodded, clenching his jaw against his pain.

"Listen to me," Kori said. "This man here is brutal." She gestured to Yainar. "He will enjoy torturing you till you tell the truth."

The wounded man said nothing, but she saw in his eyes that he understood. He breathed deeply, gathering his courage. He was not going to talk; he was going to endure whatever Yainar chose to inflict on him.

"Just tell us where the rest of your warriors are," Kori said. "That's all he wants to know."

The wounded man quickly shook his head.

"What are you saying to him?" Yainar demanded. "Some of the words are clear, but the rest are not."

"I'm asking him what you asked him." She felt as if she was being torn apart, seeing the wounded man's stoic bravery and knowing there was nothing she could do to prevent what was about to happen.

"So he won't tell us?" Yainar muttered an oath. He seized the spear in the wounded man and leaned on it, driving it deeper.

Kori squatted back down beside the man as he writhed on the ground, still with his jaw clenched tight, refusing even to scream. "Just tell me!" she cried. "Tell me anything!"

Yainar paused and the man relaxed for a moment, taking desperate breaths. Suddenly he turned to Kori. "If he removes the spear," he gasped, "I will tell you what you want to know."

Kori looked at him doubtfully. Then she turned to Yainar and told him what the warrior had told her. Yainar stood weighing the words. "All right," he said, "but it will be worse for him if he doesn't keep his word." He took a firm grip on his spear, braced himself, then wrenched it free.

The warrior gasped and slumped back with his eyes closed. For a moment Kori thought he had fainted. She moved closer to him and shook him by his good arm. Yainar frowned and stooped over the man, peering at him in the firelight.

Suddenly the warrior's eyes opened. He vented a terrible cry and seized Yainar's spear in both hands, ignoring the pain from his ruined shoulder. Yainar was caught off balance, leaning forward. The warrior dragged the spear down, and Yainar was unable to stop him. With furious strength, the warrior plunged the tip of the spear into his own chest, into his own heart.

Blood spurted in a thick fountain. Yainar jumped back,

cursing. The warrior let out a triumphant shout and his face showed a terrible pleasure as his life drained out of him and he died, staring at his tormentor.

Yainar's fury was a terrible thing to see. He seized the spear and stabbed the lifeless body again and again, till his strength was exhausted and he slumped down, leaning on the wooden shaft and gasping for breath.

His men watched him uneasily, none of them daring to speak. Kori turned away from the shredded corpse, clutching her stomach, trying not to vomit. The air was thick with the smell of blood and other body fluids. All she could think about was that any of the warriors could just as easily have been Uroh, and if Yainar had tried to torture Uroh and defile his body like that, she would have sacrificed her own life just to stop him.

Yainar paused. He cast aside the dead man's spear and turned away, shaking blood off his hands. His face was calm now; his rage had passed like a storm. "It's unfortunate," he said, "that the whitebeast defied us." He grunted to himself. "I underestimated their courage. Since they tried to kill us on the island in our sleep, I thought they must be cowards."

"Maybe we should go back to the island and tell what we've found." It was Nikoro speaking. His words came out in a rush, and Kori saw that he was trying not to look at the dead men in the clearing.

Yainar eyed Nikoro for a moment, and he saw the fear in him. "I think *you* should be the one to go back to the island," he said. "We'll drag the canoes to the river and link them with thongs. The current will carry you downstream. All you'll need to do is steer yourself."

"What about the rest of you?" Nikoro looked from one face to the next. "Will you stay here?"

"Euri is a fine tracker," said Yainar, nodding toward the shy man standing away to one side. "At least a score of whitebeast warriors came here after they fled from our island, and apparently they left the canoes here and went deeper into the forest. Such a large number of men must have left a trail that will be easy to follow."

Siew looked at him uneasily. "I think we should get help," he said.

Yainar laughed without humor. "Of course we should get help. But Hurinara made it clear to me that he'll risk no more hunters on the Western Shore till we actually find the white-beast warriors."

Siew looked thoughtful. "So what do you suggest—we track them and then send word back?"

"I see no other way," said Yainar. "Do you?"

Siew thought about it some more. Finally he nodded. "We'll do as you say."

Kori saw Euri nodding his agreement. As for Derneren—he wasn't even listening. He was standing to one side, looking down at one of the dead warriors and nudging the body with his foot. Kori guessed that Derneren was so simple-mindedly loyal, he would go along with anything that Yainar decided.

"It's agreed, then," said Yainar. "Nikoro will take the canoes back to the island, and we'll continue." He squinted through the trees toward the east, where faint gray light was showing among the leaves. "The sun will be up soon, and for all we know, the warriors may return here. We should move quickly now."

Each of the canoes measured at least two man-lengths from end to end, and they had been hewn from massive pine logs. They were so heavy that the five men and Kori were barely able to drag them, one by one, out of the clearing and down to the river.

The sun was shining brightly by the time the task was done, dimming the yellow glow from Mount Tomomor. Kori watched Yainar moving from one canoe to the next, carefully tying them bow-to-stern. Then he stepped back and paused.

"I believe there's one more thing," he said, "that needs to be done." He turned to Siew, Euri, and Derneren. "Come," he said. "Back to the clearing." He glanced at Kori and Nikoro. "You wait here."

Kori's shoulders ached from the effort of dragging the canoes, and her hands were red and sore. She tried not to think about the forest behind her, and she tried to forget about the atrocity she had witnessed in the clearing and the constant distant rumbling of Mount Tomomor. She sat on a rock and looked across the river at the forest on the opposite shore, and she tried to think of nothing at all.

"Kori?" Nikoro moved closer to her. He seemed shy about dealing with her—shy about dealing with any woman, Kori thought to herself. Perhaps that was why he followed Yainar: he saw Yainar's easy confidence and imagined he could acquire some of it for himself.

"What is it, Nikoro?" she said. She wasn't sure whether she disliked him or pitied him. All she knew was that she didn't want him near her.

"Do you still believe there are—that the Old Ones, they don't exist?"

It was hard for him to speak the words. His large eyes moved anxiously, expecting to be punished.

Kori looked at his pale, feral face. She chose her words carefully, knowing that if she said anything shocking, he would probably repeat it to other villagers after he got back to the island. "I'm not sure if the Old Ones exist," she said. "What do you think?"

"Don't know." Again, he glanced quickly around. "Never thought I'd be here on the Western Shore. But it doesn't look so different from the Eastern Shore." He licked his thin lips. "Yainar says we should be able to hunt here if we want. He says we've been too fearful of the spirits. The spirits are our friends, not our enemies."

He was looking to her for reassurance. He wanted her to

confirm what Yainar had told him. In months to come, if the whitebeast warriors could be conquered, there'd be a lot of young men like Nikoro looking at the Western Shore and hoping for an opportunity to prove themselves. Kori realized that this was how the Island Tribe's superstitions would be overcome: not by argument or thought, but through the desire to explore and conquer.

She heard a noise behind her. She turned quickly, but saw that it was only Yainar and the three other men returning from the forest. They were moving slowly, breathing hard as they dragged the dead warriors after them, leaving a rich red trail across the green foliage.

Yainar heaved one of the dead men into each of the canoes, then turned to Nikoro. "Make sure that Hurinara sees them," he said. "Do you understand?"

Nikoro nodded. "Yes, Yainar. Of course."

Yainar paused a moment. "And you should take our own canoe back with the four that the warriors stole. We can shout for help when we need to get to the island later."

"I don't like that," Siew said. "I don't want to be stranded—"

"And I don't want the warriors to come back here, find our canoe, and steal it." Yainar strode over to it and tied it to the others. "Go, now," he said. He waited and watched while Nikoro stepped into the first canoe and pushed off from the shore. The five canoes were soon drifting with the current, moving away from the bank, into the middle of the river.

Yainar turned away, then, seeming just as calmly confident as before. "Come," he said, heading back into the forest.

35

The whitebeast warriors had made no attempt to conceal the path they had taken. It was so clearly marked, Kori herself could have followed it without any help. Grass was trampled, twigs were broken, and green leaves lay on the ground where they had been torn from low branches.

"It worries me," said Siew, "that these warriors are so sure of themselves."

"It doesn't worry me," said Yainar. "The more sure of themselves they are, the less they will be expecting us, and the more vulnerable they will be. They certainly won't expect us here while Mount Tomomor is flaming." He gave Siew a sly, calculating look. "They think we're all superstitious fools."

Kori remembered what Uroh had told her—that there were other scouts like him on the Western Shore. The whitebeasts had reason to be sure of themselves: they had learned this territory well, and their scouts were well practiced at watching without being seen.

She mentioned her thoughts quietly to Yainar when they

stopped to eat a small meal around noontime. They had come to another clearing in the forest—a natural one, this time, surrounding a pool fed by a narrow stream. Huge boulders were strewn around as if a giant had tossed them down, and each of Yainar's men climbed one of the big rocks, looking out over the forest while they ate their rations.

"I understand that we face risks here," Yainar said quietly to Kori, where she sat close by. "But if my hunters are scared, they're of no use to me. They must be confident—cautious but confident. Otherwise, they will lack courage."

"So," Kori said, "you think one thing, but you say another. To your men, to Hurinara, and to all the other people in our tribe."

Yainar shrugged. "Of course. I already told you that. In fact, I suggested you could learn from it."

"And what of me?" Kori went on, forcing herself not to be angered or repulsed by what he said. "Do you deceive me, too?"

He smiled faintly. "I choose not to. It pleases me more to see how the truth punishes you."

Kori turned away. He was right, of course; she felt humiliated by the way she had to submit to him, knowing his real character. "If you ever reach your goal and lead our people," she said, "perhaps there'll be no need, after that, for your lies."

Yainar finished eating some smoked venison wrapped in sweetgrass and licked his fingers. "You speak without thinking," he said, tossing the remnants of the sweetgrass aside. "A good leader must always lie to his people. Most people are foolish, and they act foolishly. A good leader should protect them from the truth for their own good."

Kori felt her anger rising. There was no point in pursuing this; he was deliberately provoking her, and if she responded angrily, he would never begin to trust her. But could she ever convince him that he had finally broken her spirit? She sensed he wouldn't free her until such a time.

She tried to calm herself by enjoying the sunlight where it struck down into the clearing. She watched two blue jays chasing each other, dancing in the air, moving so quickly she could hardly keep track of them. That was all she really wanted, she thought to herself. To be free to dance with her mate and couple together and roll and tumble under the sun. She felt a wave of sadness from the knowledge that this joy had been stolen from her.

The ground suddenly trembled. Birds all around her leaped into the air, filling the forest with their cries. Kori quickly grabbed the rock she was sitting on, afraid of being thrown to the ground—but the quake was a tiny one, and it was soon over.

"Time to move on," Yainar called to his men. His voice was loud and confident. He climbed quickly down from his perch, leaving her to follow slowly and clumsily, hampered by the thongs linking her wrists.

She joined the men as they gathered together, and she sensed that they were not as confident as they'd been before. Their superstitions were barely contained by their courage, and they weren't happy to be moving closer toward Mount Tomomor. The cone at its summit was now rimmed with lava. Kori herself felt intimidated by the sight, and she knew that if she felt this way, men who still believed in the Old Ones must feel far worse.

By late afternoon the trail became harder to follow. Several times everyone had to stop and wait while Euri searched carefully, taking a few steps, then backtracking, sometimes getting down on his hands and knees to touch and sniff the ground. It was gravelly, here, and the vegetation was sparser. Also, the light was growing dim.

Kori knew from her previous journeyings that the western

edge of the forest was now not far away. Beyond that would be the rocky slope where she had met Uroh—although she was much farther north, here, than she had been then.

She wondered how Yainar would proceed when they reached the barren rock. Euri's tracking skills would be useless, and it surely wouldn't be safe to venture out into the empty wilderness.

Yainar called a halt at dusk, when they reached a flat-topped outcropping of rock that was wide enough for all of them to climb onto. It was wedge-shaped, sloping down toward the east. Its other three sides were almost vertical.

"This is a fine resting place," said Yainar, leading the men onto it and throwing down his bedroll. "We will only need to keep watch to the east. The slope will conceal us in shadow from the flames on Mount Tomomor, and our enemies will be easy to see if they approach us."

Kori saw that his followers were not reassured. She noticed Siew placing his palm on the rock and frowning as he felt it trembling gently with the force of Mount Tomomor's eruption. The forest, too, looked ominous in the fading light, and Kori remembered how scared she had felt on her first night alone on the Western Shore, when she had still been gripped by her own superstitions.

"You think we're safe here from forest creatures?" Siew said, setting down his pack.

"I've seen no sign of any," Yainar said with a shrug. He unpacked his firesticks and sat cross-legged in the center of the sloping rock, gathering together some twigs and dry leaves.

"I saw tracks," said Euri. "Lion, deer, wolf, bear—and others I couldn't recognize."

"Well, all creatures fear fire," said Yainar. He started work, spinning the drillstick between his palms.

"All normal creatures," said Siew.

Euri gave him an uneasy glance. Derneren, as usual,

seemed to be paying no attention. He was sitting near the top of the rock, opening a little parcel of deerskin and pulling dried fruit from it.

"You spent many nights here, isn't that so?" Yainar said to Kori. His face was stern and his eyes stared hard into hers, warning her.

"Many nights," she said. He was right, she realized: his men would be less useful if they were afraid. There was no point in terrifying them by describing the giant wolves she had seen. Her own survival might depend on their courage.

Yainar nodded decisively. "So," he said, "we will be safe enough."

Once again, Kori saw his men lose some of their fear at his words. Their shoulders straightened; their faces relaxed. She felt pleased—until she realized that she had helped him to reassure them by concealing truth that would cause fear. Did that mean he had corrupted her? The thought was so distressing, she thrust it aside. She took her bedroll all the way to the top of the sloping rock and laid it there, as far from Yainar as possible. There were so many things that she didn't want to think about now. The only way to escape from them was in the solitude of sleep.

She lay down, too weary even to eat. She watched the men as they squatted around the fire with their weapons close by. She saw Siew, Euri, and Derneren turning their faces toward Yainar as he started speaking—it was a hunting story, probably, or one of his father's exploits. The fire was burning brightly as the sun slipped behind Mount Tomomor, and the men were nodding, grinning, warming themselves not just with the fire but with the calm, friendly confidence that Yainar conveyed to them.

But behind her, Mount Tomomor still vented its discontent.

36

In the middle of the night she lay sleepless. It had seemed so easy to close her eyes and escape from all the worries and dangers of her life, but for some reason, her slumber took her only halfway through till dawn. She found herself suddenly wakeful, clear-headed and restless, tormented by everything she had tried not to think about before. While the moon climbed among the stars and Mount Tomomor murmured behind her, once again she saw in her imagination her father lying covered in blood . . . warriors moving from one home to the next, killing her kinfolk indiscriminately . . . her mother reaching out to her . . . Yainar torturing the warrior in the forest. . . .

Kori sat up and looked out at the trees bathed in wan radiance from the volcano. She told herself that the past was of no concern to her now, and she should think only of the future. Yet that was so uncertain, so dark and threatening, it offered her no comfort at all.

She noticed a movement and tensed, then realized it was only Derneren edging closer to the fire, warming himself while he kept watch. His back was turned toward her, a bulky black silhouette. The other three men were lying close by, and Kori heard their steady breathing.

She heard something else: a faint scratching sound. Some small creature was foraging down on the forest floor, behind and below her. And yet, the noise sounded closer to her than that. She frowned, turning her head. For a long moment there was silence, then the same faint rasping noise as before.

She rolled over, wondering if she dared to look over the edge of the rock where she lay. But—why not? The side of it was so steep and sheer, no creature could possibly climb it.

She wriggled out of her bearskin, turned on her stomach, and peered into the shadowy darkness. At first she couldn't understand what she saw: a bulky shape that seemed to grow out of the rock itself. Then she drew in her breath in surprise as she realized an animal was somehow clinging to the stone and had already climbed more than halfway to the top.

She opened her mouth to call out to the men and warn them—and the animal turned its face up toward her and she saw that it was a man.

She was too scared to speak. For a long, frozen moment, she and the man stared at each other.

"Kori," the man whispered in the darkness.

Kori's strength fled from her arms. She found herself slumping down, gasping for breath. In the light from Mount Tomomor, there was no doubt. It was Uroh gazing up at her.

Now she wondered if she was really awake after all. But the rock was hard and rough under her hands. The air was cold in her lungs, and she smelled the sulfurous fumes from the mountain.

"Kori! Come down to me!" he whispered to her.

She looked quickly around, half afraid that she would find one of the men staring at her—or, worse still, Yainar standing over her, glowering, his spear held ready. But no; the three figures were still sleeping by the fire, and

Derneren was sitting with his back turned, calmly watching the forest.

Kori peered at the rockface where Uroh was clinging. There were many fissures in it. Really, it was not so hard to climb. But did she dare try to descend it with her wrists still bound together?

She had to speak to Uroh. She couldn't imagine turning away from him now, sending him into the forest after he had followed her here and bided his time, then risked his life like this.

With infinite caution, she turned and swung her legs down over the edge of the rock. Uroh helped her: he guided her toes into secure footholds. She lowered herself, bit by bit, trying to make no sound. She took a last look at the men by the fire, making sure that they hadn't heard her and were not looking at her. Then she dropped down till she was hanging by her hands from the edge of the rock.

She couldn't lower herself any further. Her wrists were tied so close together, she couldn't hold on with one hand while she moved the other. Meanwhile, Uroh had climbed down to the ground. She felt him tugging at her ankles, urging her to descend the rest of the way.

She could let go and drop, but that would make far too much noise. She hung helplessly with her shoulders hurting and her hands growing weaker. She willed herself to hold on, but sooner or later her fingers would lose their grip and she would fall.

She felt a wave of panic. Then she felt his hands reaching up, seizing her by the hips. He took her weight, and he lifted her down.

Suddenly her feet were on the ground and she was turning toward him, finding him facing her, his body miraculously warm and real and close to hers. She threw her bound wrists around his neck and pressed herself against him, clinging to him, feeling a great wave of mixed emotions: pleasure, relief, caution, and doubt.

His arms circled her waist, holding her, and she felt his cheek pressing against hers, his lips on her neck, her shoulder, her mouth. Kori kissed him—then pulled away. It would be so easy not to think, and just surrender to the physical joy of having him close to her. But she couldn't allow herself that luxury.

He sensed her holding back. "Are you all right?" he whispered. "The men who are with you—are you their prisoner? When I started following you before you camped here, I saw your hands bound together. Kori—"

"Just a moment." She pulled her bound wrists up from around his neck and placed her finger to his lips. "Wait, Uroh. This is so sudden, so difficult for me."

"Difficult?" he was staring at her, looking worried.

"There is something I must ask you," she said, "before anything else."

He nodded quickly, and waited.

She had to summon more courage before she could go on, because she was so afraid of what she might hear from him in return. Finally she looked up, directly into his eyes. "Do you realize what happened on the island?"

He hesitated. "I've talked to the other scouts," he said. "I've not seen the warriors. I hear there was a fight, and our men were driven off. I hear that two were killed and one was injured. That's all I know."

Kori eyed him cautiously. "They murdered more than twenty of my tribe," she told him. "They crept in and went from one hut to the next, killing everyone in their sleep—men and women, even babies. They killed my father and my mother."

Uroh was silent. He turned his head and she felt his body tensing, pulling away from her.

"Listen to me!" she whispered urgently. "This is not something you can avoid, Uroh. Your people did a terrible, cowardly thing."

"Yes. You're right." He took her hands in his, and she felt him trembling. "But it was not my choice. I had no control over it. I wasn't there, and I couldn't have stopped it even if I'd known what they planned to do."

All of these things were true, she realized. "But you did know it would happen," she whispered.

He shook his head violently. "I knew my people would attack, but I didn't know anything more till the night you heard me talking to Onnoru. Kori, I'm a scout, nothing more! The warriors scorn me. They tell me nothing."

She pulled back a little and looked at his face. His eyes were wide; he was staring at her plaintively.

"Well," she said a little more calmly, "you still lied to me when we lay together on the slopes of the mountain. You lied about your tribe in a dozen different ways."

"Yes, you have already accused me of this, and I have admitted it." He sounded tormented. "But Kori, you know I wanted you so much, I was afraid to say anything that would turn you away. And you told me you hated your people. You said that they'd cast you out, and you never wanted to see any of them again. You told me they expected you to *die* on the Western Shore. Isn't that so?"

"I was wrong about that," she admitted. "It turned out that my mother just wanted to intimidate me, not kill me." She sighed. Her anger was spent; she felt only regret. She wondered what she would have done if Uroh had warned her that her tribe was in danger, on the first night they met. Would she have left him and gone back to the island? Perhaps. But would her people have listened to her? No, that was out of the question. Could she have protected her tribe? Could she have saved her mother's life? She had to admit, it was very unlikely.

"I suppose it would have happened this way, no matter

what we said or tried to do," she murmured, half to herself.

"Kori," he whispered, "please forgive me. Lie with me here, just for a moment."

She lay down with him on the ground, he embraced her, and now, finally, she felt her anguish and her indecision and her heartache being lifted from her. She clung to him, realizing how much she had missed him and how she needed him.

"These men with you," he whispered to her. "What are they doing here? This is so dangerous, Kori. If my people knew—"

Should she tell him what Yainar had come here for? She hesitated, then realized that if she didn't speak of it, she would be doing just what she had accused Uroh of doing: she would be concealing a danger to *his* people. Quickly, then, she told him of the plan to track the whitebeast warriors.

"Yainar thinks that once he finds them, he can bring more hunters from the island and stage a surprise attack," she said. "He thinks he can kill them all, and his people will revere him and make him their chieftain."

Uroh was silent for a long moment. "I thought everyone from the Island Tribe was too scared to set foot on the Western Shore."

"They were. But some of the men grew bolder, seeing that I survived here. And Yainar has no faith in the Old Ones. His only faith is in himself."

Gently but firmly, he took hold of her upper arms. "Kori," he whispered, "come with me now. Leave these people. You don't belong with them."

His words excited her, but then, just as quickly, she felt familiar doubts. "We've talked about this before," she said. "You know there's nowhere we can go, no way we can survive the winter alone together."

He grunted impatiently. "We can take a canoe from your tribe and travel downriver. I've thought about this, Kori. Your people know how to catch fish—you have this skill yourself, don't you? We can take some food from the stores of your tribe and fish from the river as we go. I've heard that the land is warmer to the south. Down in the lowlands, there's no snow at all. We can find a new place of our own—"

She shook her head violently, trying to drive away the vision he was conjuring for her. It was too tantalizing, too seductive. "Don't give me hope unless it is rooted in truth!" she told him. "I don't believe you've ever been to the south. You're saying things as if they're facts, but they're not, they're just more dreams."

"But I've listened to travelers—"

"If it was so warm and pleasant in the south, why didn't these travelers stay there? Uroh, you may be right, but we can't know that any of these things are true. I'm not even sure we could take a canoe safely down the rocky rapids that lie downstream. No one in my tribe has ever dared to try it. That alone could kill us, and even if we survive, there are fewer fish in the winter months, and no game for us to trap or hunt in the snow. And still you want me to risk both our lives for this?"

He was silent for a long time, and she knew he was retreating from her, clinging to his dream, refusing to acknowledge what she said.

"I think my people may be able to defend the island," she went on more gently, "now that they know your warriors exist. I think I can be safe there, Uroh. And you will certainly be safe in your tribe."

"But what about us!" he blurted out.

"Hush," she told him. She paused, listening intently. Had she heard a sound from the rock above her? She held her breath, listening again. Surely, if one of the men discovered that she was missing, he'd shout to the others. The continuing silence above was some guarantee of her safety.

She turned back to Uroh. "Why does there have to be violence between your people and mine?" she asked him. "The island is large enough for many more people. Don't you think it's possible for our tribes to share it? Have you thought of that?"

He looked at her as if she were a fool. "That, Kori, is truly a dream."

"You could go to your people and suggest it," she urged him. "Tell them our chieftain and his wife are dead, but their daughter wishes there can be peace. Tell them that!"

He shook his head. "I know what their answer will be. They won't trust your tribe. They'll expect you to seek revenge."

She sighed with exasperation because he was right. "So at least let's try to delay any bloodshed. If we can last until the spring, maybe then I would go south with you, Uroh. But not now, with the winter snows just ahead. I've made so many rash and hasty decisions in the past weeks, and I've suffered for them so much, and I don't want to make another choice now that could cause us both to die for no good reason."

He nodded slowly. "But you'll wait for me? Kori, is there any man in your tribe you care for?"

So that was what he was afraid of, and that was why he was so full of urgency, so desperate to take her away. "I despise the men of my tribe," she whispered to him. "And I swear I will save myself for you, Uroh."

She felt a pang as she said that, knowing that Yainar had forced her to have sex with him, and knowing that it would happen again, and again, as long as she was under his power. But her loyalty was only to Uroh, and surely that was what really mattered.

"All right," Uroh said, "if you promise to keep yourself for me, I'll go to my people as you say." He hesitated. "But how shall I ever find you and speak to you again?"

Kori thought for a moment. "Yainar can't keep me a prisoner forever," she said, nodding to the bonds around her wrists. "When he allows me some liberty, I'll go to the southern end of the island at night. There's a high rock there, higher than any other point on the island. I'll stand on it in the moonlight wearing a white deerskin so you'll be able to see me from the Western Shore."

"And if I see you, I'll call to you," he said. "I'll give an animal cry, twice or three times. And then you'll come to me?"

"I'll swim if I have to," she said, speaking with all her heart—although, at the same time, she wondered if this was just another fantasy. With each day that passed she was seeing more clearly how weak she was compared with the forces around her: the warriors with their spears, the elders of her tribe, and the young hunters dreaming of conquest. Even the implacable changing of the seasons was a force she couldn't fight.

She caressed Uroh's face. She would do everything she could to be united with him again, but she was beginning to wonder if he had been right when he'd told her they were fated to be together. The forces holding them apart were so strong, she no longer felt the same faith as before. It was hard for her to have faith in anything at all now .

He kissed her long and deep, clinging to her, not wanting to let her go. Finally, though, she freed herself. "I must go back," she said. "They'll take turns standing guard, and when that happens they could easily notice that I'm missing. I don't want to rouse their suspicions all over again. If I do—well, I don't know what will happen to me. I'll be kept prisoner again, or worse."

Uroh nodded, avoiding her eyes. "I just want to be with you," he whispered, running his hands up her arms, savoring the touch of her.

"And I want to be with you. I'm glad you found us, Uroh." She hesitated. "Are any of the other scouts still roaming the forest? Will we be in danger?"

He shook his head. "I think they've all returned to the camp that my people have set up. It's on the mountain slope south of here. Your hunters can't possibly track my people onto the rocks there, and there's no way to ambush them."

Kori nodded, feeling relieved. "So there'll be no more bloodshed," she said, half to herself. "At least, not here on the Western Shore." She stood up, forcing herself to think calmly and clearly and not be ruled by her emotions. "I need you to help me back up," she said.

Once again he kissed her. This time, though, he seemed to accept that he must say good-bye. He released her and she turned around; he reached down, took her by the hips, lifted her up, and she just managed to get her hands over the edge of the rock. He shifted his grip to the soles of her feet and thrust her farther upward till she was resting once again on top of the rock.

She lay still for a moment, trying to quiet her breathing. She saw that nothing had changed: Derneren was sitting by the fire with his back to her, and the other three men were sleeping.

Kori squirmed around and looked over the edge, down at Uroh. This was her last chance, she realized. She could still go back to him and run away with him; she felt a great yearning inside her, urging her to climb back down and do just that. But where would they run to? She wouldn't be safe from his people, and he wouldn't be safe from hers. Yainar would surely come looking for both of them, and Kori still remembered his terrible vow to kill Uroh as slowly and painfully as possible.

With a great effort of will, she suppressed her desire to be with Uroh. She waved to him, and reluctantly, he waved back. He lingered for a moment, staring up at her.

Then, silently, he slipped away into the darkness under the trees.

She felt a terrible wrench of sadness. Had she made a mistake? Well, it was too late for second thoughts. She would simply have to wait, now, to learn if her decision had been wise.

37

She woke with a sore throat and a heavy pain in her chest, making her feel as if she was suffocating. She sat up, coughing, blinking as the air stung her eyes. The whole world was a dim yellow-gray; the wind had shifted during the night, engulfing them in fumes from the volcano.

Kori saw a figure looming over her. "Breakfast," said a voice—Derneren's voice. He gave her a few chunks of rewarmed meat on a scrap of bark. "Yainar wants to go soon," he told her, moving back toward the fire.

Kori forced the food down, rolled up her bearskin, and then joined the men. She found Yainar checking their weapons and their packs, calmly ignoring the choking fumes. "Can we really find our way through this?" Kori asked him.

"The day's getting brighter," he said. "Euri doesn't need to see far ahead in order to follow a trail. And the mist will help to conceal us."

So they continued moving slowly through the forest. Yainar was right: Euri was able to follow the trail. Soon the forest started thinning, as Kori had expected. The soil became stonier, and there was hardly any underbrush. Then they emerged on the rocky slope that curved up to the summit of Mount Tomomor itself.

The fumes were worse here. The fountain of fire at the summit of the mountain was dimly visible directly ahead, and everyone could see that the forest had ended. Kori watched the men standing on the barren rock, looking around, realizing where they were. Even Derneren seemed nervous, and she noticed him glancing back toward the forest as if he was eager to go back to it.

"There is no way to track the whitebeasts from here," Euri said apologetically, although he sounded glad to be able to state the obvious.

"We'll try moving south," said Yainar. "We'll stay just inside the edge of the forest."

Kori saw Siew and Euri glance at each other. "They might be anywhere out there." Siew gestured toward the barren slope.

"Yes, they might be," said Yainar. "But that's what we have to discover, for the safety of our tribe." He waited, staring directly Siew, challenging the man to back down.

Siew glanced again at Euri, but Euri avoided his eyes. Looking irritated Siew turned to Derneren. "What do you think?" he asked.

Derneren paused. He seemed reluctant to speak. "I think we should do what Yainar says," he answered.

"May I speak?" said Kori.

All four of the men turned and looked at her. Yainar gestured impatiently. "What do you have to say?"

"This land," she said, pointing to the ground where they stood, "was once lava. It cooled and turned to rock."

Siew laughed. Euri looked at her uneasily. Derneren seemed indifferent, but Yainar was cautious and alert. "Explain yourself," he said.

Haltingly, she told him what Uroh had told her. She showed where the forest had taken root in earlier lava flows, splitting them into fragments. She pointed to a place where a lava flow had ended. The men were reluctant to believe her, but Yainar was soon convinced by the evidence in the land before him.

"I don't see what difference it makes to us, though," he said when she had finished explaining herself.

Kori pointed up to the summit of the mountain. "The lava is flowing, there. See?"

They peered through the drifting fumes. The wind gusted and the haze lifted, and in that brief moment everyone could see a mosaic of red. The surface of the lava was black where it had cooled and solidified, but there were cracks in the crust, and the lava beneath was the color of fresh blood. It was oozing slowly down the mountainside, steaming in the morning air.

"This is already the second day," Kori said, "and the mountain is as angry as ever. We may not be safe here."

"Still, it flows slowly," Yainar said. "And look: if the white-beast warriors camped up on those rocky slopes, the lava could force them down here, too." He turned back to his men. "I say we follow the edge of the trees a way south and see what we find. If the smoke doesn't lift, or if there seems to be danger from the mountain, we can retreat toward the east."

He waited, looking at each of them in turn. None of them spoke against him, but Kori saw the uncertainty in their faces.

By noontime the air had grown worse. The lava had crept visibly closer, and the wind blowing down the slope was hot against Kori's face. She was starting to feel anxious; if the whitebeast people had camped on the mountainside, in anticipation of eventually seizing and occupying the island, they would be forced by the lava to leave their camp. She feared blundering into them in the choking yellow haze.

Siew and Euri were obviously concerned about the same thing. "I care as much for our tribe as any man," said Siew, while they sat amid the saplings at the edge of the forest, grimly eating another portion of their rations, "but there's no trail to follow. We won't see anyone till they see us, and then it'll be too late." He rubbed his red-rimmed eyes, then turned and spat, trying to get rid of the foul taste of the air. "We'll be no use to our kinfolk if we throw our lives away."

Yainar listened impassively. He turned to Euri. "You agree?"

Euri avoided his eyes. "I think so," he said, in a voice so quiet, Kori could barely hear it above the low rumble of the mountain.

Yainar turned to Derneren. "What do you say?"

Derneren was silent for a long moment, staring at the spear he held in front of him. "I don't like it," he said finally.

Kori saw a muscle twitch in Yainar's cheek. His fist tightened on his spear, and she could sense his frustration. Still, when he spoke his voice sounded no different. "Only a foolish leader refuses to listen to his men," he said. "As you wish. We'll turn back. For now."

Euri and Siew glanced at each other, looking relieved. Derneren nodded to himself. Together, the three men turned away from the mountain.

Yainar stood to one side, watching them as they started walking down the slope, deeper into the forest. Then he looked sharply at Kori, and at that moment she saw the anger revealed in his face.

He strode toward her. He seized her robe and dragged her up to him till their faces were almost touching. "You should learn to keep quiet, woman," he told her. He gave her a little shake, then released her and stood glaring at her, clenching his jaw. "You made them nervous," he went on, "with your talk."

She eyed him apprehensively. "But I was concerned for our safety."

"Quiet!" he snapped at her. He paused a moment, trying to calm himself. "Maybe I should take my knife and cut out your tongue," he said, turning away from her.

The way he said it chilled her. There was no doubt in her mind that he was capable of such a thing, and she knew she wouldn't be able to defend herself if he turned on her.

"I don't believe I scared them," she called after him, "but I'll speak more carefully in the future."

He ignored her, leaving her to follow as he walked down the slope, away from Mount Tomomor.

The noise of the mountain still sounded behind them, providing some sense of direction, but they could no longer see the sun. In gaps between the trees, the sky was heavy with clouds above the yellow plumes of smoke. The forest was now a dim and sinister place where tree trunks loomed unexpectedly in the grayness and every direction looked the same. Kori saw the men moving with less assurance, glancing uneasily to either side. Once in a while they paused and debated the right path to take, and even Yainar seemed uncertain.

They followed a slope that seemed as if it should take them toward the river, then discovered that it was a shallow fold in the land, ending in a small mountain stream. The sight of water was welcome, since everyone was thirsty. But when Kori drank from her cupped hands, she found that the water tasted foul, polluted by the same sulfurous stench that pervaded the air. She forced herself to drink some anyway, but she felt a growing anxiety. Obviously they wouldn't be able to reach the river before dark, and almost all their food was gone. She imagined herself blundering through the for-

est, poisoned by the water, unable to find her way home—
and she thought of Uroh. Was he somewhere close by, suffering similarly? Were his people trying to find their own
way through the forest?

The place had become eerily quiet. No birds were in the
trees; they had fled from the smoke. No squirrels leaped
from branch to branch, and no creatures foraged through the
underbrush. She felt as if the animals had abandoned the
land because they knew a truth that the humans didn't yet
comprehend.

"We'll have to camp here," Yainar said finally, when the
light had grown so dim that it was impossible to carry on.
"See, there's some dense underbrush that'll hide us. We'll
take turns on watch. We'll be safe enough."

No one said anything, because clearly there was no alternative.

Yainar built a fire, and that helped to drive away some of
Kori's fears. She looked at the faces around the flames and
found them reassuring, even though she saw that the men
were just as uneasy as she was.

"We'll move on as soon as it gets light," Yainar told them,
sharing out the last of the rations. "We'll reach the river
before noon. We'll get fresh supplies from the island, then
we can wait there, or head back up here if the weather clears
and the lava stops flowing."

Derneren grunted in agreement, but Euri and Siew said
nothing. They ate in silence. Clearly, in their minds, the
tribe's superstitions had been confirmed: the Western Shore
was not a place where any human being should be.

38

This time, she was too fearful to sleep. She listened to the trees creaking and their leaves shivering in the wind. She heard the men coughing around her, and she felt the ground tremble beneath her. Her eyes were red and swollen, now, and every breath was painful. She huddled under her bearskin, feeling deeply weary and desperate to forget the world around her. But when she did finally drift off for a short while, she found herself dreaming of warriors creeping through the trees, closing around her with their knives and spears gleaming in the firelight, their eyes full of murder and their minds full of hate. . . .

She woke with a little cry and lay for a moment remembering where she was, blinking away her vision of impending death and taking quick, desperate breaths. There were no warriors; just Siew taking his turn on watch, sitting near the fire, staring into the forest with a spear clutched between his big hands.

Kori told herself that there was nothing to fear—at least, nothing more than the other times she had been in this place. But then she heard something like a footstep on the forest floor.

She told herself it was her imagination. But she saw Siew tensing, turning toward the sound. Then there was another sound—and another. Kori's skin prickled. Fear clutched her throat as she wondered if her dream had been a warning. Clumsily, she stood up. With her hands tied, she was in no position to defend herself. She saw a bunch of spears standing beside Siew and wondered if she should go to them and saw her bonds against one of the flint points. She was convinced, now, the whitebeast warriors were close by. They were circling around—

She didn't have a chance to complete her thought. There was a sudden flurry of rustling sounds and a small creature burst through the underbrush, running mindlessly toward the campfire.

It was a rat, Kori realized. Its eyes were gleaming with terror. It only seemed to see the fire at the last moment. It veered around it—and then it was gone.

Kori looked at Siew and Siew looked back at her, both of them too surprised to speak. Then another creature came diving through the forest, a woodchuck this time. It burst into the thicket, stopped as it saw the human beings, and stood for a moment panting. Then it leaped as if it had been stung. It ran across Yainar's bedroll and disappeared away into the night, while Yainar grunted with surprise and sat up, grabbing his spear and looking quickly around.

The forest was suddenly full of sound. Another rat came racing through their camp site, then Kori heard heavier footsteps. She cried out in shock and fear as a young deer leaped among them, its flanks heaving as it took desperate breaths, its legs scored by bramble scratches. It eyed them in panic, then jumped away, crashing through the foliage.

"Wake," said Yainar, shaking Derneren and then Euri.

"Wake!" Yainar stood and cocked his head, then sniffed the air. "Do you smell that?"

Kori breathed deeply. Her mouth and nose were so sore from the sulfur fumes, it was hard for her to smell or taste anything—but then she caught the scent. It was the smell of wood smoke.

"The lava has reached the forest," Yainar said. "The trees have caught fire, and the underbrush is dry. There's been no rain for many days." He pointed up the slope. "Look!"

Faintly, through the dark web of trees, Kori saw an orange glow.

"The wind's blowing hard," said Yainar. "And it's blowing toward us. Quickly. Stow your things."

Kori dropped to her knees and fumbled with her bedroll. She cursed the thongs tying her wrists. "Help me!" she cried, turning to Yainar.

He hesitated for only a moment, then strode across, pulling out his flint knife. He seized her hands, dragged them up, sawed the blade between them—and she was free. "Don't betray me," he warned her before he turned away.

She felt a wave of relief at being able to use her arms again. Then she caught another whiff of wood smoke, and she flinched as another deer came crashing through the forest, followed by dozens of small rodents.

"Which way?" Kori called to Yainar as she stood up, throwing her pack around her shoulders.

He hesitated.

"We must move downwind," said Euri. "It doesn't matter where the river lies. The fire is all that matters now."

"Euri is right," said Yainar. He pushed quickly out of the thicket where they had spent the night.

Kori found herself half running, stumbling through the darkness. The glow from the fire was so dim behind her, the forest was still almost totally black. She heard the men ahead of her and to either side of her staggering through the foliage, cursing as they became tangled in underbrush and bumped into trees. More animals were moving among them; she heard them underfoot, and she smelled them.

It was easy to get lost. She heard Siew shouting out and Yainar shouting back. Derneren was just ahead of her—or was that him to her left? Yainar called out again and she tried to move toward his voice, then found herself blundering into him.

"Wait!" he called out as the other men moved ahead. "Wait, the wind is shifting!"

Kori stopped. She licked her hand and held it up, turning it slowly. Yainar was correct, she realized. Then, with horror, she saw that the orange glow of the forest fire was no longer just behind her. It was also burning to her right.

"This way!" Yainar shouted. The glow was bright enough now for Kori to see him, a tall, dark shape among the trees with his sheaf of spears slung under the pack on his back. And here came Derneren and Euri, running toward him, with Siew just behind, his eyes gleaming in the orange light.

All of them started running. Kori could hear the fire, now, crackling and roaring above the murmur of Mount Tomomor. The wind blew in furious gusts, faster than she could ever run. The animals around her were yelping in fear: opossum and badgers, skunks and rabbits, bobcats and squirrels, hundreds of creatures all moving side by side, predators ignoring their prey as they fled from a common enemy that threatened to devour them all.

Kori dodged among the trees, running as fast as she could, but the fire was moving faster, fanned by the wind. She felt the warmth of it on the back of her neck, and it sparked such fear in her, she was clumsy and lost her footing. She tripped and fell. She glanced behind her, picked herself up, and ran on.

There was a sudden huge crashing sound on her left. She looked and saw some of the giant wolves that she'd encoun-

tered on her last journey to the Western Shore. The terrible
creatures were thundering through the underbrush, howling
as they ran. Kori saw Yainar staring at them, his face blank
with astonishment. Then the wolves were gone, lost among
the trees.

The land started sloping down. Kori found herself running out of control, unable to stop herself as her heels
pounded into the hard, gravelly soil. She cried out in pain as
her shoulder hit a tree and she bounced away from it, trip-
ping through vines and brambles. Somehow, though, she
went on running—then suddenly she saw pale light among
the leaves.

She felt a burst of hope. She heard Euri up ahead of her,
shouting something. "The river!" he cried. "The river!"

She burst out of the forest onto the riverbank and barely
stopped herself from plunging ahead into the water. The
river was a flat gray shape in the pale light of dawn. She
found Yainar standing alongside her, gasping for breath.
The other three men were a short distance away. The island
of her tribe was in the distance, directly opposite. She realized with confusion that she was standing not far from the
thicket where Uroh had hidden himself.

She turned and looked back. The fire was raging; she saw
the flames dancing high into the treetops, two or three times
the height of a man. Thick black smoke was billowing close
overhead, and through it she saw the peak of Mount
Tomomor. The mountain was lined in crimson, now, belch-
ing yellow flames into the sky.

Meanwhile, the wind was still blowing hard and the forest
fire was still advancing. All around Kori, animals were leaping off the rocks and swimming mindlessly into the river.

She turned quickly to Yainar. "Should we follow them?"
she said.

He turned toward the island and cupped his hands
around his mouth. "Help!" he bellowed. "Over here! Help!"

The other men joined him, and Kori added her voice, though her throat was still horribly painful. She edged toward the river as she felt the heat of the fire growing stronger on her back. She heard the cracking and crashing of burning timber. Meanwhile, out on the island, she saw tiny figures moving to canoes at the dock. They were the men who had been on sentry duty, she realized, guarding against the whitebeast warriors.

Kori waited, glancing nervously at the burning forest. The heat was unpleasant now, and the sight of the fire was terrifying. She slung her backpack down and threw off her robe. It hurt her to abandon the bearskin that her father had given her, but she saw no choice. She saw the men discarding their own possessions, although Yainar clung to his sheaf of spears.

Together they clambered over the rocks and down into the water. It was shockingly cold, but she didn't care. She edged out into the river, glancing back apprehensively as she saw the first tongues of flame reaching out to the dry grass at the edge of the trees.

Somewhere, she knew, Uroh must still be on the Western Shore. And so were the people of his tribe.

39

By the time the first canoe reached them, the river was bordered with a wall of flames towering into the sky, gradually spreading farther up- and downstream. Huge billows of smoke rolled across the water, and Kori's face felt scorched by the heat. Trees were falling, burning, and the river hissed as embers and flaming branches plunged into it. Meanwhile, the water was dancing with earth tremors and churning around the hundreds of panic-stricken animals swimming blindly away from the shore.

The canoe that came to Yainar and Kori contained just one man, a hunter named Fiwar, whom Kori knew as a devout believer in the Old Ones. His face was blank with terror as he stared at the towering flames, and he gestured desperately, making the canoe rock wildly. "Get in!" he shouted. "Quickly, get in!"

Kori hauled herself up and over the side and Yainar did the same, dumping his big bundle of spears in the bottom of the boat. Siew came wading over, and Derneren, and Euri, and now the canoe was fully loaded.

"Quickly!" Fiwar shouted, wielding his paddle and trying to turn the canoe against the current. "Help me get back to the island!"

Yainar ignored him. He stood up in the center of the canoe, his bare chest beaded with water, gleaming in the dazzling orange light from the flames. His leggings were sodden, his moccasins were missing, and his braids had unraveled, leaving his long, wild hair streaming in the wind, but none of this concerned him. He was turning slowly, squinting through the choking clouds of wood smoke and sulfur fumes. "We should move farther downstream," he said.

Fiwar looked at him in disbelief. "Have you no respect for the wrath of the spirits?" He dug his paddle deep, turning toward the island.

"Take it from him," Yainar said to Derneren.

Derneren moved toward the rear of the canoe, making it lurch with every step. Fiwar stared at him fearfully and gave a defiant cry, holding the paddle out of reach, but Derneren simply seized the man by his hair and dragged him forward till he fell down in the bottom of the boat. Derneren stooped, took hold of the paddle, then kneeled close by the man, paying no attention to his pitiful protests.

Meanwhile, another of the canoes that had set out from the dock had also arrived to offer help and was just a few strokes away. Two women were in it: Nenara and a small, shy girl named Tirar. "Go back," Yainar shouted to them, "get every hunter and bring them here." He pointed south. "See there?"

Downstream, the fire hadn't reached the river yet. Some deer and other animals were gathering on the shore under the trees, milling about in fear. Among them, Kori saw the flash of white fur.

She felt an awful pang of dismay. "Whitebeasts," she murmured to herself.

"The fire will force them into the water," said Yainar. "If

we move quickly, we can kill them all." His eyes were sore from the fumes and his face was red from the heat of the fire. Wet strands of his hair clung to his forehead. He had a wild and crazy look, his bloodshot eyes staring wide, his blistered lips pulled back from his teeth. In the light from the wall of flames his face looked demonic. Nenara and Tirar stared at him in fear.

"Quickly!" he shouted at them—and they hurried to obey him, turning their canoe and paddling back the way they'd come. Kori looked at the island and saw the people of her tribe massing along the shore, staring in fear at the burning forest and trying to understand what was happening.

A deer splashed through the water barely an arm's length from the canoe where Kori sat. It was cavorting wildly, desperate to escape the terrifying flames. Yainar picked up one of his spears, took hold of it by the very end of the shaft, and casually impaled the deer. It struggled wildly as he dragged it into the canoe and threw its body down. The animal made keening noises and flailed its legs. Yainar stabbed it in the neck, then fell onto it and used his knife to slit its throat. The creature's struggles became feeble as its lifeblood poured out, pooling around Kori's feet.

Yainar looked up at her, then at his men in the canoe. His face had turned an even deeper red and he was panting fast. He gestured at the dead animal. "This is what we will do," he said, "to the whitebeast warriors. They will all die." He turned suddenly back to Kori. "All of them. Do you understand? Every last one."

His words had their intended effect. She felt them as a blow to her stomach. She imagined Uroh retreating from the terrible flames, being forced into the river, turning and swimming desperately out toward the Eastern Shore—and Yainar coming upon him, standing up in the bow of the canoe, impaling Uroh like a piece of meat.

Yainar was watching her, taking pleasure in what he saw.

He slowly grinned. Then he turned his back on her. "Derneren!" he called. "Take us farther downstream. The whitebeasts will try to escape us. Some of them will lurk in the water among the rocks near the shore till the flames die down. Some will try to reach the Eastern Shore. Some will swim with the current." He turned to Siew and Euri. "I want them all, do you understand?"

The men shouted out their assent. The fear that they'd shown in the forest had disappeared, easily displaced by their desire for vengeance.

Meanwhile, down by the water, Kori saw the first of the warriors in their white bearskins retreating from the flames, stepping into the river.

Within a short time the river was filled with canoes, and every canoe was filled with men from the Island Tribe, all of them brandishing spears. Young hunters, children five years old, elders who could barely stand—every male from the Island Tribe came out to share in the vengeance, and all of them were shouting their hatred for the whitebeast warriors.

Kori felt sick as she remembered her futile hope that the tribes could coexist peacefully. Uroh had been right: that was the most impossible dream of all. The faces of the menfolk around her were lit with the same hunger she had seen in Yainar. Their urge to kill was screaming so loudly inside them, they could hear nothing else.

Many of the men were spearing game in the water as they moved toward their enemies. Kori saw rabbits, deer, even a young mountain lion impaled and dragged from the river in an orgy of bloodshed. There would be no shortage of food for the winter now.

The whitebeast people saw the canoes converging, and they realized they were trapped. Their whole tribe was there: women, children, warriors, old men, and babies. With the fire still raging in the forest and the flotilla of canoes forming a semicircle blocking any escape across the river, there was no possible hope for the people in their white furs. Still, they didn't give up. Women dove into the water carrying their children while men on the rocks hurled their spears, trying to hold the Island Tribe away long enough for some of the women to swim to safety.

Kori ducked down to protect herself inside the shell of her canoe. But the spears from the warriors were poorly aimed, thrown in fear and desperation. Only two people in the canoes were injured, and their companions quickly stanched the blood and wrapped the wounds. Meanwhile, the heat of the blaze was an inexorable force. One by one, the whitebeast people waded into the river to escape being burned alive.

Now the massacre began. With exultant cries the hunters jabbed at the people in the water, slicing their hands and arms and faces, till a huge pool of red spread across the river. The warriors fought back as best they could, diving under canoes and trying to overturn them, reaching for spears and trying to seize them. But all these efforts were futile.

Yainar plunged his spear into one man's face, pulled back, then took the shaft in both hands and drove it down into the man's chest. The warrior flailed and screamed and made desperate noises as water entered his open mouth. Yainar nudged the man away, leaving him to float away and die downstream. He turned to his next victim, a woman clutching her baby, and he killed them savagely, without hesitation or remorse.

One warrior grabbed a spear that was floating in the river and hurled it up at Yainar, but the motion forced him backward in the water and his spear flew wide. A moment later he was screaming, impaled by two hunters, one spearing him in the back, the other in the chest.

As the water churned, frothing pink around the struggling bodies, Kori told herself not to look. She covered her ears with her hands to shut out the triumphant yells of the hunters and the terrible screams of their victims. She feared what she might do if she saw Uroh being killed. She imagined herself rising up, seizing a spear, hurling it at any man who dared to take Uroh's life—

The vision was so vivid it made her tremble, and she realized she had become infected with the same bloodlust and craving for revenge that had taken hold of everyone around her. Unlike them, however, she yearned to strike out only at the one man standing closest to her, who was raining death into the churning river where bodies thrashed in agony in the roaring glare of the forest fire.

A warrior came swimming desperately past her boat, his face contorted with panic, his mouth gaping wide. He grabbed the side of her canoe for a moment, and his hand was so close to her, she could have touched it easily. For a moment she looked into his eyes—and then Derneren leaned over, seized the man by his hair, and casually stabbed him in the neck. While blood fountained from the man's jugular vein, Derneren pried his hand from the side of the canoe and used the end of his spear to club the warrior, knocking him back down in the water where he started choking on his own blood.

Derneren glanced impassively at Kori, then moved back to his position at the rear of the canoe.

The first part of the fight was the worst. Within a very short time, as the whitebeast people threw themselves into the river, most of them were killed.

Some warriors managed to break through the flotilla of canoes and started swimming desperately away, but the hunters quickly pursued them, catching up with them as easily as wolves chasing crippled deer. Kori heard hunters shouting, competing with each other to kill the last of the whitebeasts. One warrior was trapped between two canoes that came up either side of him, and the hunters took pleasure in tormenting him, inflicting dozens of small wounds while he struggled and tried desperately to free himself, screaming in pain the whole time.

Then, finally, it was over. Everywhere Kori looked, bodies were floating in their furs, leaking blood and drifting slowly away with the current. The sides of the canoes were colored a rich red; the hunters, too, were spattered with their victims' blood. Forty people of the Island Tribe had massacred more than a hundred men, women, and children.

One man could take the credit, for he alone had seen the tribe gathering on the shore. He stood, now, with a spear in each hand, grinning with pride. Derneren called to him, shouting his approval. Yainar raised both his arms, threw his head back, and gave an exultant animal cry that echoed across the water. And suddenly everyone was turning and cheering him.

Kori was sitting an arm's length away. Some spears were still lying in the bottom of the canoe, and with hardly any effort she saw she could seize one, raise it, and plunge it into Yainar's back before anyone could stop her. She shuddered, because she felt so tempted. Without a doubt, she knew this was the best thing she could do for her tribe. She trembled to think what would happen now that Yainar had proven himself and had become a hero. She knew his sadistic spirit would not be satisfied by this victory for long. He would want to exercise and prove his power, pitting men against each other, conquering more territory, perhaps seeking out the other tribes that Uroh had mentioned. The people of the Island Tribe would learn to fear strangers instead of fearing the Old Ones. They would compete with each other and distrust each other where once they had been quick to trust and forgive. Their menfolk would become warriors. Their womenfolk would be abused.

Of course, if she killed Yainar now she would be torn apart by men filled with righteous rage, but that didn't seem such a terrible fate. Uroh was dead, she had no doubt of that.

Yainar had been thorough, seeking and killing every last member of the whitebeast tribe, just as he had promised. Even small children trying to hide among the rocks at the shore had been forced out and murdered, for fear that a child who lived might become an adult one day and take revenge on the Island Tribe.

Somewhere in the great mass of blood-soaked bodies floating slowly away, Kori knew there lay the body of the only man who had ever truly cared for her.

With a terrible wrenching feeling she realized that if she had only run away with Uroh as he had wanted, he might still be alive now. They would have had time to reach the river long before the fire started. They would have had a chance to seize a canoe and fulfill Uroh's dream of going south.

She found herself crying. She had failed him, seeking security instead of yielding to his bold fantasy. She had sent him back to his tribe, and to his death.

Feeling a heavy weight in her chest she took hold of the ornament he had made for her—the little white bear on the thin leather thong. She lifted it up, over her head, and she cast it into the river. For a moment she saw it slipping away beneath the surface, sliding through the water. And then it was gone.

Of course, she was more secure now than if she had tried to flee with Uroh. She could pair with Yainar if he still wanted her—and he probably did. She could become the chieftain's wife, like her mother before her. And if she was cunning enough and tenacious enough, maybe she might even exert some influence over her tribe—though Yainar would be far less tolerant of that than Rohonar had been.

Kori saw why her mother had used the Old Ones for guidance. The spirit world was the only refuge beyond the power of men, the only way a woman could seize any power for herself. Did that mean that Kori, now, would have to start pretending to hear the voices of spirits if she wanted to moderate Yainar's dreams of conquest? The idea was abhorrent. But as she sat in the canoe watching Yainar grin and nod to the people cheering him, she realized she lacked the cold-blooded courage to kill him and sacrifice herself to the mob. And since this was so, she saw that in the years to come she would have to surrender her principles and make humiliating compromises if she was to have any hope of helping her people.

Yainar turned to her as the canoe carried them back to the island, and he smiled slowly at what he saw. "There's no need to bind you again," he murmured while the people on either side still cheered him. He bent down and cut away the last remnants of the thongs around her wrists.

Kori looked at him. "Is it so obvious that my spirit is broken?"

He reached out with a bloody hand and patted her cheek—the same cheek he had slapped not so long ago, when she had argued with him. "The women of the tribe will envy you now," he said, while Derneren, Euri, and Siew paddled the canoe with powerful strokes. "They may even try to compete with you, to take me from you."

She looked at him wearily, wanting to tell him that she'd be happy if some other woman stole him away. But he would be angry if she said that—and in any case, it wouldn't be true. If she was going to have any freedom or influence, she would need his help to repair her reputation, and she would need the respect that she could only gain by being his mate.

"Perhaps you no longer need me," she said.

"Oh, no. You are still Immar's daughter—although of course there are other women, younger women like little Tiola, who still appeal to me."

His smile had turned into a predatory grin. She suddenly saw how he was planning to torment her in the months to come. He would use his new position of power to tantalize her and humiliate her. He would try to make her so desperate she would beg to be paired with him.

"Remember," he said, leaning closer and murmuring so that only she could hear him, "you are all alone now, Kori. No one else is your friend. And if you turn against me, it will be easy for me to destroy you." He glanced at her body, and she saw in his eyes the same dispassionate interest he might show toward an animal he had just killed. He was her owner, now—or that was how he saw it. And as he eyed her breasts, then her thighs, she had no doubt he was thinking about the way in which he planned to use her later that night.

He stood up, then, and waved both arms to the crowd of women who had gathered at the island dock, cheering as the canoes came in. Kori turned her face away and stared at the Western Shore, where the terrible fire was finally burning itself out, leaving behind a vista of thin, charred, blackened spikes and dunes of ash. The air still stank of woodsmoke and there were some isolated patches of flame, but the conflagration was over, because there was nothing left to burn.

Farther away, Mount Tomomor continued venting its own bright jet of flame, but the wind had shifted and the sulfurous fumes were dissipating. When Kori looked up she could even see patches of blue sky above her.

The canoe bumped against the rocks in the dock and the men leaped out. Derneren and Siew stood either side of Yainar as the cool morning air was filled with the cries of the women and cheering from the rest of the hunters coming back from the river. Siew glanced at Derneren, the two men nodded to each other, and they bent down and lifted Yainar up onto their shoulders. Kori watched as they carried him up the slope toward the Meeting Place and the crowd followed, cheering Yainar and ignoring her as if she didn't exist.

Other canoes were being tied alongside hers. A few men glanced at her curiously as they picked up some of the game they had speared in the river and carried it with them, striding after the cheering crowd. Kori saw that many more animals still lay around her in the canoes, abandoned in their own blood.

Well, there was no point in sitting here. She didn't think she could bear to watch the victory celebration, and she certainly didn't want to squat here in discomfort under the morning sun.

She got to her feet, feeling empty inside and deeply weary. She walked up the slope toward the village, then found herself following a familiar path among the huts, seeking the one that belonged to her.

When she finally came to it she paused outside for a long moment, trying to decide whether she really wanted to go in. She thought back to all the times when she had ducked through that little doorway with Oam, ready to bed down for the night. She saw herself running out when there was an earthquake, joining the rest of the tribe in the Meeting Place, seizing an Anchor Stone and feeling afraid of the spirits but reassured by Rohonar's strong, fearless figure.

Well, Kori thought, of course he had been fearless; he had known that there was really nothing to fear, because Immar had embroidered the myths that frightened her people into submission. Deliberately or accidentally, Immar and Rohonar had evolved a perfect arrangement for maintaining peace in the tribe. Immar scared the people; they turned to Rohonar, and he reassured them.

Well, that was all in ruins now. Kori wondered if Immar's spirit was watching, crying out in torment over the fate of the tribe.

Perhaps, Kori thought, she should feel guilty, but she had done the best she could, and the forces she had faced had overwhelmed her. She turned back to her hut, summoned her courage, and bent down, pushing in through the doorway. She dragged the door flap to one side behind her, letting in some bright light and fresh air. She glanced down and was relieved to find that the warrior she'd killed here had been taken away. The floor was still stained with his blood, but even that was barely detectable, since someone had sprinkled fresh black sand over it.

Kori looked around at the hut, remembering how she had been a captive here, remembering how her mother had come to her here—and remembering further back to all the times she had lain on her bed in the dark, listening to the sounds of the night, trying to free her mind and share her mother's talent for hearing the voices of the Old Ones. She smiled at her own foolishness. She had heard nothing for the most obvious reason: there had never been anything to hear.

She went to her bed and lay down, enjoying the comfort and familiarily of it after sleeping outside on the Western Shore. Her eyes hurt and her throat and lungs were still sore from breathing volcanic fumes and woodsmoke. Her legs ached from her panic-stricken run through the forest. Her shoulders hurt from where she had dangled by her hands from the sloping rock, waiting for Uroh to help her down.

But she didn't want to think about Uroh. She needed to sleep.

40

Someone was touching her face. She woke with a start, thinking she was out in the forest. She was ready to fight, shout, free herself—

Then she realized where she was. But someone was here with her. He was leaning over her, pressing his hand over her mouth. It must be Yainar. The idea filled her with anger—and fear. She wondered if he had come back here to take revenge on her again for the time she had left him tied naked on her floor. She reached for his arm and jerked at it as hard as she could, trying to drag his hand away.

"Kori! No!"

The voice was a whisper. Then she realized: the words were spoken with the accent of the whitebeast tribe.

Kori stared up, trying to see the man's face, but the room was dark. It was evening; she must have slept through the whole afternoon. She felt disoriented. Her thoughts churned in confusion.

"Don't make noise." Slowly, the man pulled his hand away.

She took quick little breaths. "Who are you?" she whispered.

"It's me, Uroh," he said.

"No." She shook her head violently. "You died." She realized this must be his spirit, and he had come here to reproach her for the way she had forsaken him. She couldn't bear it if he blamed her for his death. She tried to struggle away from him. "Please!" she cried. "I'm sorry—"

"Kori! Kori, I am alive!" He seized her and shook her.

She struggled more, then fell still. She could smell him, she realized. He was made of flesh and blood. "Uroh?" she whispered.

"Yes, Kori." But there was no pleasure in the way he said it. His words fell heavily.

Kori raised herself on one elbow. She reached out to touch his face. "Uroh, hold me!"

He hesitated, then put his arms around her. But he moved stiffly, without joy.

She kissed his face. She felt a wave of relief, and of hope—and just as quickly, a sense of dread. "You'll be killed if they find you here," she whispered urgently. "They killed everyone. Everyone!"

"I know." He pulled away from her. "I saw."

"Were you there? I searched for you! I was so afraid—but where were you? How did you get here?"

He moved a little distance away from her. "After I left you in the forest," he said, "I never managed to reach my tribe. I saw the lava flowing, and I realized it would force my people to leave their camp, so I went down into the forest, hoping to meet them there. But the smoke and fumes were so heavy, I became lost. Eventually, late at night, I reached the river opposite your island. I hid there till dawn—and I saw my people massacred."

She realized he was bitter, angry in the same way that she had felt angry when his people had killed hers. She sensed him glowering at her.

"I couldn't stop it, Uroh!" Kori protested. "I was one women among two score of men with spears. How could I possibly stop them? And are you forgetting how your people attacked mine? They would have killed us all if they'd had the chance."

"I know that." His voice still sounded grim, and she realized it wasn't directed at her; he was angry with life itself.

"So tell me now," she said, "how you escaped death, and how you managed to get here."

He gave a curt nod. "While everyone's attention was diverted by the killing, I swam to your island. I had to, to escape the fire. I crept through the trees, and I hid and watched, and I saw you enter this hut. But I didn't dare come here till it was dusk outside."

"You've been on the island all afternoon?" She was horrified by the risk he had taken.

"I'm a scout," he said, sensing her thoughts. "I know how to hide myself." He breathed deeply and turned, looking around the little hut. "So here I am now," he said. "The last of my tribe. The very last one."

"What are you going to do?" Kori asked. She still wanted to hold him and feel him hold her. She wanted to break the dark shell that he had suddenly built around himself, and rediscover the gentle man who had seemed so devoted to her. But his manner was so forbidding, she found herself not daring to approach him.

"I'm going to do what I told you about before," he said. "I'll steal a canoe and go downriver. There's no other hope for me now."

There were no more dreams in him, she realized.

"But—do you want me to come with you?" Her throat clenched as she spoke. She found herself grasping her robe, fretting with the edge of it, trying to see his face in the dimness.

He was silent. He sat without moving.

"Uroh!" she whispered. "I must know—"

"Of course I want you!" He spat out the words. "Why else would I be here? If I wanted to leave on my own, I would have gone by now."

Finally she understood. Slowly, hesitantly, she reached out, groped in the dimness, and took his hand. "I'm sorry," she whispered. "I must have hurt you when I refused to go with you, after you found me in the forest."

He grunted. He said nothing.

"I was afraid," she said. "I'd been so impulsive, I'd made so many hasty choices, and—I wanted to be safe. I wanted *you* to be safe! I thought if we could just wait till the spring—" She got up on her knees and moved to him, embracing him. "I'm sorry, Uroh."

He sighed and she felt some of the stiffness melt from his limbs. He did still care for her, she realized—so much that he had risked his life coming to her hut. He was just afraid of being hurt by her again.

"Well, you have to make one more choice now," he said. "If security means so much to you, you should stay here with your people. Otherwise, you can risk everything and come with me." He drew a shaky breath. "There will be no more chances to make this choice, Kori."

She felt a pang at the thought that if she left now, Yainar would have no check on his power. But then she forced herself to admit that, in truth, she might never gain any influence over him. He was a tough, shrewd, vicious man; could she ever really compete with him?

And clearly she had no friends. The island was her home, the only home she'd ever known, but she could never be happy here.

The choice was so obvious, she felt foolish to be thinking about it at all. "Of course I'll come with you," she said. And as she spoke the words, all the weight of her sadness and despair slid away from her.

"You mean it?" He sounded gruff and cautious.

"Of course I mean it!" She seized his face and kissed him hard on the mouth.

He hugged her. "I didn't think you would," he whispered.

She gripped his hands in hers, not knowing what to say. She felt scared but excited. "We should leave as soon as we can," she said. "Every moment you're here, there's a greater risk of someone finding you."

"All right." He nodded toward the door. "You go first."

Kori ducked outside. She paused for a moment, listening and sniffing the air. She frowned. She heard the noise of chanting coming from the Meeting Place, but it wasn't the happy sound of victory that she'd heard before. It was one of the old chants, seeking mercy from the spirits. She wondered what could possibly be happening. How could the mood of the people change so quickly? And what could they have to fear, now that their enemies had been exterminated?

She noticed a strange smell in the air, like the smell of vegetables being plunged into steaming water. The ground was still trembling. Mount Tomomor, she realized, was still erupting. She peered over the huts and saw its peak glowing in the darkness, brighter than she had ever seen it before.

She glanced quickly around. The shadowy spaces between the huts were empty; all the villagers seemed to be in the Meeting Place. "Come out," she whispered to Uroh.

He emerged silently beside her. She was relieved to see that he wasn't wearing his white fur anymore; he had stolen a robe of the type that her tribe used. His hair was still cropped short, but in the darkness, if he kept his face tilted down, he might not be recognized.

Kori started toward the dock, but Uroh seized her arm. "The canoes have been moved," he whispered to her. He guided her back under the trees and started heading toward the eastern side of the island.

"Why would anyone move the canoes?" she asked him.

"What's happening? And why is everyone in the Meeting Place?"

"The lava from Mount Tomomor has flowed so far, it has reached the river. The molten rock is entering the water, turning it to steam. Your people shouldn't be wasting time chanting, they should leave their island while they can and take refuge on the Eastern Shore."

"But the island is safe," Kori said. "The river protects it."

Uroh laughed softly. "The island is made of volcanic rock. Did you never notice? Lava flowed here once, many generations ago. It may flow here again."

Kori tried to imagine it. The idea was inconceivable. Always, she had been taught to believe that the island was sacred ground, chosen by the Great Spirit for his people.

"My people will never leave the island," she said. "It's not possible for them. They have always been here. They will always be here."

Uroh looked for a moment in the direction of the Meeting Place, where the voices were rising and falling in steady rhythm. "They're stupid," he said.

"No." She said the word sharply, then realized he was only saying aloud what she had thought herself in the past. "No," she said again more gently, "they have been lied to. Lies have made them afraid, and fear has made them stupid."

Uroh shrugged. "You may be right," he said. "But if you're coming with me, the beliefs of your people don't concern us anymore."

He sounded grimly practical again, and she saw that he had changed. "You're no longer the dreamer," she said, staring up at his face.

He looked momentarily embarrassed. "There is no more time for dreams," he said. "Not since I saw my people die."

She felt sad—yet glad. If he could be rooted more deeply in the real world, she would trust him more. "So where are the canoes?" she whispered.

"That way." He pointed east. "But I already stole one and moved it to the southern tip of the island. Near the high rock—the place where you said you would stand and show yourself to me in the moonlight, do you remember?"

"Of course." She hugged him quickly. "We should get supplies—"

"I already did. It was easy enough; none of your people are in their houses. I have furs, spears, knives, dried fruits, fresh game—and a thing made of thongs knotted together, for trapping fish, I think."

"A fishing net," said Kori. She felt suddenly overwhelmed by what he had done. "Thank you," she whispered to him. "Thank you!"

"If we find the southern lands that I spoke of, you can thank me then."

"All right." She took his hand. "There's a path we can take around the edge of the village. No one should be on it as late as this. As you say, they're all in the Meeting Place. Quickly! This way." She hurried ahead, leading him after her.

They ducked under more trees and skirted the outermost circle of huts. Briefly, in the distance at the center of the innermost circle, Kori glimpsed figures squatting around the fire, their hands linked, their bodies swaying together, their voices speaking in unison. She thought of Yainar and saw he had not been able to dislodge the old superstitions so readily after all.

There were some more scrawny trees south of the village, and then the ground became so stony, only sparse grass grew here. This barren patch of ground was brightly lit by the glare from Mount Tomomor, throwing every ridge and pebble into sharp relief. Kori quickly guided Uroh down to the river edge on the east side of the island, where they were hidden in shadow. As she stepped from one rock on the beach to the next, she noticed the dark water moving strangely, surging up and falling back. She paused for just a moment, squatted down, dipped her fingers in the river, and found that it was warm to her touch.

"The canoe is just ahead," said Uroh, pointing past the end of the beach, where the high rock at the southern tip of the island stood as a dark silhouette against the yellow glare that Mount Tomomor was painting across the sky.

He led the way now, climbing across a low promontory. Kori knew there was a narrow inlet just beyond. It was a perfect hiding place. She leaped up beside Uroh, and then she stopped, staring, afraid to believe what she saw.

To her right was the high rock, standing four times as tall as a man, rising up from the body of the island like the head of a sleeping giant. Where she stood with Uroh was a small flat table of rock that was strewn with fist-sized stones and crisscrossed with fissures where grass and weeds had taken root. To her left was a path leading down to the inlet, and she saw the canoe lurking there in the shadows, rocking gently as the river surged and fell. But at the beginning of this path, blocking the way down, a man stood in the darkness, his feet spread, his arms folded around his spear.

"Derneren," Kori whispered to herself.

She glanced quickly at Uroh and saw that he was standing in shadow. Derneren only had one eye; his vision was poor. And he showed so little interest in the world, she hoped he hadn't even seen Uroh. Even if he had, he surely wouldn't imagine that Uroh was from the whitebeast tribe. The whitebeasts had all been slaughtered in the river; Derneren had helped to make sure of that.

Kori felt Uroh tense, ready to move forward. She reached for his arm and clutched it, holding him back.

Boldly she walked out and stopped just two paces from the big, ugly hunter. "What are you doing here?" she said. She felt some right to be bold, because Derneren had seen Yainar remove the last of her bonds. He knew she was no longer a prisoner in her own tribe. He had seen Yainar treating her as his woman, probably his mate-to-be. Surely, Derneren would have some respect for her now.

Derneren blinked at her slowly. Then he jerked his head toward the high rock.

Kori turned and looked. She saw a movement. A shadow detached itself from the side of the rock and became a human figure, tall, muscular, walking with calm authority. The yellow glare from Mount Tomomor touched the side of his face and Kori saw the familiar features: the heavy jaw, the wide mouth. He had rebraided his hair since she saw him being carried off to the village on the shoulders of his men. He had washed the blood from his hands and arms, and he was wearing a new robe, a fine elk skin embellished with zigzag patterns scorched into the hide. Like Derneren, he held a spear, and as he stopped, facing Kori, he turned it between his hands, idly rubbing his thumb over the edge of the flint tip. "Where are you going, Kori?" he said softly.

Staring at him, she felt her hopes die and her spirit weaken. She had no spear to defend herself, and neither did Uroh. She silently cursed Uroh for being so sure of himself and so reluctant to fight. Did this mean there would never be another time when she would enjoy the special, secret closeness they had known out on the rocky slopes of Mount Tomomor? If there was such a thing as fate, as Uroh said there was, her fate seemed clear enough now. She was fated to stay here on this island. No matter what she did, she always found herself forced to return.

And yet, Uroh might still escape. Yainar was looking at Kori, not him, and she drew some small hope from that. In fact, Uroh was standing so far back in the shadows, he wasalmost invisible.

"I asked a question, Kori," Yainar said, frowning at her. "Derneren told me a canoe was missing. I sent him to look for it, and he found it in the inlet. I see you were coming here to use it. So, where are you going?"

She tried to think. What should she say? If there was no hope for her now, could she at least tempt Yainar and Derneren to return with her to the village?

"Kori!" There was a new edge in Yainar's voice. "Answer me!"

She knew she couldn't lie to him outright; he always detected her evasions. "I don't belong here," she told him. "You know that. Once before, I wanted to leave. And—and this would have been for the best. You'd have less trouble without me."

He smiled faintly. "But you are mine now. You belong here with me."

She shook her head. "I'll never belong here." She gestured past him, toward the village. "The people of the tribe haven't changed. This morning they worshipped you; tonight they worship the spirits. They still harbor the same fears—"

"Oh, but I've decided to encourage their superstitions. It will be useful to me. I might even listen to the Old Ones myself, Kori." His eyes hardened as he stared at her. "It's better for me to have that power than a woman, don't you think?"

She closed her eyes for a moment, realizing that he had already foreseen her faint hope of finding a way to influence her people, and there would be no way, ever, that she could challenge him. She wondered if there was any way—any way at all—to avoid the life that she foresaw with him. "All I want," she said, "is to be free—"

His hand was a blur as he reached out and seized her by the hair. He twisted his fingers till he saw her wince and gasp. "You will do what I say," he told her, still speaking softly. "And you will never be free." He twisted harder and, through the pain, once more she saw the hunger in his eyes. "Kneel, Kori," he said, bearing down with all his weight. "Kneel before me. I want to hear you pledge yourself to me, here and now. I want to hear you promise to obey me. And if

I don't hear you say these things, I will punish you. I will hurt you till you learn to serve me."

She clenched her fists, knowing she didn't dare to strike him, but wishing she had had the courage to kill him while his back was turned in the canoe. She imagined herself thrusting the spear; she saw it penetrating his back between his shoulder blades—

Then she heard the sound she dreaded most: Uroh's footsteps moving toward her.

"No!" she shouted, hoping Uroh would understand that she was talking to him, not Yainar.

Uroh ignored her. "This is not right," he said softly.

Yainar's hand relaxed and Kori found herself suddenly set free, but only for a moment. "Hold her!" Yainar snapped at Derneren, and before Kori could turn around she heard the big man set aside his spear and felt him seize her upper arms, pinning her from behind.

Kori saw Uroh walking forward, insolent in his lack of fear, looking Yainar directly in the eye.

"You speak like a whitebeast." Yainar's voice was a whisper, full of disbelief. Quickly, he brought up his spear.

"Whitebeast?" Uroh laughed. "Yes." But his smile slowly faded. "You killed all the people of my tribe," he said. He kept pacing slowly forward and didn't stop until his chest was almost touching the point of Yainar's spear. He stood, then, with his arms hanging casually by his sides. "But you have no complaint against me. I was merely a scout. I hurt no one. So, I am not your enemy." He nodded toward Kori. "You should set her free. You have no right to act this way."

Kori couldn't tell how much Yainar understood of Uroh's speech. Just Uroh's existence and his tone of voice seemed more than the hunter could bear. She saw a muscle twitch in Yainar's cheek; she saw his anger surging. His hands tightened on his spear, and the tip of it trembled. Yainar bared his teeth. "Are you the one she coupled with?" he demanded.

Uroh shook his head. "I don't understand the way you speak. Just put down your spear and let us pass, here."

Kori wanted to scream at him, to scold him or beg him or do anything to make him stop what he was doing. But she saw something in him now that she had never seen before. Behind his self-effacing manner, Uroh was stubborn and fearless. Of course, she should have known that. How else could he have followed his own path, defying the customs of his warlike tribe?

Yainar shifted his weight, and the muscles bunched in his arms. "You are going to die," he said. He jerked the spear, piercing Uroh's robe, jabbing him sharply in the chest. "You understand that, don't you?"

Uroh barely flinched. He gave Yainar a slow, insolent smile. "Fighting," he said, "wastes the strength of a man."

Yainar's muscles flexed. "She will see you die!" he cried out. He shifted his grip, ready to plunge the spear deep into Uroh's body.

With no warning—no change in his expression and not a flicker in his eyes—Uroh suddenly dropped into a squatting position. In one smooth motion he ducked under the spear and ran. He loped across the small rocky table and disappeared around the high rock, out of sight.

Yainar's face was a picture of outrage and confusion. "Hold her!" he shouted at Derneren. His eyes were wild, and there was spittle at the corners of his mouth. She had never seen such fury in any man. He turned, then, and went after Uroh.

Derneren hesitated. He obviously wanted to see what was going to happen. Finally he lifted Kori by her arms and carried her forward with him.

As she rounded the high rock, she saw the Western Shore. She drew in her breath in shock. The land was completely bare; all remnants of the burned forest had been swept away. There was nothing but a black wasteland, now, gleaming dully in the glare from Mount Tomomor. And the contour of the shore was outlined in livid red. Lava was oozing slowly into the river, causing it to boil. Huge clouds of steam were rolling away on the wind, and the surface of the water was dotted with hundreds of dead, scalded fish.

Kori heard a sound from above, and she craned her neck around. She saw Uroh leaping up the high rock, moving as gracefully as if he were dancing. And then, in the yellow light from the flaming mountain, she saw Yainar going after him. The hunter was pulling himself up with one hand, still holding his spear in the other. On the flat top of the rock, Uroh paused and calmly waited for him.

Kori was painfully aware of her helplessness. "Uroh!" she cried, not knowing why she spoke or what she wanted—just wanting him to know she cared for him.

Yainar clambered up to the top, moving cautiously now, obviously suspecting a trap. Kori saw him placing his feet far apart, once again leveling his spear at the man opposite him.

"I wonder why you hate me so," Uroh said, his voice still sounded casual, showing no trace of fear. He tilted his head to one side, studying Yainar. "It's true, of course, that I coupled with Kori. Many times. My seed is in her; did you know that? When she bears her child—"

Yainar shouted in fury. He charged forward, holding his spear like a lance aimed at Uroh's chest.

Uroh dropped into a crouch. As Yainar neared him he reached up, seizing the spear just behind its point. He braced himself and pushed sideways with all his strength, and the spear turned like a spoke in a wheel. Yainar's forward rush was deflected. He shouted in surprise and outrage as he found himself teetering on the outer edge of the rock.

Uroh smiled. He came up out of his crouch, used his legs to push himself forward, then threw his weight along the line of the spear.

Yainar staggered, unable to catch his balance. He stepped

back to brace himself—and his foot trod empty air. He tumbled backward, screaming as he fell. Kori watched his dark silhouette writhing, twisting through the air, till he hit the river with a mighty splash. And now his screaming changed in pitch. He was shouting in agony. The water flowing down this side of the island was bubbling and steaming in the cold night. Yainar was being scalded alive.

"No!" Derneren shouted out from behind Kori. His grip weakened, and she seized the moment. She bent forward as far as she could, then tossed her head backward, smacking it into Derneren's face.

He grunted in pain and surprise and released his grip on her completely. She hesitated, seeing Yainar down in the water, still screaming, trying to claw his way out, but the rocks were sheer, with no handholds. In desperation he turned and started swimming with the current. The water flowing down the other side of the island was barely warm; if he could swim around the southern point, he could still save himself.

Without looking back at Derneren, Kori turned and ran. She saw the big man's spear where he had leaned it against the side of the high rock, when he had first seized her. She grabbed it and ran on down into the shadowy inlet. Her feet skidded over loose stones; she flailed to keep her balance. She skinned her hand on an outcropping, but barely noticed as she threw herself forward.

She seized the thong mooring the canoe and jerked it free. She threw the spear in, jumped after it, grabbed the paddle, and started urging the canoe out into the river. It was heavy and unwieldy, and it rocked wildly under her, but the current helped her—and there was Yainar, just as she had feared, swimming around the point.

Kori wished she had Uroh's calmness and discipline. She was gasping for breath and her hands were shaking. Her mouth was dry, and her whole body felt as if it was burning up. She set aside the paddle, seized the spear, and stood up in the canoe, trying desperately to keep her balance. She focused on Yainar in the water ahead of her. Even in the dim yellow light she could see that his face was contorted in extreme pain, while his skin had turned bright red and was blistering. He looked up and saw her looming over him. "Kori!" he cried. He held both arms out toward her, kicking his legs to keep himself afloat. "Kori, don't!"

For a moment she felt her resolve weakening. She despised the desire for revenge. But then she remembered seeing Yainar torturing the whitebeast warrior in the forest, and she remembered his face as he had threatened Uroh, and she realized that for Uroh's safety, for her own safety, for the safety of her tribe, Yainar could not be allowed to live.

"No!" he cried, as she raised the spear high.

She paused just a moment, because she wanted him to know the fear that the whitebeast warriors had felt that morning, when he had been the one slaughtering them without remorse.

At the last moment, he ducked down under the surface to evade her. But she was almost close enough to touch him, and she couldn't possibly miss. She thrust the spear with all her strength, and it slipped cleanly through the water and plunged deep into Yainar's belly.

Shuddering, weeping, Kori jerked the spear free. Yainar rose up and flopped back on the surface, clutching the wound, staring up at her with disbelief.

"You are evil!" she cried at him. This time when she rammed the spear down, she aimed it squarely at his handsome face.

Yainar screamed—then, abruptly, the scream died. Kori let go of the spear shaft, feeling horror at what she'd done. The point had plunged deep into Yainar's skull, killing him almost instantly. Kori saw his body floating away, the spear still embedded in him, casting a long, thin shadow over the churning water.

Kori slumped down for a moment, clutching herself and shivering. Her body no longer felt hot; she was cold with shock.

She realized, then, that the canoe was drifting. Uroh was still back on the island, unprotected against Derneren. Clumsily Kori seized the paddle and started working hard, turning the canoe, taking it against the current. To her left, along the Western Shore, she saw more lava pouring into the river, throwing up so much steam that it briefly covered the entire island.

She looked toward the inlet where the canoe had been moored, and she saw a figure standing there, barely visible in the shadow. "Uroh?" she called hopefully.

"Yes." It was his voice. She felt a wave of relief. And then, as the canoe came closer to him, she saw Derneren lying at his feet. "What happened?" she cried.

Uroh stepped over the hulking man. "He ran after you, down to the water. He ignored me. So I came up behind him and hit him with a rock."

Kori blinked. "You killed him?"

"Perhaps." He swung his leg over the side of the canoe, and from the way he moved, she saw he was inexperienced and clumsy. "Careful," she warned him, reaching out to steady him.

"I'm all right." But he was moving unsteadily as he squatted down with her.

"You were scared," she said, in sudden understanding.

"Of course I was scared!" He looked at her as if she was crazy. "Your friend almost killed me with his spear!"

She shook her head. "You seemed so fearless—"

"I learned to seem fearless with men like that, long ago. It rouses their anger. Their anger makes them stupid, and I turn it against them." He slumped down. "Did you kill him?"

"Yes. Yes, I killed him." She drew a shuddering breath. "That's three men I have killed, Uroh. Two from your tribe, one from mine. There must be no more."

"We will do whatever we have to do," he said, "if our lives are threatened, we will defend ourselves." He gestured toward the river. "Quickly, now, before any other people from your tribe find us here. They may all start fleeing for safety soon."

She pushed the canoe back out and guided it into the center of the river. As it moved from the shadow of the high rock, into the water that had flowed down the Western Shore, she felt the heat penetrating the wood under her feet. Fortunately, the wooden shell was thick; it would protect them.

"Look there!" she cried.

A bigger mass of lava was oozing inexorably into the water. The river frothed up in a huge bubbling, foaming mass. There was a hissing, roaring sound. A high wave came surging toward them and Kori cried out in alarm as it lifted the canoe, then set it down again, leaving them rocking wildly but still upright. She yelped and flicked water away from her hands where it had scalded her.

Then she looked back and saw that the river no longer flowed along the western side of the island. It was completely blocked by the mass of oozing black rock with a web-work of luminous red lava showing beneath the crust. And still the flow hadn't ceased. It was advancing onto the island itself.

"They will all be killed!" Kori cried.

"You don't believe they will try to save themselves?"

She shook her head helplessly. "Not until it's too late. They believe their legends, Uroh. It's inconceivable that the Old Ones would destroy their own people."

She cried out again as trees on the island started bursting into flame. Then she turned to Uroh with sudden intensity.

"Listen to me, Uroh! Lies made my people afraid, and fear made them stupid. Never lie to me again, Uroh. Promise me that. Whatever our future is, it cannot be built on lies."

"Yes, I promise that." He moved toward her, picking his way carefully across the furs and provisions on his hands and knees. He reached Kori and kneeled in front of her, looking her in the eyes. "But you must make a pledge in return," he went on. "Be brave enough to dream with me, and have faith in me."

She looked down, feeling ashamed of the way she had rejected him after he risked his life seeking her out in the forest. "I understand you better now," she said. "I see that even though you are a dreamer, you have great courage. I do have faith in you, Uroh."

"Good." Uroh turned toward the vista of destruction. He looked at the flames leaping from Mount Tomomor, the vast wasteland of black lava, the steaming river strewn with fish, and the island consumed in flames. "There are two things more to say, Kori. First, we will never know what forces there are in the world, causing such terrible things to happen. There may even be Old Ones; who can tell? And second, all this—" He swept his arm around. "All of it would have happened if you had done nothing at all. There are forces so great, we cannot hope to oppose them. And sometimes there truly is such a thing as fate."

She looked one last time at the island, then turned away. She picked up the paddle and dipped it cautiously, guiding the canoe down the center of the broad, dark river, leaving the ruins of her tribe behind.

"So let us hope," she said, "that when we reach the South Lands, fate will be kinder to us there."